Nicholas Lim

THE PATTERN MAKER

Richmond Press

First published in Great Britain in 2014
by Richmond Press

A Richmond Press Paperback

1.0.3.1

ISBN 978-0-9928119-0-7

Richmond Press
A division of ICraft Solutions Ltd
6 Bourne Gate
25 Bourne Valley Rd
Poole
BH12 1DY

For Ali

ACKNOWLEDGEMENTS

They say it takes a village to raise a child. I've learned the hard way that much the same is true of a book. I would like to thank my agent Judith Murray at Greene and Heaton for her repeated careful readings and insight. I would also like to thank Richard Skinner and the Faber group of 2012; without the stimulus and stamina provided by the fellow writers I found at the Academy this book might not have crossed the finishing line. Thank you also to Becky Swift at The Literary Consultancy; winning the Pen Factor competition was a very helpful stepping stone on the way to publication.

My editorial debts are legion but I would like to thank in particular Simon Rigge of Sheldrake Press for the opportunity he gave me to work with him years ago and for his editorial motto, "Prune and unify", which still haunts me. And thank you to my first readers, Caroline and Felix Milns, Jill Paton Walsh, Carolyn Smith and Joel Moskowitz, who all gave me much useful advice as well as that invisible but most vital of supports, encouragement.

The cover of this edition is by the gifted photographer Patrick Dodds. The design is an example of his particular alchemy in combining the memorable with the simple.

Above all, I owe special thanks to my wife Ali without whose editing skill, support and love this book would not have been completed.

Nicholas Lim

"Every epidemic begins with a first infection, a first death."
Dr Christine Garrett, Senior Epidemiologist
West Sussex Primary Care Trust, July 2011

"Where the skull divides there lies the Gate of God."
The Taittireeya Upanishad

Chapter 1

The morgue of the Brighton Royal is set apart from the main campus, screened off by a line of Holm oaks. The complex provides for all the needs of the hospital's corpses, from cleaning, autopsy and viewing through to disposal. It was where Dr Christine Garrett felt most at home.

"You must go deep enough here and here."

She made two swift cuts diagonally from each shoulder to the bottom of the sternum. She continued the last incision vertically down the abdomen to the pubic bone with a slight deviation to avoid the navel.

"You working late again tonight?" The intern Rafal Dudec waited for a glance from Garrett but her gaze remained focussed on the quick, definite movements of her hands.

"Yes."

"I saw the Multiplex has started late screenings. I was wondering–"

"You'll notice the blood at the nose and mouth. A common result of passive congestion caused by a lowered head position." Garrett's knife parted yellow fat and whiter tissues from chest wall, rib cage and diaphragm. "Worth noting. The bleeding can cause diagnostic confusion. This woman was found yesterday floating face down off the end of Brighton Pier."

Dudec nodded, quick bird-like nods. "Two drownings." He glanced at the next table. "Looks like it's going to be a busy bank holiday, Christine. Do you go to the cinema much?"

"No. I don't have the time."

"Well there's nothing on right now. But next Saturday–"

Garrett shifted her grip on her knife and pointed with the tip. "Dudec, can we concentrate on this post?"

"Yes of course."

"Remember, the chest is always opened before the abdomen."

As Dr Garrett skinned the body's front, her sixteen-inch blade touched once or twice against the chain mail glove on her left hand. The chink of metal on metal was audible above the

1

ever-present hum of air conditioning in the autopsy hall. The fans produced ten complete air changes per hour, but the smell of bleach, meat and opened bowels was constant.

"Isn't it easier to use a scalpel?" Dudec said.

"It's the usual choice. I prefer this knife. Either way, work with the edge not the point."

"Right."

"Up like so." Garrett folded chest skin up over the face, like a winding sheet, and down the sides of the trunk.

"I'm off on holiday next week," Dudec said.

"Good for you."

"It's a cruise. Only thing is I get seasick."

"Sodium pentothal."

"I heard that too. But my ex is coming. Not sure a truth drug would be a good idea. Any other suggestions?"

Using heavy curved scissors two-handed, like pruning shears, Garrett cut the ribs along both chest edges. Each bone gave way with an audible crack to leave a row of whitened ends.

"For seasickness? Sitting under a tree?"

Dudec blinked then grinned. "Okay."

Garrett lifted off the detached chest plate and stopped.

From neck to groin the major internal organs were visible, packed inside the body cavity like belongings in a suitcase. The lungs were darkly blotched. The spleen was enlarged and sooty grey. But it was the liver – charcoal dark as if scorched, and grossly distended – that held Garrett still, as if at attention.

"My God!" Dudec lowered his head. "What is that?"

Fluorescent tubes in the ceiling ticked arrhythmically with heat and light.

"When you said diagnostic confusion–?"

Dudec was known for his smart mouth. As long as it matched his work that was fine by Garrett. She put down the chest plate and re-read the admittance notes.

"The cause of death wasn't drowning was it?" Dudec pointed. "Every major organ has been infected by something or other."

Garrett picked up the long prosector's knife and began cutting again.

"I am freeing the organ block whole. It's the quicker procedure."

"Christine, do you have an idea what this is?"

Garrett shook her head.

"No. But I agree with your assessment of infection. The number of organs affected and the state of the liver and spleen – the vascular filtration units – suggests it's blood related."

Dudec looked excited. "This could be something new!"

"Rafal, when you hear hoof beats," Garrett held up her knife like a warning finger, "Think horses before zebras."

Dudec fiddled with a line of scalpels. He took a deep breath, like a little boy.

"I guess you see a lot of unusual cases, huh?"

"More than general practice. Epis move around different hospitals. Does path work interest you?"

"Um, not really. I'm more interested in going into the other end of things, maybe obstetrics."

Garrett recognised the thought. Her specialty, epidemiology, dealt closely with patterns of health in populations, particularly causes of death. Not as common an interest as natal care. *The other end of things.* She divided the last attachments – pelvic ligaments, bladder and rectum – with one slash of the knife and carried the organ block to the dissection area.

"That liver looks scorched. Barbecued!" Dudec said. His voice wobbled with excitement. "I've never seen anything like it – have you?"

The mass of sooty meat, yellowed around the edges, began to overflow Garrett's hand as she cut around the organ. She glanced up at Dudec, shook her head then stepped on a microphone foot-switch.

"Twenty-eight by twenty-four by twelve centimetres. Weight two thousand five hundred and fifty grams."

"Er – that's enormous." Dudec looked at Garrett as if she had asked him a question.

"Pronounced yellowing in the outer tissues characteristic of bile build-up."

Garrett completed the initial organ dissection.

"Rafal, do you know how to prepare quick-freeze sections?"

He nodded.

"Liver first please."

Garrett moved round to the head. The eyelids, where rigor had first appeared, had re-opened on relaxation of the small muscles. The eyes were the deepest royal blue. They reminded her of the lazuli robes of a Madonna that had hung in her room as a child, the colour of unquestioned faith. Around the iris the cornea showed yellow, signs of jaundice.

"Aren't you going to do these sections with me?"

"We still haven't established cause of death."

Garrett made a single deep cut across the crown from ear to ear and pulled the front flap of skin forward and down over the cadaver's face, then selected a small handsaw and addressed the exposed skull. She glanced at a plaque set high on the facing wall, etched with black lettering. *Hic locus est ubi mors gaudet succurrere vitae.*

Garrett cut through the exposed skull bone around the equator of the cranium. She took care to make a small notch, not for medical reasons, but so she could restore the head shape in case relatives viewed the body. She stared for a full minute before dictating.

"Calvarium off. Cerebral hemispheres appear grossly swollen, with meningeal congestion. Colour abnormal. Black."

Dudec looked up from his tissue sections. Garrett severed the spinal cord and tendon-like dural reflections between cerebellum and cerebrum and lifted out the brain. She peered into the head cavity. "Skull vault appears normal." She carried the brain back over to the dissection area. Dudec came over to see.

"Jesus Christ."

Garrett kicked the mike switch. "Cause of death: brainstem dysfunction. Tonsils of the cerebellum are softened and herniated."

"Yeah! Crushed to a pulp. That must have been some pressure. This brain's imploded!"

Garrett stepped on the mike switch. "Rafal, please?"

"Sorry."

She deepened the small incisions she had made in the base of the brain. "Pons, medulla oblongata and bulb are also all herniated. Cause: intense intracranial pressure." She paused to adjust her face mask. Fingerprints showed up redly on the filter paper below her eyes.

"There is widespread thrombosis, haematomas, haemorrhaging." Garrett pointed out to Dudec dense clusters of purple spots, like flea bites, all over the brain's surface. She began slicing sections through tissue and found penny-sized areas of paler tissue. "Localised cell death is visible in scattered infarctions throughout."

"What the hell is this?" Dudec took a step back from the blood-smeared steel of the examination table.

"There is oxygen starvation, blood vessel ruptures, a clearly lethal increase in cranial pressure."

"A black brain."

Dudec looked at her. His eyes had a shifty, overwide look.

"You said blood-borne diseases. I can think of HIV, hepatitis B, hepatitis C, malaria. And also West Nile virus and the viral hemorrhagic fevers." Dudec looked at Garrett, cheeks flushed. "Have I missed any?"

Garrett understood Dudec's fear. The same emotion lapped at her too. But she knew how to deal with it, concentrating on near, necessary objectives and schooling herself with her science and reasoned facts. Normally, she would send the worker home. Fear was contagious as disease.

Garrett smiled. "Remember Rafal, horses not zebras."

She maintained eye contact and raised her eyebrows. Dudec took a breath. He visibly steadied himself, roused himself to nod.

"That's it. Now I need you to help me. Where are you with those sections?"

"Umm, the liver. I've frozen and sliced four–"

"Good. Let's stain shall we?"

They worked in silence for a few minutes.

"You must think me a bit of a wuss."

"No I don't. You have an imagination. You need it for the job."

"You don't scare easily do you?"

Garrett placed a slide onto the lowered stage of a scope and added a drop of oil. "Right, let's have a look at what we're dealing with."

She made fine focus and diaphragm adjustments. Her body became still.

"Well?"

Garrett nudged the stage slowly back and forth.

"See anything?"

Garrett stepped aside. She watched Dudec's hunched shoulders. She knew what he was studying. Scores of pale lilac forms, mostly round, some crescent-shaped, some distorted into ovoids or spheres like unopened shells. Within each pale shape further forms, coarse rice-like granules stained to reds, darker cinnamon, soot...

"I know what this is." Dudec continued to peer down the binoculars. Garrett waited. "It's malaria." He looked up, triumphant. "Yes, must be."

"I agree. The pathology matches cellular identification. The liver is the first target of attack for the malaria parasite, where it starts to breed. And I'd say, from the state of the brain, we're looking at a cerebral malaria."

"The colour is due to the malaria pigment."

Garrett nodded. "Haemozoin. Did you see almost every single blood cell is colonised, deformed by the infection?"

Dudec looked back into the scope. "Yes. Yes, I see." He straightened and glanced at her. "Have you worked with malaria cases before?"

"I was in India for two years with the WHO SEAN. I'm not an expert but I saw a lot of malaria infection there."

"Like this?"

Garrett studied the sectioned brain on the steel counter. She thought of the slide images. "No. The pathology is extreme and the parasite blood colonisation – I've not heard of parasitemia approaching a hundred percent. We must be dealing with some new virulent strain. Most likely a holiday import." She looked at Dudec. "Remember, it's only transmitted by the mosquito insect vector."

He smiled his relief. Garrett returned to the opened body. She circled it twice, often bending down for a closer look, her movements careful and unhurried.

"What is it?"

"No bite marks."

"Perhaps the infection was contracted early?"

"Perhaps," Garrett conceded.

"The immune response could have subsided before death?"

Garrett nodded, still staring at the body.

"Or this was a relapse after long intermission. Malaria can be chronic."

"Maybe." Garrett sighed. "Look why don't you start typing up the notification for CDSC while I clear up?"

"Ok. You want to grab a coffee first? We could do with a break I think."

"Thanks Rafal, but no, I want to finish up here." Garrett glanced at the table with the remaining post under a blue plastic sheet.

"What about that one?"

"Tomorrow."

After Dudec had left, Garrett worked in silence. She closed the autopsied corpse and sluiced down the floor. She cleaned and sorted instruments ready for the next day; when she had finished, the stainless steel tools lined up in neat ranks in their racks.

On her way out, as she passed the last body waiting examination, she heard what sounded like a sigh, almost a protest. She came from a Dissenting people – who would not cross the road at ladders, consult tea leaves or shy from black cats – and she dismissed her gut reaction, reminding herself of the normal action of bacterial decomposition in the digestive tract after death.

It had been a long day. Tomorrow was fine. No need to rush.

***

The hospital chapel, a brick fragment of the original Victorian hospice, was attached to the morgue. Garrett paused at the door to make sure there was no one inside. She could hear nothing. A draft of cool escaping air smelled of candle wax, incense and dust.

She walked down the epistle aisle. Her heels tapped on familiar dates: 1917, the Spanish Flu; 1945, the tuberculosis epidemic.

She thought about drowning statistics. There were around four hundred across the country each year, a significant number alcohol-related, many due to concussions and broken necks after falling or diving; very few occurred in swimming incidents.

On the walls woodcuts of the Stations of the Cross marked the progression of another death. She crossed the transept and sat down in one of the front pews. She rubbed scrubbed fingernails with a thumb.

A crucifix was fixed high on the back wall of the apse. *The Passion*. She disliked the word. Garrett studied the injuries. The cause of death was indeterminate: either the wound in the side, if it had perforated the right lung or pericardium, or else cardiac arrhythmia or infarction provoked by hypovolemic shock, dehydration and exhaustion asphyxia. With limited ability to push up with the feet, each active diaphragmatic respiratory effort would have been tiring and agonizing. She felt annoyance at a customary inaccuracy: the ligaments and bones of the wrist can support the weight of a body hanging from them, but the palms cannot. *One faith against a whole earth's unbelief, One soul against the flesh of all mankind.*

She studied the conformity of the head and thought about the skull vault she had just opened. She needed a second opinion.

Door hinges squeaked from somewhere behind her and Garrett heard two sniffs and then humming. She glanced around the chapel. There was only one exit door. She sat perfectly still, eyes closed like a child hoping.

"Hello Christine!"

"Hi Arthur." Garrett frowned. The man was normally like clockwork. This was not his regular time.

"It's a busy evening! I've just seen Jim Da Costa in ER."

"What was he doing there?"

"I was just passing through. I didn't ask." The Chaplain slid into the pew beside her and launched into a rambling story about palliative care and then one about hospital catering.

"But anyway, enough of me. How're you, Christine? Working late?"

"Yes, long day. Just off home."

"It's good to catch you. You know my colleague at Guy's tells me that he sees you often in his chapel."

"It's quiet there."

"Like here." The Chaplain tilted his head and sighted along his nose as if through a glass to scry objects out of the normal view. "I often think of you in your room, me in mine." He glanced around his chapel. "I noticed you returned our cross. Your walls must be completely bare now."

"They're not bare. There's a plaque."

"A plaque. Right. What does it say?"

"Hic locus est ubi mors gaudet succurrere vitae." Garrett waited a moment to tease the clergyman. "This place is where death rejoices to teach those who live." She shrugged. "You'll find it in autopsy rooms everywhere."

Garrett tried to identify the smell the chaplain had brought in with him. Was it incense or aftershave?

"Any news of your son?" His voice was quiet.

"No."

"It must be difficult for you." Garrett turned her face away, but he continued to speak. "I was talking to Eva last week. You remember the trouble her cousin had, with those same people? Well, she told me a bit more about this clinical psychologist they used; apparently he's something of an expert on them. I think he may be able to help."

"Thank you but–"

"I've got his card somewhere here. She gave it me. Now where the devil – ah-ha! Prenderville. That's right. Please, take it. Eva says he's a miracle worker. Her cousin swears by him; doesn't know what they'd have done without him. And he has contacts. Anyway, he might be helpful."

The chaplain left with his usual over-familiar squeeze of the shoulders. In his absence Garrett heard a record of other absences in quick succession as if spliced newsreels. She listened to them and waited. Sometimes now, occasionally, she heard just the silence. It was what she came here for. What was the word? νοούμενον. The thing itself. Garrett stood up and patted pockets for her car keys.

She stopped her battered estate car at the bottom of the exit ramp, at lights on red. An ambulance turned into the entrance and headed towards A&E. There was no other traffic on the roads; that was one advantage of working late – the quick run home. Garrett stared at the red traffic light and saw again the malaria pigmentation illuminated on the slide.

What was a lethal strain of cerebral malaria – with parasite levels she had never heard of – doing in England? The returning thought annoyed her. She had a knack for leaving work at work.

"Horses, not zebras."

The lights turned amber then green. Garrett shifted into first.

It was an import or relapse. Garrett glanced in the rear view. Deaths by drowning were mainly male; ninety-five percent of swimming-related deaths were male. So by the numbers, the she should have been a he. Unusual, but then again, not that far off the curve.

The lights turned red again.

Garrett reversed up the exit ramp. At the top she made a one-point turn.

She walked around the table three times before starting, by her fixed habit.

The second body was of a tall, well-muscled young man. The head looked back at her with the blank regard of a statue.

Dreadlocks snaked away in rough ropes. But what caught Garrett's attention was the colour of the skin – all the colours – of intricate tattoos, livid in places like bruises. Rare un-inked patches appeared as the bare canvas of a painting in progress.

Garrett continued to circle the table. She bent to inspect the blue fingernails of a strong hand; well-defined tendons linked knuckles and finger joints. There was ante-mortem bruising in the palm; non-circulating blood from damaged veins had pooled in the capillary beds. The hand held a brief image of final pain, of a grip strong enough to break skin.

One fresh tattoo stood out on the left shoulder, the healing incomplete. Garrett approached for a closer look then took a quick step back. Her lips opened. Her pulse, rarely above sixty-five, reached a hundred and forty.

The new tattoo was of a small eye, the pupil black and iris a veined green, surrounded by rays like a child's sun.

Garrett held herself still for a full minute. Her breath entered and left her in small gasps. She waited for her heart to calm before continuing.

She prepared the post instruments with quick efficiency. The routine of it calmed her further. She slipped on her glove and selected the prosector's knife.

After the Y incision she did not move for a long time.

***

"Fifty cc, Benzodiazepine."

The consultant anaesthetist hesitated and asked Mr Da Costa to repeat his prescription.

"Yes, Benzodiazepine," Da Costa said. His voice was sharp, clear about priorities. If they didn't thin the blood immediately, they'd lose the patient.

Isolation Room 401L hummed with activity. Da Costa, the Brighton Royal's Head of Clinical Pathology, had been called in to help with an unusual case.

A currently-unidentified female in her mid-twenties had been found five hours earlier wandering delirious on a beach. By the time she had been admitted to the hospital, she was suffering from seizures. The fits had steadily escalated in severity until the patient had begun repeatedly to lose consciousness. Initial blood work had shown, in addition to high levels of alcohol and traces of Diethylamide, the presence of malaria parasites.

"Fifty cc, Benzodiazepine," the anaesthetist intoned, measuring out the dose. A nurse prepared the woman's right forearm. The needle slipped into a vein.

As he watched, in a dry, black and always-sane corner of his mind Da Costa mused on his prescription and the pharmacological peculiarity that the most effective drug for thinning blood was also a popular and powerful anti-depressant. Watching the girl he noted that mood alteration was not a rapid side-effect.

The girl's eyes were open, staring unseeing at the white-tiled hospital ceiling. Occasionally she would blink in spasms that convulsed her whole face. Her mouth was half open, lips stretched back over her teeth as if in parody of a diva mid aria, but in truth frozen in the rictus of a pain which gripped her entire body. Her hands clenched bed sheets, knuckles down. Only her legs moved, kicking out spasmodically like the limbs of an experimental frog whose nervous system continues to fire after its spinal cord has been severed.

"Temperature is now 106, pulse arrhythmia increasingly pronounced," the anaesthetist observed.

Da Costa's gaze flicked over to the monitor displays. He noted the increasingly erratic waveforms on the ECG. "Increase IV quinine dihydrochloride to twenty mg and maintain hydration, Dex ten."

An intercom beeped.

"Jim, the CBC smears are ready."

"Thank you Janice."

Da Costa punched up the results on a monitor at the foot of the bed.

The anaesthetist came to stand with him. "Christ. Platelet count twenty bph! Paresitemia ninety-five percent! I've never seen anything like it! Her blood is completely colonised."

Interrupted by sudden movement, the two men turned. The woman had convulsed, her whole body in spasm. The nurse and both residents held her down as another convulsion shuddered down through her body. Moments later she was still, and the air was filled with the ECG's continuous hum of lost pulse.

Da Costa moved to the bedside. "Twenty mg BP," he ordered calmly. "Go to slow IV, benadryl, cortisone and amniophylline."

"She's going cyanotic."

"Positive pressure oxygen. Charge."

The woman's lips were turning blue and her eyes no longer blinked. Her body spasmed now only under the repeated shock of resuscitation attempts. The team worked efficiently and without mistake to the legal limit.

In the pause after death no-one spoke. Da Costa stared down angrily at his empty hands. He always felt anger. He had figured out once, a long time ago, that it was really helplessness. Not that the knowledge helped. The anger did not change with understanding.

The continuous tone of the ECG filled the air like a reproach.

***

"Gladys. Got your message."

"Well?"

"We lost her."

Da Costa dropped down heavily into one corner of a large leather sofa opposite the desk of Gladys Morgan, the Brighton Royal's day manager. Morgan's PA poked her head around the door.

"Christine Garrett is here."

"Send her in."

"Er, and Colin Jenkins is on the line again."

"Not *now*."

The sharp word dismissed the PA too. Thin and bony, and with a smile full of teeth, Morgan was sharp at all her edges. The nurses called her The Shark, and had invented various carnivorous explanations as to why she was still childless.

"Come in Christine. You've caught up on Jim's case?"

Garrett nodded to Da Costa.

"Look you two, I'm looking at three fatal cases of malaria in twenty-four hours. What the hell is going on?"

Morgan looked at Da Costa. Da Costa looked at Garrett.

"For God's sake Jim," Morgan said. "You saw the admitted patient. You start."

"Initial visual blood work appeared to show malaria *falciparum* parasites–"

"–but there are significant anomalies," Garrett said. "In my opinion, enough to call the diagnosis into question."

Morgan leant forward.

"Really? Well if it's not malaria then what is it?"

"At the moment, I couldn't say."

"What shall I say to Jenkins?"

Garrett glanced at Da Costa then said the last thing Morgan had expected to hear from her. Hospitals – particularly large general hospitals with the staff and budgets of small multinationals – were notoriously self-sufficient. They built their reputations on what they could handle.

"Ask him for some help."

Dudec sat on a white plastic chair in the cramped pathology admin office typing data into a form. When Garrett had returned from her meeting with Morgan he had volunteered to add the priority lab request to the CDSC notification. He was regretting wanting so much to please. He hated forms.

The computer gurgled for a moment as the anti-virus program started its daily scan. The machine was old and very slow. Dudec completed the forms, attached them to an email, hit *Send* and stood up. He could hear Christine Garrett in the adjoining room. He wondered if he should suggest a quick drink. He noticed a single golden hair on the carpet. It was hers. He thought about the way she moved around the autopsy tables, beautiful and strict. He shook his head. *Stop it.* Time to shut down and go home. He turned round, stabbed an impatient finger at the computer's power switch and headed for the door.

The anti-virus scan had not completed. It had taken so much of the machine's resources that the notification message remained unsent when the computer shut down.

Chapter 2

Imagine you are riding the waves of your breaths. Breathe in...Out... In...Out...You are floating on the seas of sensation. Now imagine a coastline, cliffs in the distance. You see a sandy beach. Breathe in...Out...

You arrive on the beach. A path follows a stream inland. Take it. You walk under trees then come out into a valley. What do you see?

Christmas turned his head slightly, eyes closed. He saw what he always saw: sheep, trees, flowers.

There are fields with sheep. Orchards. Flower meadows.

Christmas took a shuddering breath filled with sadness. He would never make the journey again.

Continue on the path up into the valley.

A sharp pulse thudded in his temples. The air came and went from him in short pants. Repeated shivers ran through his body.

You reach the source of the stream where the water runs clear in pools that reflect the sky. You have arrived at the place of faith. You see sets of stone steps cut in the earth. They lead down into confusion and darkness. Choose.

He chose the path of action, as he always did.

Good. You have chosen well. There are candles. Light one.

The candle flame was white, like the thudding pain in his head.

You are in a maze with corridors branching in all directions. Follow the sequence of personal growth as you have been taught. Find your way through the darkness.

He opened his eyes. Pale whites stretched to the horizon, the light of English seaside summer mornings.

You stand in the Circle of the open secret, where the Unseen is made visible.

Christmas studied the cooling distances. Bible white, sea and sky. As above, as below. He closed his eyes again and waited. His head was aching. Sweat cooled his back.

This is where the central truth can be revealed to you.

He watched his breath.

"Sorry – are you working?"

In…Out…

"Hello?"

In…Out…

"It's too early."

"He's got his sign out. Scuse me?"

Christmas opened his eyes. A woman in a pink beach dress knelt in front of him. Behind her a man held a Frisbee with two hands; he was looking away. The woman gestured at a cardboard sign propped up on pebbles.

"Hi. Are you working?"

His fingers found the buttons of his music player and stopped the track.

"What do you want done?"

They discussed prices.

"How long will it take?"

Christmas looked at the woman and estimated her pain threshold. "Maybe an hour."

It was still early on Brighton's Palace Pier beach. The tide was in, the sea flat beneath a white sky. Scattered irregularly along the dunes, fluorescent-coloured sleeping bags twitched and rolled like the pupating cocoons of some exotic giant moth.

Christmas sat cross-legged on a striped cotton mat at the top of the highest dune. His eyes, widened in concentration, were of a startling green, the colour of glass pebbles found on the shore and held up to the sun. Barefoot and shaven-headed, wearing faded jeans and a cotton waistcoat, he was weathered down like an old piece of driftwood. Between his legs a power cord snaked down to a small battery-pack.

He held a buzzing needle over the outstretched arm of the woman in the pink dress. Her skin was good to work on, smooth and unmarked. Sheets of muscle bunched and folded like heavy cloth over his shoulder blades as he worked. His movements held the compact threat of a boxer.

He lifted the needle's tip. "We're done."

She blew out her breath. "Nice one."

"That's twenty-five?"

Christmas waited while the woman searched in her waist pack. On her right forearm a small butterfly gleamed wetly. Many more insects stood out across the caramel skin of the tattooist; separate swarms of flies encircled left and right forearms; half-a-dozen beetles spotted his chest and abdomen; a large moth shadowed his neck. The woman counted out five blue notes into his hand.

"Don't forget, the Thousand Names of God." Christmas held out a leaflet. "Here, take this."

"I don't–"

"Just read it in your spare time."

"I'm not really… Well, okay. Thanks. How long till it's fully healed?"

"Couple weeks. Best you cover it. Don't pick. Don't scratch. No swimming."

He adjusted his ear buds, ignoring the thanks. His customer turned away.

Latin plainsong echoed out across the unbroken mercury surface of the sea, backed by a drumbeat and a flute. When he held out both hands and flexed muscles, a swarm of flies settled on his right arm; beetles scuttled across his chest and abdomen, crawling down under his jeans and waistcoat as if seeking shade.

The sun, a perfect pink disk, slid up out of cloud like the opening of a great eye. Words from Sri Ramakrishna rose in his mind. *Longing is like the rosy dawn; then, like the sun, comes the vision of God.* When he bowed, a deep bow from the waist, his tattoos were brought to sudden illuminated life, like panes in an Advent calendar opened all at once, Christmas morning. Arms raised, he called out in a clear voice.

"Sri-kalki. Arshu! You who showed us the unseen through the Eye of Faith: many are Your names and infinite the forms through which You may be approached."

An old woman, up to her waist in the flat sea, glanced over her shoulder. She raised a hand to her blue shower cap for balance as she stared at Christmas, then turned and stepped out into deeper water. Her dog, a black and white border collie, ran back and forth along the shore, barking and snapping at invisible enemies.

All along the beach the overnight sleepers were waking – rolling, sitting up, splitting the sides of their fluorescent cocoons to stand two-legged, blinking at the sunrise. New arrivals were spreading out over the flats, intent on securing a pitch for the day. Up on the boardwalk a hotdog vendor pushed his cart between drifting holiday-makers. Shopkeepers were opening, putting out signs, hoisting awnings, laying out tables and chairs, securing their trading spaces for the day.

He could see the old woman with the blue shower cap doing a slow crawl fifty yards out, watched over by her anxious dog. Should he go for a swim, before the real heat? He turned off the music and stood in one smooth motion.

He swayed on his feet. Blood thudded in his skull. He sat down again.

The muscles in his legs ached. He could hear his quick breaths. He stared at the water's edge. His time of trial was coming. Maybe perform his Dues?

Breathe in, deeply and smoothly. Now breathe out. Do not try to control the breath. Just watch. How it is. However it is.

The sun rose, yellowed and gathered strength. The sea was suddenly molten, heaving heavily as if out of sleep. It was going to be another scorcher. Christmas put a cold arm across his hot neck. Sweat poured down his back.

The Palace Pier stretched out into the sea like an anchored liner. Pale strings of multi-coloured lights beaded the ivory superstructure. How many times had he sat on stones and gazed at the same floating whites, of Indian ghats, Greek fishing villages, Venetian palazzos? Aged and feminine, the pier seemed like some grandmother spirit brooding over her waking children. He could see movement beneath the wrought-iron arches of the pier.

Was that Jade?

How was she doing this morning? She had been worse last night. Drunk, feverish, they had lost each other near Juicy Fruity's last night. Christmas held his knees. Moisture trickled wherever skin touched. He raised his shoulders. If only the aches would go. Were they getting worse? He had been warned.

The sun's disk brightened, shrank, became an invisible point. The last cotton-white clouds began to fray at the edges and disappear. Out across the beach the noise reached the continual scream of a school playground. Christmas shivered in the sunshine and drew a hand across his forehead. It came away shiny. He shaded his eyes, scanning the crowds. His glance alighted briefly on each person, probing momentarily for opportunity.

***

Dr William J Prenderville's practice was in north Oxford. It was only two hours from Brighton. Garrett parked outside a tall residential house, an Edwardian end-of-terrace building that leaned a little crookedly over its neighbours.

In his seventies, Prenderville was now semi-retired, a part-time clinical psychiatrist and Oxford lecturer. Garrett knocked on an orange door. It opened almost immediately.

"Carl, get down! Now!"

"Hello!" Garrett caught the sharp paws of an ash grey Persian. She knelt and when the cat stood still for her, picked it up and handed it back to its owner.

"Thank you."

Dr Prenderville was tall, with a long face. He moved with a slight limp, favouring his left leg. With one hand he combed white curls across a spider angioma high on his forehead.

"Christine Garrett?"

"Yes."

"Please come in. I won't be a moment."

Prenderville showed Garrett into a study. A long récamier couch and a wooden ladder-back chair faced a desk. Irises stood in vases on occasional tables between glass-fronted bookcases. The grey Persian and what looked like its twin, only snow white, drifted into the room. They floated around her legs and nibbled at furniture, silent as fishes.

While she waited, Garrett walked down shelves reading titles. 'God's lamps', 'Self and Belief', 'Feet of clay: a study of gurus'. The books were grouped by subject and sub-subject: Schizophrenia, the Holocaust, Thought Reform / Coercive persuasion / Deprogramming / Exit counselling.

She picked out one of Prenderville's own, 'A Study of Modern Cults', from a row of twenty copies, and riffled pages.

> *What is a cult?*
> The term is usually pejorative, denoting a group whose beliefs or practices are considered strange. I define a cult more specifically to be a group led by a charismatic leader who employs techniques of thought reform. Such groups typically exhibit many of the following behaviours: demands for purity, continuous confession, exclusive membership terms, production of transcendent experiences, no-

> complaints cultures, planned spontaneity, imposed punishments and rewards, closed repetitive language, personality worship, doctrines superseding experience or persons, milieu control, sacred science...

Garrett took out her phone and redialled a number.

"CDSC Colindale, how may I help?"

"Simon Kirkpatrick please."

The telephone system began to play Kenny G. Four bars into 'The Girl from Ipanema' the music was interrupted.

"Simon Kirkpatrick, CDSC."

"Simon, it's Christine Garrett from Sussex Epidemiology."

"Christine, yes. I got your voicemails."

Three of them. "Thank you for taking my call. We referred some malaria cases to you yesterday–"

"Well I looked – we've not received anything from first line support."

"A priority lab request should have been sent to you last night with the notifications."

"I'll look again."

Garrett heard faint clicks of a mouse. She thought about Rafal Dudec. Had he not sent it? It was possible. *Damn.*

"Can't see anything." The man sounded bored. In the pause Garrett heard paperwork shuffling in the man's mind. She needed him to push a button. He was probably staring at it on the screen in front of him. She prepared for a game of bureaucratic chess. Love it or hate it, everyone in the National Health Service knew how to play.

"No. Nothing."

"Perhaps there's been a mistake at our end. I'll check. Would you be able to put in an emergency lab request? It is an urgent case." Garrett gesticulated as she spoke and moved in reversing circles with small stopping steps, balanced trim on her feet for any direction.

"We haven't even opened a case file yet. Without the notices and the E244 requisition form–"

"Did you receive a call from Colin Jenkins?"

"The Sussex county medical examiner?"

"Yes."

"Is this what he was calling about? I was at lunch."

"I have the biopsy material ready. As soon as I know the lab, I can–"

"As I say, we've had no paperwork."

"I'll send you the forms today."

"You've actually been coming through to the wrong person. I'll be away for the long weekend. Going forward, ask for Clarice Konstantis. Please take down this case reference."

Garrett ended the call. She stared down at the book in her hands.

> *Sacred Science*
> *A marriage of the religious and the rational*
> A four-hundred-year retreat of competence has left its mark: most modern religions attempt at least passive reconciliation with science. Such accommodations are rarely simple because, beyond the embarrassments of history, there is theology. To claim to know anything of the mind of God is an assertion of authority; such authority – if it is to have consequence in the temporal world – must negotiate with scientific truth and its technical utility.
> Many cults attempt a more active marriage of convenience, using a technique of mystical revelation I call sacred science...

Prenderville re-entered the room. Garrett put the book back.

"Please, have a seat."

She chose the chair.

"Now, what can I do for you?"

There was a moment of silence.

"Would you like some tea?" Prenderville asked.

"No thank you."

"Water?"

"No. Thanks." Garrett felt for her mobile. She considered turning it off.

Prenderville waited.

"Thank you for seeing me at such short notice."

Prenderville sat back. "Not at all."

Garrett held her fingers and watched the sunlight on the window glass behind Prenderville's head. She remembered what she had learned when she had looked up the psychiatrist, that his daughter had entered the Unification Church of Sun Myung Moon thirty years ago.

"Jason is due to call me, in twelve days. I haven't heard from him in six months. If he does call, I'm not sure what to say to him – what's the best thing."

"What do you want to say?"

"Come home." *I've kept your room just as you left it. Your car's in the garage.*

When Prenderville gave a nod Garrett added, "But I can't say that. He'd resent it."

I've missed you. What have you been doing? What have they done to you? Have they hurt you?

"I want to ask him if he's alright." Garrett looked up at Prenderville. "I think he would resent that too."

"Tell me what happened, from the start."

Garrett considered the unwelcome request; as a doctor she would have asked for the same.

"Alright. Five years ago David my husband – Jason's father – died in an accident, a car crash. Jason was sixteen at the time and he found it very difficult to cope with. He and David had been very close. When he left school – before university – he went travelling. Against my advice." Garrett hesitated. She forced herself to go on. "Our relationship had deteriorated. Anyway, for two years I received regular postcards and e-mails, from all over, Italy, Greece, Israel, Thailand, Korea, India. Jason started to describe visits to ashrams and alternative communities, and I heard from him less and less. Then a couple of years ago, he turned up out of the blue at our home in Brighton. He'd run out of money. He stayed with me about a month."

Garrett watched one of the Persian cats bob along the bottom of a bookcase. It stopped and looked up at her with two large blinking purple eyes.

"They were difficult times."

"Difficult how?"

"He would appear and disappear without notice. I suspected he was selling illegal drugs. He denied it. We argued. A lot. Then he disappeared completely. No word. No calls. No e-mails. Four months later he reappeared. I barely recognized him. He had shaved his head and wore Indian clothes. He had a number of tattoos. He seemed mentally unstable."

"In what way?"

Garrett dropped her head as though ashamed at something she'd done. "He told me I was only to call him Skyler from now on, and that Jason was dead, and I wasn't his mother. He would stare for ·hours at a single object, a window, a tap, a flower, a mug of tea. When I asked him what he was doing he would say things like, 'You wouldn't understand' or 'You must learn to transcend yourself, mother' or 'Contemplating reality'. He had obsessive rituals around certain events – sunrise, sunset, mealtimes – when he would say names and phrases again and again, like prayers."

"Do you remember examples?"

"Yes I remember. They were like broken records. Arshu! Father of Light! Triple-born Jewel! He had one phrase 'Goo-roosh-ree-kal-ki Arshu' which he was always saying. When I asked him what it meant he just smiled."

"Guru-sri-kalki," Prenderville re-pronounced the first syllables. "They are the words that begin the Arshu Purana, part of a prophetic scripture written in Sanskrit. A rough translation is 'Divine father incarnate.'"

"Divine father," Garrett repeated.

"I recognise it because it is part of a common Asari prayer: 'Gurusri-kalki Arshu! You who showed us the Unseen through the Eye of Faith, many are Your names and infinite the forms through which You may be approached.' Arshu is the leader of a community called Asari."

Garrett felt a flash of anger. "Jason began asking me for money. Increasing amounts. When I finally refused that was when he left. Actually I will have that water if I may?"

Prenderville walked with a slow uneven step, a hand down by his right leg. Garrett drank half a glass.

"Thank you. I waited another month. Then I made a mistake."

Prenderville returned to his side of the desk.

"I went through things he'd left in the loft. There were blister packets of various drugs. Sheets of LSD. He had used our house as a dealer's store."

Garrett stopped and watched the cats circle, allowing their aimless movements to calm her.

"He had kept a diary. I discovered he had not been happy. It was upsetting to read. Not that I should have. I learned about this group Asari, how he joined up. The meetings, the drugs, the Disciplines as they called them, the donations, the vows of loyalty, bizarre rituals around this leader, Arshu. There were pages and pages about one morning Jason thought he had stepped on this man's shadow. Fears at what might happen." Garrett shook her head. "He had to write confessional essays all the time, about what he feared most, hated most, wanted most–"

"It all frightened me, really frightened me. I knew from the diary that Jason was staying at the commune's temple in Brighton. It's a block of flats; you can walk straight in. I found him sitting on the floor of a concrete cell meditating. He refused to come with me. They have armed guards."

Garrett considered her clenched right hand then took a sip of water.

"I had a fight with one of them. They evicted me. Jason met me outside the gates. He was upset, I think at least in part at how the guards had treated me. He told me never to come back. I refused to promise. We came to an agreement. He would call me once every six months. So far he has kept his word. Twice."

Prenderville contemplated Garrett for some time before speaking.

"What your son described in his diaries–"

"It was wrong of me to read them."

"It is understandable. You said you were afraid for him–"

"It was wrong."

Prenderville waited a moment then said, "Such an act is usually regarded as a violation of trust."

"And going to visit him in that temple was stupid." Garrett shook her head. "It pushed him away."

"Possibly. But you have maintained contact. Which is a considerable achievement. More than you perhaps realise. May I ask what prompted you to visit me now?"

"I'm investigating a new outbreak. It is medically unusual. One of the victims is a member of Asari. The coincidence spooked me a little." Garrett stopped. She stared at her hands. "I wanted to contact Jason. To see if he was all right. But I can't."

"It must be hard, coming here and talking about him."

Garrett's head came up. "Do you know anyone who has left?"

"I have counselled nearly a dozen ex-members of Asari."

"Might I speak to them?"

"I can try to arrange it."

"Thank you. If he calls – do you have any advice on the best thing to say?"

"Just listen. Encourage him to speak. Accept what you hear. Of course use your own judgement if there is an implication of harm to anyone else, but otherwise just listen. Maybe try to talk about shared experiences. But not too much."

Garrett nodded then looked away.

"Can I tell him I love him?"

The psychiatrist's smile was like the touch of winter sun, cold, white. "Just that is surely never wrong."

Prenderville cleared his throat then added, "But without 'buts' or advice if possible. I would not offer him rooms, or cars, or money. If he asks for a place to stay that is different. If there is any indication he wishes to leave Asari, you can be supportive. If you wish me to, I would be happy to help in such circumstances."

Garrett's hands twisted into a nest of nails and knuckles.

"If he doesn't call–"

"I would strongly advise against repeating your visit."

"Can we not do something, to get him out?"

"Against his will? Remember he could always go back, unless you intend to imprison him yourself. Coercion doesn't work on its own, not for parents or for cults."

"Is there nothing we can do?"

"Not directly. He will always be free to choose."

Garrett thought about that for a long while. When she spoke again it was as though from far away.

"He was such a pious little boy. I brought him up a very strict Catholic. He took catechism, First Communion, Confirmation. He attended a Jesuit school. He was in the choir and served at Mass every Sunday. It was just the way I was brought up. Perhaps–"

"It's not your fault."

Garrett held still. She trembled slightly, like a glass full to the brim.

"Perhaps I could have prepared him better."

"It's not your fault."

"But there must be something, some defence–"

"Only one that I'm aware of." Garrett looked at Prenderville, her eyes suddenly focussed. He too was sharp, motionless in his chair. Garrett heard in his voice words he had paid for, had earned the right to say. "It is the superstitious, the literal and the faithful who are vulnerable to exploitation. The only defence I know is teaching people to think for themselves. To question. To reason. It's the only thing I've found that works."

Prenderville limped over to a bookcase. Garrett began to knot her fingers again.

"But Jason is already–"

"Mrs Garrett, how is your son's physical health?"

"What do you mean?"

"I mean, does he suffer from any chronic conditions? Is he physically fit? Does he rely on medications?"

"No medications, no chronic illness."

Prenderville picked out a book. "Based on current research, sixty-nine percent of people who enter cults leave eventually of their own accord. The average stay is between three to six years. From these statistics, your son is likely to leave this commune within the next few years. It is then that he may be able to recognise the connections between you. It is then that he will need, and may be able to accept, your help, support and love."

Prenderville returned to his chair. He pushed the book over the desk top.

"This might be helpful."

Garrett took the book.

"Be patient," Prenderville said. "Wait."

Garrett contemplated the pain of the last two years, the continual, almost physical, sense of loss. Parents always worry, about a child who doesn't sleep, or is sleeping too silently, is too hot or too cold, about a chesty cough, vaccinations and schools. But these last two years had been like living with a sort of death when no-one had died, an accident always happening, out of sight, an endless waiting, listening for phone calls, doorbells, watching for e-mails, texts, letters that never came. She measured her strength out against the coming years. He might need her. She must wait. Yes, she would wait.

Garrett unplaited her fingers and sat up straight. "When did the last person you know of leave?"

"Oliver Weightman. His cult name was Nilesh. He was a brave man."

"Was?"

"Oliver died six months ago from a drug overdose, apparently self-administered." Prenderville opened the drawer of a filing cabinet behind him. "What I am going to tell you is prompted in part by the nature of your attempts to make contact with your son. I believe you have been very lucky."

Prenderville handed Garrett a piece of paper. On it was a crude crayon drawing, of a primate animal – a monkey? – impaled on a long pole.

"This was found on Oliver's body."

"What is it?"

"I believe it's a warning. The drawing is a well-known reference to an Indian farming practice called 'Monkey on a stick'." Garrett looked blank. "When monkeys invade banana plantations, farmers kill one of the animals and put its body on a stick in the middle of the field to warn the rest of the troop off. Oliver's dead body was found soon after a visit from some friends, members of Asari."

Garrett stared at Prenderville.

"You think he was murdered?"

"Yes, I do."

"Do you have any evidence?"

"Only circumstantial. The type of drug used. The time of his friends' visit. An action inconsistent with the progress he had been making. Previous warnings."

"Warnings about what?"

"Oliver was once a journalist. Around the time of his death he was writing a series of pieces on Asari. Only one was ever published, in a periodical. I have seen drafts of the other articles. They were all highly critical. Also–"

Prenderville moved awkwardly in his chair.

"Soon after Oliver's death I was hit by an unmarked van. It didn't stop. Then I received a letter warning me to stop exit-counselling with members of Asari. The letter also expressed concern about the recovery of my damaged leg. It was a crude threat."

Prenderville leaned forward in his chair. "How much do you know about Asari?"

"I've tried to find out what I can. They are very secretive."

Prenderville nodded. "Fanatically so."

"Jason's diary has told me the most. Asari is a cult."

"The term cult is not well defined. But yes, the Asari community exhibits behaviours characteristic of modern organizations described as cults: charismatic personality worship, totalist doctrines, milieu control–"

"Milieu control?"

The Persian with the purple eyes leaped onto Prenderville's lap. It gave a yawn then settled with a leg resting on the desk top, as though making a point.

"The term describes all the ways physical and communications access is restricted. Typically it involves a place – a farm or compound – with a defined perimeter, and rules forbidding ownership of mobile phones, the use of computers... The outside world is a potential alternative authority and must be excluded. For this group, Brighton is where they try new outreach programmes – street campaigns, yoga classes, meditation retreats – but their base in Wales is where they exert complete milieu control."

Prenderville watched his cat fold an ear over with a paw, three times.

"Not all so-called cults are malign. But I believe Asari is unusual. In Oliver's articles he made a series of serious claims: that the group was involved in the illegal drugs trade and criminal theft, used violence to support those activities and recruited with extensive use of thought reform techniques. There are a number of ongoing police investigations. My exit interviews confirm Oliver's concerns, as well as others."

"Such as?"

Prenderville got up, the cat spilling to the floor with a yelp. He limped over to a window. "Many modern cults hold deeply alienated world views together with a corresponding millennial doctrine or prophesy: that is, a belief in a coming transformation of society, without which current problems are intractable and after which all things will be changed. The centrality of such doctrines is a good index to the possible harmfulness of a cult, to its members or wider society. For Asari, these beliefs now appear to be dominant."

"I don't think that was always the case. From what I can gather, Asari began as an ecological group experimenting with communal living and science to create a sustainable lifestyle."

"What happened?"

"How did the well become poisoned?" Prenderville looked out of the window and sighed. "We can only guess from other cults. Each is different. The Dravidians and MRTC began to self-destruct when their visions collided with reality; the Krishnas were corrupted by sex, drugs and money; the People's Temple followed their founder into breakdown and final suicide; likewise Heaven's Gate. Asari? I don't know."

"What is clear is that the group is very well-funded – through endowments and drug running – conventionally amoral, scientifically literate and extraordinarily well-organised. Everyone is a member of a House, named like ministerial departments, for Theology, Health and Knowledge, Agriculture, Education, Right Force, Justice, Children."

"Jason's diaries mention Education."

"It's an extraordinary social construction." Prenderville looked out of the window and straightened up, as if an old soldier coming on duty. "My present concern derives from interviews with Oliver and other ex-members. The cult appears to be in the advanced planning stages of a major operation."

"To do what?"

"A recruitment campaign maybe, acquisition of funds or land, something more violent perhaps. I don't know."

As Garrett drove away she noticed one of Prenderville's cats on top of a wall. It lay in the sun licking its whiskers and watching her with a large purple eye.

Chapter 3

Two hundred miles off the Javanese coast, the Indoex continental pollution cloud is visible as a brown haze. The WHO officer stood in the prow of the small ferry, feet between rusting tangles of anchor chain, eyes on the muddied horizon. Ahead, the Kepaluan volcanic crater, Gunung Neira, rose up ash-grey.

The ferry tilted on a slow swell. Spillage oil reflected back iridescent on gently-heaving surfaces of water. The volcano was a welcome sight – a promise of landfall – but it cast a looming shadow, reminding the WHO officer of the reason for his journey. From three of the surrounding atolls, thin grey lines rose into the sky, perfectly straight against the blue. An image flashed across his mind, of the flat lines on the EEG of a lost patient.

A sudden breeze was warm. The sun dazzled in bright flecks on the water. The officer thought of the infamous Chikungunya outbreak on Reunion, infecting over a hundred thousand islanders, traced to two young girls. Isolated from continental infections, with narrowed immunity, he knew island communities were accidents waiting to happen. For medical researchers, islands acted as Petri dishes: small real-world laboratories for passive experiments. Only passive: deliberate introduction of infectious agents had never been sanctioned.

Closer now, he could see the black slopes of the volcano. The smaller islands were visible, hovering in the surrounding sea like attendant guards. They made for the nearest of the atolls and a horseshoe jetty jutting fifty yards out into the water. There was no-one in sight.

The officer squinted against the midday sun and thought about what the ferry captain had told him.

The captain made the trip two or three times a month. On his last visit – two weeks ago – some of the islanders had been complaining. The pearl fishing was suffering because of a recent fever that had come to the island. Many were laid up in bed. He had picked up one passenger, a man he had taken out the previous month, who had said he was on a pilgrimage. The captain had suggested starting with a hospital. He had not looked well either.

Up by the tree-line four wooden sheds faced out to sea, the vacant eyes of their open windows staring back unblinking. Behind them the thatched roofs of a village were visible through a palisade of palms.

As they pulled in, boats rocked gently at their moorings. The sun glittered on the water. Shoals of fish flickered in the aquamarine shallows, brightly-coloured against the white sandy bottom. There was still no-one in sight. The captain gave a sudden cry and raised an arm to point at something in the water ten feet from the end of the jetty. He gunned the engine and swung alongside.

It was floating half-submerged, like a piece of driftwood. But not driftwood. A brown back, face down. The officer ran down the side of the boat and peered at the corpse. It bobbed gently in the water. There were no visible marks of injury. With the magnified awareness of shock, close up, he could noticed rainbow shoals of small fish circling, darting in to touch the skin. Gentle nudges, like kisses. Nibbling.

"Doctor!"

The captain stood frozen upright in bright sunshine, pointing at the walkway. Three more bodies lay sprawled at intervals along the uneven run of slatted wooden planks, motionless, in awkward heaps, the closest a few feet from the ferry's gunwales. Similar shapes were scattered over the ground, small mounds of arms, legs, heads and torsos heaped anyhow like untidy piles of clothing.

"I must examine the bodies."

The captain looked uncertain.

"I must find out what's happened. That's why we've come! Please wait for me here."

The WHO officer hefted his pack, stepped up onto the boat's gunwale, balanced, judged the gap, then jumped.

In the silence he could hear the slap of water against the ferry's metal hull. His ears strained to hear another sound – a raised shout or cry perhaps, from the direction of the village. Any human noise. But there was nothing, only the lapping of the water and the intermittent cries of the gulls overhead. The captain stood unmoving at the wheel of his boat, wide-eyed, staring at the bodies along the shoreline.

The officer turned and walked up the jetty.

***

The operations centre of the World Health Organization, South East Asia Network, is a cramped, florescent-dim basement just off Mahatma Ghandi Marg in New Delhi. From his raised desk beneath a wheezing air conditioning unit, Amitabh Kumar, night-shift duty officer, watched a dozen operators playing computer games, emailing friends, taking the odd support call. It was a quiet evening.

Kumar was proud of the room and his place in it. It was no small responsibility to oversee the hub of a healthcare network serving two continents, fifty million square miles, four oceans, eleven countries and nearly two billion people. It was the boredom he couldn't stand.

He lit his nineteenth cigarette of the shift. Five large time-zone clocks showed how slowly ten hours could pass when nothing happened. He had spent most of the night trying not to watch the row of synchronised red second hands.

He stared sourly at a new email. It was from his manager, Samir Sharma. Just texted in. "Do NOT go home before seeing me. We need to talk about Kepalua."

Typical Samir. Do this, need that. Kumar wished he could just delete the email and go home. He wanted a shower badly. He stared at the wall clocks and remembered the original support call from Kepalua, six nights ago.

It had been another quiet shift just like tonight. Singapore had patched a shortwave radio broadcast through from a group of Indian Ocean islands. Kepalua? It was not in a risk zone. The report shouldn't even have been escalated to them. But he remembered the panic in the nurse's voice. So frightened the report had made little sense. He heard again the silence when the connection had been lost, then Singapore Relay's attempts to re-establish contact, "Trying... Trying..." The six red second hands of the wall clocks had swept round and round like the clear signal line on an empty radar screen.

On an impulse Kumar crossed to a large wall map. The eleven SEAN WHO member countries were pimpled with coloured pins representing all current outbreak reports. Off the south coast of Java in the middle of empty blue was a single white pin next to the N of Indian Ocean.

"Middle of bloody nowhere," Kumar muttered to himself. They had sent out a junior inspection officer.

"Amitabh!"

One of the tele-operators made her you're-in-trouble face. Kumar sighed.

"AMITABH!!!" The shout echoed down the hallway.

***

The WHO officer knelt at the first body. The head was twisted round at an impossible angle. The lips were blue. A trickle of blood had congealed to black on the chin. The hands had a yellow tinge to the skin, nailbeds were blue.

Competing theories raced with the officer's heartbeat. The majors: yellow fever, dengue, typhoid, malaria. Possible minors: chikungunya, West Nile, Trypanosomiasis, Leishmaniasis.

He walked over to the second body. An adult male, the same pathology: blueing of nails, lips, around the mouth and nose a rusty smear, yellowing skin, the rigor of sudden seizure. The third body, of a young girl, was the same.

He straightened and looked out along the shoreline. Five more bodies were scattered along the beach, one in the porch of a seafront hut, the corpse folded over a rail like a blanket left out to dry. Where was everyone?

***

Samir's door was half-open. Kumar's knock was answered immediately.

"Amitabh!!! That officer you contacted in Yogyakarta. Where is he now?"

Kumar blinked. "I don't know exactly. You remember, I checked with you before I–"

"Well I suggest you find out." Sharma tossed a printout over his desk. "Read that."

It was an email. A few sentences in, Kumar began speaking aloud to fill the silence. "...after a fishing trawler picked up an islander from Kepalua who reported many unusual deaths. The account part-confirms the support call from the MSF nurse. Due to the potential health risk, we have instigated a forty-mile perimeter quarantine around the islands." Kumar glanced up at Sharma then back down at the page. He felt his palms begin to sweat. He swallowed. "Investigations should only proceed jointly with CDSC personnel and local backup. Please acknowledge immediately."

"Amitabh. Just tell me you waited for formal clearance before sending our officer out there."

Kumar swallowed again. He cleared his throat.

"Amitabh? Tell me what I want to hear?"

Kumar re-read the last lines of the e-mail. "I, er, I, umm, I think a ball got dropped."

"A what?"

"That day was the big rush for the Gujerat quake. I–"

"Get on the phone. Call everyone we know in Jakarta and on that coast. Try and trace the boat he used. Get a name. Get a radio frequency. We must make contact before he reaches those islands. Before. Do you understand?"

Kumar nodded.

"Why are you still standing there? Get on with it man!"

***

The WHO officer worked fast, taking blood and tissue samples. The drone of the cicadas from the surrounding forest filled his ears. The meaty stink of a corpse filled his nostrils.

At the back of the officer's mind a warning bell was ringing. With narrowed isolated immunity, island communities were accidents waiting to happen. But where were the survivors? Natural diseases, even new, virulent strains, did not exterminate. He had to get the biopsy samples back to a lab.

He ran back through the village square. Half-a-dozen thatched huts were still-smoking ruins. As he cleared the tree line he saw the ferry. It was in open water, coming about, the captain at the wheel staring away from the island.

"WAIT!"

He sprinted down the sand. The ferry continued its rotation, the ship's prow turning out to sea. The captain was not looking back.

"WAIT!! WAIT FOR ME!!!"

Chapter 4

The headquarters of CDSC, the UK Communicable Disease Surveillance Centre, in Colindale north London, is a modern ziggurat of glass and steel, a fifteen-storey tower block that rises in narrowing terraces out of the surrounding maze of red-brick Victorian semis.

Simon Kirkpatrick, senior project manager in Surveillance and Reaction, stood in silence beside his desk, head down, hands clasped together in front of his stomach. His hips moved back and forth, back and forth, in small swaying motions. With a sudden jerk his clasped hands swept across his body and his tongue clicked once. A golf ball rolled in his mind across the floor past his desk with a swerve under the window into a hole where the waste paper bin stood. *Have it!*

Pop!

The computer on his desk emitted a sound like a rude schoolboy flicking a finger out of his cheek. Kirkpatrick returned to his chair. He scanned a new email. Subject: *Brighton malaria case*. It was from Dr Christine Garrett. Already? This woman was a real nuisance. He glanced at the wall clock. Quarter to five. Golf practice tonight. He needed it with the bank holiday match coming up! He logged on to Sentinel and started to create a new case file.

He worked fast, importing Christine Garrett's documents. He clicked *Initial analysis*. A progress bar began to fill up.

Through a plate glass window he could see three cubes along to where Clarrie sat hunched over her keyboard. He still couldn't understand how Ms Liu had already made grade 4. She'd only been with CDCS four years. It had taken him seven! Seven years hard graft. And she didn't even put in the hours. She was often late and left early. She was rarely on-call at weekends. She was always going away! Work-life balance she called it. Work hard, play hard, recharging the batteries, blah, blah, blah! Listening to her was like reading one of those women's magazines. Nothing but clichés.

Sentinel initial case analysis complete: new CLC required.
Kirkpatrick frowned.

Sentinel was the CDSC's new outbreak management system.
The key to its incident tracking and alerting was the CLC: the
Cluster Lead Case. Each case was ranked and automatically
linked to related cases in a cluster; every cluster had a Cluster
Lead Case. As the software manual put it: *"This single point of
control defines responsibility, ownership and overview."*

When the notification threshold for a cluster was reached,
Sentinel automatically alerted the responsible case worker.

The system had replaced a dozen older applications and had
been live since March. They still had CDSC Ahmadabad as
manual back-up – offshore case workers who monitored the
system round the clock – but they were increasingly seen as
unnecessary.

A new cluster? Yes, that made sense: this incident was an
anomaly, with no related cases. Kirkpatrick clicked *OK*.

He glanced at the clock. Five already. He should be leaving.
Let's expedite shall we?

Most of Kirkpatrick's favourite words began with the letter
e: enable, effective, efficient, energy … and if they didn't,
someone often put an e in front of them for him: e-medicine, e-
healthcare, e-processing, e-solutions…

He opened the incident summary, skimmed the first few lines
then the odd word here and there. He was prompted to review
the attachments – meeting minutes, lab reports – and decided he
couldn't be bothered. The incident sounded like a whale-sized
red herring.

He confirmed the allocated lab: Porton Down, for two
members of staff, thirty-five hours total, contact George Skinner.

Alert thresholds: default. He set the responsible case worker
to Clarice Liu and clicked "Publish".

Done. He stood and practiced a few more putts then returned
to his desk. He clicked the Receive button. Twice. Where the
hell was Clarice's acknowledgement? His phone beeped at his
waist. He looked down, cancelled the golf reminder and glanced
at the clock: 5:15. He would be late for his lesson if he didn't
leave *now*. He stood and walked over to the water dispenser in
the corner of his small office. Clarrie waved at him through the
glass. Kirkpatrick gave her a serious nod. She nodded back,
mock serious. At last. *Home time!*

A few minutes after he left his office a new email arrived, an out-of-office notification from Clarice Liu. *"I will be out of the office until 2 September. (Catching the sun in Crete!) If you have an urgent query, please contact the CDSC Colindale office where another member of the team will be happy to help. Kind regards."*

Clarice Liu had a philosophy: once she'd set her out-of-office she was officially not at work. No more emails. No more computers. If someone couldn't be bothered to check her calendar or her email replies it wasn't her fault.

***

A line of Jubilee-blue benches faced the cliff-top railings above the Promenade. Garrett sat on one of the benches writing names in a notepad. She had begun to draw connecting lines, a sparse, broken web strung between facts. The first autopsy – Spyder and the second – Grant – both dying on Palace Pier beach. Da Costa's case – Lizzie: found on the same beach. Spyder, Grant and Lizzie. Three deaths, within a week of each other. All dying in Brighton. All visiting this beach. This place was a common link. It was why she had come here, to find connections.

After a while she put down her notepad and walked over to the railings. Behind the Big Wheel she could see a parade of stalls, a one-storey, barrel-roofed terrace that extended between the rides out into the pebbles at the top of the beach. Colourful and isolated, the line of low shops appeared like a stranded train of circus wagons, a caravan come to a halt and rested for so long the vehicles had lost wheels and taken root. At the end of the rundown parade Garrett could make out a juice bar, coconut shy and cafeteria. A bald-headed man sat in the shade bent over the outstretched arm of a kneeling young woman. The arm was twisted round, palm up. The pose reminded Garrett of a doctor taking a pulse, or nurse giving an injection.

She leaned on the railings and waited – for what she couldn't say exactly, but she knew it was what she should do. For her, medical instinct was a sort of listening, and over the years it was a knack she had come to accept like an article of faith. It was what she had built a reputation on at the Sussex CDSC, called in by experienced doctors, by local hospitals, to trace the invisible infection source, find the missing vector, where others had failed. And years of knocking on doors, interviewing relatives, peering into microscopes, dissecting entrails – had taught her that the tougher medical puzzles were tough because in such cases previous experience was as much a hindrance as guide; you had to let facts speak for themselves, to listen afresh.

She sat back down on the bench with her notebook open in her lap. She was conscious of a clock ticking somewhere in her mind, and a need to find something more concrete than conjectured lines drawn in pencil on a page. She tried to curb her impatience with this case: impatience was the enemy of listening. *Remember, connections present indirectly, like symptoms in a body.*

She remembered the quiet of the hospital Chapel. She found the card the chaplain had given her and placed it face up on the notebook, beside the name Spyder. *Dr. Prenderville. Psychiatrist and Research Fellow. Stonehill College, Oxford.* She thought of Jason. Where was he? Was he ill? Was he safe?

She took out her phone and found his address book entry. Trusting blue eyes stared out of the screen at her from under a brown foppish fringe. That image was from a photo taken four years ago. Why hadn't she updated it? Her finger moved towards the call button as if to touch someone. Panic drew the breath from her. She mustn't. She put the phone away.

Although it was early evening, the fairground was still in full swing. She could hear a miniature train clanking past. Faint screams floated up from the rocking chairs of the Big Wheel as it spun, and stopped, and spun again.

Jason had been such a noisy toddler, no hint in those early years of the quiet pious boy to come. Her thoughts shied at the memory, as though retreating from a hole with unstable edges, and she frowned down at the web of lines she had drawn, trying to concentrate on the problem to hand. In that brisk turning away she recognized the survivor's instinct, a hardness inherited from her mother. She was grateful, accepted the selfishness, knew it had kept her alive and not yet made her mean; but she could wish for some other use to put that tough streak in her.

A seagull made a slow arc around her head, resting on the cliff-top air currents with bent wings. It landed on the end of the bench and turned its head to stare at her with a yellow eye. Garrett blinked first. She began to doodle a design at random on Prenderville's card.

The noises of the fairground rose and fell. Tired, sunburned holidaymakers trickled constantly up the cliff stairs. After some minutes, Garrett stopped doodling and looked at what she had drawn. It was an eye, surrounded by rays like a child's sun. Garrett watched the beach from her bench. She saw a liquid immiscible with the facing sea, a tide of people draining back from compartments of sand and stone between breakwaters, a multicoloured stain seeping back across the flat heights, the rising dunes, back to the tracks of the miniature railway. Garrett stood still as a fly fisherman on a river bank, or a hitch hiker beside a quiet road. Her phone began to ring. She ignored it. She tried to stay aware of the broken lines in her notebook. She felt close to something not yet seen. Patterns rose in her mind, slow, shy as wary trout, suggesting effects and causes.

All her life she had seen patterns and the explanations behind them. Scientific just-so stories, mathematical and mundane. A fading stain on wallpaper around a light switch – to her mother, irritating dirt – had been for her the visible spoor of countless hands, normally distributed. The route her rambler took up the front wall was a living manifestation of averages: of phototropic behaviour summed across days. The hollow in the stone step from her kitchen into the garden counted generations of footsteps in aggregated functions of friction. Clover patterns in a meadow betrayed nutrient deposition; a line between stiles the pollination of boots; clouds the condensation gradients of thermodynamics. All day, every hour, she saw such repeating meanings.

An intern had once pointed out after a lecture she had given on outbreak causes that she appeared to believe in and talk about patterns much as the religious believed in God: patterns explained; patterns were beyond good and evil; they pointed to a truth beyond themselves; they shaped everyday thoughts, like a morality. Garrett had replied that in that case the Devil was coincidence.

She took out her phone and thumbed keys. The missed call was from an unknown number.

A memory sudden as summer rain came to her. Of afternoons sitting at the back of a school library, shading her page from the sun. She had been a shy girl, the quiet one, never the volunteer. And then one hot summer – like the one they were having now – she had discovered a relief, scratching marks in pencil, finding in the personless words of mathematics a silence free of bruising playground chatter and skipping conversations. Garrett could still remember the deepening silence over the hours as a tangle of symbols simplified down the page; conversations – that is how she had seen them, regardless of with what – all ending in certainty, like the prayers her mother had plaited through their lives, and that she in turn had plaited through Jason's.

At school she had discovered computers – for her, a sort of mathematics in motion, subroutines simply equations in action. Drawn to the most challenging computational problems, for her master's she had specialised in the new science of bio-informatics. Then soon after starting her first job her career took a more practical turn when a pathologist suggested a medical degree to complement her theory with practice. By natural steps she found her way into epidemiology, its combined disciplines of medicine and maths the perfect vocation. Looking back, she felt she had been lucky to find a profession in which her x's and y's touched lives so directly. It had carried her out of the library back into the world.

Her phone began to ring again, her bag chirruping as though hiding a trapped bird. It was the unknown caller.

"Dr Garrett?"

"Speaking."

"It's George Skinner from Porton Down. I was given your contact details by Colindale. I gather you have some malaria material you want us to take a look at?"

"Yes. Thanks for calling. We've done peripheral smears and quantitative tests. I'd like an OptiMal Assay and maybe ICT. And frankly, I'd appreciate a second opinion–"

"Well we are very busy at the moment. As soon as we receive the samples–"

"You're just outside Salisbury aren't you? Why don't I bring them over to you tomorrow?"

Chapter 5

The Central line mid-morning on a weekday was always packed as it passed through the City of London. When the businessman got on the first carriage of the eastbound train to Ealing Broadway he was pleasantly surprised to find a seat. He made a table of his briefcase on his knees and opened his laptop. A bead of sweat dropped onto the keyboard. Annoyed, he wiped it away with a thumb.

Two young businesswomen hung from straps in front of him.

"Anyway when he said she said that, I said you're having a laugh mate."

The businessman hunched over his laptop. He tried to block out the chatter of the other passengers. As he typed a password he sneezed. Three million droplets of water and mucus left his mouth at two hundred miles an hour. Fifty micrometres in diameter, they shrank as they dried to nuclei a tenth the size each containing a micro-ecology of organisms that moments previously had been internal to his body.

At Chancery Lane the women were replaced by young men in shirtsleeves carrying jackets over their shoulders.

"E-readers are killing that business model. Newspapers are closing faster than pubs. And real journalism started dying a decade ago. Face it, the written word is dead."

"I haven't been feeling so well myself lately."

"Ha ha."

The businessman pulled out a handkerchief and wiped his forehead. He stared at the damp cloth. A dull rhythmic pain beat in his temples. He could see sweat beading the back of a hand. He wasn't right.

Truth was, he hadn't been himself for some days. Not since his trip to Brighton to see Fiona. It had started with a sore throat, then the chills. Now this fever and coughing. He tried to dry his hands on the wet handkerchief and wondered about cancelling his three o'clock. All those investors! He couldn't. He frowned as he tried to remember where they were supposed to be meeting.

The young men had got out at Oxford Circus. In their place was a couple wearing matching t-shirts and trainers, arguing loudly

"I'm not coming. She's spoilt everything."

"Look Jess, people have gone to a lot of trouble. Forget her. Just enjoy yourself. For once! Christ, life is short."

The businessman began to cough, over and over, deep retches from his stomach. When he took his handkerchief away from his mouth it was spotted with blood.

"Hey fella – you okay there?"

"I'm fine. Thanks."

A few hundred droplets escaped the businessman's mouth with each word. He began coughing again, five thousand droplets a cough.

"You don't sound it."

"I'm okay." He buttoned up his jacket. It didn't stop the shivers. Or the knifing pain in his head. His breath came and went in shallow pants. When the train stopped and the couple got out he followed.

He couldn't understand the signs on the walls. The colours were confusing; and the letters wouldn't join up. Tunnels and stairs led him round and round in an underground maze without exits. When the sliding doors of another train opened in front of him he got on. The carriage was half full. He stayed standing, holding his briefcase with his right hand.

A group of smartly-dressed young people sat around him in a group.

"It's not religious extremism per se that's dangerous. The more fanatical a Jain is, the less an insect has to worry about."

"Here we go."

"It's the born-agains that make me nervous. Look at Bush after he swapped Jack Daniels for Methodism – he went on a Crusade."

"That's America for you. You know what a Texas governor once said about lessons in Spanish? 'If English is good enough for Jesus it's good enough for us.'"

The businessman twisted on his strap. The voices were coming from all directions. He wanted to move away but the carriage was now full. He stared at an advert for a dating site. He wondered if it was worth trying. Just the thought of meeting someone new was exhausting.

"Apparently Spain translates more books from English in *one year* than the entire Arab world has since the ninth century – in a millennium."

"Is that true?"

The businessman closed his eyes; he had read the dating site advert twenty times. The chatter continued. It was impossible to block out completely.

"Faith prefers respect; it's a confidence thing. You know that joke from the Irish Troubles. When a journalist at a checkpoint says he's an atheist, he's asked, 'Is that a Catholic atheist or Protestant atheist?'"

"Maybe it's not a joke."

The conversation continued to rise and fall around him. The fever was getting worse. He thought about letting go of the strap. His right hand squeezed the handle of his briefcase tighter as he tried to control his coughing. An aerosol of inhalable droplets hovered around him, a personal cloud spreading through the sealed metal carriage of fifty passengers. Shrouded in a smog of each other's fluids, they shared more than conversation. Air in the human nose and trachea moves at about a hundred centimetres a second. Large particles stick to the mucosal lining; smaller – less than five micrometres – are sucked into the lower branches of the lungs and settle out by sedimentation when the air is calm between breaths.

The businessman remained on the tube network for an hour. When the fever subsided his mind cleared enough for him to find a taxi back to his bedsit in Maida Vale. The cab driver wanted to take him to a hospital. He refused. Back home he took aspirin and sat himself in front of the television. He wondered if he was up to working. The fever returned.

Throughout the final seizures his right hand maintained its grip on the handle of his briefcase.

Chapter 6

Garrett pushed her estate through the bends and straights of the single carriageway as it climbed up from the Sussex coast to the Salisbury plain. On the passenger seat beside her was a cool bag, large enough for two six packs, labelled 'UN 3373'. It contained racks of tissues and blood from her three most recent autopsies.

"In one hundred yards, bear right onto the A413."

The car sat-nav's voice was canned like laughter and just as fake. As it ended, another recorded voice faded up in the car's interior. Garrett fast-forwarded past an intro to a new WHO podcast. She was aware she was behind in her listening. In a normal week, she would catch at least a dozen briefings.

"With international air travel, an infected person can carry a disease from any point of the globe to any other in less than thirty-six hours, a time shorter than most incubation periods. So travellers can depart, arrive, and begin infecting without even knowing that they are sick. The number of international migrants is estimated at over three hundred million a year: nearly a million a day."

Garrett turned the podcast off. It was too general. She knew the stats already. And she couldn't concentrate. She switched lanes, turned onto the A road and picked up speed. Smooth tarmac snaked ahead of her. Simon Kirkpatrick at CDSC had finally assigned a lab – Porton Down – and arranged a meeting. She suspected that without the support of Jenkins he wouldn't have bothered. She thought about her destination. Although a military base, Porton handled a lot of referred civilian cases. She had never visited before but had often worked with their researchers, recently on a cholera case. For a tropical disease like malaria, it was probably the leading research centre in the UK so she was not surprised they had been given the work.

"Approaching junction 8. At the roundabout, take the third exit onto the B342. Estimated arrival time nine minutes."

Humped, bordering fields stretched ahead to either side. A memory unspooled on the unwinding, grey ribbon of road; another drive, to a holiday cottage in Cornwall. The images that survived – jumbled, fragmentary – puzzled her sometimes. Their tent shivering with laughter; outside sheep bleating like children; cold feet leaving black prints on wet grass. Garrett leaned over the steering wheel and overrode the automatic gearbox to shift a while with and without the clutch. It was calming.

"Warning. No map data available. Please return to previous junction. Warning..."

Garrett started. She slowed late to pull into an unmarked lay-by. All buttons on the sat-nav unit were unresponsive. Something had given it a fit. She pressed Restart.

"Warning. No map data available. Please return to previous junction. Warning..."

"Okay, I heard you the first time." She switched the unit off, pulled out a road map and looked up her location. The area was covered by what looked like a national park, a large greyed-out box marked "MoD land".

Garrett reversed, shifting gears with the slightest whine of synchromesh. Fifty yards back a large sign marked a left-hand turning. Garrett stared. 'dstl. Porton Down.' Somehow she had missed it.

Garrett drove the new road more slowly. After some minutes she came to a stop at a road barrier.

MINISTRY OF DEFENCE
dstl. Porton Down.
South entrance.

Restricted land: keep out.
This is a Crown road. MoD regulations apply.
Unauthorised persons entering this area
may be arrested and prosecuted.

A guardhouse stood directly ahead. To either side, as far as Garrett could see, an endless chain-link fence divided rolling grassland.

A uniformed man approached. She opened her window. Birdsong and the day's close heat poured into the air-conditioned interior of the car.

"Af'noon ma'am. Can I help you?"

Garrett passed over an email printout. "I'm here to see a Major Skinner."

She followed the soldier over to the guardhouse. She was asked to fill in an id form. Then a vehicle form. Then a visitor's form. Army bureaucracy appeared to rival the health service.

Along one wall a bank of six monitors faced inward, each full of small windows displaying text and blinking lights like a workstation on a city trading floor. "That's a lot of screens to watch," Garrett commented. A soldier swung round on a swivel chair.

"Can't even get cable." He shook his head.

"What are they for?"

"We're a monitoring station." The soldier turned to the screens and proceeded to name them, like naughty children, with wags of a finger. "HQ. Squadron. Fence. Land sensors. Gates. Bio labs. Anything happens on the base, we see it here."

Garrett thought of her satnav system. "Does it work?"

"Sure."

Garrett looked out of the guardhouse door to the chain-link fence. She had a childish flashback to crayon pictures of moats, portcullises and crenulated walls.

"Dr Garrett. Please wear this at all times while you are here." Garrett accepted a plastic laminated ID card, blank white, with a copper chip embedded in its centre.

Her phone began to ring.

"Excuse me–"

"Go ahead."

"Christine Garrett?"

"Yes."

"It's Dr Prenderville here."

Garrett turned her back on the monitors.

"Do you still wish to meet with someone who has left Asari?"

"Yes."

"I had a call this morning from a client of mine, Michael Boorman. Says he knows your son. He's willing to see you."

Garrett found Prenderville's card and scribbled an address and phone number on the back.

"Let me know if I can be of further help."

Garrett stared at the name she had written down. Jason would see any contact as a violation of their agreement, a trespass. Was that fair? Fair? To want to see him? It was natural, for God's sake.

Another soldier approached. "My apologies Dr Garrett. It appears there may have been a mix-up over times. Major Skinner's giving a talk at the NOTAF conference. He's expecting you, but I'm afraid he won't be done for an hour or so."

The soldier at the screens pivoted on his chair, a slow back and forth rocking, as if on a porch. She became aware she was being studied with a confident, straying glance, all over, as though for risks. She forced eye contact. The soldier smiled.

"Sarge, no point the lady waiting here – she's been cleared. And my shift's up." The officer gave a single nod. Garrett heard unspoken words pass between the men, brief as a blink. *Fair play*. She controlled a flash of disdain.

The soldier stood. "Come on, I'll take you up there."

Chapter 7

"Chrissy! Chrissy! Can you hear me?"

Christmas sat cross-legged on a mat in a shrinking slice of shade where the beach sloped up to meet the black-tarred deck under the Palace Pier. Behind him, at the highest point under the eaves, a purple sleeping bag wiggled on the pebbles. One end shifted slightly and long brown hair spilled out like a hank of seaweed.

"Chrissy, I've got the sweats again."

Christmas bent towards a Tilley stove, lit it and balanced on top a Billy can.

"Did you hear me? I think my temperature's back. I feel really bad again. What about you?"

Christmas turned the stove's flame up to maximum then returned to his shaded mat. He coughed once and spat. Rusty phlegm hit a well-used target rock. Further down the pebbles a man in a pinstripe suit rolled out from under an overcoat, looked up and gave a wave.

"Everyone's got the sweats today Jade." Christmas rubbed his forehead, smudging beads of moisture into a shiny smear. He stared at the back of his hand. Water covered the skin.

"You're not even in the sun! Look at you!"

Jade zipped the sleeping bag open to her waist and sat up. Black-wet strands stuck to her forehead. She waved at the man in the suit.

"Hey Jimmy!"

The suited man was folding his coat with the precision of a butler.

"Chrissy, I feel like I'm burning up, like my head is going to explode."

"I told you: do a Sit. Do the Awakening."

Jade pushed up onto her elbows. Her body was wet with sweat. The sleeping bag beneath her was drenched. She stared down from her spot under the eaves of the pier, huddled in the last thinning slice of shade. She twisted fingers through her hair, knotting up stray strands into tight plaits.

"No Chrissy that isn't right."

"We already talked about this."

"But I'm dead sick. And I think you are too. If you're ill you can't *think* yourself well. Not if you're really ill."

"So you don't believe Arshu?"

Jade sighed. "I'm saying let's get help."

"Right thoughts. Right prayer. Right belief, Jade."

"Christ."

"You don't try. You have the help you need. It's called faith."

Jade stared at Christmas for a long time then shook her head. "You can have too much faith."

Christmas closed his eyes.

"I tried calling the Valley yesterday." Jade flopped onto her back. "Still couldn't get through."

Christmas said nothing.

"Why doesn't someone answer? You know don't you? Why can't you tell me? Zoo Crew haven't seen anyone neither. I was up there last night, spoke to Cherry."

"Last week, Lizzie said–"

"Lizzie! Lizzie this, Lizzie that, I'm fed up of Lizzie! What does that woman have, hey? Where is she? Did you see her last night?"

"I haven't seen her in days."

"Since you were all over her like a rash."

"Your jealously is wrong. People are not possessions. Remember what Arshu says: Love is not owning. You get me?" Jade didn't answer. He smiled. "Good. Because you and me, that's how it has to be." As he rhymed, his head jutted back and forward, rap-style.

Silence.

"I'm off tomorrow," he said.

"Where you going?"

"Glastonbury."

"I'll come."

Silence.

"No wellies this year! And the extra Monday. They were smart to move it, hey?"

Silence.

"You wanna be careful Chris. They're tough on dealing there now."

"That's not why I'm going."

"Chrissy, no one's interested you know. No one is listening."

"You know what your problem is, Jade? Maybe you took Sanyas, years ago, but now you believe in nothing."

Christmas crossed his legs and rocked from side to side to find the balancing point. He gazed above Jade's head, his eyes focussed at a distance. "Something extraordinary is happening. Something you can't imagine."

"Yeah?"

"Yes. The world is about to change. Forever."

Jade yawned. "Here we go."

"You understand nothing. *Nothing.* About the truth, about what is holy, about what is happening," Christmas bowed his head, "and the price that must be paid."

"Guess I must have just missed it."

"You don't know what's going on because you chose not to listen. Others will."

Jade sat up. "No they won't. You know why? Cos it's boring. Your ideas are boring. You're boring. Arshu's boring. That's why I left. Don't you get it? No one gives a fuck."

At the mention of Arshu Christmas closed his eyes. He said, "No. You don't give a fuck."

"And you don't give a fuck about me. Same thing."

The can on the stove gargled like a baby. Steam curled cloud-white in the sunshine.

"Don't you see? I can't make you like me. I can't make you want me, listen to me."

Jade's mouth folded in at the lips and she began to cry, softly, into her hair. After a while she stopped. She could feel sweat starting out all over her body. She squinted. Christmas was coming in and out of focus.

"Arshu isn't a saint you know. He's not God. Not like you all want to make him! Arshu is just a man!"

"Jade."

"He's just a man. He goes for a crap like the rest of us."

"Shut up."

"He does! He's probably going for a crap right now."

Christmas watched the water begin to bubble in the can. His tattooed skin glistened as though oiled. Flies, high up on an arm, trembled in annoyance.

"Arshu's going for a crap!"

"I said shut it!" Steam poured into the air in a steady stream. "You don't talk about him that way!"

There was a sudden puttering rumble, then fizzing like a poured drink. Christmas cursed and moved towards the stove. Jade began to shout.

"I'll talk any way I want! You can't stop me!" Jade began to sing in a terrace chant. "Arshu's going for a crap! Arshu's going for a crap! La laa laa la! La laa laa la! Arshu's going—"

Christmas changed direction. He crawled over the pebbles, tin mug in hand, moving three-legged like a monkey up into the narrow roof space.

Jade drew her sleeping bag up to her nose. "Chrissy—"

Christmas shook his head.

"Chrissy, I was only messing."

He balanced the mug between stones by Jade's head then reached out his right hand, burying it in her hair. She closed her eyes. His fingers combed softly. "I know you feel bad baby, but you can't speak like that. It's," he hesitated, "Disrespectful."

"My temperature's all over the place, Chrissy. I'm burning up!"

Christmas's hand closed. He twisted and pulled.

"AhHHH!"

Christmas tightened his fingers further and drew his fist towards his face, rotating the girl's head to put an ear close to his mouth. Imprisoned in its sleeping bag cocoon, her body jerked spasmodically.

"AhHHH! CHRISSY!!"

Below them, the man in the suit and hat called out a question.

The flies shivered again on a bicep. "Shhhhh."

Jade's body went rigid. Her mouth opened in a silent plea.

"You listening to me Jade?" He did not relax his grip or raise his voice. Jade nodded. "Look at me!" He turned her to look at him. "No more disrespect to what is holy." She nodded again, tiny easing jerks of her head. "No. More. Disrespect." His hand remained bunched in her hair.

Below them, the suited man approached with a rattle of pebbles.

"No more disrespect. Right?"

"Yes, alright."

"Right?"

"Yes, yes, I'm sorry. I didn't mean it, Chrissy."

"I don't care what you mean or don't mean. You have no idea what is going on. I say the world is about to change. It is.

And you could have been a part of it. You are not. That was your choice. But you will show respect. Do you understand?"

"Chris? Jade? Umm… You okay there?" The suited man stood beneath them, panting and plucking uncertainly at his eyebrows.

Christmas rotated his wrist. "I don't hear you."

"YES!!! Chrissy. Yes! Yes! Alright!!"

"Ahh Jade? You sure you two are okay?"

Christmas released Jade's hair, dropping her head like a bag of rubbish. He picked up his mug and crawled back to the stove. He adjusted a knurled valve under the Billy. He coughed twice, looked back at Jade and spat. When he wiped his forehead the back of his hand came away gloss wet. He glanced out towards the beach. The sun was high.

"It is time to perform my Dues. I must sit."

He settled himself cross-legged on his mat and closed his eyes.

***

"Every thirty seconds somewhere in the world a person dies of malaria."

On the stage at the front of a small auditorium, a uniformed speaker stood at a glass lectern beneath a projector screen. Major George Skinner, Head of Parasitology, Porton Down, was trim and clean-shaven. He delivered his statistics without trace of nerves, his words clipped into pieces by their consonants, commanding attention.

"There are five hundred million infections and up to three million deaths annually. Some epidemiologists estimate that the disease may have killed one out of every two human beings who have ever lived."

The magnified image of a single stained malaria parasite loomed over the room like a rose window. The auditorium was silent. The forty-strong, mostly-uniformed audience smelled of starch, hair wax and money. Skinner had their attention. But then what was more relevant to a soldier than death?

A row of Colonels, Lieutenant Generals and Brigadiers stood up at the back, smart as salutes, as Garrett strode along the nodding line. She settled in a seat.

"By body count you are looking at the animal most deadly to our species ever to have existed."

"So what?" A two-star General sitting in the front row sounded bored. "We ain't planning an invasion of Bug World, are we?" There was scattered laughter. Encouraged, the General looked around and added with a broad grin, "Last I heard, they ain't interested in democracy." More laughter circled the room, fluttering up into the dark of the higher benches like moths.

Skinner smiled. "General Wilson makes a fair point. Why are we here, gentlemen?" He paged through to a slide showing statistics. "Malaria is a two-and-a-half-million-year-old weapon present in eighty percent of our likely zones of conflict. It has proved more deadly to Anglo-American military personnel than the combined armed forces of the Third Reich and Soviet Union."

Silence returned, sudden as the draining of a cup. General Wilson shifted in his chair.

"In the last century, malaria took the lives of more British servicemen than were killed by the Whermacht."

The auditorium was quiet. *Malaria is a weapon.* Garrett thought of the chain link fence surrounding the Porton base. She had the curious sensation of having stepped into a parallel world.

"We need an effective defence. So you understand what you are being asked to fund, I'd like to take a moment to explain our recent breakthroughs."

Skinner showed a slide of an insect. "This is the vector. Remember the mosquito is not the disease–"

"It's the transporter," said a British officer in the front row. Someone laughed.

Skinner nodded with approval. "Yes, if you like, it's the bird that makes the drop." He advanced a slide to show a worm-like cell with a darkened perimeter and complex internal structure. "But the attack starts here, with the ookineete cell form. It's been described as Nature's most precisely-engineered killing machine." Skinner traced a route with his finger in the air. "This cell travels through mosquito tissue from gut to salivary glands–"

"–some sorta super virus." General Wilson interrupted. He sounded dismissive.

"No. Viruses are simple." The general looked like a schoolboy who had joined in by mistake and regretted it. "The malaria parasite is much more complex, a protozoan with multiple cell forms." He advanced the slide. "The ookineete produces this: the sporozoite, the next stage of the attack. They are the Special Ops."

Against a stained purple background a cluster of seven spherical, balloon-like shapes floated.

"There you go! Seven-man squads. These guys follow airborne service regs!"

The quip from an army chaplain – whose medical corps uniform included a dog collar – drew general laughter. Again Garrett had the sense of a parallel world. Jagged impatience struck through her.

"Except these aren't just foot soldiers. Think of them as completely autonomous units, with combat and command capabilities, built-in counter surveillance and an armaments factory all rolled into one. If just one reaches your liver, it will produce an army of ten million."

Someone joked, "Hey, we need to teach our paras to do that."

Impatience hardened into anger in Garrett as she listened to the lesson in the dark. Malaria research was being judged by medical illiterates. The unnatural conceit of her thought warned her that she should take care with herself.

An officer at the front asked, "What's the end result?"

"It depends on the strain."

"Worse case?"

"Without medication, with some of the newer strains of *malaria falciparum*, from the first signs of symptoms a soldier may be dead within twenty-four hours."

One of the audience members gave a low whistle.

"Why don't we leave this research to the civilian health services?" General Wilson asked. Skinner hesitated.

"If I may?" Garrett's musical voice carried through the hall. "Malaria is not a first world disease. And as a researcher once told me: pharmaceutical companies simply aren't interested in developing drugs for people who can't afford shoes."

"I believe the Wellcome Trust is a major researcher," the General interrupted, his response delivered in a magisterial tone reserved, Garrett suspected, for insubordinates, politicians and women.

Garrett ignored Skinner's rising arm. Her voice rang clear as a tuning fork. "Worldwide cancer research expenditure runs at around thirteen *billion* dollars. Just five years ago, annual malaria funding was in the millions."

"Was it," the General said.

"Yes. If for one day we had the death rate of sub-Saharan Africa in the UK or US – that is, in twenty-four hours, sixty-two thousand infections and three hundred and fifty deaths – then perhaps you could rely on civilian research funding."

Wilson looked poisonous, like a bullied bully, combative but unwilling to take on hard facts.

"Which is why," Skinner had raised both hands and waved one, palm flat, "We are asking for your backing. Dollar for dollar, it's the most cost-effective spending decision you'll make this week."

Chapter 8

The intern at the Epidemiology Department of the Sussex and Surrey NHS Trust was methodical by nature. He had seen the priority broadcast requiring early reporting on all UK malaria cases and made a mental note. In the last twenty-four hours, four autopsy reports had defined malaria as cause of death at the Eastbourne and Hastings General hospitals. In his opinion, at least eighteen more infection cases involved symptoms suggestive of the same connection. He entered all case histories with care and accuracy into the Sentinel computer system. There his responsibility ended.

The Sentinel escalation protocols were automated. Each new record triggered an e-mail to the inbox of the registered case worker at CDSC Colindale. Mobile devices, issued automatically to such staff, ensured instant notification.

Unfortunately, Simon Kirkpatrick's oversight had not been corrected. The case worker registered for malaria alerts was still Clarice Liu, officially off-duty. Just arrived at her hotel on the south coast of Crete, she was unaware that her inbox was filling up, and that on her bedside table in her empty flat in Ealing, west London, her work mobile was spinning and buzzing like a trapped mosquito.

***

"You nearly pushed my pitch off course," Skinner sorted notes like cards on his lectern, as though dealt a bad hand.

Garrett answered from her seat at the back of the cleared hall. "I answered a question with facts."

"In my experience, facts are a matter of opinion," Skinner said. A mobile phone gleamed in his hands, briefly consulted. "As it happens your intervention was a gift. Civilian funding is a kicker objection, and General Wilson doesn't like to argue with women. At least in public. Dr Garrett?"

"Yes."

He stepped down from the stage.

"George Skinner."

"Christine," Garrett allowed.

"There was confusion over times. Apologies. We were expecting you. I understand you have biopsy material for us?" Garrett lifted her bag. "Let's go over to my lab."

Garrett followed Skinner by car out towards a small complex of two-storey flat-roofed buildings set apart from the main army base and encircled by grassland and steel fencing. A chimney stack rose a hundred feet into clear air, shining like a needle in the sunlight. At rising intervals, cables anchored the metal column to surrounding roof points. The arrangement looked fragile, the chimney improbably tall for its restraints.

"It's an exhaust outlet. From the biosafety labs."

There was a military gallantry to Skinner's door-holding duty. But his uniform irritated Garrett. Medicine required imagination, not drill. She tried to dismiss the feeling and failed. She got out of her car and stared upward.

"The air is thoroughly sterilised before venting: it's drawn through ten feet of activated charcoal and a formalin bubble chamber then heated to two hundred degrees." Garrett suspected Skinner had done the talk before. He sounded like a tour guide. "That's the reason for the stack height, because of the superheated gases."

"Exactly what sort of pathogens do you handle here?"

Skinner led the way towards the largest building in sight, a grey, windowless caterpillar of repeating concrete sections. "Anything and everything. Something comes up no one recognises, if it's potentially infectious, or civilians don't want to handle it, it ends up in that building."

"We're also a level-five storage facility. I'm only aware of three such: this one; the Americans' Fort Detriek; and Corpus 6, in Koltsovo, Russia. Have you ever worked in bio-safety zones?"

"I'm familiar with level two and three procedures. I've used them once or twice, for notifiable diseases." Garrett shook her head. "I've never heard of level four. Or five."

"They're military classifications," Skinner said. "We have ongoing defence research – developing vaccines, prophylactics, containment measures – for Ebola, anthrax, smallpox, cholera... Some of those can only be handled safely with highly-specialized procedures. And someone discovers something new, ten to one it ends up being analyzed by one of us. If Armageddon happens, we will see it start here."

Garrett ignored the pride in Skinner's voice. She could see distortion caused by the heated exhaust air above them. She glanced behind her, counting fences back out to the access road and motorway.

"And your malaria work is done here too?"

"Yes," Skinner said. "My lab handles the parasite-based diseases. We don't use containment measures with malaria of course. There's no need, it's not contagious."

Skinner passed his ID card through a reader beside a revolving glass door.

"All building entry and exit points are controlled by card access. Entry here requires a specific security clearance. I've been told you've been cleared."

A security guard sat behind a reception desk, chin on chest, face whitened by some concealed light. Garrett could hear sports commentary. A machine gun was propped up against the desk beside him. A hand unclasped from behind his head in distracted acknowledgement.

"Hi George."

Skinner crossed a tiled lobby to a steel bank of lift doors. He pressed a call button and stood upright as if the building was calling him to attention.

"There are above-ground labs but all the isolation areas are in the basement. An underground design is essential for our levels of biosafety."

There was a long ping, reassuringly-normal, like the cheerful ring of a bicycle bell.

Doors closed behind them. The floor juddered once and Garrett's stomach lurched. She noticed a panel of buttons beside a metal intercom grill, for one basement level, a lobby and two upper floors. As they continued to descend she asked, "How far underground are these labs?"

"About four hundred feet."

The image of a castellated keep drawn in gray crayon flashed across her mind again. Garrett felt weight collect suddenly in her shoes. The doors opened onto a curving corridor. Shiny battleship-grey paint covered the walls and floor and squeaked underfoot. Skinner led the way, talking enthusiastically. His patter was fluent. She got a sense that he was boasting, showing-off. *Boys and their toys.* She was faintly amused, and felt lighter for it.

"This lab complex is only five years old." Skinner turned sideways to talk to Garrett as he walked, crabwise. "The design is based on the ring architecture we found at Corpus 6 in Russia."

"This is the perimeter access corridor." Skinner pointed at a door sign, 1II. "There are seven numbered sectors covering differing specialties: One is for Bacteriology, Two is Parasitology – my sector. Three's Virology etc."

"Sectors run inward towards the hub across concentric rings of increasing safety. The outer labs are rated to biosafety level two. Those with inner access doors lead onto the level three suites and staging areas, which in turn lead on to the level four lab ring, and, in some cases, level five, the central storage hub."

"The design ensures higher-rated agents are enclosed in more, and successively-restricted, containment environments, like Russian toy dolls. Each lab is maintained at constant negative air pressure relative to its outer neighbour, and all vent through a single central shaft to the chimney, so air only ever flows inward. That will be much like the civilian level three labs you may have used."

Civilian. Garrett said nothing. Skinner gestured at the surrounding walls. "We have many additional safeguards. For example, where we are now, the corridor, all the labs, ops rooms, service shafts, ventilation system – this whole subterranean complex is surrounded by a metre-thick concrete sheath nine hundred feet in diameter. In the event of a contamination incident all exits are automatically sealed, the lift shaft we just used is filled with a high-pressure Styrofoam-derivative that sets like rock in under thirty seconds. Here we are."

Skinner stopped by a door marked 2II. He passed his card through a reader.

"Welcome to Parasite World." The entrance made a peculiar sucking sound as it opened, like an intake of breath.

Chapter 9

"Next!"

Surgeon-Cmdr Charles White replaced a green file on top of a pile of discards and accepted a new document from his aide.

"A routine Sentinel notification."

James Hanratty – a young man of pale complexion and slickly-black hair – settled back in his chair. A minute passed, the only sounds the ticking of the mantel clock, the muted rumble of traffic passing down Whitehall outside the Metropole building, and Hanratty's occasional nervous cough. *Malaria.* White gazed out of a window, trying to remember something. He sensed his junior's impatience.

The Metropole overlooked Trafalgar Square. The tall sash windows of White's office were thickly double-glazed. White reached forward for a fountain pen. Beyond the sleeve end of his navy jacket a starched-white cuff appeared, links twinkling. Links. Yes: links were his job. The pun pleased him. He glanced up at the crest on the gilded picture frame of the Queen on the wall, at the motto of his service, *"Regnum Defende",* below the winged sea-lion. The heraldic animal represented Department Five's historical links with all three armed services. Links everywhere. He returned to the file. He was day-dreaming.

"Is there anything more on these malaria cases?" he asked, scribbling a note.

"The CDSC have asked the hospital concerned for a pathology report."

White poked at pieces of paper with his fingertips. As a senior defence analyst, clearance Ultra, his chief responsibility was giving advice. These summary judgements were based on interpretation of intelligence information which, in all shades of grey, passed unceasingly across his Whitehall desk. Scientific facts, expert testimonies, opinions, conjectures, confessions, lies, counter-lies, rumours: the challenge did not lie in a shortage of information. No, no. His fingers nudged cautiously at the slips of paper floating around on the surface of his desk like tiles in a board game.

The challenge lay in the interpretation.

The young man coughed, then said, "Just a health matter I think. We could look into it, but maybe that would be a duplication of effort."

"Hmm."

White stared out of the windows again. The problem with advice was that it couldn't be taken back. Once given, it acquired a life of its own. He had found that out to his cost.

He was well aware of the mantra that had circulated the Metropole after his mistake five years ago: 'Damned if you do, doomed if you don't'.

Five years? Was it five years since that summer? And not a day since that he hadn't thought of it.

They'd been having a heat wave just like now. A report had come in of four unexpected deaths from flu at a hospital in Newhaven on the south coast. Initial lab results had confirmed the influenza was an unusual orally-transmissible Type A, Subtype H1N1 strain. New cases were being reported hourly. An epidemiologist had traced the outbreak to a battery chicken farm and discovered bio-safety violations. When he had realised no-one else had put together the picture White had immediately raised a COBRA alert to request a cabinet-level briefing.

The epidemiology report proved to be incorrect but only after a £150m EU export ban and the slaughter of half a million birds. Had he been wrong to sound the alarm? Even now, he still thought he'd done the right thing. It had just been bad information, and bad luck for him.

"Chicken Charlie" – he had just about lived that nickname down. In the shake up two years ago he had been passed over for Department Head. Before Newhaven that would have been a surprise, but no-one had needed to explain.

Still, it could have been worse: his advice could have turned up as a paragraph in an over-edited government dossier; he could have ended up in a muddy wood with a hole in his head.

He settled back down to read the file. Someone had to do it. Government needed advice to govern. It was his job. His duty. The words of the toasts from his navy days came back to him, together with a memory of Caribbean nights at sea: "Sweethearts and wives (may they never meet)", "Queen and Country".

He checked an inward sigh. He was aware of Hanratty waiting and wondered why he was still hesitating.

He glanced up at the picture of Queen Elizabeth II on the wall. It was a reproduction, a fair copy of Pietro Annigoni's famous portrait. The stern romance of the young queen caught by the Italian painter, the set of her mouth and carriage of her head, always moved him when he studied it. He knew his response was outdated; he heard it in the rude banter of the junior staff; men like Hanratty. One of the newer intake was a confessed republican for God's sake. Time was, you could be hung for less.

Behind the portrait was a small wall safe. Old-fashioned and off-line. *Like me.* It contained codes he would not entrust to any computer system.

Still he hesitated. He re-read the file's introduction. Something nagged at his mind, a forgotten fact he couldn't quite get a hold of. Some link.

"Your opinion?"

"I don't think this one's worth chasing. A–" Hanratty paused to consult his notes, "–Simon Kirkpatick is handling the incident at UK CDSC. We were notified through his Sentinel alert. I wanted you to see it because of the Porton Down connection. They've been involved for their malaria expertise."

"Of course."

Hanratty shrugged. "It'll almost certainly turn out to be a traveller import. There are regular outbreaks of *malaria falciparum* across southern Europe."

White nodded. He suppressed a shake of the head: although he had asked for it, hoping for once to be surprised, he held Hanratty's judgment at close to nought. The young man had had the benefit of the finest education England could provide: Rugby – or was it Harrow? – then Clare College, Cambridge. The result had bred a set of correct responses fine-tuned as social machine but unfortunately not fully conscious. If he had gone into the City... but in intelligence you needed a man who could think for himself. Unfortunately there was no-one else – his number two and others were on summer holidays.

He shrugged. "Yes, all right. Just watch for now. Perhaps alert Sniffer."

Sniffer, Five's early-warning system, monitored the UK's public health networks – email traffic, databases, web site content and NHS news feeds. Set up to alert when general conditions occurred – exceeded thresholds, signature information patterns – it could also be programmed to watch for specific events, and had repeatedly proved a sensitive set of electronic ears. White was aware Hanratty was a big fan.

"The continental outbreaks are all monitored by the WHO. They'll get this report too."

"Mark for my review in seven days."

"Yes, sir."

"And I want to know immediately if any more cases come through."

"Yes, sir."

White allowed himself a small sigh. "That it?"

Chapter 10

"I'm so sorry about that." Skinner entered an office glass-walled on three sides, where Garrett sat waiting. She shook her head and smiled.

"I'm afraid you've caught us at an unfortunate time. We're shorthanded – most of my team's on holiday – so of course there's a rush on. We three are covering seven investigations, including a Chagas outbreak in Guangdong – thirteen hundred fatalities in the last six months – and a critical *Staph.* notification from eastern Angola. That was Angola!"

Skinner smiled at her and jerked his head towards the outer lab. Lit by fluorescent lights, lab benches stood in rows like pews in a church. Two white-coated researchers sat on high stools, round-shouldered over a computer monitor.

Skinner stepped backward. "Rheinnalt, can you join us please. Actually both of you in the fishbowl for a minute?"

"Yes in you come. Christine, I'd like to introduce you to Rheinnalt Bryce, one of our microbiologists. This is Dr Christine Garrett. She's here to discuss some unusual malaria cases–" Bryce looked Garrett over, from waist to hair. She saw curiosity flicker in his eyes behind his glasses.

"Christine, a pleasure to meet you. Hello."

In the starting cadence of his greeting, Garrett heard the once-upon-a-time of a story-teller.

"Christine's brought case histories, and some extra presents – biopsy samples and data. Captain Shani Zahra."

"Hi."

Zahra, short and small-framed in her white lab coat, moved out from behind Bryce with the quick careful steps of a bird. Black hair, bobbed square across her forehead, framed eyes heavy with mascara. She looked at Garrett with frank curiosity.

"C Garrett – as in RAPID?"

Garrett smiled. "That's right."

When Bryce looked puzzled Zahra nodded at Garrett. "Randomized superlinear gene detection. It's a toolkit."

"Must be five years old. I haven't–"

"We still use it."

"Shani is our molecular geneticist."

"–Malaria, Crypto, they're really George's pigeons. I'm more on the Sarcodina side of things. And Mastigophora. And Ciliophora. And mainly protein modelling–"

"Yes okay Shani."

Zahra nodded at a wall clock. "Cuito's due to call back in ten minutes. Twenty cultures have tested positive."

She glanced at Garrett then blinked as she turned back to speak with Skinner about the *Staph.* outbreak. Garrett wondered if she was a territorial kind of woman; she estimated she was in her late twenties, thirty at most.

Bryce moved around and pulled out a chair for Garrett, graceful in his movements despite his height. He stood until she sat.

"Thank you."

"Where are these unusual cases?" Bryce leaned an elbow on the table and pushed his gold-framed glasses further up his nose with the fork of two fingers. The circular lenses, hippy-messianic on a musician, lent the man a scholarly, out-of-world precision. Garrett found herself studied by magnified eyes, intense in their still regard.

"The south coast. Sussex."

"Okay, we're here to discuss a CDSC notification on a cluster of three unusual malaria cases. Let's do a quick case review shall we?" Garrett distributed copies of her autopsy reports. "Starting with Paul Fletcher. You've all got his chart. Christine, do you want to talk us through it?"

They began an extended discussion. As the lab team argued dosages and histologies, Garrett saw again the opened body, a bare arm braceleted by a hospital ID tag. She listened to the medical chatter and remembered measuring out the man's life by the wear on his teeth.

She noticed Bryce by an absence of movement. He was studying an autopsy picture of Fiona Grant. He muttered words to himself. "Ni edrych angau pwy decaf ei dalcen." The sentence sounded like a spell. It was uttered privately, under the conversation.

"Fifty percent parasetemia rising to over ninety?" Zahra gave a low whistle. "That's off the scale."

"Quinedine was finally available," Skinner said after a moment, as if satisfied. Reading on, he began to frown.

"It had no effect," Garrett said. "I am not aware of documented resistance."

"Perhaps we had a patient with predisposition factors," Skinner mused.

"Malaria mutates quickly." Zahra said. "Maybe this is a new strain."

"Or drug dosage error, or a batch problem–" Skinner said.

Garrett opened her notebook. "I've looked up the epidemiological data. There has been one malaria fatality in the UK in the past ten years. That was six years ago. A businessman returning from Thailand, already infected. There are sixty or seventy cases of malaria illness reported annually, all similar imports. Of those, less than half-a-dozen were potentially cerebral, and all but that one case treated successfully with quinines." Garrett put down her notes. "We're dealing with three fatalities in forty- eight hours."

"That's odd," Zahra said, "Both hospital cases show swollen tonsils and lymph nodes in the throat. Sounds like strep."

"Do we have backgrounds?" Bryce asked.

"Paul Fletcher was a motorbike courier for a trans-shipment company. Thirty-six, mixed race – English mother, Indian father – the only patient with a record of travel, extensively throughout Asia, though not in the last eighteen months."

"What about the other two?" Bryce asked.

Garrett shuffled more paper. "Of course we know next to nothing about the missing persons 'Lizzie'. Fiona Grant was a Caucasian woman, thirty-three years old. Single. Worked for a local pharmaceutical company. In previous good health. No recent travel abroad." Garrett put down her notes. "It's transmission that puzzles me most."

Skinner nodded agreement. "UK marsh habitats haven't been malarial for a century."

"Do you know where the last known malaria outbreak was?"

"Isle of Grain," Bryce and Skinner said together. Skinner grinned and finished, "Off the Kent coast. 1918."

They contemplated the infection riddle in silence together.

"It's been a hot summer," Zahra began uncertainly. "Perhaps there's been an unknown migration event." Skinner looked at her over his glasses. Zahra shifted uncomfortably in her chair but plunged on. "There *are* unprecedented levels of species migration nowadays. I'm thinking of the blue tongue cattle outbreak in Sussex last year." Zahra said. "That was caused by a movement of *Culicoides*."

"There are over two hundred different species of mosquito. Why the vector *Anopheles*?" Skinner asked. Bryce shook his head and smiled agreement. Garrett was less sure of dismissing Zahra's suggestion.

"What about blood transfusions?" Zahra ventured again, clearly the 'ideas' person of the group.

"The hospital blood was re-screened. Came up negative." Garrett said.

There was silence.

"What about relapse?" Bryce said. Everyone looked at him. "If the deaths were caused by relapses from older infections then there's no transmission issue: no need to look for recent infection marks or travel. Malaria can lie dormant in the liver for many years."

"Can be for a lifetime," Skinner said. "There are cases of fatal malaria recurrences from infections contracted sixty years previously. But," he shook his head impatiently, "Three relapse cases simultaneously? And all the same strain?"

"Shared IV drug use?" Zahra suggested. "This girl had traces of LSD in her blood, she was a recreational drug user."

"So far, the victims have no known connection," Garrett pointed out.

"They have now. They're all dead." Bryce said.

A phone rang in the outer lab and Zahra went to get it. She returned only to put her head round the door. "It's Cuito."

"Rheinnalt, please continue going through the case histories." Skinner stepped out.

"Well we've pretty-much covered them." Bryce put the reports down on the desk. "It's a shame the slide printouts aren't clearer. I'd have liked a closer look."

"I've got the source images," Garrett said.

"That would be useful."

Garrett passed him a memory key. Bryce swivelled his chair to face a terminal in a corner of the room. He turned his head to her, owlish behind his spectacles.

"Fiona Grant was beautiful, don't you think?"

"Yes. She was. What was it you said earlier, was it in Welsh?"

Bryce tilted his head to one side and examined Garrett along his nose, then smiled and repeated, "Ni edrych angau pwy decaf ei dalcen. It means, 'Death considers not the fairest forehead.'"

Bryce glanced out of the room to where Skinner and Zahra stood together. "May I ask, Christine, why you are so interested in this case? Surely you don't go to these lengths with every unexplained disease cluster? Visiting the reference lab, bringing samples in person–"

"No, of course not."

Garrett found she couldn't sit still, and stood up. She came to the dividing glass wall and put her hands in her pockets. In the outer lab, Zahra and Skinner were bent over a speakerphone, Zahra talking, gesticulating with her hands. Garrett noticed the lab's side walls narrowed perceptibly, like railway tracks in a painting, creating the illusion of distance. She remembered Skinner's description of the complex's ring design, and decided she was looking towards the centre of the hub. An oval hatch was set in the end wall. It had a wheeled handle like a submarine door, marked 2III, above a design in yellow, three arcs intersecting a central circle, the international biohazard symbol.

Her fingers felt the sharp edges of something in one of her pockets. She took out Prenderville's card and stared at the sketch she had doodled above the beach in Brighton, of an eye surrounded by rays like a child's sun. She wanted to speak about Jason and the tentative connection she had found. One of the dead might have known him. It had been nearly two years. When he had left the last time he hadn't even said goodbye, just raised a hand over his head. She couldn't reach him, couldn't touch him, didn't know what he was doing. At least she could speak about him. It might fill that ever-present silence she carried with her. Garrett turned a cold eye on herself and filed the edge of self-pity off her impulse before letting it be. She put the card back in her pocket.

"Working in epidemiology, you develop an instinct for what is not right. I can't put it more explicitly than that at the moment. Something feels wrong."

She watched her words mist and fade on the glass wall. The sound of typing had stopped. Garrett turned back to Bryce. He adjusted his glasses, his movements shy.

"We are sent dozens of malaria reference cases every year," he smiled when he looked at her, "All with anomalous behaviours of some kind, often lethal. That's why we get them.

They are seen once, then disappear – stray, non-viable mutations, never fully explained, never seen again. My guess is we are looking at one of those."

"I hope you're right."

Bryce returned to his keyboard. His long fingers sounded a soft rain. Garrett noticed a faded cotton friendship band around his left wrist. She watched as he moved and resized images with practised skill. The man was gone, in his place only a point of concentration, out of phase with human speech.

There was a seriousness in him she responded to. She had a sudden odd memory of lazy Sunday mornings, long breakfasts spent reading the papers with bottomless pots of tea, toast hardening in racks, watching David work. She had loved to see him researching, taking notes, typing up his articles, bent over with un-childish intent, passionate, committed. In the years after they had met, she had seen how that strength of purpose had been the way he had found to grow up, and given him a maturity beyond the limits of his character, a strength she had measured herself against and drawn herself up to meet.

Waiting, Garrett turned back to the glass wall. She tried not to think about how far they were underground, the weight of rock around them, the dark in these labs at night.

"I don't mean to discount your instinct. Nor the three deaths you have seen." The soft music in Bryce's accent brought Garrett back to the table. She sat down. A projector flickered on as Bryce's fingers moved in impatient rushes. "I mean, we are lab researchers. We study cells and molecules, not people. But we're not disconnected."

Bryce stopped typing. He turned his hands palm-up and studied them. "It's an odd power, don't you think? We sit down here in splendid isolation, pulling our molecular levers and our mathematical pulleys. And because of what we do, something happens – or we understand something – up there in the real world. We depend upon that connection just as surely as a mechanic on a wrench." Bryce returned to his keyboard.

"In my work," Garrett watched Bryce's fingers as she spoke, "in epidemiology, the key – the power if you like – lies in understanding those connections: the symptoms and infection vectors, patterns in the data–"

Bryce raised his eyebrows.

"*Patterns.* Hmm, that's a good word Christine. Their regularity always suggests cause, no?" Bryce hit runs of keys, short acciaccaturas, in quick succession. The wall screen lit up to show a three foot-high image of blood cells. They shivered, once, twice, clusters of freckled pale cells enlarging each time, as if growing. Bryce selected one freckle. The magnified image of a single stained malaria parasite loomed over the room like a rose window. "Their beauty certainly speaks of one."

Garrett sensed the brief vertigo of the converted. She had an impulse to tease, to replay an old argument. Each Sunday morning David had driven her to Mass with Jason. He had sat in the pub for an hour before driving them home, always asking 'How was the blood today?' It had been the only real disagreement between them.

"Beauty? Do you mean a *first* cause? Are you making a *theological* argument? "Garrett mimicked Bryce's raised eyebrows. "Don't you know James' riddle? – What does the great world-carrying turtle stand on? And if a greater, what does that turtle stand on? I mean really Rheinnalt, can it be turtles all the way down?"

"Are you offering me an *atheistic* argument?"

"Atheist makes me sound like a member of some Russian sect, a Karamazov, all pride and sensual sin."

Bryce nodded. "It does, doesn't it?"

Garrett checked herself. She wondered at her sudden openness. "Can you track across the blood?"

"Sure."

"You see the variation in forms? Look – tiny rings and spheres, banana shapes – trophozoites, merozoites, sporozoites, gametocytes. I noticed them this morning but they are much clearer here than in my printouts."

"Hmm. Normally, only one parasite form is seen in the blood at any one time: trophozoite broods causing hot fever, gametocytes cold sweats—"

"Yes, I know—"

"It's rare but this breakdown of brood synchronisation has been recorded before as a side-effect of high infestation rates."

"I didn't know that. Can you put samples from the others alongside? Same mag. I'd like to compare."

Bryce fiddled. The display split, and split again, forming a triptych of three windows. "Pretty much the same."

They began an exhaustive blood study. Bryce gave up first, straightening to massage a shoulder. "Well, I don't think there's much more—"

"Wait a minute. Back up a bit. No, there."

Garrett walked over to the screen and pointed. "What's that? Can you enlarge?"

The screen shivered. The blood cells grew.

"More?"

The screen shivered again, cells growing until less than forty of the pale lilac balloons were visible.

"How is it you're not losing definition?"

"I'm using a military image-enhancing program. It was originally developed for missile guidance but some bright spark spotted we could use it."

Garrett's lips thinned. Inches from her nose, a dark spiky ball floated amongst larger blood cells. It looked out of place, floating loose like a mine. Garrett pointed.

"What is that?"

Bryce frowned. He said nothing.

"Can you enlarge further?"

"Hang on, just have to convert–" The image shivered then began to grow again. "We are at times seven hundred, enhancing now to fifteen hundred." The black parasite began to fill the screen. Details began to blur. "We're at the optical limit," Bryce announced.

"It doesn't make sense," Skinner was staring at the screen. He and Zahra had rejoined them while Bryce had reformatted the image.

"Ovoid, interior apicoplast, thickened exterior with spike formations: it's definitely an ookineete," Skinner said.

"Don't ookineekes only exist in the vector?" Bryce asked.

"Yes. In the mosquito host." Garrett pointed. Her arm extended through the cell wall of the rogue cell, three feet into the magnified interior. One side of her body and half her face was speckled blood-red.

"Can we go back, look at the other samples?" Garrett asked. Fifteen minutes of painstaking study revealed just three more of the rogue cells: a pair together and another isolated cell.

"Perhaps they're just part of the mixed broods," Bryce suggested.

Skinner nodded. "When the lifecycle clock becomes unstable I suppose any plasmodium cell form could be produced."

"Or maybe there's another enzyme present, triggering the change," Zahra said.

"We're guessing," Garrett said. She pursed her lips, thinking. Skinner opened his mouth to speak but Garrett continued. "I suggest you centrifuge the blood, separate out cells by mass."

Skinner closed his mouth, nodded. "I would–"

Garrett interrupted again, "A Buffy Orange test would be best."

"Just what I was going to suggest," Skinner said. "Good idea."

Zahra looked from Garrett to Skinner and back. Between two beautiful women there is a moment soon after meeting when they must decide whether they will be friends or enemies. Zahra smiled at Garrett. "Good idea."

"Let's also get high quality stains and images: blood and tissue," Skinner said. "And we need some proper electro-mags of the interiors of those cells. Okay good–"

"We are looking at three cases," Garrett said, "Three fatalities. No natural disease can afford to kill all its hosts." Garrett held up a hand to forestall objections. "I know it's a tiny sample. Even so. That's too lethal. So this cluster must be an outlier. Just for my peace of mind, can you start an RNA probe? I would like to identify the exact strain we are dealing with."

Skinner inclined his head, a slight movement of courtesy. "Of course. It's routine."

He sighed and picked up a clipboard.

"Shani, the Angola *staph.* cases are the highest priority. And the Chagas second. But start the tissue prep." Skinner shook his head at Garrett. "The material workup is labour intensive. And given how short-staffed we are right now… Christine, I know it's the bank holiday weekend. I don't suppose–"

"I can give you a few hours this afternoon," Garrett said. She saw Skinner jump at the offer. "But I'm driving back down to the coast this evening. I want to look into the circumstances surrounding the deaths."

"Surely the lab investigation is the priority?" Bryce was frowning at her. He clearly couldn't see the point in knocking on doors.

"Lab and field work go hand in hand."

"But the initial prep takes the time–"

"I hope to be back tomorrow afternoon."

"We shouldn't discount on-the-ground investigations." Skinner said. "Thank you Christine. We'll take all the help you can spare. Okay. Let's get started then, shall we?"

"Deuparth gwaith yw ei ddechrau," Bryce said. Seeing Garrett's blank look he added, "Starting the work is two thirds of it."

"It sounds wiser in Welsh," Garrett said. Bryce smiled.

"Don't encourage him," Zahra said, following him out.

Skinner watched Garrett's eyes track Bryce through the glass walls. "I hope Rheinnalt didn't spook you. He can be a little... intense, on first meeting."

Garrett glanced at the projector screen. "He was helpful."

"He's a good microbiologist. Not as good as he thinks he is but you get used to him. Well, we have. Rheinnalt is Rheinnalt."

Garrett stayed behind re-reading the case notes. When her thoughts idled they turned to Bryce. She found herself wanting to continue the discussion they had started, if only with herself. The loose end of it was like a stray hair on her lips.

Chapter 11

"Peshawar – that's where you can get real dysentery."

"You stayed at the Khyber Hotel?"

"Course. Best banana pancakes, man."

"Better than the Pudding Shop?"

"You eat anywhere in Istanbul you'll have the trots. Guaranteed."

Jade sneezed.

"You alright back there?

"I'm fine. Thanks."

"You don't sound it."

"I'm okay." She pulled her sleeping bag up to her ears. It didn't stop the shivers. Or the knifing head pains. Her breath came and went in shallow pants.

Smoke hung in the air in twisted, sinking ribbons. A Kashmiri prayer shawl hung over the seats in front of her. She watched it sway to the movement of the coach as she listened to the other passengers. From where she lay across the back seats she could see only the tops of heads.

"Better than at Amir Kabir?"

"Better."

"Better than The Matchbox in Kathmandu?"

"I'm telling you they're the best. End of."

Jade closed her eyes. She had hitched a ride out of Brighton that morning with the crew of a London to Sydney tour bus.

The chatter continued. It was hard to put the words together.

"Cakes in Pokhara."

"Or Surat Thani."

"Mekong and coke, mate."

"Just the Magic Bus."

Jade felt the sweat on her back. The fevers were getting worse. She wanted to go home.

The Bus was going close.

"Hasn't run for three years. Couldn't get Iranian transit visas till last month."

"Or the Crown. Be in Delhi in about three months. Only twelve countries to go!"

Jade got out near Dover. It was hard to stand, harder to lift her pack. She got angry when helped. She wandered for hours, drifting aimlessly along the front, reluctant to leave the sea.

It felt like a last link to Christmas. Such a bastard. And he didn't care. That hurt the most.

"When your down, and troubled, and need a helping hand, and nothing, nothing is going right."

The songs on her player looped and looped. She started to enjoy shouting when people tried to speak to her. Occasionally she stopped to sit on a bench, to cough and retch.

"You just call out my name, and you know wherever I am, I'll come running, to see you again."

"Lizzie?" she whispered. "Where are you?" She felt tears on her cheeks. She doubled over, spitting gouts of red saliva.

She heard the sea. The sea!

She steered by the promenade railings until she found a staircase. The steps were steep and narrow. She slipped and hit a small concrete landing.

"Shit!"

She stood. Her ankle was not right. She realised she'd lost her pack. Blood pounded in her temples. Sweat gathered in beads along her forehead. She heard the sea again. She got up and continued down, favouring her left foot.

At the bottom of the stairs a small sandy beach sloped down to rock pools. The narrow compartment was shut in on one side by a breakwater and on the other by a high curving wall of concrete, lime green at the base. Jade stared up at the wall, trying to understand why it was there. At the edge of the rock pools a rusting container lay half-submerged in sand. Around it was strewn old fishing tackle and plastic rubbish in heaps. There was no-one in sight. Somewhere out to sea she could hear a ship's horn.

The sea.

She took a few tentative steps away from the stairs. She could just see the waves. A weaving path of wet sand shone between outcrops of sharp black rock. She thought of the cooling water and broke into a hobbled jog.

"And you know wherever I am," Jade half-shouted, half-sang, "I'll come running!"

Her fall was awkward, arms still spread-eagled. The ground that came up to meet her was unexpected. She lay still, dazed. Her eyes brightened with the pain in her head.

"Close your eyes, and think of me, and soon I will be there, to brighten even your darkest night."

"Lizzie? Mum?"

Blackness rushed in. Her limbs began to jerk, movements of spasmodic reflex, disconnected from her mind. After some minutes she was still.

Carol King continued to sing on a loop. Out across beach the tide was coming in. Foaming water filled the rock pools and ran fast along the gleaming channels of sand.

***

"Home time."

Garrett glanced up. Bryce was waiting by the door.

"I've just got one more tissue section to prepare."

"Come on, it's late. It'll wait. Araf deg mae dal iâr." He waited for her to look up then added, "The way to catch a hen is – slowly."

Garrett sighed and nodded. She had wanted to complete the Buffy Orange test but it had taken longer than expected.

They left together. Out of a lab coat, Bryce looked different. He wore a collarless rough-weave linen shirt that looked unexpectedly – Garrett searched for the word – trendy. Yes. That was it. Trendy. It was a surprise.

He stopped by his car.

"I want to show you something. Why don't you follow me?" When he saw her hesitate he added, "It's not far out of your way."

Bryce drove through the compound gates and turned away from the main Porton campus. Garrett followed. Behind her, to her right, the sun was an orange glow low on the horizon. The road ran across open grassland and after a few hundred yards Bryce turned off onto a gravel track. Garrett stopped at the junction.

She could see a low brick building on a slight rise of land perhaps a mile down the track. Bryce's car, a hundred yards away now, had not stopped. Garrett thought of the fence encircling the MoD land, and the guardhouse and soldiers. She frowned at the distant building, released the brake and turned onto the track. She would go that far and no further.

As she approached she could see there were no doors or glass in the windows. Weeds sprouted out of the roof. Bryce stood by his car and gestured like a car park attendant for her to pull up alongside.

"What–"

"Shhh." He put a finger to his lips. He took her hand and led her into the building.

"What is this place?" Garrett whispered.

Bryce drew her over to a window. He stood behind her. She gazed out through an empty window frame.

"What?" her voice was sharp. She didn't know why she was here and felt that holding his hand had made her complicit.

Bryce said nothing.

"I think I should–"

"Shh!"

She caught the excitement in his voice. He turned her by the waist to point where he was looking. She wondered if she should be angry that he had touched her again. She thought of David.

She decided to leave.

"Can you see her?" Bryce whispered. He raised his arm to point.

She frowned. Out over the grass the ground undulated in natural furrows. She could see nothing. Then, as she lost her patience, she saw a slight movement. A small grey creature scurried low over the ground.

"Oh."

Garrett watched as the animal froze. Motionless it almost disappeared, its buff, brown-streaked body merging into the colours of the grass and earth. Fifty yards away, she could just make out long knobbly yellow legs, and wings held half-lifted in a curious arrested pose.

"What's it doing?" she whispered.

"There's a ground scrape – a nest – there."

Right on cue, two little sand-coloured chicks scuttled into view. When Garrett started to speak Bryce put a finger to his lips again and whispered. "They're very shy. Jumpy. Come on." He led the way out of the building.

He crouched down by the west-facing wall. When Garrett hesitated he gestured with his head that she should sit.

"If we're still they may come close." He pointed at a nondescript expanse of stony ground.

"At this time?"

"They're nocturnal."

"What are they?"

"Stone curlews. *Burhinus oedicnemus*. A breeding pair. Very rare."

"How rare is very?"

He drew his legs up beneath him and settled his back against the wall.

"Over the past fifty years numbers have declined all over Europe." He grimaced. "Loss of suitable habitat. Norfolk still gets a few visitors on reserved land, in summer – it's a Palaearctic migrant. Over there they call them Dikkops, or the thick-kneed bustard."

Garrett sensed he was showing off and suppressed a smile. She sat down. He gestured at the grasslands in front of them.

"But with the right conditions the birds return. They demonstrate conservation works; I like that about them." Bryce stopped. She waited but he didn't continue. The silence deepened.

"How did you find them?"

"Spotted one from the car." He broke off. "You hear?"

Garrett listened. A soft, repeated banshee call echoed out across the greying grassland. Kur-lee. Kur-lee.

"I see the name is–"

"Shh."

Garrett waited. She became embarrassed then saw he wasn't. Suddenly she realised how tired she was. It'd been a long day. She rested her back against the rough wall and closed her eyes. The brick still retained some of the day's heat. She felt a vertebra in her neck pop softly as the muscles in her shoulders relaxed. When she opened her eyes again Bryce hadn't moved.

Somewhere in between noticing his calmness and opening her eyes she realised she had become comfortable. She studied the grass. She could see no movement. She wondered how long they would have to wait. She thought about being held by the hand and turned at the waist. On the tanned back of his hand where it rested on his knee Garrett noticed fine gold curls. He nodded very slightly. She looked up.

In front of them, not ten yards away, a queer creature bobbed over the ground. Garrett could make out much more clearly now the knobbly yellow knees and large yellow eyes. *Nocturnal.* The bird held an insect in its beak. Another bird bowed deeply, touching the ground with his bill, his fanned tail held high in the air. The chicks scurried around the courting adults, always on the move.

They watched for some time, until the birds drifted away, grazing across the stony ground.

"I wonder why they breed here?" Garrett asked.

"This is good country for wildlife. Most of it's untouched since Porton Down was set up nearly a hundred years ago." Bryce spoke in a normal voice, relaxed now he had seen the birds up close. "Last summer, there were over forty species of butterfly logged. That's a UK record." He raised his eyebrows in appreciation and explained. "No pesticides. This is about the most undisturbed countryside in England."

"Is none of it cultivated?"

"Over by there, to the west, there's Arlington farm, but that's only a few fields. Ah, it's amazing how beautiful nature is, given a chance, hey? This place is more untouched than the Brecon Beacons. You could call it a small piece of Eden."

"Have you seen the birds in Norfolk?"

Bryce smiled and Garrett was embarrassed by her curiosity. "Am I a birder? A twitcher? I suppose so. My father was." He hesitated then rushed a little, as though to beat a question. "He's dead. He died many years ago. But he taught me a lot. I think it's why I like this place so much. I feel close to him here. He would have liked to see these birds. Of course he would never have had the chance. But I think he would have liked the idea of this uncrowded land."

He seemed to want to say more but didn't.

The sun had set; overhead, the sky was already black. A cluster of stars, oval, like an eye with an empty centre, shone faintly above the northern horizon. Garrett wondered where Jason was. She wanted to speak about him. Bryce was silent still. She noticed that while talking their bodies had leaned together and touched lightly at the shoulders. She moved away.

"Come on, it'll get chilly," Bryce said, standing, "and you've still got a drive ahead of you. I'll speak to George about getting you digs on-site if you like."

"Thank you for showing me the birds."

Chapter 12

Hot metal boomed like a Caribbean steel drum. Garrett knocked again on the dented panels of a twenty-foot-wide entrance gate. Rusting razor wire looped in undulating coils above her head like a vicious, oversized Slinky.

"Hello?!"

"Hello? Is there anybody there?"

Garrett had been woken early that morning with a call from Eastbourne District General; they had wanted her help with an emergency response training exercise. By lunchtime she had returned to the Brighton Royal and, with Da Costa's help, obtained contact information for the malaria cases. Frustrating calls had discovered nothing about 'Lizzie', the missing person. Fiona Grant's ex-husband, speaking over a crackling line from Cape Town, had been curt and unhelpful. That left Paul Fletcher. Two unreturned messages to his girlfriend 'Cherry' had brought Garrett to this gate.

A concrete wall stretched out to either side topped with twinkling glass and black tufts of Buddleia. Across the road a builder's skip, piled high with bags of rubbish, was alive with flies. What possible connection could a young professional like Fiona Grant have with a man from this place?

Garrett strolled back and forth in front of the gates. She remembered her husband's ability to slow her down, his cautions and suggestions of patience. Investigations always start like this. Dead ends may not be what they seem. Garrett watched the flies. She remembered his persistence too, his endless questions. "Why? Why? Why?" Like a little boy. Questions that had often got him into trouble. Once, after a drunken meal and an argument that had left him too romantic, he had told her that in the ever-varying Because, Because, Because of her science they fitted together perfectly. It didn't matter who was right, who was wrong: he was the Why to her Because, she the answer to all his questions. Glib. The words of a writer. She had pulled him by his uncombed blonde hair, kissed his eyes and told him to shut up.

"Who is it?" A voice spoke from behind the gates.

Garrett bent and posted words slowly through the gap. "My name is Dr Christine Garrett." She could see the toecaps of heavy boots. "I called and left messages. I'm looking for a woman called Cherry."

One half of the double gates swung open. A tall, heavily-muscled man stood in the entrance. He wore oil-stained jeans, a white T-shirt and a red bandana knotted across the top of his right arm.

"You here 'bout Spyder."

"Paul Fletcher?"

The man pulled the gate open wide. "Better come in."

He led the way over the concrete apron of a station forecourt past two rusting petrol pumps. The whitewashed walls of a bungalow reflected back the sun like a blank sheet of paper.

"Who are you?"

"The name's Fly. CHERRY!" Fly's voice was raised like a father's. A wooden signpost read 'Zoo Crew Clubhouse'. Underneath someone had scrawled in black and silver paint: *Abandon all hope, ye who enter here.*

"Coming!"

A head disappeared at a door. Fly gestured at an old blue sofa. Garrett hesitated then sat down in the sagging dip. Behind her the corrugated metal clubhouse roof ticked away in the sunshine.

"Spyder was Cherry's partner."

"Yes, I was told."

"She's taking his death hard. Blaming herself."

"Blaming herself in what way?"

The girl reappeared. A wide-chested black Staffordshire terrier was jumping around her heels. Fly looked at Garrett. She had the fleeting impression of having been weighed, placed in the pan of carefully-calibrated scales. "Take care with her."

When the dog saw Fly it jumped. Cherry checked the animal's weight with a leash thick as a stirrup leather wrapped around her knuckles; the jerk ran through her body.

"Let me take Rocky," Fly took the leash and snapped it hard to restrain the heavy dog. He put an arm round the girl and squeezed her shoulders before he left.

Cherry stood square in front of Garrett. She wore grey jeans and a black check shirt. Straight henna-orange hair framed an open oval face.

Fly called out from the doorway, "Can I get anyone a drink?"

"Thank you!" Garrett replied. "Coffee. Two spoons, black, no sugar."

Cherry shook her head.

"You the doc who left a message?"

"Yes. Cherry?"

"That's me. What do you want?"

"I'm Dr Christine Garrett. I'm an epidemiologist—"

"What do you want?"

"Please, won't you sit down with me?"

Cherry perched on the edge of the sofa. In front of her a crate of empty beer bottles gleamed in the sun like a treasure. Garrett met Cherry's eyes, the same bottle brown, surrounded by fine sun wrinkles, unfriendly, appraising.

"I performed the post mortem examination of Spyder."

"Uh-huh."

"Do you mind if I ask you some questions?"

"You seen 'im. I haven't. Not for two days. That's not right."

Autopsy pictures from the case file flashed across Garrett's mind. Young. Strong. Outwardly healthy.

"I'm making sure we understand exactly why Spyder died."

"He was my man."

Cherry stared Garrett down. Garrett remembered again the intimate examination she had performed. She looked away first.

"I understand—"

"Go on, ask your questions."

Garrett took out her notebook. "We believe Spyder was killed by a cerebral malaria. Do you know if he had ever had malaria before?"

"Yeah. Once."

"When exactly?"

"Four, five years back. After a Goa Christmas."

Cherry's voice was flat, emotionless. She could have been giving directions to a passerby. Her gaze was fixed on the empty beer bottles. Where the girl's sleeve had ridden up her arm, Garrett noticed a long oval bruise along the cephalic vein bisected by a straight line of spots like acne. Similar spots marked other veins.

"Did Spyder fall ill while you were out there?"

"No. Was 'bout a month after we got back."

"What happened?"

"Doc told him he'd stopped taking the pills too soon. Come summer, he was better."

"What about any other illnesses?"

"Spy wasn't never ill."

"Nothing? The flu last winter? Anything with a fever?"

"I told you. No. He was never ill."

"Before he got ill this time, what was Spyder doing?"

Cherry shrugged. "The usual."

"What's that?"

"It's a busy time. Last few weeks he was working with Fly getting set for Glasto." When Garrett frowned, Cherry said patiently, "The festival. We run a caff there."

Garrett questioned Cherry further about Spyder's illness, and then about Fiona Grant and Lizzie. The girl recognised neither name.

"What about outside work? Did he do anything special in the last month?"

"No."

"Go anywhere?"

"No. Well, couple weeks back we went to see Jade at the Brighton festie. He was *fine* then! Smoking, drinking like a horse down the beach." Cherry lifted her head. "More than Christmas, and that's saying something."

"And when did Spyder first become ill?"

Fly reappeared and placed a mug of coffee on the ground near Garrett. He moved with his eyes down and returned to the clubhouse without speaking. Garrett took a sip and turned the mug in her hands. Painted on the side was a gold eye, many-spoked, circled by religious logos. It was a copy of the tattoo on Spyder's shoulder. Garrett's stomach muscles shivered then tightened. The gilt paint of the image glowed a little unreal in the sunlight, like luminescence at night.

"Bout a week ago."

"What?" Garrett looked up from the logo on the mug. She forced herself to concentrate on Cherry.

"That's when it started. He was sweatin' something terrible. Then coughing. Spitting. Said he must have picked up some bug. That was unusual. Spy's never ill! And he's not the sort to complain. I should've made him go to the docs. I jus' thought–"

"You were not to know how ill he was."

Garrett waited but the girl did not look at her. Her beginning flare of protest was gone; talk and logic couldn't bring him back.

"Has anyone else been ill – with a temperature, fever – that you've heard of?"

"No."

"Anyone at all?"

"No."

Garrett put away her notebook.

"That it?"

"Yes. Thank you. I may need to ask some more questions later."

Although the sun was dipping low in the sky, it was still hot on their shoulders. On a distant rise of land, Garrett could see a field of wheat gilded by the late sunlight. She turned her mug of coffee round and round in her hands. When she spoke, her eyes were unfocussed.

"May I ask you a question, about something else?

Cherry brought her tongue up in front of her top teeth. "Lady–"

Garrett raised her mug. "This logo. Do you know anything about it?"

Something bent Cherry's lips then was gone, vanishing like writing on water. She shook her head.

"Do you?"

Cherry shook her head again. She leaned back and rested a crooked arm along the top of the old sofa, as though around someone beside her.

"Guru-sri-kalki Arshu," Garrett pronounced the syllables carefully, exactly as Prenderville had sounded them.

"They're a bunch of freaks. Don't waste your time."

"My son's there."

Cherry stared.

"In Asari Valley. For the last two years. I saw the same tattoo on Spyder's shoulder. Why?"

"He lived there. A few summers back. Not for long."

"Would you tell me what happened?"

"It was after a bad time between us. For a while I thought I'd lost him to that crew of nutters. Then he wrote me, said he wanted out, said he was scared to leave."

"And?"

"I went and got him."

"You went to Asari Valley?"

"Yep."

"Why didn't they throw you out? They did–"

"Thought I was joining up. I stayed a few days. Then we left. One night. Just walked. Big full moon party. No-one noticed. They were all on the beach, high, stoned. We had a little trouble after, but they know to leave us be now." Cherry lifted her chin towards the clubhouse. "Fly takes care of his own."

Garrett's hands tightened on each other.

"Did you meet anyone called Jason? Or Skyler? Blonde-haired boy? Man."

Cherry shook her head.

"Did Spyder mention–"

Cherry shook her head again.

"Do you know anyone else there?"

"A few."

"Are you in contact with them?"

"No."

Garrett stared unseeing at the rusting petrol pumps on the forecourt in front of her. Cherry studied Garrett. Her shoulders dropped a little. "You ever hear from–"

"Jason. Once every six months."

"Must be hard."

"Yes."

"People leave. Eventually. When they get tired of the bollocks. The preaching. The guru crap. The working for free. They get help and–"

"I know."

There was silence. Garrett rehearsed a strength she didn't feel.

"Spyder," Cherry stopped, then began again. "Spy loved it to begin off with. The parties, the free trips – the girls, I bet – the free booze. He was even into all the meditation. He always was a spiritual boy. That crazy mum of his brought him up a Buddhist. That's how they get you. Early. When he joined Spy was going through a bad patch. Couldn't find work–"

Garrett held still, not listening to Cherry until she had identified the pain, sharp, like a splinter left to fester. It was guilt.

"You know he could drink a bottle of vodka straight and not slur a word." Cherry was gazing fondly at the crate of empty bottles. "Man, he loved his booze." Pride made Cherry sit up. "He wasn't ever mean with it – he was a happy drunk. You know I still got half a bottle of Becks in our room, on his table. Not like him. Not to finish it."

They sat together for a long while in silence.

Cherry began chanting softly, her head raised as if calling out across distance. "I Spy, My Spy. I Spy, My Spy. I Spy, My Spy, on the sea shore."

Garrett watched two men on the other side of the forecourt securing the loaded roof rack of a white Landrover with sheet and ropes, the old way. One of them was whistling a tune through his teeth. Fly reappeared to check on the work. As he walked back past them he jerked a thumb towards the Landrover. "Skylark's ready!" Cherry smiled at him and Garrett said, "She's alright," as if she were. When Cherry spoke again her voice was bitter.

"Doc? You know why it happened?"

"We don't have all the answers just yet," Garrett began.

"I should have got him to the hospital earlier."

"Cherry, it—"

"If I'd made him go, the day before—"

"From what we know, it wouldn't have made any difference."

But Cherry wasn't listening. Garrett waited.

"You think everything happens for a reason." Cherry began softly. "You know: you do something good for someone, eventually something good comes back. You do bad, bad'll happen to you." Cherry's head came up, her voice rising. "Seems right, doesn't it? But Spyder and me, we never did nothing wrong."

"No one can be blamed for Spyder's death. Not you, not him, not anyone," Garrett said.

The two women sat side-by-side on the sofa staring into the same place. In the distance, beneath a falling sun and a sky faded to cotton-washed blue, a combine crawled across a field of shining wheat like a silent, fat beetle. After a long while Garrett began to speak, her voice matter-of-fact and tired, as though describing the beginning of a long day. "I lost my husband. Two years ago. His death was an accident, a car crash." Garrett watched the combine harvester make its turn. "He was a reporter. He was driving to interview a contact for a story when his brakes failed; his car hit a parked coach. He was taken to hospital in a coma and died without regaining consciousness."

Garrett looked at the ground, unseeing, her body rigid, hands clasped together in front of her as if hiding a surprise from a child.

"Afterwards, I found a reason to blame the police, then when that turned out to be unfair, I blamed the man he was going to meet, the editor he was writing for... Finally, I blamed myself, for my encouragement of his interest in the story, for not being there, for a hundred reasons. It doesn't help. It," Garrett hesitated, "It just confuses."

"What was his name?"

"David." Garrett began rubbing her hands together. "It was a local accident. The body came to my hospital late and I was the only one on duty. I did the autopsy myself. He was so broken. He had been... the steering column had smashed into his sternum, punctured the lungs, liver and heart. But his hands were fine! Not a mark. They looked just like he was alive." Garrett stared down at her own fingers. "I often think of his hands."

After a moment Cherry asked softly, "You're a doctor – you must have figured out why things like this happen." Garrett looked up and saw Cherry's cheeks were wet. "What did I do wrong?"

"Nothing." Garrett took Cherry's hands in her own, her grip firm. "A cellular infection is an act of nature, like a flood or earthquake. It isn't true that healthy people are good or beautiful people better, or ill people are bad, or that there's any achievement or sin in dying from a natural cause."

"So it's all just luck?" Cherry said bitterly.

"Well disease doesn't choose." Garrett hesitated. "When someone dies, that's not the end of them. It seems like it at first. But it's not."

"What d'you mean?"

"They live on."

"You mean some kind of resurrection? Or like a ghost?"

Cherry withdrew. She clasped her elbows with her hands, arms in front of her, like a shield against temptation. She began to tremble, a shivering that ran all through her body. Garrett remembered her own tightening grip, when David had died, and felt a sudden love for the girl, for the adamant way she held herself, the thin set of her mouth that shaped smiles she couldn't feel. She had not asked for consolation, only answers.

"I see David in the oddest things. A lost scarf, how someone is telling someone off at a bus stop, watching the evening news. For God's sake, I can still hear his grumbling! Every day I see him all around me. And I am David in so many small ways. How I cook a meal, read a newspaper, write a letter–"

Cherry still held her elbows tight. Garrett knew what she was thinking. It wasn't enough. She just wanted him back.

"The blame, the guilt, it just gets in the way. If you–"

"Doc, do you mind if we don't talk?"

They sat together on the old sofa. The sun was beginning to set, doubling the shapes of things in long shadows. Behind them the clubhouse roof still ticked on like an arrhythmic clock in the last heat of the day. In front, surrounded by a dozen or so bikes and cars, the two rusting petrol pumps on the station forecourt looked like a couple of defiant one-armed gunfighters making a last stand.

Chapter 13

You are in a maze with corridors branching in all directions. Follow the sequence of personal growth as you have been taught. Find your way through the darkness.

Christmas listened to his shallow breathing. His head ached. He stopped the track. He was too tired to make the trip.

He shifted on the pebbles and scanned the beach below. Cold tickled his spine where sweat cooled. His time of trial was close now. Maybe perform his Dues? He didn't need so much concentration for that; or his player. He closed his eyes. Some things you know by heart.

Breathe in, deeply and smoothly. Now breathe out. Just watch. With complete acceptance, without judgement. These are the Dues of Awareness.

He felt the threat of heat as the last light from the sun reached under the pier. He remembered a sunny morning back in the Valley, in the House of Healing. Arshu had brought them together in the great Greenhouse. Just the Five: he had spoken to them alone. Five chosen for glory. Five men of faith who would change the world. It had been hot, the sun casting rainbows through the glass. Arshu had stood on a raised bed of flowering grasses and told their future. Only then had Christmas truly realised his destiny. With the memory of that sing-song voice a chill trickled down his back.

"Let us pray. Come with me now! Put your hands together before we start."

"You stand here, on this day, this hour, filled with light and laughter. Why? Because today we start something wonderful. Something beautiful. Something the world has been waiting for."

"A parasite which was once holy has spread like a rash to cover the face of our Great Soul, Mother Earth. She is sick, sick to death. She cannot breathe, her children are disappearing, she has a fever – she is dying from a pestilence that breeds without

*ceasing, billions upon billions, day after day. That Great Soul –
she needs our help."*

*"Brothers! The time has come to face our responsibility.
Each of you has been prepared. You have trained hard. Now you
must act: with one mind, heart, faith – pray with me a moment!"*

*"Thank you. Today we go where none can follow. Many will
try. None can stop us! Many will try. All will fail if we remain
true to each other. Will we be thanked? No. We will be hated. It
does not matter."*

*"Let us talk of death. Do not fear that great illusion. Today I
make you this solemn promise: when the journey is over, I will
be your guide and for a thousand lifetimes your feet will not err!
Think! You lose one life and win a thousand with me."*

*"We step out onto a forgotten road. Our destination lies in
shadow, in the silence of fallen stones, of empty cities and
broken nations. Choose your shoes wisely. Ready your hearts for
loss. Pack as if you will never return."*

"Go now. Do your duty. And you will live with me forever."

The first of the Five had already shown the way with a martyr's
footsteps. Where was he now? Jakarta? Beijing?

Christmas opened his eyes again. His legs ached like he'd
run a marathon. Cross-legged, he tried to settle more
comfortably on the stony ground.

Up under the eaves of the pier, almost out of sight, a man and
woman nestled half-naked in a pebbled dell of their own
making. Christmas watched the couple shift position, stomach to
back. The woman's dark hair made him think of Fiona and
Lizzie. Girls girls girls. He grinned despite his aches then shook
his head. Jade. Her jealousy had been poison. It was wrong
thinking. People were not possessions.

His fingers searched for the buttons of his music player.

Chapter 14

Mark Boorman lived in a vicarage on the edge of a small village on the South Downs, barely ten miles inland from Brighton. As she queued with the early morning commuter traffic, Garrett remembered Dr. Prenderville's words. Asari tried out all their new ideas on the South coast. New ideas. Like dividing children from their mothers.

Boorman's mother was not what Garrett had expected. A severe-looking woman, neatly dressed in a green twin-set and with an old-fashioned manner.

"Won't you please take a seat?"

Garrett was shown into a sunny high-ceilinged drawing room. Tall French windows opened onto a paved terrace. A clarinet was propped against the arm of a striped green-and-white sofa, like a mislaid walking stick. On a pedestal stand beside a piano was a wide-throated glass vase with an arrangement of Madonna lilies.

"Mark will be down in just a moment."

Mrs Boorman behaved as though Garrett were a client come for an appointment, and left her waiting alone.

Garrett walked around the room. Framed pictures on the piano showed a growing boy, at his youngest posing in a white suit with his mother, titled 'First confirmation'; a little older, he was a uniformed schoolboy surrounded by monks; and much taller and older still, in a caftan.

"Christine Garrett? I'm Mark."

A thin man in loose cords and a baggy jumper stood in the doorway, one bare foot resting on the other. Dr Prenderville had said he was in his early thirties.

"Hello Mark. Thank you for agreeing to meet me."

They sat down together.

"You wanted to talk about Skyler?" Boorman's voice was soft, educated.

"Jason. Yes. Did you know him?"

"We were friends."

Garrett nodded quickly. "How is he?"

"I haven't seen him since March so I can't give you any recent information."

"Was he well–?"

"Last time I saw him we were in a vegetable garden weeding and digging a trench." Mark didn't smile. "We were trying to find a break in a water line."

"Gardening? Jason was gardening?"

"Everyone takes a turn in the gardens. Self-sufficiency is one of the principles of Asari."

"He never showed any interest in our garden at home. We grew vegetables too. I'm sorry – I'm just trying to understand."

"That's all right. Understanding Asari is not easy, even if you've been there."

"What did you talk about when you last saw him?"

"We argued."

"About what?"

"He'd just done a meal run. He'd been asked to leave food outside a locked room in the science block. We were arguing about something he'd seen. It had disturbed him."

Boorman looked around the room, frowning. He went over to the piano and came back with a glass ashtray. He took a packet out of a pocket and tapped out a cigarette. Garrett controlled her impatience. She waited until Boorman looked ready to speak again.

"What had disturbed him?"

"He was concerned about the woman and child he'd seen inside the room." Boorman exhaled smoke. "He'd noticed them there a week earlier and they were sitting in exactly the same places, as if they hadn't moved. He said they looked trapped. I told Skyler they shouldn't treat Sikanda's family that way."

"Who?"

"Sikanda. I don't know his real name. He came to Asari Valley two years ago. We were told he was some high-powered scientist working with Osei – our Head of Healing – on a special project. Something big, a secret project, that's what they said, all the Sanyasins and the House leaders." Boorman sucked hard on his cigarette. "You have to understand Asari is riddled with secrets. There are secrets within secrets. But in this case some of the people that do know what they're about – Osei for one – were saying it too. He said that we must have faith in the Leadership. He said a time of great change was coming, a Cleansing, a Transformation that would give Arshu his proper place in the world. It was probably all rubbish. Anyway the last year I was there that project became an obsession. We were making preparations as though there were a flood coming. There was even talk of leaving the Valley."

"This special project – was Jason involved?"

Boorman shrugged. "I don't know. He had become more senior than me so he wouldn't have told me everything, not because we argued, that's just how it works." Boorman contemplated the glowing end of his cigarette.

"Why did you argue?"

"I said that it looked like the rumours were true. That Sikanda and his family had become prisoners, after trying to leave. I thought it was wrong for us to imprison anyone. Your son accused me of not having faith, of doubting Arshu. He spoke of higher causes, said the end would justify the means. I disagreed with him."

Garrett sat back slowly, like a collapsing balloon. What was Jason mixed up in? Where was he now? What was he doing? Whatever it was, he was beyond her help.

A memory returned of a long winter filled with three-year-old fevers; for two months he had slept only if within reach of her. Through the sleepless nights she had listened to the sounds he had made. When he had become disturbed she had placed a hand on his hot back and waited till he had grown calm. For a moment she let herself hate Boorman, for not being Jason here with her. She tempered her will with the cooling anger, with a need to understand.

Boorman waited in the opposite corner of the sofa. Garrett stared at the rainbow reflections cast on his feet from the vase on the piano.

"Do you mind my asking, how you became involved with Asari?"

"Through the London Spiritual College. I was studying for a doctorate in Psychic Healing. A guy called Kirtananda came to speak a few times. I got to know him. He was hip and tough, not like the usual goons. I could see he'd been around the block, knew what was what. I respected him. And he gave out a lot of free drugs; he said his acid was fast food enlightenment, a short cut for Westerners lost in their materialism. I don't think they were his words – he spoke a lot about his Teacher. He invited me to a free retreat. I went with him to Asari Valley and didn't leave for two years."

"Why did you stay?"

Boorman stared at the carpet. His cigarette dangled forgotten from a limp hand. Birdsong and, farther off, the seashore sound of a lawnmower being pushed and pulled, drifted in from outside.

"At the start it was good. Free meals, free booze, free sex, free drugs, amazing parties. We had fun. There was a real community, shared understandings, lots of lame jokes. You have to imagine a place without television, the Internet, advertising, telephones. We made our own music, food, clothes, stories – world really. I liked the rituals, early morning, lunchtime, evening. And at first, I loved Arshu. I fell for the spiritual line." He shivered then snorted. "Of course I did."

Boorman stopped again. Peace and domestic silence rushed in.

"I was always religious. From school I went straight into the seminary. By the time I got to the Spiritual College I could pray my way into believing just about anything." Boorman looked down at himself, his face full of disgust, his voice bitter.

"What do you mean, anything?" Garrett cast her question low, just in front of him.

"Have you read G.K. Chesterton? He said, 'When people stop believing in God, they don't believe in nothing – they believe in anything'. Well it sounds true, and clever, but he was wrong. The truth is the exact opposite, and not as pretty. When people stop thinking for themselves, stop being sceptical or critical – when they choose or are brought up to believe in things without a shred of evidence, that's when they can believe in anything. And that anything can be searching for you. It comes knocking. Because it wants you for its own ends."

Boorman stabbed out his cigarette in the glass ashtray. "Don't think these people are superstitious idiots. Far from it. They know exactly what they're doing. Especially the Instructors. They understand the 'journey' you must make. Every step is managed, calculated in careful order."

"What journey?"

Boorman sat up. "First thing, they get you to write these autobiographical essays, about what you believe, your childhood, your problems. The more confessional, the more guilty, the more you are congratulated and rewarded – and the less you are left with. Before you realise, you have given away all your privacy. Of course they don't tell you that."

Boorman spoke now with a sneer of open anger. "They start by honouring your 'faith tradition' – whatever it is, Christian, Buddhist, Islamic, Jewish, Hindu... When you are ready, they invite you to 'transcend', to see the limitations of your old ways of thinking, suggest you act out your progress by performing rites of deliberate sacrilege. I burned a bible. It was at a full moon party. Jesus! We made a fire on the beach. I remember the smoke smelled of glue. It nearly made me sick." Boorman shook his head. "That's when I began to stop communicating with my family and my friends back home. I was doing it all willingly. Guilt, continual confession, hard labour penance, the rewards of approval, sex, drug ecstasies – believe me, it's hard to compete with Arshu's lessons and gifts and revelations. And of course you're isolated out there. Everyone around you is conforming like mad."

Garrett could smell cut grass through the open French windows, and under that, the heavier smell of the lilies.

"It's a joke, isn't it? I thought Asari was revolutionary, would give me new freedoms. But it was the most reactionary, conservative place on earth. They don't tolerate a word of dissent. It's a dictatorship of faith. Total belief."

"Of course they encourage humility. I understand why now." A clenched hand twisted inside another. "It is an overrated virtue, and cultivated a certain way can rob you of independent conviction. Of course that's why it's so useful."

"Have you heard from anyone since you left?"

"They sent me a card. With this in it."

Boorman stood up. He took a saffron-orange slip of paper from his wallet and handed it to Garrett. A single sentence had been written on it.

"The story is not yet ended, it has not yet become history, and the secret life it holds can break out tomorrow in you or in me."
Gershom Scholem

"Do you know what it means?"

Boorman looked as though he were about to spit on the carpet. "Did Dr. Prenderville tell you about Nilesh – Oliver Weightman?" Garrett nodded. "They never let go. And neither can you. I saw it while I was there. People who had left, coming back, sometimes after years away. That scares me."

"I'm frightened too. For Jason."

"It's – it's difficult to adjust, outside." Boorman scuffed his foot. "When you are there, everything is done for you. Even your thinking. It runs deep. I don't think I'll ever be completely free of the place. Of what happened to me."

Boorman looked out of the window. "I think there is a part of human nature that wants to be a slave. In some ways it's easier. To be told by a priest or a guru, a mullah or rabbi what is true, what to believe in. Unfortunately, those people mostly do it for their own reasons and interests, not yours. Whatever they say, usually the influence or power they want is not in the hereafter or in heaven, it's right down here on Earth."

Chapter 15

The blood droplet trembled as it grew. The scarlet of strawberries, it ripened over seconds into a single three mille sphere. Touched to the centre of a glass slide, it began to spread out from the end of the needle. Garrett used a cover slip to drag a red smear. Her gesture was deft, practised, creating a faint single-celled layer.

The sample was from the missing persons – Lizzie, as they were calling her. Garrett had driven on to Porton Down after visiting Mike Boorman. She worked with troubled concentration and in silence, alone in the lab. Bryce was in level four. Skinner and Zahra had gone to a meeting on the Cuito case.

The PCR work required accurate preparation and after an hour she took a break. The others were still not back and she wandered around the lab. The thought of negotiating airlocks and lifts to reach fresh air was off-putting.

It was quiet, the circulating air in the underground room chilled and odourless. She stopped at Bryce's desk. A docking station, keyboard and mouse were lined up on a clean uncluttered surface. There were no sentimental family photos, no fluorescent sticky notes or half-drunk cups of tea. The only other objects on the desk were a spare laptop battery and a small potted orchid; a spray of tiny open-mouthed orange flowers hung from a single jointed green stem. Garrett bent forward. There was no scent.

A set of printouts was tacked haphazardly to the wall beside a large wall-mounted projector screen. They were pictures of the Cuito pathogen. Garrett stretched her neck and shoulder muscles. The images had been the subject of heated debate between Zahra and Skinner. Beside them was a poster depicting Mendel's Law of Independent Assortment. In the upper right corner, a gold-edged portrait of the Augustinian monk, gardener and mathematician glowed like the icon of a saint. Garrett remembered undergraduate lectures on the father of genetics, descriptions of how he had divined his inheritance laws through cultivation of twenty-nine thousand pea plants in his Abbey garden.

"Isn't he just the picture of innocent contemplation?"

Garrett wondered if Bryce had intended to startle her. He stood at her back, so close she half-expected to feel his words as breath on her neck. Perhaps he just disliked formality.

David had. Meeting him at the airport after a three-week field trip he had held up a finger and said, "All right, we'll ask your father first," replying to her parting suggestion as if he'd never been away.

Garrett considered Bryce's question. She remembered what Skinner had said. A little intense, but you get used to him. Rheinnalt is Rheinnalt.

"Most people would say that's what he was."

"Then most people would be wrong."

"Why?"

"You forget where you are Christine. This place is built on Mendelian genetics and it's anything but innocent. It's true, we've not yet destroyed cities – unlike physicists – but our power is greater." Garrett remembered the men at Skinner's funding lecture; overfunded boys with dangerous toys. "The diseases we hold in our freezers threaten more destruction in one test tube than any bomb. These cells adapt and reproduce indefinitely. Your malaria strain is part of a family that's almost three million years old. Its ancestors have been dividing by binary fission every fifteen minutes for over two billion years. Most people are naïve."

Garrett did not immediately reply. She had read up on Porton Down. Whistleblowers. Covert programs. Anthrax experiments on servicemen, poison gas, weaponized smallpox. Official denials together with Whitehall justifications of secrecy, capability, national security. The implied uses of her sciences had appalled her. Reading the reports, she had thought of her science and felt a hot shame. Science. Reason. The grail words receded, like upheld light before the grasping fingers of an imperfect knight.

"Ah, there you are!" Skinner bustled through the outer hatch followed by Zahra. "We have some results for you. Not sure you're going to like them mind."

They assembled in the meeting room. Skinner passed around printouts.

"We have run RNA matches. Unfortunately we didn't get a hit." Skinner shrugged. "Happens from time to time with the standard malaria probes. There is great variability in the malaria *falciparum* genome. Fortunately we have a reference chip." When Garrett frowned Skinner nodded at Zahra. "It's used with the gene analyser."

Garrett looked up from the printout. "You have an analyzer?"

The massively-parallel gene pattern recognisers were new but she had read of them.

"Shani's baby."

"We call ours Sherlock," Zahra said proudly. "Only three in the UK. Only had him a few months and he's already proved himself. Last week, in thirty minutes, he found a DNA sequence for a rare Sarcodina that would've taken us months to find. With the DNA reference chip, he can test against thousands of strains simultaneously."

Skinner spread his hands. "Looking at my worksheet, we need all the help we can get. Unfortunately Shani is booked for the next couple of days. But if you can still help out, she has time to give you an intro. You only need the basics to set up the test."

"Well you are privileged," Bryce said. "Shani hasn't let anyone else near her new toy so far. Sherlock!" He raised his eyebrows.

Zahra showed Garrett the basics, how to define programs and submit jobs remotely from secured on-site workstations. "And we can write our own algorithms. Look."

Garrett leaned forward, her interest caught by the search code. Zahra's approach was unsophisticated. Garrett made suggestions on matching sequences. She noticed the younger woman was impatient, quickly irritated by her own mistakes.

Garrett became conscious of Skinner hovering behind them, and his growing interest in the clock on the wall.

"Where is the actual physical sampling done?"

"Level four unfortunately. So we can test any agent. We can remote in from here to run analyses but that's where the physical kit is."

"I have PCR product ready from Fiona Grant."

"Good. I'll set up the *falciparum* chip and kick-off processing of our baseline Brighton data. Be a minute."

Garrett picked up her samples. She found Zahra standing by the inner hatchway punching codes into a keypad.

"Bloody PINs."

"Telephone number? Birthday?" Garrett suggested.

Zahra closed her eyes. Her lips moved silently. She tried another number. The door hissed. She smiled and nodded at Garrett. "Anniversaries of a sort. But we have to alternate them to pacify the security geeks. Okay, let's suit up."

Garrett followed Zahra into a room with lockers and changing cubicles. An observation window ran the entire length of one wall. Garrett walked over to it.

"That's our level four. Parasitology has no level three because of our larger level two." Zahra pointed to a glass plate on the wall covering two handles, yellow and red. "A few things to run through. These alarms are for hot agent breaches. You'll see them in every room."

"Yellow secures lab by lab by the last man out. It can be reversed by pushing the handle back up. We've had three yellow alerts since I've been here," Zahra raised her eyebrows, "All minor accidents in Sector Six."

"Red is for level four or higher containment and cannot be reversed. The whole complex is sealed on a timed protocol: level four in one minute, the sector in two, the whole facility in ten. Door locks and air flow isolation are automatic and will not allow manual override."

Garrett pictured again the containment circles Skinner had described – the surrounding concrete sheath and earth and the bio-secured entrance hatches.

"How many of those have you had?"

"None. Only drills."

Blue biosafety suits of unusual design hung flaccid on pegs beside the lockers, like the discarded chrysalises of man-sized insects.

"Now what can I get into? I've put on so much weight," Zahra muttered. Garrett watched her hold a biosafety suit up to her neck and smooth it down over her body. Her hand cupped her stomach as if holding an ache.

"So how come you're working a bank holiday weekend, Christine? I mean, I know it's an interesting case, but–" she paused then added, "Well, it's not all about work, is it? You've got to have a life."

Garrett nodded gravely. "You're right."

"You must really like your job."

"Yes. Do you?"

"I did. I loved it! I was always happy to work the long hours. They never really bothered me."

"You're talking as if you've stopped," Garrett said.

"Am I? I suppose I am." Zahra laughed. She glanced around the walls and sighed. "Don't get me wrong, the army's been good to me."

"Some people would find this lab environment stressful. There are different sorts of research–"

"No, I like it here. The work's interesting. But you know, you get to the stage when you think about other things, don't you? Not just work, work, work." Zahra took a deep breath. "Can I ask you something?"

"Shani, sorry I need you." Skinner called from the doorway. Bryce climbed through the hatch in front of him. "Christine, Rheinnalt can take you through to level four."

Zahra shrugged her displeasure; she rolled her eyes as she walked back past Bryce.

"You've drawn the short straw Christine, you've got me. Has Shani found you a suit?"

Garrett shook her head. Bryce crossed over to the rack, selected a safety suit, held it up in mid-air and studied Garrett's size.

"You can have any colour as long as it's blue." Garrett forced eye contact. "This should fit you."

"Thank you."

He turned back to the pegs. Garrett suited up. She emerged from the changing cubicle to find Bryce standing by two large bins sorting through gloves, galoshes and helmets. He picked out a white metal dome with a clear visor. "I'm afraid we have to wear these. Have you worked in a bio-containment lab before?"

"I've done some culture work in level three labs."

"The procedures here are more restrictive, but you get used to them. Power switch and air sockets here, on the side. There are lines in all the labs." He motioned for Garrett to try on the helmet.

"These units have a reserve lung, that's why they're a little heavy. You'll see the chin plate holds the readouts."

Garrett looked down her nose at a set of lime green LEDs.

Operating mode: ISOLATION. Air remaining: 1 hour 16 minutes.

Bryce tapped keypad buttons at another hatch, spun the handle wheel and stepped through into a small airlock. Garrett followed. The scrubs turned out to fit badly and the plastic galoshes were cold on her feet. Bryce closed the hatch. The lights flickered and went out.

The black of the airlock was featureless. In the second it takes for the heart to adjust, Garrett reached for the wheeled handle behind her. A scream fled silent down the yards of her nerves. Eyes wide open, she registered two things: that the tiny LEDs on the chin plate of her helmet now read an hour and a quarter; and that her hand rested on an arm. It was warm and still as a stone rail. Another hand came to rest on hers.

There was a click. The main lights flickered back on. Garrett removed her hand from under Bryce's.

Entry protocol complete. Door locks are released.

"I should have warned you." Bryce turned his whole body towards her as he spoke, cumbersome in his suit.

They moved into level four. Bryce showed her how to plug in her helmet.

Operating mode: CONNECTED.

The loudest noise in the lab was the humming helmet. The conditioned air tasted metallic.

Sherlock turned out to be an unexciting grey box controlled by twin monitors and a keyboard. Bryce showed her where to place her PRC product. They worked side by side in silence for a while.

"You don't like the dark do you." His words sounded tinny through her helmet speakers.

"No."

Garrett considered Bryce's earlier courtesy. She shifted her feet in the cold galoshes. "When I was seven years old, I got myself trapped for nine hours underground. Since then, I've never liked dark spaces."

"How did it happen?"

"It was a silly mistake. I was looking for new beetle species."

Garrett heard a quiet laugh. She stopped to decide whether to take offence then smiled. "The crypt was one of the best places for them! It was disused, the old pews stored there were rotten. Perfect habitat. I had already found one pretty good ground beetle when I saw a *Panagaeus cruxmajor*. The Crucifix Beetle! Very rare. I didn't have a free hand so I popped it in my mouth.

When it squirted acid I dropped the torch and the bulb smashed. That's when I found out the door had locked when it closed."

"You feel fear but you don't scare easily, do you Christine? Lucky for us you are still prepared to help us here."

When Bryce spoke next his voice was quiet, as if farther away. "I found, if you wait, the dark always passes."

Beside them were two large glass-fronted freezers. Garrett could see test tubes and labelled slides racked in ranks like toy soldiers. She felt Bryce watching her through his glass visor.

"Our containment freezers. They're rather full at the moment. Shani's doing a cross-domain pathogen study with Sherlock. Cholera, Ebola, Tularaemia, Typhoid, Hantaviruses, Botulinum Toxin spores, Encephalitis, Anthrax, Nipah, the haemorrhagic viruses, Poxes, Yellow fever, MDRTB…you name it, we've got it in there. The most lethal collection in history." He placed a gloved hand on a glass freezer top. "Remember Mendel's peas in his Abbey? Perhaps his being a monk wasn't a coincidence. Think of the community here as monastic, these samples lighting our way, like candles." His voice was mocking.

Garrett laughed. "The Porton monastery?"

"In a way. And we're not the first. If you think, directly above us, scattered over Salisbury plain within twenty miles of here, are Avebury, Stonehenge, Sarum. Similar centres of contemplation in their time. Lenses you might say."

Garrett breathed in tasteless air and felt the inhuman constancy of the lab's light and temperature. In here there was no day or night, there were no seasons. She felt a sudden impatience at Bryce's facile connections. When she turned to face him the lights of the lab reflected in their opposing visors. "I disagree. Science is not the same as faith. What you believe you prove. The rest is superstition."

Bryce's suit swayed from side to side. "If you don't mind my saying so, you sound angry."

"Do I? Yes, you're right. Lighting a candle didn't save my husband; better understanding of infection in coma patients might have."

Garrett slowed down a little, shocked at herself. She took a deeper, air-conditioned breath. When she spoke again it was more softly. "Centuries of faith haven't changed the lives of millions. Public healthcare programmes do. I've seen the difference that can be made."

They worked in silence a while before she spoke again.

"We deceive ourselves easily. Science disciplines the human imagination."

"Anger can blind," Bryce's reply was soft but firm. "It prevents faith in something greater than ourselves."

Garrett sighed. "I've had this argument before."

"Who with?"

"My son."

After three hours they stopped for a break. When the door closed behind them the lab returned to quiet. Above the faint hiss of air filtration units, Sherlock hummed briefly to itself as the platters in its disk bays answered a request for data. After some minutes the overhead lights clicked off.

The only remaining illumination in the lab came from two orange LEDs glowing on the freezer cabinet doors. The only remaining life in the lab was shelved inside.

The top rack held a tube containing a 50cc solution of Influenza A type H1N1; cultured from tissue from an Inuit woman buried for a century in the Alaskan tundra, it was a strain of Spanish flu that had infected one in four living humans within three years and killed a hundred million. The shelf below held the world's most complete collection of *Filoviridae*, including samples from Côte d'Ivoire and Ebola: haemorrhagic viruses with, in some cases, fatality rates above ninety percent. The lower storage areas held boxes and vials of other rare pathogens. The countless microscopic killers waited motionless on the freezer shelves, their life suspended in the cold. The sequences digitised on Sherlock's discs held coded representations of the sleeping creatures, digitised shadows of their twisted nucleic strands.

The Analyzer disks began to stutter, a staccato beat that lengthened into a continuous static burst. A new analysis initiated from the outer lab had completed and the results were being written to disk, long strings of base acids, the coded shadow of a new organism.

Chapter 16

Fifteen UK National Health Service Trusts had reported Sentinel alerts in the last twenty-four hours against the original malaria broadcast warning of the sixth August. They stretched from Dorset on the South coast to as far north as Leicestershire.

On a normal working day, the regular contact between county health authorities would have been enough to raise suspicions that something unusual was going on. Unfortunately, meetings were at a bare minimum. Local epidemiology departments and General Hospital reporting units were running skeleton staffs over the August bank holiday weekend.

In any case Sentinel, the CDSC's national disease analysis system, was relied on to raise the alarm. It had done so in the recent past, with signal success during two flu epidemics, a legionnaire's disease outbreak and a cluster of nationwide food poisoning incidents. The escalation service was fully automated and proven.

But it wasn't foolproof. The UK malaria outbreak had started with just three cases in Brighton, Sussex, on the South coast of England. No one was aware that the national count now stood at thirty deaths and a hundred and twelve identified infections. The counties with the highest infection rates were Sussex and Ceredigion in Wales.

***

Garrett picked up a four millimetre cube of Paul Fletcher's heart tissue with a pair of plastic forceps. She dipped the sample into the steaming mouth of a glass beaker half-full with liquid nitrogen. After a silent count, she transferred the frozen block into the cryostat chuck of a microtome.

The Buffy orange test had confirmed mixed broods but found no more rogue cell forms. Skinner had just shrugged. Garrett had decided to prepare more tissue sections. Across that afternoon as she had worked, she had caught herself straining to hear background noises – the rumbling of traffic, planes going over, birdsong. But two hundred feet down, the subterranean room was quiet as the grave, the circulating air chilled and odourless. She felt isolated, as if on some voyage through a void for which she had not prepared.

She set the microtome's cutter to 5 microns and hit a switch. The diamond cutter began to whine. A thin ribbon of material peeled away like smoke, so thin it was transparent, the colour of greaseproof paper. Garrett watched, satisfied. A muted, interrupting squeak startled her a little, and she half-turned, to see Zahra enter the lab.

"Christine! Did you hear? Sherlock got a match!"

Garrett turned off the cutter.

"Let me show you!"

They sat together at a keyboard.

"I've only run analyses so far for Grant's material. But four separate sequences confirm Sumatra-7: a rare, lethal South East Asian strain of cerebral malaria. Look."

Zahra waited while Garrett reviewed the data and references. Garrett frowned.

"It doesn't seem right."

"I know the pathology is not exactly the same. It's good we've found a match though, no?" Zahra said. "It's progress."

"But remember the blood films? And the rogue ookineetes?"

"We discussed that. George thought it might be because there's very little Sumatra-7 data."

"Even so." Garrett stood a moment without speaking. She made a decision. "I'd like to run the other two cases. Can you show me how to set the analysis up?"

Zahra showed her how to navigate the Analyzer's genetic repository. "You need to prep the PCR product and submit it in level four, like you did with Rheinnalt."

Garrett nodded. She returned to the lab bench. She muttered ingredients as she began mixing a solution. "Five microlitres proteinase, sterile water, heart tissue–"

Zahra settled on an opposite stool. They discussed pathological anomalies and RAPID, Garrett's gene matching software toolkit. Eventually Zahra stirred herself to work. She selected a glass slide from a rack and clipped it onto the stage of a microscope. She stopped to watch Garrett load a centrifuge with lysate.

"Do you have any children Christine?"

"Yes. I have a son."

"What's his name?"

"Jason."

"How old is he?"

"Twenty-two."

"My God!"

Garrett smiled. She opened the centrifuge and considered the eluted DNA. She began mixing amplification reagents. Her hands moved with a disciplined precision to match her speed.

"Were you frightened when you were pregnant?"

"Yes. There were some complications in my second trimester. I thought I would lose the baby."

"That must have been awful."

Garrett set a timer for thirty cycles and flicked a switch. Primers and polymerase began to act as molecular scissors on target DNA, snipping target genomes into tailored pieces.

"It was."

"Did you always want children?" Zahra bent her head to select an objective lens.

Garrett studied Zahra a moment. She put a test tube back in a rack.

"Yes."

"And was the pregnancy planned?"

"No."

"So did you think about not having it?"

Garrett watched Zahra peer into the microscope.

"No."

"Have you ever regretted it?"

Garrett thought about the pain of the last two years, the violent arguments and brief, stilted phone calls. "No never."

Zahra sighed. "Of course not. That's what every mother says." Her fingers whitened where one hand gripped the lab bench. She looked up at Garrett. "I'm pregnant."

When Garrett said nothing, Zahra swung away from the microscope. "It was an accident! And it's such bad timing!"

"Why?"

"I'm not ready." Zahra looked around the lab then at Garrett. "Did you feel ready?"

Garrett smiled. "No."

"I'm too young. Plus, the father–" Zahra stopped speaking.

"What does he say?"

Zahra snorted. "He doesn't want to know. My mother says we've got to get married but even if he would, I don't even like him! She says I don't realise how hard it is raising a child, that I won't cope on my own. Do you think that's true?"

"It is hard. But mothers usually find a way. How far along are you?"

"I'm twenty-one weeks!" Zahra glanced at the clock, as if she was in a race. "I feel sick all the time! And my dad! He's the worst! You know he called me a slut. He says abortion is *haram*, forbidden." Zahra put a hand on her stomach. She looked at Garrett. "He says I'll go to hell. Do you think I'll go to hell?"

"No."

Bryce stepped into the lab. "Still here?"

Zahra bent towards Garrett and whispered, "Please don't mention anything." She turned off her microscope and stood up. "Yes I'm late! Home time."

"Has George fixed you up somewhere to stay yet?" Bryce asked Garrett.

"Yes." Garrett nodded once at Zahra. "It was good of him."

"It's the least we can do. We have the facilities. Lots of researchers stay over. And it'll save you a three-hour commute."

"He said South Row?"

"I'll walk you over. Be good to get some fresh air."

Garrett took a deep breath. It was a relief to be able to look up and see distant objects and the horizon beyond walls. She could smell dust and grass. The time in the containment lab with its elaborate isolation and investigation apparatus seemed like a voyage in some alien craft.

The long summer's day was over but the memory of heat was still in the ground. Bryce guided Garrett through Porton Down's campus-like area of tree-lined lawns and regimental buildings. He had promised a short walk to her accommodation.

A few late-leaving cars rolled slowly around curving access roads, their paired headlights gleaming in the twilight. Two cyclists glided ahead of them like low-flying insects, wheel spokes flashing like light trembling on water, silent except for the greeting tinkle of a bell. All the movements of the evening seemed to have adapted to the tired end of a long day. Garrett curbed a childish impulse to swing her arms and break into a run. She reached up to massage the back of her neck.

"Lab work can be tiring," Bryce said. His Welsh lilt deepened and rolled his rrrs.

"It's good to be out."

"It's easy to lose track of time down in those labs. They're like casinos. White light and stale air."

He veered to his right, and steered Garrett by the elbow around a dip in the pavement. He raised an arm to point across her chest. Grassland, visible between buildings, rolled to the horizon like a grey sea. "Up here you can breathe."

They walked silently together a while. Bryce took a spur road out towards a line of buildings on the campus perimeter. High and flowering grasses bordered the road, a vast hay meadow gone wild. Occasional chalk outcrops showed through the vegetation like scars, or patches of baldness.

"Rheinnalt – that's northern Welsh?"

"Very good. My family are originally from Ceredigion, that's on the North West coast. I go back when I can. Most weekends."

"That's a lot. I suppose there isn't much research work around Cardigan Bay."

"You'd be surprised–" For a moment Garrett believed him, then was astonished at herself. Bryce smiled. "No."

"Of course that's no excuse. To the true Welsh I'm a traitor for leaving. But then, as my ma used to say, Y mae dafad ddu ym mhob praidd."

When Garrett looked at him, he added, "Every flock has its black sheep."

"How long have you been working here?"

"Couple of years."

"What brought you?"

"I was already working with George on some outsourced research. A position came up." Bryce smiled. "I'm not the saluting type. You can probably tell. But I'm on a civilian contract and the facilities here are the best."

Bryce started describing equipment. Garrett considered how men liked to show women how their toys worked, and stopped a smile.

"I'm boring you."

Garrett shook her head. "No, I'm sorry. I've been thinking about what you said about Mendel, about the dangers... Somehow, I can't shake off the feeling that something is happening, something we don't know about yet."

"Something unseen? Sounds a bit superstitious to me. Have you any evidence?"

"Yes, okay I deserved that," Garrett's brief grin faded. She turned her head. To the west, a single thunderhead rose tall and white on the horizon.

Garrett recognised a cumulonimbus, the tallest of all clouds, full of rain and ice. She estimated the cloud base at around three thousand feet, the top perhaps thirty thousand or higher, shorn off flat by high wind. Above ten thousand feet or so the cloud would be pure ice crystals.

"I had a dream last night." Garrett kept her eyes on the distant cloud. "I was back in my kindergarten playground. It was break time. One of the boys had a box of matches. While I was watching him playing, I noticed his arms were covered in thin scales. When I looked closer I saw his skin was made of matches. I looked at myself and my friends. We all were. The teachers were made of larger sticks, of explosives. And the ground and school buildings were pure phosphorous. And this little boy was striking match after match after match, trying to light one. I ran towards him, shouting, calling out, but he couldn't hear me. Then I saw his face. It was Jason, my son. I screamed. Then I woke up."

"It was a catastrophe dream," Bryce said quietly. "A projection of fear."

"It was horrible."

"I know you feel strongly about this case. I don't understand why exactly, but–"

"When I did the autopsy, I saw something on Paul Fletcher's body." Garrett stopped speaking. Bryce led the way towards an isolated row of houses facing fields. She liked the way he didn't feel the need to fill each silence.

"He had a tattoo on his right shoulder. It was an eye, stylised. I recognised it. It's a logo."

"Of a brand you mean?"

"No, it's the sign of a religious organisation."

"What religion?"

"Well, it's more of a cult."

"What's it called?"

"Asari."

"How did you recognise it?"

"Jason my son is a member."

Bryce nodded. "I understand. Of course. Your interest in this case is natural."

Garrett frowned.

"You're afraid for your son."

Bryce shook his head slightly. The glints from his glasses kept time to the soft, steady rhythms of his speech.

"Yes, I'm worried about him – and if he's in trouble I'm worried he won't call. There's a distance between us right now." Garrett looked away. "Sometimes I think it's my fault, because I didn't... I can't listen the way he needs me to."

"The mother-son bond is very hard to break."

"What do you mean?"

"It is the strongest relationship we have – so it's natural. I understand your fear. But you mustn't worry."

"I can't stop."

Bryce was silent, for once without a ready answer. When he spoke again it was with unusual reserve. "Sometimes understanding isn't enough is it? Seeing effects and tracing causes – it doesn't always change how we feel."

They walked together side by side. She kept her eyes on the pavement in front of her.

"What did you mean, 'The dark always passes?'" Garrett said. Bryce was silent for a long while. Garrett wondered if she'd offended him.

"Missing people can be one of the hardest things we bear, don't you think?" Bryce spoke softly, as if from far away. "And if your pain separates you, you become divided, always a fraction of yourself. But when you face your fears," he turned slightly towards her, "the loss, the dark passes."

Again Garrett sensed the curious intensity Skinner had mentioned and wondered why she didn't mind.

"Back there in the lab, in the dark when the lights went out, you were strong even though you were frightened. You faced your fear. That took courage. I felt it." Bryce hesitated, for once awkward, and Garrett liked him for it.

"We haven't known each other long, Christine. But perhaps we share more than we realise. I have been through my own dark times. You know, our fears don't have to be faced alone."

He stopped at the first gate in a knee-high picket fence bordering a row of crew-cut lawns. Crazy-paved paths led up to a line of semi-detached houses with pebble-dashed walls. It was as if one side of a sixties suburban street had been picked up, flown cross-country and dropped into a field.

"Here we are."

Bryce indicated the first house, distinguished from the others by its size and build. A leaded fanlight gleamed above the door. "You'll be comfortable. I've stayed a few times here myself."

"Thank you." Garrett unlocked the front door.

Bryce hesitated then entered first. "I'll check the utilities for you."

Adjoining rooms were furnished but empty as a hotel suite. A carpet covered the wooden hallway floor. It was expensive. Garrett counted eleven colours in the intricate floral patterns.

"There's tidy then," Bryce returned from the kitchen. "Well I'll say goodnight."

"Goodnight." She noted a twelfth colour. She waited.

Bryce turned in a slow circle. "Do you like it? It's Persian."

Garrett held the knotted repeats of leaves and flowers whole in her mind. The pattern was soothing. "It's beautiful."

"Although it looks perfectly symmetrical, it isn't." Bryce began walking the perimeter of the carpet. "There is in fact a deliberate error–"

"–in Islam, it is blasphemous," Garrett picked up the thread unbroken, "to create perfection."

Bryce smiled at her. Garrett looked away and said, "It's actually a common weaver's superstition. Found also in Native American spirit beading and the quilter's humility square."

"I didn't know that but somehow I'm not surprised you do." He placed his left foot beside a tulip design the size of a small hand. The stem was crooked. "A concealed flaw. Appropriate, no?"

"To what?" Reluctant but wishing to see, Garrett came to look more closely.

"Isn't that what you do?" His voice dropped. "Search for the patterns and breaks?" Bryce stepped behind her. His aftershave smelled of cut grass. The muscles in her back tensed. "Search for order in the muddle of things?" Garrett felt his hands on her waist. She held still.

"Find beetles in the dark?"

Bryce turned her gently to face him. Garrett wondered if we always remember where we are first touched. David had held her chin first. She shook her head.

"Don't."

The reflection in his glasses, too bright, confused Garrett for a moment. Then she saw his eyes, half-closed, as if focussed on a distant object. They seemed to see through her. He brought a finger to her lips. "Shhh."

"Don't Rheinnalt."

Bryce's eyes still had a faraway look. She wondered if he were dreaming. Slowly he leaned forward to kiss her, his movements like a man under water.

"Shhh."

Unhurried, eyes still half-closed, he reached for her chin.

Her slap was harder than she intended, and loud in the hallway.

"I–"

He stepped back, shook his head. She watched his eyes widen and focus. There was a red mark on his cheek. A look – was it sorrow? Or a queer kindness? – passed over his face.

"Don't be afraid Christine."

He took another step back. He smiled at her. She didn't want him to speak, but when he did his voice was kind.

"If you wait the dark always passes."

When she said nothing he spoke again, his voice falsely light, "I'm sorry. I–"

He stopped. She felt his awareness of her grow sharper still. His body thickened as it absorbed her anger. He inclined his head and stepped off the carpet.

"I understand. Don't worry, I won't bother you again. Good night."

His heels sounded bare wood then stone. Garrett waited a long while before she stepped to the door. The front garden was deserted. There was no-one on the access road. She rubbed the side of her waist where he had held her.

Damn.

She sat on the front step and watched the sun set over the grasslands. To the west, the distant thunderhead caught the last of the light. From the cloud's base Garrett could see protruding mammatus, the strange appendages that indicated the atmosphere was unstable; they meant rain. The cloud glowed darkly red.

It was time to go back to Brighton, back to field work. She would leave in the morning.

Chapter 17

The morning light threw shadows without edges across the walls of the cell. Cracks branched against a damp sky of plaster. The breathing of a family repeated in sighs from under coarse blankets in a steel-framed bunk bed.

Professor Stephen Richardson knew in the bunk above him his daughter Adele had her pillow pulled round over her ears. His wife lay beside him hands folded across her chest, her body not touching his. What time was it? Eight? Coming up to nine? He reflected he hadn't slept in this much since a student. Undergraduate days. Happy days, when they were young and energetic and free, with nothing forbidden, everything possible.

Whispered words replayed in his head on a loop. *An outbreak. In England. The south coast.* His eyes climbed the cracks in the wall. Sweat seeped into the stale bedding as his thoughts circled again, around his wife lying silent beside him, his child above, the surrounding walls of the cell, the compound, the world outside, London, England. He was helpless in the face of the impending catastrophe.

He blinked hard, trying not to feel sorry for himself. He thought of propagation speeds and population densities, of international airports and hub cities. Beneath the sheets his fingers closed and opened like claws in time with his shortening, shallow breaths. The warning words from a famous confession repeated silently in his ears. *"We knew the world would not be the same. A few people laughed, a few people cried, most were silent."* Oppenheimer's words continued, a relentless whisper. *"When you see something that is technically sweet, you go ahead and do it and you argue about what to do about it after."*

Could the rumour be a lie? No. Whatever else he was, Osei was not a liar; and he would know first. Richardson tried to regain control of his breathing. He unclenched his fingers, forced his thoughts beyond paralysis, beyond the cell walls.

His eyes focussed on a series of three-letter words scratched on the plaster wall by his head. CAT, GAG, TAG, ACT. Not quite anagrams. Nearly. He closed his eyes again.

"Daddy?"

His wife rose from the bed. Richardson followed. He swayed on his feet, rubbed the hair on the back of his head where his scalped itched. His daughter was half-hidden at the back of the top bunk. She peered at him over her pillow.

"Morning Adele."

A metal desk, a chair, and the wide double bunk bed stood on a concrete floor. The otherwise-bare room was lit by a single fluorescent tube in the ceiling and the morning light from a barred window. Through the bars the geodesic roof of the House of Healing was visible. Above it Richardson could see the steel chimney stack of the lab where he worked.

He watched his wife get dressed. He noticed she moved like an old woman in the mornings now. She sat down at the table, straightened her back, settled her hands in her lap and stared at the wall in front of her.

"Daddy."

Richardson smiled. "Yes Adele?"

"Yesterday Mummy made me go through all my alphabet. Ten times. One-oh times. A, B, C, D... She says I have to do it every day." She swung her long yellow hair back and forward in a slow pendulum motion, "Do I?"

Richardson tried to improve on his smile. His daughter's voice filled him with worry. She was seven years old, going on four. The regression appeared to be accelerating. She emerged from behind her pillow and began to climb down from the bunk. Her mother looked up.

"Yes Adele." The order was flat, emotionless as a speaking clock.

The young girl looked at her father then climbed back quickly into bed. Richardson wanted to go over to comfort but he knew his wife would forbid it.

Muffled words sounded through the cell door. "Five minutes Sikanda!"

He dressed.

"Is that my breakfast I see? Just let me eat Adele."

Richardson crossed to the table where his wife sat and an uneaten plate of food waited. Thirty-year-old habits turned his face. His wife remained motionless.

"I had to stay late in the lab," Richardson said softly. "Thank you for saving the food."

"It was brought by the guard."

There was no place for him at the table. Richardson took the plate over to the window and ate standing. A white trail of exhaust drifted away across the morning sky from the steel chimney stack. Richardson watched the faint constellations hang in their places in the lightening sky. Somewhere behind him he could hear his wife cough.

He returned to the table. There was no sound from the upper bunk.

"Gudrun, I am worried about Adele. Her speech is worse," Richardson whispered. His wife moved so he faced her back. He wanted to reach out and touch her. They had not touched for a long time.

They were breaking down. He certainly was, and his child too. Only his wife was surviving, become hard, almost inhuman. She protected Adele in careful ways, keeping to a routine, running lessons, a school timetable, supporting her successive accommodations, even this regression.

Richardson remembered earlier times, innocent times, just after they had married, what they had said to each other, before they had had Adele, that as long as they stayed together they could face anything. They hadn't known then what he could do.

Richardson blinked rapidly. The thought of what was happening gripped him again.

Not all was lost. Someone must be investigating the outbreak on the south coast. He prayed for a scientist, not some overworked nurse or field doctor. Please God it was someone smart with experience, who understood outbreak management; someone who knew the importance of finding first cases and could find one of them alive.

Approaching voices echoed in the outside corridor. He saw his wife glance around the room. He knew she still hoped to escape. The idea frightened him.

A key screamed in the door lock, iron on iron. Blankets moved in the top bunk.

"Don't go Daddy."

"I've got to work Adele. I'll see you tonight."

He looked down at his wife. She remained at the table, eyes fixed on the wall, her back straight.

Chapter 18

The small rectangle of plastic looked like a credit card. Except that the chip etched on the substrate was an opaque matt black and large as a thumbprint. Zahra turned her head to catch the audible click of a clean seat as she settled the card into a mounting.

She wriggled down into her chair like a racing driver into a cockpit. "Ok, let's check who you are." She pecked at the keyboard with two fingers to configure the processing sequence. "Twenty-three thousand strains should catch you." At her elbow, the mounting locked shut, isolating the chip while current was supplied.

On arriving, Zahra had found a box of peppermint tea next to her keyboard. Garrett had sent her an e-mail that began, "It doesn't work. But a cup of tea can help in other ways." Christine must have driven to a local shop to get the gift that morning. It was true: ginger tea, peppermint tea, vitamins, antacids, she had tried them all and none of them worked; she still felt sick. Zahra had smiled.

Garrett had returned to the lab the previous evening to write a search sequence to apply additional checks. Her e-mail suggested Zahra try it when checking the two new samples. Zahra had just tested her code; it had worked without error and she had to admit Garrett had improved on the approach. Some parts she didn't fully understand. She was surprised Garrett hadn't stayed to help interpret the output.

Processing... Checking chip integrity... Applying current... Please wait... Applying current...Analysing electrode responses...

Zahra watched the onscreen hourglass fill with binary sand as Sherlock read chemical syllables from the cut strips of malarial DNA.

Translating... Translating...

The processing was quick. The analyzer's chemical sequencing mimicked reproduction in its unzipping of the twin nucleic ribbons and the massively-parallel chip core allowed a fluent reading in minutes of the fifteen sequences of a thousand base pairs from Garrett's biopsy.

Translation complete. Analysing... exceptions reported...

Zahra viewed anomaly reports from Garrett's search as they came. Nothing much. Some unexpected data but all in junk DNA. Zahra clicked through to see a dump of nucleotide sequences.

AGT CAG AGT CAG AGT CAG AGT CAG AGT CAG AGT CAG AGT CAG AGT CAG AGT CAG **AAA CCC AAA CCC AAA CCC CAG AGT CAG AGT CAG AGT CAG AGT CAG AGT CAG AGT CAG AGT CAG AGT CAG AGT CAG AGT CAG AGT CAG AGT CAG AGT CAG AGT AGT CAG AGT CAG**

Zahra frowned at the anomalous sequence highlit by Garrett's code and the repetitious starting pattern. Unusual. She had not seen it before. She pulled at her lower lip. She stopped when it began to hurt. Who to ask? She couldn't pester George about every tiny thing. Rheinnalt was working on the far side of the lab. He might be able to help. He was good with computers. But as well as weird the man was annoying. The way he had cozied up to Christine. So obvious.

Analysis complete. Perform additional exceptions analysis?

Zahra hesitated. All sorts of oddities were seen in junk DNA: hence the name. Junk encoded for no active proteins and served no known practical function; the genomes of mature species were full of junk. Unimportant, evolutionary dead-ends.

Zahra breathed in sharply. She put a hand on her stomach. What was that? Wind? No. It had felt alien, like a thump inside her. A kick. She closed her eyes. She thought about a tiny foot. She squeezed her eyes more tightly closed as they filled with tears. What was she crying for? She waited until she fell calmer. When she opened her eyes she saw Rheinnalt staring at her. She glared furiously at the exceptions report on the screen. What was she doing?

Yes. Junk DNA. It wasn't important. Zahra closed the exceptions report and returned to the main results window.

Species: Falciparum. *Match:* **Sumatra-7**

There it was again.

"George, we've got a repeat match on the Brighton strain."

Skinner looked up from a tray of tubes, hands full.

"You're meant to be working on Cuito?"

"I just ran the match for Christine, that's all. I don't think she'll be pleased. She insists something else must be going on."

Skinner put down his tray and sighed. He nodded reluctantly.

"I was reading up on the phylogeny of *Plasmodium* last night," Zahra shoved her keyboard away like an empty plate, "And malaria seems uniquely prone to cross-mutations and jumping species. One study suggested human malaria's virulence was due to its recent transfer from migratory European songbirds."

"Susan Tollen."

"Yes," Zahra looked annoyed.

"She was not the first to make that claim."

"She pointed out that because many mosquito species feed on multiple hosts – mammals, birds, reptiles, humans – alien transfer events occur all the time." Zahra's voice rose. "I was thinking, a bird-malaria type-scenario would solve the transmission puzzle! There are dozens of candidate mosquito strains in southern England, not just *anopheles*."

"As they say, variation is the one biological constant." Skinner's voice struggled with patience.

"But if it were true," Zahra persisted, her face suggesting a girl who had done her homework and not got what she wanted. "A new cross-species malaria would be the epidemiologist's nightmare. AIDS, smallpox, polio, Ebola: they were all caused that way. And it doesn't take much. A few alterations to a haemaglutanin protein–"

"Shani–"

"–when *Yersinia Pestis* mutated to become orally infectious it created the bubonic plague."

"Shani, I've told you before, we can't shout 'Pandemic!' every time we see strange pathologies."

"I know. But I understand a bit more what is haunting Christine about this case. She is obsessed by it isn't she?"

Skinner did not reply.

***

The roads west of Porton were twisting and this early in the morning mostly clear of traffic. Garrett pushed her car fast through the corners, glad to be leaving. She had a backlog of work she wanted to clear at the Royal. A campervan held her up for two miles. The toot of an oncoming lorry forced her to check, brake hard and drop back. The single carriageway offered few chances to overtake. After two more tries, she stopped forcing the pace.

She reached the town of Boscombe. Porton was only a few miles behind her but already she felt calmer. Off to one side of the road she glimpsed a squat church steeple rising through trees, a stone dart aimed upward. She slowed, stopped, got out of the car. Her feet walked her through a wooden gate and led her across mowed grass littered with toppling stones. A small parish church stood under yew trees, a neat house of rubble masonry with dressed stone lintels and window frames. *Why do I come back?*

After David's death she had gone to church and wept. She had called out to God, then raged against him. In the silence of her prayers she had asked questions, and waited.

The grassy courtyard was quiet. Garrett walked towards the church.

While waiting she had worked and in that distraction found a sort of peace. There, among the ill and the dead, she had turned her scientific detachment onto herself. Through that objective lens she had seen a simple idea as if for the first time. Community, consolation, nostalgia, promises of reward or punishment: they were not reasons to believe something was true. Belief in the Christian God was an accident of birth; it was not supported by evidence. It was unscientific. She had stopped going to Mass.

She approached the arched entrance. At her feet clumps of yellow flowering herbs pushed out of the grass. She recognised *Hypericum perforatum* – Chase-devil or St John's wort. Its cancer-inhibiting properties had recently brought the plant into the news feeds. Half-forgotten lines surfaced in her mind. *Pick simples for a cancer.* She glanced up at the Chi Rho inscribed on the arch keystone. *A purpose more obscure.*

Staring up at the weathered carving, she remembered childhood Sundays. The sacraments weren't like her theories. They were shared old steps, more like a social dance, with meanings worn smooth with use. She pushed at the door.

The air inside was cool. She crossed the transept. Even as she genuflected she wondered if it showed more than respect. *Physical memory is not wholly to be trusted* she decided as she rose from a half-crouch. It might allow you to play a memorized piece of music – or drive from Brighton to Porton Down with hardly a conscious thought – but before you are wholly aware it can kneel you before a God you no longer believe exists. She sat in one of the pews at the back and listened to the thickening silence. It was peaceful in the church. Nothing moved.

After some minutes she looked round. She had half-expected a conversation. David's ghost had been with her that morning, together with the anger that always came with him. Memory of another presence had been there too, of Jason, mistrustful, holding himself at a distance, out of reach. It had filled her fists with frustration.

A small altar stood at the end of the central aisle covered with a simple white cloth, a table awaiting setting. She suddenly realised why she had loved the gospels so much. They were a master pattern, a way of understanding told in a story of human proportion. She bowed her head over her empty hands clasped like a child's around a found treasure.

Sunlight fell on Garrett's upturned face, stained through the leaded figures of the four evangelists. *So fix our eyes on what is unseen. For what is seen is temporary, but what is unseen is eternal.* What if that were true?

Was her lapse other than she had supposed, simpler than her rational arguments? Had she allowed anger and resentment to foster sin? Had scientific detachment and her pride in knowledge cut her off from a living faith, from a personality behind the facts of the world?

She remembered her argument with Rheinnalt Bryce the day before. It itched like an insect bite. Her models of infection and protein expression gave predictions and identified compounds that saved lives. As Bryce had suggested, this queer grip her medical maths had beyond the tip of her pen required explanation. How did her mind-made levers move objects in the world?

The crucifix high on the wall of the apse filled her vision. She had the sudden image of herself suspended between two worlds, as if a diver seeing both corals and sky. She moved her head as if to shake something free.

Even if she considered an unproven origin for the patterns she studied, the journey would hardly be started. To return to a place kneeling in front of a cross? That would need a confrontation with a Creator who appeared to be incompetent, indifferent or worse.

The image of a man as God hung in front of her. Perhaps she could just take what was useful, and not trouble with the hows and whys? The thought rang hollow. Some instinct warned her that what she was facing would demand of her a greater understanding.

She stood and crossed over to the gospel aisle. Halfway up, a cluster of patched flags drooped from poles in the windless air. Retired regimental colours. Garrett recognised the long shadow of Porton, five miles down the road. She remembered her anger seeing in Skinner's lab the intrusion of military purpose into her scientific world. Here too.

At the end of the nave a large painting of dark oils hung from the back wall. In front of it, intricate swirls of inlaid coloured tiles patterned the floor. Garrett drew closer.

She recognized a type of maze, a prayer labyrinth. As a young girl on a French exchange holiday she had discovered the one in Chartres Cathedral and been entranced. Separated from her group, she had not noticed their absence until she had solved the puzzle and entered the six-petalled stone rose at the centre.

This one was smaller but complex. As she studied the twists and turns, her preoccupations – the memory of her sudden anger with Bryce, the endless waiting for a phone call that never came, the current medical case – fell away. For a moment, she was happy.

She stepped forward and threaded her way through the tiled spirals without hesitation or retreat, like a chess master moving against a club player. The turns narrowed. At the last, her eyes lifted towards the painting on the back wall positioned to face the puzzle's centre.

An inscription at the top read "The light of glory everlasting". In the middle, Christ hovered between broken gates below a golden sky. In his hands he drew up a man and a woman by their wrists. Below was a dark cave, its black interior tessellated with figures of the damned. The lowest crouched in corners manacled to rocks.

The faces of the chained were turned away. There was a second quote from St Aquinas below Christ's feet. "Shame for their unbelief." Garrett drew a cold, dusty breath. The message of the Harrowing was unequivocal. Rejection of God was the sin that could not be forgiven. She would find no comfort here.

Chapter 19

It was a cold night. The broken glass and bars of the cell window let in a breeze. Richardson could feel it on his face. The sky was clear, a three-quarter moon visible above the trees. The light would be useful. He listened as he worked. The sea, a background fizz of white noise, was some help too.

"Shit!"

Pain scraped his knuckles. Richardson looked down at the broken halves of a fork. Blood trickled between his fingers. He hit a brick with his fist then rested his forehead on the rough wall.

"Be quiet."

The tone of his wife's instruction suggested it should not need repeating. She sat at the table behind him watching with cold eyes.

"Sorry."

"How much longer?"

"Maybe tonight."

Richardson crossed to the bunk bed. From above came an occasional snuffle and snore. Adele was sleeping. He pulled the lower mattress away from the wall, reached into an open seam, swapped the broken fork for a spoon, and returned to the window.

It was his wife who had spotted the chance. She had noticed when a different person returned to collect their meals, and saved a fork, hiding it in the mattress. That night, four weeks ago, she had put him to work at the window.

He hacked between bricks. The bars were fixed on the outside. He removed and replaced more mortar each night. Already, he had loosened the courses across two bars beneath the window frame. Freeing a third bar would be enough.

The worst part was not his scarred hands, it was the scraping silence. His wife directed him with few words, more with her eyes. And over the weeks he had worked on the window she had worked on their jailer.

Richardson had been forced to listen to her methods. She had recently managed to convince the young man – Sky she called him now – to let her leave the cell with him. Twice. Coming back, she had said nothing. Had she gone to his room? Had she undressed, closed her eyes, with him? So far, she had only managed to leave in daylight, with others watching.

Each night these past weeks she had played another game, another sort of seduction, with Adele. 'Mousy mousy' she called it and there were only two rules: you must keep up with Mummy; and you mustn't make any noise, however surprised, or hurt. She had the child chase her round and round the room and rewarded her with chocolate – a gift from the young man no doubt. *Sky.*

Richardson hacked free another few grains of cement. He was close now. He would finish his work before her. Maybe by morning.

It was quiet in the woods. When Kirtananda came out of the trees the sea was suddenly, surprisingly loud, but in here nothing stirred but water.

He leaned on his spade and surveyed his work. He gave a low grunt, satisfied. The valley stream ran down the slope along its usual course till it met his makeshift dam of mud and stones. A small pool had formed above the obstruction and the overflow trickled down through the surrounding trees, creating a wide area of sodden earth. Three deep trenches marked the bare stream bed below the dam. The two largest holes – seven feet long – he had dug side-by-side; the third, half that length, ran across their ends; they formed a crude hieroglyph, the shadow of a trilith, on the earth.

All the guys were out, only Sky left here with him. He would use the boy. Of course he could clean up on his own. He needed blooding. This was a good opportunity. Belief was one thing – the lad had plenty of that – real loyalty was something else. You had to feel it, earn it. Prove it. Not just think about it.

This job would do the trick. He had the right bait and the right hook. And if the boy ducked – if his acid-cooked brains shut down, or he bottled it – never mind, he would do it himself. Killing wasn't something he enjoyed. That wasn't his kink. But it didn't bother him either. He had learned that in Iraq.

Was it twelve years ago? Those parched, fly-blown months full of corpses; he could still hear the muezzin in his dreams, calling to the faithful across bombed cities. He watched a trickle of water spill over the top of the makeshift dam; the thin vein, silvered by moonlight, escaped into the trees. In the desert, water was always beautiful. Here, the wood around him was thirsty, alive and drinking.

Small arms would do, and the plastic, and Sky. All back at the House. He began to climb up through the trees. The dam would hold a while yet.

Imagine you are riding the waves of your breaths. Breathe in...Out... In...Out...You are floating on the seas of sensation. Now imagine a coastline, cliffs in the distance. You see a sandy beach. Breathe in...Out...

You arrive on the beach. A path follows a stream inland. Take it. You walk under trees then come out into a valley. What do you see?

Skyler turned his head slightly. He saw what he always saw: a quilt of fields and orchards.

There are fields with sheep. Orchards. Flower meadows.

Skyler decided tomorrow he must make this journey in the flesh.

Continue on the path up into the valley.

The air came and went from him, fresh and warm, like new-made bread. He was filled with a sense of peace.

You reach the source of the stream where the water runs clear in pools that reflect the sky. You have arrived at the place of faith. You see sets of stone steps cut in the earth. They lead down into confusion and darkness. Choose.

He chose the path of Contemplation, as he always did.

Good. You have chosen well. There are candles. Light one.

Skyler smiled. The candle flame was yellow. It was always yellow.

You are in a maze with corridors branching in all directions. Follow the sequence of personal growth as you have been taught. Find your way through the darkness.

Skyler stared at his eyelids.

You stand in the Circle of the open secret, where the Unseen is made visible.

As above, as below.

This is where the central truth can be revealed to you. What do you see?"

Gudrun.

He studied her face with his mind's eyes. He could remember every detail, hovering above him. The straight nose, flushed cheeks, curving open lips, a strand of blonde hair escaped from her plaits, and those blue eyes, so clear yet unreadable. She'd said she loved him! Was that true?

No. She didn't. Not really. She just wanted to escape. She'd say anything.

But when she was with him, it seemed so much like she loved him! And she'd told him she did. Maybe she did.

She was interested in him. Last time, she had asked why he respected Arshu so much. He had begun to explain the teaching, the paths. He had told her that he was an Instructor. He had become embarrassed.

He thought again about teaching anything to those clear blue eyes and shivered. What was she doing at the moment? She was with her husband. Doing what? She said she didn't love that man any more. Was that true?

He thought of his own wife given to him by Arshu. Obedient, a housewife, tending to his physical needs as the Rules dictated. Compared to Gudrun she was barely more than a dog.

He remembered Arshu's lesson on sex. *With all desire comes attachment and suffering. That is why control of the sexual impulse grants spiritual power.*

Sex. It had been the cause of his only crises of faith. The first had come hearing the rumours of coercive sex with female novitiates, of hidden rooms in Arshu's private apartments where the strictures of the ascetic life were loosed, lubricated with alcohol – drugs of all kinds – meats, sex and electronic entertainments. But he had discounted the gossip as malicious, motivated by spiritual jealousy.

The last crisis had come a year ago with the police. They had entered the Valley with a search warrant and taken two members of Asari by force, Derzelas and Eshmun, the crèche managers. The local health authority had prosecuted Eshmun with rape of minors and Derzelas for wilful medical neglect of children. "Your prayers should complement — not compete — with proper medical care," the judge had told Derzelas at his sentencing hearing in Cardiff. Arshu had declared the secular authorities would repent their blasphemy. When Derzelas beat the charges and was moved to the crèche of another House, the rumours restarted.

If you notice your concentration has wandered, return to the breath...

Skyler heard a distant knock at a door.

...without reacting, without giving yourself a hard time. Breathe in...

"Hey Sky!"

The knock at the door repeated. Skyler ripped off his headphones and opened his eyes. The room snapped into focus. It was bare, monkish, with unvarnished wooden floorboards. There was a bed, a shelf of books propped up on bricks, a low table cluttered with smoking equipment. Through two windows the trees and fields of the Valley were visible, and halfway down the sky a horizon of blues where it met the sea.

"Sky! I hear you in there! Wanna do a bong?"

"No thanks."

The door opened and a short, bull-chested man with close-cropped red hair walked in.

"Sure you do."

Skyler turned sideways. "I'm busy right now, Kirt."

Kirtananda studied him, head tilted to one side. His intense whitened eyes were close-set to his broad nose. He carried a small khaki knapsack over one shoulder. When he spoke, corded neck muscles moved inside a rainbow-coloured collar.

"Doin what?"

"Studying."

"Yeah? Studying your feet?"

Skyler closed his eyes and took a breath deep into his diaphragm. "You wouldn't understand."

"Hey! Don't come all holy man with me. You forget I am sanyasin and a Head of House. Show some respect!"

Skyler opened his eyes to see what Kirtananda was doing. The man scared him.

"I got a tola of Rishi black."

Skyler hesitated. Kirtananda opened his right hand. It held a brown, cling-wrapped stick of hash.

"Where'd you get that?"

Kirtananda grinned and went over to the table. "Jeesus man, you got enough hubblies?"

Skyler prepared a pipe. Kirtananda let Skyler do most of the first bowl. They settled on the bare floor under the layers of smoke.

"Good?"

Skyler grinned. He rocked on an elbow, eyes closed.

"I got one last cake of it. You want it? Too heavy for me."

"Yeah? Thanks man."

"No worries." Kirtananda scratched his chin. "Hey Sky, you're okay you know?"

Skyler nodded.

"I can see why Arshu chose you. I hear you've been invited to take Sanyas."

Skyler opened his eyes.

"Your faith is strong."

Skyler struggled to a sitting position.

"He can sense that you know," Kirtananda said.

"Yeah? I was surprised. I mean, I know it's an honour. In the Hall, when he called us up in front of everyone I was surprised."

"I know."

"But then, everyone left and it was just you guys, and me. I–"

"Sure, it's tough being left behind."

"Yeah, but I don't really understand – why me? I mean I'm not a doer. I'm not a fighter. Not like you, and Rayan, and the others. Don't get me wrong, I'm not criticising. I understand the Path of Action. Remember I'm an Instructor. But it's not me. It's not my way."

"You think you must only travel one path? Remember the Succession." Kirtananda held Skyler with his white crossed eyes. "Arshu has been a warrior."

"That's different! For his Master there was a war to fight."

"There's always a war." When Skyler reached for his pipe Kirtananda stopped him. "I need you to help me with something tonight."

Skyler frowned.

"Don't worry. It's just a small job."

"Job?" Skyler eyed Kirtananda nervously. "What sort of job?"

"Arshu has asked us to send Sikanda on, to join him in the Exodus. He's concerned about security here."

"Sikanda?" Skyler looked alarmed. "Just Sikanda?"

"Yes." Kirtananda smiled. "You must carry on looking after his wife and child. They come with us when we go. It's not time to leave yet."

Kirtananda watched Skyler thinking. For a monk he sure thought slow.

"You like her don't you?"

"Arshu asked for this?"

"Looks like she likes you too. Nothing wrong with that."

"Did he?"

"Sure." Kirtananda took a pair of miniature cymbals out of a pocket. The clear note he struck sounded formal, as though ending an audience. Before it had faded Kirtananda stood. When Skyler looked up at him he said, "Come on."

"Now?"

"Yes now."

The forest was dark and too quiet. Skyler cursed Kirtananda. What the hell was the man up to?

When they had taken the scientist from the cell, Kirtananda had grinned at Skyler like it was just a game. Skyler had felt relieved. At least the man was acting like they were on the same side.

"Here. Take this."

At first, Skyler had thought Kirtananda was passing him the promised hash cake. But hash wasn't cold, wasn't a heavy piece of metal.

"I'll go ahead with Sikanda. You watch my back. If he runs, shoot."

"No, Kirt I–" Skyler had found it difficult to think after the pipe.

"Arshu was clear wasn't he?" Kirtananda hissed. "He is your charge. He must not be allowed to escape."

Skyler had kept quiet. He remembered the stories about Kirtananda. He believed them. The man ran gangs and dealers. What was he planning tonight? He remembered Arshu's private words to him before he left: *Sikanda, his family, they do not understand fully but they are part of our family now and they must stay with us – that is your responsibility.*

He could see Kirtananda through the trees, pushing Sikanda on in front of him. Whenever Sikanda slowed, Kirtananda gave him a savage poke in the back. Skyler watched as the man cried out and stumbled. When he fell Kirtananda kicked him to his feet.

Skyler hung back. He gripped the gun in his hand. The weight of it was frightening. Kirtananda and Sikanda were walking faster now, up a gentle incline through thickening trees. Skyler looked down at his feet. They were wet. The ground was soaked with water. Why? He tried to clear his smoke-filled mind. He didn't understand. Everything was happening too fast. What should he do?

A cry came from up ahead.

"Sky!!"

Skyler began to run.

A dozen yards ahead, on the edge of a clearing, he could see the two men. Behind them, a pool of water, silvered by moonlight, lapped against a low wall of mud and stones. Sikanda was on his knees holding Kirtananda by the waist. Kirtananda was clubbing him. When Sikanda tried to stand Kirtananda spread his arms wide and gave a great shout.

"Waaaa!"

Sikanda ran. Kirtananda pointed his gun and fired. Sikanda ducked into the trees.

"Skyler! Shoot him! Shoot!"

Skyler stepped out from behind a tree directly in front of Sikanda. The running man screamed and veered away.

"Sky! Remember what Arshu said! Shoot him! NOW!"

Skyler thought of Gudrun. He raised his gun. He pulled the trigger. Sikanda fell. Stood up. Again Skyler pulled the trigger. The power of the recoil was shocking.

When Sikanda got up this time he didn't run. He stood still, bent over a little, holding an arm against his side as though ashamed of something. A shot spun him around. Another pushed him back against a tree. He moved as if punched by an invisible opponent.

Kirtananda loomed out of the dark. He pushed Skyler in front of him. They stood over the scientist as he lay on the ground holding his side. Kirtananda shot him two more times in the chest. The man continued to breathe.

"Bloody one sevens."

Kirtananda shoved his gun in his waistband and unslung his knapsack. He knelt by the dying man. Quickly, he rolled Sikanda's now-still body in plastic sheeting. He looked up briefly. Skyler had gone.

He dragged the body to one of the graves in the riverbed.

"Go!" Skyler flung out an arm then turned and ran.

Gudrun guided Adele with a hand at her back. Outside, she knelt down by the child and smiled.

"Are you ready?"

Over her daughter's shoulder, a hundred yards away, she could see the tree line.

"Mummy–" Gudrun focussed on her daughter. She managed a smile. "I've decided I don't want to play the game today. Can we go back inside?"

The sounds of the night squeaked and sighed all around them. Above the distant sound of the waves she heard gunshots. Gudrun's stomach heaved with fear. The mad dog of a man would be coming back for them. They had to hurry!

Gudrun nudged her daughter with her elbow. She held up a whole bar of chocolate, smelled it. "Mmmm."

Adele held out her hand. "Mummy!"

"Only if we play the game. That's the rule." She waited. She tried not to move.

"Okay."

"Remember, quiet as a mouse!"

They walked hand-in-hand across open ground towards the forested sides of the valley. The dome of the night sky glittered above them. It was a sight she hadn't thought she would see again except through bars.

When Steven had been dragged out of the cell they had been lucky: the scarred wall under the window had not been noticed. With quick, desperate fingers she had made good the brick joints, as she had made Steven do every morning. She had waited for him to return, waited for the thugs with their sharp suspicious eyes. Instead Skyler had arrived. He had opened the door, his face turned away, unable to look at her, eyes full of a terrible shame. His words, whispered over Adele's head, echoed still in her ears. *Your husband is dead. You must run. Run! Run for your lives.*

They reached the trees and found a clear sandy trail, heading north inland and south towards the beach, just as Skyler had described. Gudrun headed south, down to the sea, leaving clear signs for a hundred yards – a torn sleeve on a thorn tree, on bordering barbed wire, footprints in wetter ground – then turned around. She knelt and held her daughter by the shoulders. She breathed in the smell of the girl's hair.

"There's more chocolate at the station. So quick as we can! No stopping. No noise. We must follow Daddy's star – there. Let's go!"

They began running north.

Kirtananda loosed the dogs. They ran towards the trees led by their tongues – two blueticks, a redbone and three ridgebacks, a tight chasing pack. The ancient sound of their excitement echoed off the valley walls.

Kirtananda squatted in the open doorway. He studied the ground. It had to be Skyler who had let them out. The lad was nowhere to be seen. Hiding somewhere. Give him time. He'd done okay. Now he needed to understand what it meant. To understand everything had changed. Everyone was different, but Kirtananda judged he would need a day or so.

He lifted an ear. The dogs' barking had changed; deep-chested, retched howls carried over the fields. They were calling to him. They had found something.

It took just an hour to catch them – they had nearly reached the coastal road. He settled the dogs then barrowed the bodies back to the river. That was the hard work. Dead weight was heaviest to shift. At least he had dug the holes first. When it was finished all he wanted to do was sleep.

He sat with his back to the banked earth and rolled a well-earned smoke. It tasted good. He wondered where Tarin was. Christmas as he now was, one of the Five.

He missed the man. When he had told him about his blood group – and that he had decided to be one of the Five and accept *Neshmet*, the Holy Death – Kirtananda had been dismayed. They had served together years ago on the same tours – fought together, even gone to jail together once. He had brought him to the Valley and made him his lieutenant. He would miss him. He had trusted and relied on him: there was no more useful man to have at your back when things got rough. And things were going to get very rough.

"The world is about to change", Arshu had said, the last time he had gathered the Heads together. Damn straight. Only that handful and a few chosen sanyasins – the inner circle – had been told. A few hadn't been able to handle it. They were gone.

Kirtananda contemplated the holes in the riverbed. Now was the waiting time. It wouldn't be long. The chaos that was coming, even Arshu probably hadn't guessed what it would be like.

He could. He was a soldier. He'd seen hell before; heard it, smelled it, tasted it in the air. Cordite smoke. Bodies lying on the ground like broken toys. Fathers holding dead sons, talking to them. Screaming mothers, holding fistfuls of hair in front of their eyes. Torn human flesh, the smell of bleach on concrete.

Through the trees the sky was lightening. A bird began to call. After some minutes there was a short, repeated answer; then the whole forest began to sing.

As if to join in the chorus, one of the open graves gave a moan. The sound brought Kirtananda to his feet. He examined the three bodies in turn. When he bent over Sikanda he got a shock. The man's eyes were open; they blinked at him through plastic; his mouth moved. Kirtananda hunted in the trees for his shovel. He was angry. The man's refusal to die was a surprise. He hated surprises.

Four cuts with the shovel into the mud at the middle of the dam cooled his anger. He watched the water break through. In moments the graves and the whole riverbed were covered by the stream as it rushed down along its old course towards the sea.

Chapter 20

Christmas emerged from the shadow beneath Palace Pier. He took a long drag on his cigarette and shivered. He could feel the fever sleeping in him. *Finish the snout. No rush.*

He looked along the beach. The sky was the palest blue, white along the horizon. He heard the rumble of morning lager in his stomach and took another drag on the cigarette. *Breakfast of champions.*

He bent to peer in under the pier floor. The weight of his pack pulled down on his shoulders. He felt moisture trickle down his arms. *I've performed the Arshu Awareness. Twice.*

He straightened up. His cigarette smoked with faint heat between his fingers. *Disease is the tax the soul pays for the body.* Ramakrishna's line rolled round and round his mind like a marble in a glass bowl. *These sweats – yes, they are price I must pay. No matter. This is the holy time of the Chosen!*

At the top of the beach a refuse lorry moved slowly along an access road under the chalk cliffs. A vast flock of seagulls wheeled overhead as if above a fishing trawler. *Wish I could be flying up there, in the cool.*

Christmas watched Jimmy the Suit collecting abandoned deckchairs into stacks. Up and down the dunes. The sight tired him. Everything tired him at the moment. After a while Jimmy gave a noticing wave.

The Exodus was already under way: Osei and Kirtananda, the last House Heads, they would be going soon. Jade and Lizzie too. So many going without him. An emptiness filled him, and something else he wouldn't name, deeper than his tiredness. His head thudded. His arms were wet where they rested against his legs.

The trouble with Acceptance – it was a healing spell, but you could apply it to anything. It could make you numb. Christmas closed his eyes and tried to concentrate on his breathing. He wished he was back in the silence of Asari Valley. No television. No internet. No mobiles. Such silence. The thought that he would never return there made him feel very alone.

Arshu said you carry your silence within you. But there was a silence he heard in the Valley which he had found nowhere else. On each return – every time he rode the rolling road out of Aberystwyth, saw the first glitter of the sea from the cliff top and followed the familiar wooded turns of the stony footpath down into the valley – Christmas loved the feeling of passing over, into a place held apart. *As above, as below.*

Over the years his meditations had got stronger. With each Retreat his self-control had increased. When he had been Chosen, it was like all his birthdays in one, like when his father had come home that year. He had never expected it. One of the Five! Chosen by Arshu himself. He had felt such peace!

He understood now. It was just a word. But the feeling! He'd never been chosen for anything before. Not like this. Finally he understood what it was all *for*. The meaning of life. The *purpose*. What was it Arshu had said? *When you are ready, the purpose will appear.*

Yes it was frightening too. Losing his name: he had been surprised at how much that had hurt him. Tarin. A good, strong name. A name he had earned. Arshu was right: all attachment is suffering.

Then there was the approaching pain. But that was okay. He was expecting it and had been trained to cope. And simple pain was nothing compared to the responsibility he had been given. One of the Chosen Five. A Christmas for each continent, bringing Rebirth, healing the world – the forests, the warming, the species, Arshu had explained it all.

Maintain the Discipline. Keep moving. Keep breathing. It was his only work now. To live. To breathe. To spread the Word. As long as he could. To the end.

Holy work. He looked out over the beach to where Jimmy was still stacking chairs. The first arrivals were climbing down the cliff steps, lugging their beach gear. *Nasari.* Outsiders. The faithless. He flicked his cigarette butt into the pebbles. Somewhere up in the town an emergency siren wailed.

He was on a sacred path, with footsteps to follow. Arshu had promised. For the next thousand lives he would be there leading him higher; because he was one of the Chosen. Christmas trembled with the thought of it. That a being such as Arshu would delay his departure from Samsara a thousand lifetimes to be his guide!

Even Kirtananda had been impressed. Impressed but sad when he had heard the news. The thought of his friend made him smile. He would miss the old soldier.

He began climbing, long rattling strides up the beach. The effort forced him to gulp air like a landed fish. He reminded himself each breath was holy. At the edge of the fairground, two stalls switched on their displays side-by-side, suddenly colourful. A ride began to move, its empty seats spinning silently. Christmas reached the first line of shops along the seafront and stopped in at a cafe.

The owner was expecting him. He wheeled out a motorbike from the back of the store. Its chrome and black coachwork gleamed in the morning light.

"You alright Chrissy? You look like shit."

"Fine. Rough night." Christmas leaned on his knees to catch his breath. He spat. Pink saliva hit the cement. He straightened and strapped his pack to the back rack.

"Where you off to then?"

Christmas swung onto the bike and kicked the stand. "Heading over to Glasto."

"Jade left her diary here. Will you see her–"

The bike's engine caught first time, the big four-stroke settling into a low popping beat. Christmas grinned and shook his head. "Time to spread the love."

The caff owner grimaced and looked back over his shoulder. "Nowadays, the only thing I get to spread is butter." He raised a hand as the bike moved off. "You take care yourself Chris."

Christmas rode slowly along the seafront. Reaching the access ramp up to the cliff-top he picked up speed, overtaking the climbing refuse lorry with a sudden burst of acceleration.

***

The bone-white line of Palace pier extended out into sparkling water. Garrett fingered the beginnings of a blister on her left heel. Her shoes were white and her ankles hot. She was beginning to know this beach too well.

She had slept angry. Four hours knotted in the sheets. Then waited like a hunted animal for dawn, her right hand a fist held ready by her cheek. Rising, she had headed straight for the beach. This place was the point of connection.

She rubbed at her heel again. She must have walked over ten miles across the same patch of hot pebbles.

"Melonade!" The waitress rollerbladed to a stop in circles. She had the bounce of a darts compère.

"Thanks."

Garrett picked up her drink and retreated to a line of deckchairs.

It was midday. She had emailed Skinner a promise to return soon to review the DNA analysis. It was probably ready. An image of Rheinnalt Bryce returned, of his stepping around a dip in the pavement, for her to notice. Why did he do that? Was it calculation? No. That was unfair. What was it then? Their meetings had unsettled her.

She dropped down into her chair and pulled out her notebook. *Concentrate!* She sucked thirstily at green ice.

Her book was full of new scribbles. She had talked to every beach regular prepared to stop and exchange a few words. A hotdog vendor, lifeguard, fairground attendants – many had heard of the deaths. A few had witnessed surrounding events. This beach... she felt it was important, in some way she should trust. She sucked repeatedly on her straw, as a smoker on a cigarette for distraction. Rereading her notes, she felt thoughts adjust focus, like the millimetrical to-ing and fro-ing of a microscope's stage.

Bryce had reassured her, but she couldn't shake off her sense of foreboding with this case, that somewhere out of sight, unseen, a terrible thing was taking shape, that she was the only one in place trying to see; and that now, when she needed it the most, her skill had deserted her.

Her notes suggested nothing new. She decided to carry on walking and talking. It had not yet proved useful, but she knew from experience sometimes you just had to make up a catching pattern. She must be a grass spider, a conscientious weaver with eight eyes, waiting for some movement, some caught signal. The ice began to gurgle. She peered into clear crystals and put the empty beaker down.

"There's a bin over there."

Garrick blinked into the sun. An old man in a faded and frayed suit was standing over her. He was barefoot. A tattered straw hat covered his head. He gestured with a hand up the beach. "I'll take it if you like."

Garrett watched the old man track over the pebbles and back.

"Done."

Bushy grey eyebrows gave a conspiratorial lift. He settled into a neighbouring deckchair. Garrett opened her mouth then closed it again.

"Well, here we are."

The man dropped crossed arms on his legs a few times with the happiness of it.

"Beautiful day."

He looked around as if waiting for the entertainment to start. The sea sparkled. The pier stood white and unmoving against the shore. The man rocked in the sling of his chair, seemingly content with what was on offer.

"Thank you."

"Not at all. Not at all. Consider it a quid... a quid–" He smoothed his eyebrows hurriedly with both thumbs and tried again.

"Let's consider it a quid–"

"–pro quo?"

"Yes!" The man agreed with the gravity of the successful. "Quite."

"What's your name?"

"Me? My name?" Fright spasmed across his face. He smoothed his eyebrows again before relaxing and smiling with a delight of childish width. "My name is Jimmy the Suit. I live here. And you are?"

"Christine Garrett. Pleased to meet you Jimmy the Suit."

"Likewise Christine. Are you on holiday?"

"No. Well, sort of–"

"You sound confused."

Garrett laughed. "Yes, I do, don't I? It is the bank holiday weekend – that's the holiday part. But I'm working on a case at the moment which I can't let go of."

"What sort of case?"

"It's medical. I'm a doctor."

Garrett sat with Jimmy the Suit and watched the passers-by. Behind a windbreak, a red-faced father was blowing up a ball. A dog ran past. The sea glittered in the sun.

"Beautiful day isn't it?" He sat back happily and spoke to the stones as if they listened. "But what are days for? *Solving that question...*"

As Garrett joined in Jimmy tilted his head towards her. "…*brings the priest and the doctor in their long coats, running over the fields.*"

Garrett smiled. "I haven't heard that in years. My husband loved it."

"I used to use him in my sermons."

"You're a priest?"

"Was."

Garrett slipped off her shoes. The pebbles were warm under her feet. Jimmy was watching the beach and the sea, humming, and nodding to himself. Garrett returned to her notebook, but the words and lines were dead on the page. She had stared them to death. She sighed.

"I'm stuck Jimmy."

"Yes." Jimmy nodded agreement, as if at something the pebbles had said.

Garrett raised an arm to clasp the back of her deckchair and closed her eyes.

"I was stuck once," Jimmy said.

Garrett opened one eye. "What did you do?"

"Good question. What did I do?" Jimmy adjusted his straw hat and addressed the pebbles again. "I waited. Until I could see clearly. Remember? Till I see what's really always there."

"*Unresting death, a whole day nearer now,*" Garrett squinted at the sun.

"How come you're here Jimmy? What do you do?"

"Oh, this and that." Jimmy nodded and shook his head at the same time. He gestured at the view. "Mainly this. Sitting. Watching. Seeing. You see all sorts here. Do you know, on a clear day you can see France?"

Garrett frowned. She couldn't see anything clearly at the moment. Was it impatience? Fear? Was it Jason again? She couldn't seem to get a hold of it. She studied the distant-silent glitter of light beyond the pier.

"Have you tried walking? Walking is a great way to get unstuck."

Garrett closed her eyes. "No joy. I've been walking all morning, Father."

"Hmm. Perhaps you're trying too hard. By the way, it's not Father any more." Jimmy rocked in his chair. "I've found this beach is very good at helping things get unstuck, if you give it a chance."

"I should warn you, I'm allergic to superstition. I'm a scientist."

"Well perhaps I should warn you, you're a doctor of medicine, I was a doctor of theology."

They smiled at each other.

"Medicine is very technical and scientific nowadays," Jimmy peered at her, "But I've always thought science is a matter, in the end, of faith. Just like everything else. Isn't it?"

"No."

"You're trying to find an answer. You can't see it, but you trust you will. You have faith." Jimmy's voice was sing-song as if he argued with a child.

Garrett frowned. "The trust I have is just a sort of common sense, expecting to see around a corner what is seen every day."

Lines from another student of medicine, a son of a Catholic doctor, returned to her.

> *Not where the wheeling systems darken,*
> *And our benumbed conceiving soars*
> *The drift of pinions, would we hearken*
> *Beats at our own clay-shuttered doors.*

Garrett felt her childhood stories reach out for her with their shadowy saving hands. She frowned down at the web of lines drawn on the page of the notebook still open on her lap and thought about Bryce's comparisons.

No! He was wrong. She was not a seer. She found causes and medical effects in the real world. Her predictions were then simply systematic guesses, a net thrown to catch facts not angels. To call that quietism 'faith' was not to name the thing she had been taught as a child.

It was not Thompson's Unseen that she drew her patterning net through; nor some world of abstracted Doubt, of wondering if Bishop Berkeley's tree grew out of mind or Mind. She trusted the ideas of her scientific ancestors, their invisible nets of evolution, atomic structure and gravitation, because of the tested evidence. The mathematical lines physicists had found to hold up the sky had proved trustworthy as a falling apple.

Yes, scientific instinct could *feel* like a sort of revelation, but only in the sense of 'I've been here before', like recognizing a timeless tune on the radio then discovering you'd never heard it before.

It was true, the face of science was forever turned towards the as-yet unseen. And because the faithful claimed knowledge of the Unseen, they would continue to argue science required faith, and continue to see the rollback of religious competence as science moved forward.

Jimmy was looking at her with a kindly smile. "Why do you hate it so?"

"It's important not to pretend to see in the dark."

Jimmy the Suit smiled and nodded. "If you let it, this beach helps you see what is hidden. That's what I've found since I've been here."

"What sort of things?"

"Each night I watch the stars. I wait and watch and peel back the corners of the sky."

Jimmy the Suit stopped to comb his eyebrows. Garrett watched two children chasing a beach ball. With each kick it sailed high over the pebbles. "And what do you see?"

"When I first arrived, mainly people from my childhood: my father, a teenage friend, a monk from my prep school – my demons. Then I saw the figures we're taught to see – Orion, Armeros, Perseus; and Christ, early on the horizon, with the evening star; then my face, staring back at me. Now I am peaceful and I see nothing." Jimmy smiled. "Now I see just the stars themselves. At night, I sit on the end of the pier and stare at them for hours, sometimes until morning. They are very beautiful."

"Those myths, I understand why they are there. They are from our childhoods. But they don't half get in the way," Jimmy said.

Garrett, surprised at finding nothing to argue with, held herself still with approval. Then she said, "I can give you a fact instead."

"Oh yes, facts are good."

"In the centre of those stars you watch, all the heavy elements are manufactured – it's the only place with the necessary conditions. And when those stars burn out, they expel this matter. Carbon, oxygen, nitrogen…" Garrett pinched her arm. "These elements are the atomic components of organic matter – what we are made of. So in fact, we are atomic waste; or, if you prefer, made from the dust of dead stars."

"What things you know. Facts you say. And yet they sound like magic. Stories that are true." Jimmy smiled. "Wonderful."

"I used to watch the stars with my son Jason when we were on holiday. He saw all sorts of things in them. Before he left."

Jimmy watched her. "You miss him."

"Yes. Terribly."

They watched the children chasing the ball. When it bounced near Jimmy got up. Garrett felt his detachment and was grateful for it. She was just another passerby on his beach. When he came back from playing he was hot and panting. He flopped back into his chair.

"What were we saying?" He stretched, a writhe of his whole body as if waking from under a duvet. "Oh yes. Missing people."

"Can I get you anything?" The waitress called out to them across the pebbles as she rollerbladed backwards along the boardwalk, bottom first. Garrett lowered her arm from the back of her deckchair and shook her head.

Jimmy threw a stone at a clump of seaweed. "Friend of mine died here last week doc."

"Oh?"

"She was a good sort, you know? Gave me this hat." Jimmy frowned under the straw brim at the sun. He threw another stone. "It's always the good ones that go."

"What was her name?" When Garrett turned to look at Jimmy her gaze narrowed, like the beam from a pencil torch adjusting in the dark.

"Her name? Yes. What was her name?" Jimmy lowered his face to his thumbs and worked his eyebrows again. "I don't remember."

Garrett held her body still, aware of Jimmy's concentration, the thin, breakable thread of it.

"I forget things. I should remember though. I noticed she was missing." Jimmy stared at the sand. "When I asked, someone told me she died of malaria, which doesn't make sense. Not here in England. Doesn't make sense at all."

Garrett shaded her eyes.

"Do you know where she died?"

"They said in hospital. Lizzie hated hospitals!"

"Where did Lizzie live?"

"Here."

"Where?"

"On the beach. She had a spot under the pier."

Garrett put her shoes back on and stood up.

"Can you show me?"

Jimmy polished his eyebrows. Garrett stood next to him on a sloping floor of pebbles beneath the Palace Pier. Shafts of sunlight divided the shadows. There was rubbish everywhere – discarded tin cans, cigarette packets, plastic food cartons, yellowed strands of toilet paper, driftwood. At the bottom of the beach the sea heaved. Jimmy watched as Garrett studied the ground.

"Looks like they're all out for the day."

"Lizzie had the top spot, with Chris."

"Chris? Her boyfriend?"

"Sort of."

Above their heads the wooden planks of the walkway rumbled with the footsteps of passing walkers.

"Do you know him?"

"Everyone knows Chrissy."

"I'd like to talk to him."

"Hotdog Harry told me he left this morning, for Glastonbury. Jade must have gone with him."

Garrett turned away. She picked a path over the stones, working upward. Reaching the top of the dune under the walkway she paused for breath. Here and there she could see black circles marking fireplaces. Pebbles rattled behind her.

"You said his name was Chris. Chris who?"

"Chris. Christmas. That's what we have to call him now. Used to be called Tarin. He's gone to the festival. Think he's after some natural healing. He and Jade've been ill. Bad sweats."

A pattern shivered, like the shift of kaleidoscope mirrors, as it formed in Garrett's mind. "Christmas?"

"Yeah. Tough guy. A bit crazy."

Garrett turned and walked off towards the open beach, pulling out her phone.

"Hey! Hey!"

Garrett continued her sliding walk across the pebbles, chased by Jimmy's cry.

"You won't find him now. Not in Glastonbury."

***

"You didn't mean Christmas *time* did you?"

Garrett stood at the door of a garage in the Zoo Crew compound. She had skipped gears and left three millimetres of tyre on the road up from the coast. Her calls ahead had got only an answering machine.

Cherry knelt on the concrete floor in front of a disassembled motorbike. Beside her Garrett could see a plastic lighter, three Tuberculin syringes, cotton buds and white tablets on a folded slip of paper. At Garrett's words Cherry looked up. She blinked sweat out of her eyes, "Hello doc."

"You said when Spyder was at the beach he was on good form."

Cherry packed up her things into a small hip pouch, zipped it and stood up. "So?"

"Then you said *Better than Christmas*."

"Yeah?"

Fly wandered into the back of the garage.

Cherry closed her eyes on Garrett, as if on an argument she had finished with. "No. Spy's mate. Christmas. Used to be called Tarin."

Fly came to stand beside Cherry. "What's this?"

Garrett took out her notebook. "Christmas is a person."

Fly nodded. "The tattooist?"

"Yes. Our missing persons 'Lizzie' also knew this Christmas; she was his previous girlfriend." Garrett raised her notebook. "And the last person to die, Fiona Grant, also knew him; she met a traveller called Chris at Sundance. I've spoken to one of her colleagues and she confirmed Chris was short for Christmas." Cherry stared at Garrett's raised notebook. "The common link isn't a beach. It's a person. All the people who died knew Christmas. He's the real connection. I need to know about Christmas and Spyder."

Fly frowned down at the young girl. "Cherry, you must talk to the doc."

"Christmas–" Cherry began then stopped. She looked horrified. "He gave Spy a tattoo."

"The Asari tattoo?"

Cherry nodded.

"Christmas is a member of Asari, isn't he?" Garrett demanded.

"Yes."

Garrett had a sudden image of Jason sitting in a cell, cross-legged on concrete, sweating, alone. *He hasn't called. Is he okay?* She let her fingernails dig into the flesh of her palms. The pain balanced the fear, calmed her a little. *Malaria isn't contagious.*

"Her son is in Asari," Cherry said quietly.

"When did Christmas give Spyder the tattoo?"

"About a week ago. I remember Christmas was ill. He was still working but he had a fever."

"I need to speak to him," Garrett said.

"Isn't he at the beach?" Cherry asked.

"He left this morning. For Glastonbury festival. I talked to Brighton police. They know him. He violated his last parole." Garrett shook her head in frustration. "I was put in touch with a sergeant in Somerset CID but he warned me that if they made a public announcement a traveller like Christmas would just disappear. They are organising a search but they've four hundred officers in a crowd of two hundred thousand."

"The cops won't find him," Fly said.

"But I must. Somehow he is connected to this disease. I think he is the index case for this outbreak. I need to find him. Fast!"

Cherry looked at Fly. "No one knows Glasto better than you do. You can walk it blind. Zoo Crew helped build the site. If he's there, you can find him."

Garrett faced Fly. "Is that true?"

"I can tell you, he'll be at Café Sanctuaire, maybe in the Asari circle or the Tipi field," Fly shrugged then added, "If he's dealing, a few other places. For sleep, he'll stay with whoever offers."

Fly watched Garrett steadily. "You've not told us everything."

Garrett opened her mouth to protest then stopped. She struggled to rid herself of the image of Jason alone.

"Is there some danger to my crew?" His eyes had the steady regard of a hunting animal.

The question caught Garrett by surprise. A clock ticked somewhere in her mind. She had to find the index case. She suspected Cherry was right: for that she needed Fly. Her reasons overrode his fears.

"No."

Her reply was simple and straight. But as she stood her ground and faced Fly her shoulders dropped.

"I don't know. I've seen what this disease can do. It's terrible." The image of a cellular mine, a spiky ball of protoplasm, superimposed on her vision. Her voice strengthened. "And we don't understand what's going on. The lab investigation is incomplete." She stopped, drew a deeper breath and met Fly's eyes.

"Is there a danger to you if you go? Maybe."

"I'm not sure. That's why I must find this man Christmas. He is involved with transmission, deliberately or unconsciously, I don't know how. I need to talk to him. Run tests. We must understand what's happening."

Something in Fly's face hardened. He turned on his heel and left the garage. Cherry stood up. She hugged her empty waist with both hands then ran after him. "Fly!"

Garrett gazed at the open door.

Damn it.

She was angry with herself. She had made a mistake. And there was something else. She held herself still until she understood. Spyder and Christmas: there were two connections with Asari now.

Inside her car the steering wheel was at cooking heat. She took out her phone. She scrolled down to Jason's number. She stared at the call button and breathed in a lungful of stale heated air. They had an agreement. But she had reason to believe he might be in danger, he might need to be warned!

She lowered the handset. Was she over-worrying? Maybe. But if she was, he could dismiss her worries. She would apologise. That would be that. What harm could come of a phone call? She thought of the tattoo she had seen on Spyder's shoulder, and the scorched ring of stones under the Palace pier, and the opened skull vault. Two connections. She had no choice. She pressed the call button.

Dialling... dialling... dialling...

"You have reached the voicemail of... *Skyler*. Please leave a message after the tone."

"Jas... Skyler, it's me. Would you call me when you get this message? Something's come up I need to talk to you about. It's Mum. Sunday. Evening. About seven o'clock."

Garrett broke the connection. She tried to control her breathing. What would he do when he got the message? What if he didn't?

Outside, the revving of motors could be heard, a growing buzzing, like the waking of bees. Glastonbury. She tore a page searching her notebook for the number of the Somerset police.

A shadow fell across Garrett's lowered head. She looked up. Fly stood outlined against the sun. Behind him, two bikers and a white Land Rover drove out of the compound gates. Garrett wound down her window and was surprised by cool wind.

"Wake up Christine!" Fly leaned down into the window. "If we're going to find Christmas before the festival ends, we'd better be off." Behind him, a man clambered up onto the tilting Land Rover roof rack. "Getting on site Sunday night at Glasto won't be quick."

Fly grinned at her and threw back his head. His roar, a rallying, parade-ground shout, echoed off the compound wall.

"All aboard the Skylaaaaaaaark!!!"

Chapter 21

"Goswami, this doctor has been seen at Café Sanctuaire. She's been asking after Christmas. Hello? Hello?"

Kirtananda bent his head and pressed a mobile hard against his ear. Zakiya stood next to him, retying his orange robe; with his shaven scalp he looked like a bloody Krishna. Above his head, Kirtananda could see the tops of marquee tents, music stages, circus big tops and the swinging propeller of a seventy-foot high silver wind turbine.

"Hello?"

"Where is she now?"

"I don't know. Our people are asking. They have the information." In one hand, Kirtananda held a crumpled printout.

"You will find her, before she finds Christmas."

"Yes Gurusri-ji." An arrhythmia of interfering drum beats vibrated in Kirtananda's chest from surrounding sound stages. He watched the slow downward sweep of the propeller blade. "What shall we do when we find her?"

"Kill her."

The fields glowed blue, orange, white, green in a thousand prismatic points. At night, peering down through the glass footwell of a police helicopter, the nine-hundred-acre site of the Glastonbury festival appeared to Garrett like some luminescent alien cell, complex, prokaryotic.

"You've got your Green Fields – Healing Field, Craft Field, Avalon, Green Futures. That brown line through the middle is Muddy Lane – best avoided. Off to the right is the Area of Lost Vagueness. Ditto."

Her tour guide was Chief Inspector Hembry – a stocky Somerset man with a grey moustache, damp hands and dry speech. His rolling rural lilt was a constant Protestant complaint in Garrett's ear.

"And top of hill – there – you've got your King's Meadow. Has a Neolithic stone circle that's about fifteen year old."

They had arrived at Glastonbury in the early evening after three hours in traffic. The first policeman hadn't heard of no search for no one. Eventually Hembry had explained that instructions had been delayed. He had offered she join one of their reconnaissance flights.

Five minutes back on the ground, Garrett realized Cherry had been right. Fly's group knew the festival better than any police squad, from the inside, as crew not guards. She searched with Fly, learning the site as she shuffled in his footsteps. He concentrated on the tented maze of cooperatives, communes and collectives that made up the higher fields – the 'Green Fields' scorned by Hembry – where he said Christmas was most likely to be found.

Garrett left voice messages for the Porton team. It was now five am and the eastern edge of the horizon was beginning to lighten. Competing light shows lit the sky. Garrett and Fly stood shoulder to shoulder, faced opposite ways, at a crossroads near the main music stages.

Maybe he left," Cherry said. She squatted on the ground beside them.

Fly turned to speak to Garrett. His words were drowned out by punk blasts from bagpipes played by a passing tartan busker with matching kilt and Mohican. Fly shouted again through his hands.

"We should check Café Sanctuaire again."

Garrett heard the strung note in his voice.

"Look, why don't you take a break? I'll go."

Fly puffed out his cheeks then raised eyebrows in agreement.

Cherry nodded at Garrett and they stepped together onto a crowded metal walkway heading uphill. Garrett pulled out her mobile and shook the device repeatedly, as if readying a thermometer. Despite the encouragement it showed five dead signal bars. Coverage had been intermittent all night and out for the last two hours.

There was a snarl-up around the cash machines approaching the Unfair Ground. They turned off into the Healing Field but their progress through the busy market was still slow. Customers crowded the stalls of amulets, homeopathic remedies, dream catchers, faith healers and potions. They stopped frequently to ask for news.

"Hello Bryony, any luck?"

"Hi Cherry! You still looking for Chris? Sorry love."

Garrett found herself staring down at a table covered in necklaces. A knotted rope strung with pretty purple gems caught her eye.

"Genuine quartz." The stall owner smiled. She was a walking advert for her own stock, encrusted with necklaces, rings and bracelets like an old wreck in a coral reef. "They're healing stones. Want to know how they work?"

Garrett backed away. "No thank you."

"Won't hurt you love."

Garrett found herself trapped between trestle tables.

"It's not complicated. You don't have to be a doctor or anything. And it's worked like a charm on my arthritis. Just boil the nine crystals for nine minutes, then drink the water for nine days."

Garrett escaped between a gap in the tables. She searched the crowds for Cherry, chased by the calls of the medieval medicine seller. Garrett thought of the pathogen she pursued. That mindless killer would not respect hopes pinned on boiled crystals. As she pushed through the long queues around the Healing Field stalls, the popularity of the place puzzled and saddened her. Perhaps centuries ago such magical theories were the best possible, the first sciences, a crude beginning; or perhaps, without a modern understanding, it made sense to turn to the subjective, to the Romantic dream, and hope the world would shape itself to will and wish. But now, today, why choose what had become daydreaming? Why turn away from the only objectivity that could be achieved, interrogating together what was real? Fear hollowed her stomach. Was Jason sitting on the floor of some cell, sweating in silence, out of reach of hospitals, protected only by a string of stones, determined faith would cure? *Where was he? Was he alright?*

Garrett found Cherry perched on a bale of straw, a thick black slice of cake in her hand. Sitting with her was a woman with purple hair holding a clipboard.

"Antonia is the Healing Field site manager. She's going to do some asking for us."

Garrett nodded. "I'm going on ahead to the Café."

Café Sanctuaire was just beyond the Craft Field. Garrett weaved her way between camps of bakers, potters, weavers and blacksmiths. No-one she asked had seen the tattooist. It was the last night of the festival. Fires were dying down; many stall-holders were packing up, eager to get off-site early. Garrett's sense of urgency increased – if she didn't find Christmas before he left, she sensed she would lose his trail.

The sky above the ridge on the eastern horizon was beginning to lighten. Garrett cut through a tangle of tents to avoid a crowd gathered around two men fighting on stilts. She was confronted by tall sculpture, a giant fly made of discarded wellington boots and bottles. Garrett walked straight under it, ducking between jointed plastic legs to reach a walkway.

She paused to get her bearings. Beside the metalled track stood a large tented stall. White dhotis and collarless shirts hung for sale on a rail. A sign advertised 'Khadi' above a picture of Gandhi at his charkha. With Ghandi's picture came an old smell, of warm monsoon rain, and the memory of long weeks trapped indoors. Garrett remembered Gandhi's refusal of penicillin to his dying wife, his insistence on Ganges water and faith. She felt the return of a terrible anxiousness touched by anger.

A woman sat at a spinning wheel in front of the tent. Her feet worked paddles as her hands paid out twine in movements of measured synchrony. She paused to beckon Garrett over. Garrett recognised her as one of Cherry's friends.

"Namaaste." The woman clasped hands in front of her chest in the Añjali Mudrā. "Did you see Christmas?"

"No–" Garrett stepped closer, "–you've seen him?"

"About an hour ago. I tried to speak to him but he was in a hurry."

"Where was he going?"

The woman gestured uphill. Garrett called out thanks over her shoulder.

He had been seen! Garrett spent an hour asking at every tent in a wide radius around the weaver's stall but there were no other sightings. Frustrated and tired, she headed over to Café Sanctuaire.

A line of pennants in front of a tall ex-Army marquee advertised Veggie Vibes and Third Eye Meditation. When they had arrived, Cherry had explained that Café Sanctuaire shared the pitch with Asari. But no-one from the Valley had turned up all festival. Cherry had wrinkled her nose. "It's odd, even for them. There's been no word. No call, no email, nothing. The Caff're worried they'll have to pay for the whole pitch."

There were half-a-dozen people inside the tent. No-one had seen the tattooist.

A band was practising together on a makeshift stage at the end of the tent. Garrett sat down on a damp carpet near the central fire, reluctant to leave a place linked to Christmas.

Songs started and stopped. The musicians were a strange mix – Flamenco guitarist, Irish drummer, didjeridu player, and two Welsh harmony singers. Garrett's sharp cataloguing ear caught at fragments of sevillanas, reels, baijans and glees. Smudged colours shaded the smoky air, agitated by a home-made light show. As her eyes adjusted, a young man materialised out of the carpet on the other side of the fire. He sat cross-legged, cowled by a red, green and yellow shawl. Only his face showed, eyes closed. Beside him a large cardboard sign was propped against a backpack like a hitchhiker's ad. A quote was visible below the top edge. *"You see many stars in the sky at night, but not when the sun rises. Can you therefore say that there are no stars in the heaven during the day? O man, because you cannot find God in the days of your ignorance, say not that there is no God." Sri Ramakrishna.*

The musicians settled down to their first song. A beautiful complex polyphony filled the tent. Garrett followed the five parts and heard with astonishment the musicians weave of their separate pieces a whole cloth. A harmony lifted her – to an English folk tune. The monk nodded time. His hooded eyes twinkled briefly orange through the smoke. Once, in her tiredness, Garrett thought she heard Jason's name. She waited through the verses but it did not repeat. Other words sounded above the music: faith, soul, heaven. Through shared imagination, art easily serves superstition. The sad confusions and alarms of the Healing Field touched her again.

"Can I help anyone?"

A young girl appeared at the counter behind the muffins and chipped mugs. She wore a brightly-patterned headscarf around her temples. A gold sun and silver moon were painted on either cheek.

"I'm looking for Christmas. Have you seen–" Garrett's phone beeped for a new text.

"Christmas is in December."

"Yes, I meant–"

"Although that's just a prediction. Personally, I don't make predictions. Never have. Never will."

Garrett noted dilated pupils, delayed reflexes. The girl was drugged. She tried again.

"I'm looking for a tattooist called Christmas."

"Sounds like he's branching out. Is he a father? Likes to dress in red? Rides a big flying sleigh?"

"No."

"Look, I don't really work here. Just helping out this shift. If it's important, why don't you ask site security?"

"I'm searching with the local police."

"Would you like a cup of tea?"

Garrett sighed. "Yes, thank you."

"We've got camomile, redbush, nettle–"

"Normal's fine," Garrett interrupted.

The girl made a circle out of thumb and forefinger and inspected Garrett through this hole for a moment. "What's normal?" She looked solemn then grinned. "One fifty please." She poured Garrett a tea.

"You're very serious. You're like a teacher, or a traffic warden."

"Thank you. I'm a doctor, and I'm looking for–"

"Are you! That *is* a serious job."

Garrett read the caption on the mug. *Careful, or your karma will run over my dogma.* She wasn't going to get much help here.

She returned to her place by the fire. She checked her phone. There was a text from Fly: 'Christmas seen at Sanctuaire. Heading over. Wait.'

Garrett stood up. The band were still playing. Three girls were buying muffins. There was no one else in the tent.

The monk had gone. His cardboard sign lay discarded on the ground where he had been sitting. Below the quote she had read were a row of prices above logos in black-ink, of a cross, crescent, lotus, auṃkāra, wheel, taijitu and star.

Rastafarian, Christian, Muslim, Shaivas, Buddhist, Confucian, Jewish – Garrett saw the monk had found his own answer to an old charge – that the religious were atheists to all religions except their own – and it was the opposite to Gandhi's, "God has no religion".

Below the logos she read the words "Tattoos while you wait".

Damn it!

Garrett ducked out of the tent. The endless queue was still shuffling. Garrett ran up and down the line. She swore and stopped. Overhead, a jagged line of orange stood out against a paling sky. It was approaching sunrise. A man in a top hat, rainbow waistcoat and purple tails swerved out of Garrett's path and overbalanced into a ditch, dragged there by a wheelbarrow full of a girl in a white ball gown. The couple lay there laughing.

Garrett looked back at Café Sanctuaire. The pavilion marquee stood out greyly in the strengthening light. A man emerged from the side of the tent carrying a backpack. Garrett held still. Her phone beeped. The man withdrew back into the gap between tents. Garrett followed. She peered into an alley walled by canvas. Guy ropes criss-crossed the air.

"Hello? Is there somebody there?"

A man moved out of the shade, tall, heavily-built with a shaven head. Garrett could see bare arms. The skin was darkened, blue not browned and mottled like a turning bruise. As her eyes adjusted Garrett could make out the tattoos. They moved like living creatures.

"Are you Christmas?"

"Who wants to know?"

"My name is Dr Christine Garrett."

The man sniffed. "I heard you looking for me. You're a cop."

"I'm a doctor. I–"

"You smell like a cop. You talk like a cop." He turned his head as if to listen. "You're a cop."

"No, I am a doctor," Garrett offered both hands, empty. "I just want to talk to you."

"Hey look I'm clean. I ain't carrying."

They both heard the lie. The man hefted his pack and took a step forward.

"I'm not interested in your drugs. I want to talk to you about an infection. Some friends of yours are dead. Spyder. Lizzie–"

The man stepped back.

"The girl you met at the Brighton festival, Fiona–"

"This is some kinda frame?" Garrett heard an effort at self-control, as if something was snapping in the man.

"–Fiona Grant." Garrett's mobile beeped again. She glanced down. "They're all–"

The blow caught her in the stomach. Garrett staggered, one step, then kicked out hard at the shadow closing over her. She heard a grunt and saw Christmas trip back over a guy rope. She doubled over. Empty lungs drew on nothing.

She looked across to Christmas. He got to his feet and shook his right arm as though loosening up.

"Christmas–"

Garrett gasped for more air to speak. Christmas lunged. She saw the danger late, the glint of light on metal and jumped back. She looked down at her left hand. A red line looped over her wrist. It thickened to a liquid and spilled over her fingers.

"Get out of my way."

"Wait–" Garrett tried to speak again. Her stomach spasmed as she retched air. She waited, to try and talk again.

The knife extended like a toughened nail from Christmas's fist. He circled. Instinct told Garrett if she lost this man now she'd never find him again. She forced herself to mirror Christmas's feet, to block the exit. She stepped quickly to her right behind a guy rope.

Christmas shuffled forward on his toes. Garrett retreated within the tangled geometry of the ropes. He feinted, feinted again then, when she slipped, jabbed the knife point towards her face. She raised her left hand to block the blow. The blade sliced deep into the flesh of her forearm. Part of her mind felt the metal edge touch the radius bone near the elbow. The knife snagged on the guy rope and fell.

A fist slammed into the side of her head. Garrett put out a hand to break her fall. A heavy boot trod down on the middle of her injured forearm. Bright pain blinded her.

She shook her head and saw the knife lying between her feet. She snatched it up with her good hand and twisted away. With quick steps she moved around the ropes. She blocked thoughts of the pain in her arm with a calculation of distances.

With a yard between them she shifted her grip, noting the blade's weight, similar to her prosector's knife but balanced more towards the butt. Christmas's eyes narrowed.

"Christine?"

She heard Fly's shout through the canvas walls of the tent.

"Here!"

Christmas sprang forward, his pack held in front like a shield, and sprinted towards the exit.

Garrett blinked past the pain. Outlined against the paling sky she could see another man standing in the gap between the tents.

"Follow him!" Garrett ordered. When Fly hesitated she said, "Don't lose him! I'm fine!"

Garrett pulled herself up one-handed. She stood on both feet, swaying as if against a wind, then leaned forward, forcing steps. She emerged from between the tents. With her good arm she searched her pockets for her phone. She moved very slowly. Pain throbbed to her pulse.

A man with a shaved head, dressed in an orange robe, walked out of the crowds towards her. Something about him was out of place, like a bouncer at a party. The man gazed down at a piece of paper. It appeared to be guiding him, like a dowser's twig.

Garrett looked down at her left hand. It was dripping blood. Too much blood. She dropped the knife. Her fingers found the brachial artery just below her left armpit and applied pressure.

She looked up. Overhead, the sky was a royal blue. A knife-thin line of red clouds scarred the lower horizon. Garrett shook her head, trying to clear it. How long had she been in that muddy, roped tunnel? It seems like years. She suddenly felt old and very tired. She noticed the approaching man. Their eyes met.

"Doctor Garrett, you all right?" A group of policemen were running up Muddy Lane led by Inspector Hembry. The man in the orange robe broke eye contact and walked past.

She gestured in slow motion up the hill.

"Are you okay?"

"Yes. Go on. Fly's chasing Christmas. Quick!"

The policemen ran on. Garrett followed with a toppling step, fighting for balance. She reached a gate and looked over. A wide grassy slope led up to a small summit encircled by stones. Two figures raced across the grass, weaving like skaters between small knots of festival-goers gathered round fires. Christmas. Fly.

The police officers followed in a tight unit twenty or thirty yards behind. Garrett swayed. *Ensure correct medical supervision.* She forced herself to move forward. Pain brightened in her arm, then through her body. She stopped. She looked across the immense distances of the field. She wasn't going to make it. *Must get to Christmas.* She pulled out her phone and tried to dial a number. *Blood sample.* She closed her eyes. *Porton.* Opened them again. She recognized the place, but couldn't remember why. A man approached her, smiling. Who was he? She had seen him before. She closed her eyes again. Tiredness, an overwhelming wave, flooded in. She let go and the ground rushed up to meet her.

Chapter 22

"Sir, I thought you should see this. Just came over the wire."

Over the wire. White glanced up from his monitor, past Hanratty to a line of small brass bells mounted on the wall beside the door, attached to nothing. To his predecessor forty years ago they had signalled the arrival of telegrams. *Tempus fugit.*

"Thank you James. Put it there will you?"

"Sir, I think you should read it now."

James Hanratty remained where he stood, a single sheet of paper held out over the desk in front of him like the baton of a relay runner. Commander White frowned. Being pushy just didn't do, not at Five. Or if it was the frustration of working Sunday... that didn't do either. The rota came with the job: security threats were not weekday-only events. White caught sight of his subordinate's face and checked his irritation. Hanratty's face was red with self-importance.

"What is it?"

"Do you remember that report about unusual malaria deaths, on the south coast? Being handled by CDSC and Porton Down."

"Yes." White reached out and took the sheet of paper.

"You asked my opinion, and I thought it was not a worry."

"Yes." James had such a *confessional* streak. White suppressed a grin. Perhaps it was the Catholic gene. Just like his father in so many ways. Funny how these things go through the generations, like a gammy leg or left-eye squint. White read the printout as Hanratty summarised.

"Late yesterday afternoon, Sniffer intercepted four separate reports on fever cases to the CDSC, from two hospitals in the Brighton area." Hanratty's voice was a little breathless, too earnest. White shifted in his chair. "One fatality so far." Hanratty added, "Suspected malaria has been confirmed by stains."

"Sir, the oddest thing is they still don't know how they caught it."

Hanratty stood waiting. "I thought you should see it immediately sir. Just in case."

White frowned down at the piece of paper. He tried to place a strange feeling, low down, in his bowels. "Why has this alert come through Sniffer? What about the CDSC?"

"Nothing from them." Hanratty coughed. "That's strange too. Their data should be better."

"Chase them please." White turned to his terminal. "I'd like to see the original reports, including lab results and hospital autopsies. Thank you James."

"Yes sir."

Hanratty left the room. White got up from his desk and strode to the tall sash windows overlooking Whitehall. Toward Westminster, he could see the Cenotaph looming like a standing stone out of the traffic, singular and white. The coloured spears of the service flags were just visible, obscuring Kipling's chiselled words.

He glanced back at his computer terminal. It sat on his desk like the flattened head of a rearing snake. Power and video cords ran down into floor sockets. Five years ago, the emerging facts of the Newhaven influenza outbreak had trickled in through those same electronic wires: four fatalities, an infection cluster on the south coast, an unusual strain...

And here were new facts. An infection cluster on the south coast, caused by an unusual strain, this time of malaria, with four fatalities so far, a question of unresolved transmission...

He remembered the original briefing now. For once, he had asked Hanratty's opinion. Partly for the young man's confidence, but also to stall. That's right. He had had a niggle.

Cars queued up in stationary lanes waiting to enter Trafalgar Square. White watched the traffic and began to bite a fingernail. His department head was back from his summer holidays Tuesday. This incident would hopefully wait till then. Or maybe it would turn out to be nothing.

A muted trumpet signalled receipt of mail. White flinched.

Jesus. Talk about Chicken Charlie! What was he scared of? An electronic message? He reminded himself that he was a Surgeon-Cmdr in Her Majesty's Royal Navy. He had served with distinction in two naval campaigns. He suddenly realised how much he hated the train in to work each morning, the waiting green files on his desk, and above all, his computer terminal.

He stared out of the window. A sudden flashback from his naval days superimposed over the Whitehall traffic. A dog day of mirror-calm seas. *Steady. Storms in teacups.*

He returned to his desk and logged on. He skimmed the brief summary by Captain Skinner. They confirmed malaria by stain slides. And unusual pathology. Mixed broods. Rogue ookineetes.

White stared around the room, eyes alighting on the row of Victorian signal bells. Alarms were ringing through his mind.

That niggle. He turned back to his screen and logged on to a secure filing system, feeling distaste for the keyboard he was forced to use like some secretary. Damn machines were taking over. Even he was reduced to relying on the things for his memory...

He typed in a few search terms. "*UK. Malaria. Transmission.*"

He rubbed his fingers. They felt cold. Four thousand two hundred and twenty-six hits.

Too wide. White clicked to narrow search terms. "*From ten years to current day.*" He hesitated, hunting through his own memory, then, on a vague hunch, added two extra keywords. "*Security breach.*" He clicked Search again then scrolled down the results page. Stopped. "Potential breach of GM protocols at Kronos malaria vaccine research laboratory." There! He clicked on a link. A single title page appeared.

White sat back in his chair staring at the screen. 24/11/2018. Two years ago. Yes. No wonder he hadn't remembered. He wrote down the reference on the top of Hanratty's printout, folded the A4 sheet and put it in a pocket. He locked his office on the way out. When the lift arrived, he punched for the agency basement stacks.

***

"Bristol General Hospital. Go!"

Harith slammed the grey panel van into a small slot in passing traffic. A car beeped. Kirtananda leaned forward in his seat and stroked the close-cropped red stubble on his head, slow, comfortable, as if at home watching the game with his dogs at his feet.

"Be there in twenty minutes Ji."

"This is easier than Glasto. We know where she is and she ain't going anywhere." Kirtananda watched Zakiya take out a packet of beedies then put them away, for the fifth time. "Chris did us a favour."

Zak and Dharma glanced at each other and grinned. Harith pulled out, accelerating up a blind rise towards a ridge top. He overtook one, two, three cars, swerved in front of an oncoming container lorry, trimmed to avoid fishtailing the back end. A retreating horn blared.

Kirtananda took his kartals out of the glove compartment. The miniature cymbals voiced muffled, stopped notes.

Tick – tick – tick. Tick.

Quiet. Sunday afternoon quiet. Smells of new linen mixed with bleach.

Tick – tick – tick. Tick.

Light everywhere. Great chunks, with pieces broken off at angles. A ceiling. Three walls. A burst of sound like a hello. Silence again, a tap shutting.

Tick – tick – tick. Tick.

That quiet again, so peaceful. Whose arm is that on its own?

Tick – tick – tick. Tick.

"Hello."

Garrett turned her head. A green graph moved on a small screen. She could still smell bleach.

Tick – tick – tick. Tick.

"How you feelin?"

Garrett tried to focus.

Tick – tick – tick. Tick.

"You knitting?"

"No, I'm making soup. Yes, I'm knitting."

Garrett watched Cherry's fingers for a while.

"Mum says I'm never happier than when I've something on my needles."

"Groggy."

"That'll be the diamorphine. They gave you a shot before seeing to your arm."

Garrett glanced down at a white bandage wound tight around her left forearm near the elbow.

"What happened?"

"It's fine. Only a cut. They put in a couple of stitches. But you lost a lot of blood."

Garrett closed her eyes. She thought of natural replacement rates: hours for lost plasma, a couple of weeks for marrow to replace erythrocytes.

"We brought you straight here."

Garrett tried to sit up. "Where's here?"

"Bristol General. Don't worry, you're doing fine. You just need some rest. No strenuous activity for at least twenty-four hours is what they said."

Garrett spotted her folded clothes on a chair. Her eyes closed on their own.

"There! Second left." Kirtananda pointed. Harith nodded and switched lanes. A queue of cars led up to the turnoff.

"Fucking hell," Harith shook his head. Up ahead an old lady in a Renault Clio had stalled.

Kirtananda glanced in the rear view. Zak was shaking his packet of beedies again. "Relax, she ain't going anywhere."

Harith nodded at the looming building. "Big hospital. We could use Rayan."

"Well he ain't here," Kirtananda said. "And we've got one defenceless woman in a hospital bed. Think you can handle it?"

"Sure, sure, no problem, Ji," Harith said hastily.

Zak grinned. The van lurched forward a few yards. "Rayan's a waste of space anyway. Guy's probably working on his tan."

"He's got plenty to do," Kirtananda said. "The House of Health and Knowledge must be cleansed."

"Cleansed?" Zak said.

"The Rebirth work is done. We must leave no trace of it behind."

"How come?" Harith said.

"Because Arshu-ji has said so."

"So when we going to join the others?"

"When we've finished what we need to do. When I say so."

There was silence.

"Rayan's getting Instruction from Sky," Zak said.

"Sure," Kirtananda nodded.

"Sky is a very spiritual man," Dharma said. "He is the youngest Instructor ever."

Dharma was not the brightest bulb in the van, Kirtananda thought.

"You know Hoshi?" Zak said. "He joined us last year. Sky instructed him. Hoshi told me he thinks Sky's enlightened."

"I heard he found out where Arshu was born," Harith said.

"Where was that?"

"Ashcroft, Liverpool,"

"You what?"

"Yeah, straight up. He went there."

"What for?"

"I guess to pray."

"I've spent time with him," Dharma said. "He's a special being – he sees patterns in things others don't. You know he's memorised all of Arshu's sayings? He's on a special path."

Dharma was soft in the head. If he was not such a good man with his hands Kirtananda would have had no time for him. But he was the best knife man he had ever seen. A useful skill. Kirtananda studied the windows of the hospital building. Especially for quiet jobs.

Up ahead, the old lady in the car in front was still struggling. She was talking to herself. He shook his head. Across the road, a tall black woman dressed in green and gold stood outside eating chicken from a box. She called out to two young schoolboys fighting in the road in front of her.

All this will pass away, Kirtananda thought. The reflection surprised him.

"What an idiot," Harith said. He pulled on the handbrake and came out of gear. They watched the old lady panicking as she struggled with her gearbox. "Someone should put that out of its misery."

Someone was going to, Kirtananda thought. A strange feeling moved him. For a moment he didn't recognise what it was.

"She's alright. Let her be," Kirtananda said. His men looked at each other, puzzled.

This red darkness is finding the index case is the key to Christmas time is a happy…

Christmas!

Garrett woke between heartbeats.

"What about Christmas?"

Cherry looked up from her magazine. "Mmm?"

"Christmas?"

"He's not talking."

Garrett picked at the sheets with her fingers. "We–"

"Trust me. Fly's tried. He's saying nothing. The cops are holding him on possession. They expect you to press charges."

"Where is he?"

"Shepton Mallet station. What do you think you're doing?"

"I'm getting up!"

"You're not. You must rest. You're hurt."

Garrett struggled upright. Pain from her left arm broke through the drugs. "He must be tested."

Cherry reached out to her shoulders. "You gotta stay in bed!"

"We need to get samples to the lab. Where's my phone?"

"They don't allow mobiles in here."

"I must–" Garrett threw off a sheet.

"All right!" Cherry looked into her eyes, like a parent demanding attention from a toddler. "If you stay in bed, I'll find you a phone, and you can call through and get what you need done. Okay?"

Garrett stared at Cherry, one leg on the floor.

"Just get back into bed and I'll go ask."

Garrett hesitated. She had been on the other side of these conversations. The only way to escape being treated as a child was to act like an adult.

"And I'll bring the phone, okay?"

Pain throbbed in Garrett's arm. She nodded. "Okay. But you don't realise–"

"I know it's important. I'll do it," Cherry patted the sheets back into place. "Leave it to me."

Garrett flopped back onto her pillows. Slowly, bit by bit, she allowed tiredness and morphine to close her eyes.

"Fuckin A, grandma's figured it out!" Harith rolled the van forward. The old lady had finally found a gear.

"Now listen up," Kirtananda looked around. "Dharma, Zak. I want you two with me. Harith, you stay with the van."

Harith whooped, "Rock 'n' roll!"

He gunned the engine. It stalled.

"Wanker," Zak said.

"You dick!" Dharma yelled.

Kirtananda grinned.

"Fuck off you guys," Harith said. He restarted the engine. Stalled again. On the third attempt he got the van in gear.

"Hey grandma," Zak said. "Shall we put you out of your misery?"

Harith turned and hit out, one hand on the steering wheel. The van wobbled. The punch missed. Harith twisted around and lunged with both hands. He caught Zak on the ear, a glancing blow.

Kirtananda laughed and grabbed the wheel as the van veered into the curb.

"You fucker!" Zak yelled.

"Okay cool it. Take the turn," Kirtananda pointed. He held the dashboard one-handed as they bumped over sleeping policemen into the hospital grounds.

Garrett's eyes snapped open. How long had it been since Cherry had left? A minute? An hour? She raised her knees. The movement made her wince.

Pain seeped up her arm. Her bladder complained too. She swung her feet onto the floor.

Walking to the window brought the blood to her head. It was another sunny day. The car park was busy, nearly full. A grey panel van indicated to turn into a bay opposite A&E. Two cars paused to let it pass. She counted ambulances, cars, bicycles, and remembered Jimmy watching his beach. *This is my beach. Hospital traffic.* The thought made her grin. When she carried on grinning, she diagnosed morphine.

She suddenly remembered her mobile. Numb fingers searched the pockets of her clothes.

The call history showed no missed connection attempts. Where was Jason? Why hadn't he called? She stared at the dial button and swayed on her feet. No. She should wait for a hospital landline.

She rested her forehead on the window. The glass was warm. Maybe get a chair. Sit in the sun and watch the traffic until Cherry came back.

Harith slotted the van into a spot in front of A&E.

"Arshu's will be done." Kirtananda struck a clear chime from the kartals. He jumped out before the brass note had ended. "Let's go!"

He headed towards the open double doors of the main reception, Dharma and Zakiya at his shoulder. Out of the corner of his eyes he tracked Harith by the van. *Good.* The familiar screw of tension tightened in his belly. He felt the butt of his silenced Glock semi-automatic lying snug and warm inside palm and curled fingers, concealed in a pocket of his zipped windcheater. He thumbed off the safety.

Garrett counted cars cruising the lot for spaces. She had been remembering queuing theory and how her first attempts at statistical programming had used the Poisson distribution.

Over by A&E three men walked away from the parked panel van. The one in front wore an odd, coloured collar around his throat. Like a priest. The shaven head of the man at his right shoulder made Garrett think of Christmas. Where was Cherry?

"Hello, could you tell me where Christine Garrett is?"

"And you are?" The receptionist looked up at her questioner, a handsome man with military hair and the whitest smile. She glanced at his two companions. One of them was dressed in an odd orange robe, his back to her, elbows on the counter. Rude.

"Stephen Garrett. Her brother. Her older brother." The red-haired man smiled again. He had a nice nose and neat teeth. One front incisor was pointed, so sharp it looked filed. "I called through earlier?"

The receptionist began typing at a keyboard. Kirtananda added, "Chrissy was admitted last night. She had an injury to her arm?"

"Oh yes, I remember. She was brought in from the festival. Here we are. Ward B, room three. Second floor." She looked up to meet the man's eyes. They were blue and very steady, friendly when he smiled. "Right out of the lifts, down the corridor, it's the third door on your left. Ask a nurse if you get lost."

"Thanks. If I get lost I'll come back and ask you." He smiled again. The receptionist grinned back, thinking how important manners were in a man. You could tell so much. She watched him walk over to the lifts and press a call button. He nodded his head towards the stairs.

"Now where are my glasses gone to?"

The nurse on the ward desk fumbled around her pockets. When she found them she checked the signature and date on the form. Garrett ignored the nurse's disapproving frown. The argument had been short. She had pulled medical rank.

"Christine! What you doing up?"

"I got tired of waiting. Where've you been?"

"Sorry," Cherry stopped stuffing crisps in her mouth. "I was hungry. I figured you'd be asleep–"

"Your friend's checking out," the nurse said.

"What?"

"I can't diagnose Christmas over the phone. I need to see him."

"You're joking! You've just–"

"I'm fine. Come on." Garrett took the top copy of the form from the nurse. "How did you get here?"

"Fly dropped me. Christine–"

"We'll get a cab outside A&E."

A man stepped out of the lifts. The nurse glanced at the clock. Visiting hours were nearly over. Another man appeared behind him. He was shaven-headed. Chemo? At a nod he waited, legs open, hands clasped behind his back, beside the open lift doors. The first man headed down a corridor as if he knew where he was going.

The nurse smiled to herself. Those two men had such a wordless understanding. Almost like they were married. Her smile deepened. Maybe they were gay.

An ambulance had just arrived. Garrett led a still-protesting Cherry through the scrum of activity to a waiting cab. A passenger was paying.

"Keep the change."

Garrett opened a rear door and slipped inside. She winced as she jogged her injured arm. A pulse thudded in her head. She put a hand up to her cheek to shield an eye from a growing headache.

"Hello girls! Where to, love?"

"Shepton Mallett please."

The cabbie jogged his rear view with a finger. When he discovered Garrett was a doctor he began to complain about his spondulitis. Garrett protected her arm with her body as they bumped down an exit ramp. Advertising hoardings, telegraph wires and the tops of buildings edged Garrett's view as they emerged onto a local High Street. She watched the turning of cloudless blue.

***

White entered the Metropole basement stacks from the top, experiencing a familiar touch of vertigo as he peered down six descending levels visible below his shoes through metal grille flooring. He passed his ID card through a reader and exited the wire mesh cage which surrounded the lift doors.

Opposite the lift was a wrought iron spiral staircase. White stepped down four flights then threaded his way across a floor of corridors laid out like a library, walls formed of files and electronic equipment. With each step, the metal underfoot ran like a tuning fork; fluorescent lights glinted through the grilles from the stacks above and below.

White felt frustration and guilt at his slipped memory. What the hell was happening at CDSC? They handled the primary data. If Sniffer had caught four cases through the background noise, how many more were there?

He stopped at a door marked 4B34. He passed his card through another reader and entered a small cubicle, empty except for a table, computer monitor, input devices and a plastic chair.

White sat in the chair. He typed in a name and password then submitted to voice, fingerprint and retina scan. He pulled out Hanratty's printout, typed in the file reference, then a compartment pass code. The screen refreshed.

> Report into potential breach of GM protocols
> at Kronos malaria vaccine research laboratory
> concerning Malaria Falciparum x Streptococcus
> Type III GM gene sequences."

"Display file?"

White clicked OK. He began to speed read.

***

"Yes he's here. Came in last night under custody from the festival. We charged him with Class A possession. It's with the CPS."

A uniformed duty officer sat behind double-glazing studying a charge sheet. A half-eaten sandwich sat in a plastic carton at his elbow. Garrett managed her impatience before speaking.

"I'm only concerned with the health issue. I asked that CDSC be informed immediately after any arrest."

The officer glanced at his sandwich, wet a finger and turned a page. "Nope. Doesn't say anything about... Ah. A message was left at CDSC for a Mr Kirkpatrick."

Garrett's felt the muscles in her neck relax a fraction. She had just finished a frustrating call to the lab at Porton. As usual no-one had picked up. She had left a brief message; her mobile battery was almost flat. She felt a running urgency and the world wanted to stroll.

"And did you get any reply?" Cherry spoke each word slowly as if asking directions of a foreigner. She stood at Garrett's shoulder.

The officer glanced at Cherry then returned to his reading. Garrett searched for patience. She was already exhausted by the short, officious exchange, after another that had been required to prove her credentials. Her left arm ached like a rotten tooth.

"Looks like he has not yet replied."

"This man may be involved in a serious public health matter," Garrett said.

"Yes. Apparently so," the officer said, still reading.

"Where is he now?" Cherry demanded.

"Jimmy, our Medical Officer, checked him over. He didn't look too clever. Running a fever. We've got him in solitary."

Garrett pressed teeth together. Pain seeped up her arm. Questions revolved like riderless horses on a carousel, about the disease, the connection with Asari, Jason... Now, perhaps, she had found someone with answers.

"Can I see him?" Garrett asked.

They followed the police officer down a whitewashed corridor to the back of the station.

"I will need a blood sample," Garrett said.

"Let's hope he gives his consent then," the officer warned over his shoulder, pleasant but superior. "They all know their human rights now you know."

"This health issue concerns a notifiable disease. Consent is not required." Garrett's voice was sharp. She was tired of bureaucratic dismissals. "I will get a magistrate's order if needed."

"I see." The officer stopped at a metal door. "What sort of... health issue are we dealing with here then?"

"I'm hoping this man will help me answer that question."

After a cursory glance through a small grill, the policeman unlocked the door and stepped aside. *At last.*

Pain, and the memory of it, surged up Garrett's arm at the sight of the figure sat at a small metal table. She stared at a shaven head pillowed on crossed arms, skin blued by tattoos, lit by a stretched square of sunlight from a small barred window.

"You've got a visitor," the policeman said. Christmas gave no reaction. "You hear me?"

There is a stillness to a dead body that is not the same as sleep. Garrett moved past the policeman. She put two fingers into Christmas's neck.

"What the hell?" The policeman sounded angry.

"From rigor and body heat, I'd say he's been dead an hour," Garrett said, after a pause. She studied a small brown stain of blood beside his mouth. "There is–" The ringing of a mobile interrupted her. It was her own. Remembering her message left with the Porton lab, she accepted the call. Good timing...

"Hello?"

"Mum? Er – Christine?"

Garrett felt the muscle of her heart shiver. The phone was porcelain cold and hard and precious in her hand. She turned her back on the policeman, Cherry and the dead man in the cell.

"Jason?"

Chapter 23

"I said I'd call didn't I?"

"Yes."

"How are you?"

Garrett glanced down at her arm. "Fine."

There was silence on the line. Garrett remembered a time when Jason talking was an incessant twitter chasing her around the house like a trapped bird. Mummy, I show you... Daddy can I... Mummy, I want... Dad, I'm going to...

"Good to hear your voice," Garrett said. "How are you?"

"Fine."

Silence again.

"What have you been doing?"

"Today? Oh, nothing much. A bit of cooking. Reading. You?"

Garrett glanced at the body of Christmas. Other uniformed police officers were approaching. She manoeuvred her way out of the cell. "Work mainly."

"It sounds noisy. Where are you?"

"Oh, it's just, hang on, I'll go somewhere quieter." Garrett walked down the corridor, away from the cells, aware of Cherry following. "What have you been cooking?"

"Oh this and that."

"Yes?"

"A curry. Some breads."

Again that silence. Garrett waited for more crumbs from his life. She thought about what Prenderville had said. *Just listen.* Don't offer him anything.

"Listen mum. I'd like to speak to you about something."

"Yes?"

"It's not easy to talk about on the phone. I know it's a lot to ask, but could you come down here?"

"To – Wales?"

"Yes. Look, don't worry if you're too busy! It was just a thought. I–"

If there is any indication he wishes to leave Asari you can be supportive.

"Of course I'll come. Are you alright? Is there anything–"

"Let's speak when you get here. How soon can you come?"

Garrett glanced down the corridor towards the cells and the scrum of officers. Cherry was watching her.

"I'm actually free today. Why don't I come this afternoon?"

"Great. Okay. See you later."

"Okay."

"Bye."

"Bye."

***

It took two hours for the police to finish their questioning and paperwork, and another hour for Garrett to persuade them to release the body to Porton for immediate autopsy. Major Skinner helped, speaking uniform to uniform over the phone. With Garrett he had been brief, surprised and concerned but harassed; Cuito and Guangdong were worse, and Zahra had been off sick that morning.

A patrol car dropped them back at the festival. Garrett spoke little on the ride over. She thought about her car; it was an automatic, no trouble for her to drive. They crossed fields of churned-up grass. Pain from the cut in Garrett's arm gnawed at her through the analgesics.

"So are all your cases like this?"

Garrett grimaced and shook her head.

"So what now?" When Garrett did not reply Cherry said, "If you like I could drive you back. Happy to."

Garrett watched the festival goers queuing on the paths around them. A young man wearing a cotton pyjama suit stood close by; tattoos patterned his neck. Garrett felt suddenly apprehensive. "Thank you but I can drive. And I'd rather be alone right now."

"That call was from your son wasn't it?"

"Cherry, it's been a long night. For all of us. Go home. Get some rest."

"What did he say? Was it about Christmas?"

"I've got to go." Garrett turned away.

"What?" Cherry said, suddenly angry. "That's it? Just like that? Don't you think I deserve to know what's going on, what happened to Spy?"

Garrett stopped. She turned back. "There is something I have to do."

"What is it?" Cherry demanded.

"It doesn't concern–"

"You know it does!"

Garrett stared at Cherry a moment then said, "Not in the way you think."

"How then?"

Garrett saw the suspicion in Cherry's eyes. She sighed. "Jason has asked to meet me."

Cherry heard the excitement and hope in Garrett's voice. She frowned. "Where?"

"Wales."

"Is that where he was calling from? Asari Valley?"

Garrett nodded. Cherry's chin lifted.

"That doesn't sound right."

Garrett began to walk around the car to the driver's side. Cherry followed her. "The Asari don't invite people, not unless they want to convert them."

"This is Jason you're talking about."

"I know Christine. But I've been to that place. I know them. They–"

"Not everyone's the same."

Cherry's suspicion reminded Garrett of the limping Oxford professor and his circling cats.

"You don't know what you might be getting into!" Cherry said. "Know what it sounds like to me? It sounds like a setup."

"Think what you want. Jason asked to see me. I'm going."

Garrett was angry now. She began to search for her key, one-handed.

Cherry walked around to face her. "Of course you have to go. But you don't have to do it alone."

Garrett shook her head.

"Look, Spy's dead. Nothing can bring him back, I know that." Cherry blinked hard. "But what killed him – whatever Christmas had – is connected with Asari. You think that don't you?

Garrett said nothing.

"I need to understand how Spy died. Why he died. I deserve to know!" Cherry stood square to Garrett. "Let me come with you."

Trust is an act of faith, not a logical exercise or an each-way bet. The two women stared at each other over three feet of churned grass. Garrett turned away first. She unlocked the car doors.

"Get in then."

Chapter 24

"Simon Kirkpatrick?"

"Speaking." Kirkpatrick adjusted his headset, settled his hips. *Elbows in, shoulders relaxed. Lucky six.*

"Hello, it's Sanjit Patel here, duty watch officer from Colindale. Yes. That's right. I've been trying to reach you. Sorry to call on a Sunday, only we've had some calls and there're a lot of open alerts against one of your projects. It's gone red."

"Red? Impossible. I would have got Sentinel alerts on this phone." Kirkpatrick shifted his weight from foot to foot and squinted down at the ball. *No more Mr Nice Guy.*

"Yes but–"

"I've had no texts, emails, calls–" Behind him Kirkpatrick heard his partner give a patient sigh.

"I think there's been a glitch in the system."

"So raise a support ticket with IT."

Why had this man had interrupted his weekend to tell him about some bug? Kirkpatrick looked down at his hands. Concentrate. Don't get distracted. Just the one shot adrift now. And this his favourite hole. He squinted at a distant flag. That double or quits had been a bit rash. Now they were talking real money. Watch the bracken, left of the fairway. A hundred and forty yards. Six iron. Yes. *Payback time.*

"Come on Simon, get on with it. Be Christmas soon."

His partner was so impatient. Kirkpatrick adjusted his grip then addressed the ball again.

"I did some checking while I was trying to reach you."

Christ. Officious sounding little man, this Sanjit. "Oh yes?"

"It appears for the last two days all alerts for one project have been forwarded to Clarice Pearson and she's on leave."

"What alerts? And which project?"

"The Brighton malaria cluster. First report came in day before yesterday from the Brighton General Hospital."

"The Brighton Royal you mean," Kirkpatrick corrected. *Just can't get the staff.* He swayed his upper torso and shoulders like a dancer. The voice behind him made another suggestion to play the ball.

"No, it was definitely the General. The Royal called yesterday. I saw their messages looking back through the alert log. I guess you didn't see those reports either."

"I think you should pay attention Simon. Not sure you can afford not to."

Was that meant to be gamesmanship? *Pathetic.* Kirkpatrick glared at ball and club head. *Okay, focus.* He paused, wound back to his full extension, swung...

"–They reported five new cases, one fatality–"

The ball rose into cloudless blue. The white speck arced up high then left, left, left...

"Then later, in the second message, three more cases, two more fatalities."

"Oh bad luck!"

The ball floated down into the bracken.

"I beg your pardon?" Kirkpatrick reached up and touched the side of his headset. "What was that? What did you say?"

"Yesterday. Looks like a total of three fatalities from the Royal, two from the General."

"Did you say fatalities?" Kirkpatrick gazed out across the fairway at the offending patch of rough.

"Yes. And you've had a dozen messages from hospitals all over Sussex. Unfortunately for some reason I can't access them. There are also related reports coming in from London, Gloucestershire and Ceredigion in Wales. Do you know who set up the Sentinel project? That's where the mistakes were made."

"What mistakes?"

"Well, to alert Clarice Liu for one. As I said, she's abroad on leave. It's in her calendar."

Something colder than a clubhouse breezer settled into Kirkpatrick's stomach as he remembered his last moments in the office.

"And it seems your project was not correctly set up on the status board." *Christ.* In the rush to leave, had he forgotten to do that too? "So we couldn't see the red light till I started digging. In the last hour we've got calls in person: a Captain Skinner from Porton Down, and James Hanratty, from MI6? And just now, the Head of Sussex Emergency Response. To be honest, if I hadn't got through to you, I was going to escalate."

Kirkpatrick turned and walked back to the golf cart. He climbed in and stared at the wheel as though trying to work out what it did.

"But I wanted to reach you first if possible. We need an escalation decision."

Kirkpatrick shook his head. "Yes okay Sanjit. Don't do anything. I'm coming in."

"Simon? What the hell are you doing?"

Kirkpatrick pressed the ignition switch. "Gotta go."

"That's pathetic! Are you worse at playing or losing? I can't decide. Even you–"

Kirkpatrick wrenched at the wheel of the cart, accelerating, swinging round towards the clubhouse. "Something's come up."

The cart sped away. His partner was left empty hands raised in a disbelieving question. Behind him on the edge of the tee the six iron lay forgotten in the long grass.

Chapter 25

They stopped at a service station for petrol. When Garrett went to pay she saw Cherry wandering the aisles, her arms full.

Back at the car Garrett put her phone on charge. She opened a packet of unsalted cashews and raisins, took a bite out of an apple, started the engine.

Cherry stared. "You like that stuff?"

Garrett considered. "Yes."

Cherry took a swig from a plastic bottle of chocolate milk. She popped a handful of bright orange cheesy puffs into her mouth, followed by a mini-pork pie. Garrett watched.

"You like that stuff?"

"Yep, tastes good and fills you up." Cherry slapped the round of her tummy. "I'm lucky. Never stays." Cherry noticed Garrett indicate to pull out, steering with the same hand. "Oh sorry, I'll drive if you like."

They switched seats. Garrett was grateful. She explained the gearbox as Cherry pulled away. Cherry drove with relaxed aggression, faster but without Garrett's accuracy. When she manual-selected second for an overtake, Garrett relaxed too. Cherry glanced across at Garrett.

"Have a mini pork pie."

Garrett tried one. She smiled. "Not bad."

"They're bloody brilliant. Spy got me hooked on them last summer." Cherry wound down a window, lit a cigarette. "So what was your David like then?" She barely paused for a reply. "Spyder was a gent. Took care of me. Was there when things got rough. Always gave the bike a once-over after I worked on it." She flicked ash out of the window. "And he loved to hold a door for me; he'd say, 'Mi'lady'," Cherry snorted smoke. Garrett remembered the strong young body on the autopsy table. "He wasn't sexist–"

"David was a journalist."

"Does that make you sexist?"

Garrett laughed. "Can do."

Cherry opened a packet of crisps in her lap one-handed. She ate between drags.

"I mean don't get me wrong, he wasn't no angel. He could be a selfish son of a–"

"David could be selfish too," Garrett said.

"Let's face it," Cherry said, "Men usually come first."

Garrett glanced at Cherry then barked a laugh. Cherry began laughing too. They laughed hard until they saw each other's tired faces, laughing out of need.

Cherry overtook a string of lorries. She drove with increasing restlessness, switching lanes in swerves. Garrett offered her an apple. She took it reluctantly.

"Haven't had one of these since I was a kid." She took a bite. She smiled. "Not bad." She took another bite and spoke between chews. "So do you have any idea what your son wants to talk to you about?"

"I hope he wants help to leave."

Cherry glanced at Garrett. "Usually they want to convert you. That'd be my guess. I say we go in with our eyes open, wait for a chance to snatch him, start deprogramming – you know about that right?"

"Yes but I don't want–"

"Sort of what I did with Spy, except he was already losing the faith. He was willing to leave." Cherry shrugged. "Maybe it'll be the same."

"I wouldn't force him against his will."

"These people don't play fair, Christine. They're bastards. You've got to fight fire with fire."

Garrett remembered Prenderville's words and said, "He must be free to choose."

After a moment Cherry nodded. They drove in silence for a while. "Was he always religious?"

"I brought him up a Catholic."

"No!"

"Yes. It was how I was brought up. My parents sent me to a convent school."

"With real nuns?"

"Yes. I almost became one myself. "

"You?" Cherry barked a laugh, "A nun?"

"It seemed logical at the time. At school I had fallen in love with both science and God. I thought I could combine them."

"What was it like?"

Garrett settled back in her seat. She felt tired and sore but comfortable. She was going to see Jason soon. "From the first day you realise how your life will change. You are given your habit: a black skirt, hat, cross, ring... You are expected to practice silence from nine at night to seven in the morning, also each day to take the Eucharist, spend time in personal meditation and join in community prayers with other sisters at the canonical hours."

Cherry snorted. "Sounds like Spyder's first days at Asari. Why did you leave?"

"I became frustrated with all the devotions. I was doing maths and biochemistry degrees by distance learning and it seemed pointless to spend so many hours contemplating statues when there were tangible, real problems to solve."

"Are you still religious?"

"Not since David died," Garrett said quietly. After a moment she added, "I'm a medical researcher and a doctor first. That makes it difficult to be Catholic on ethical grounds."

"Why's that?"

"The Vatican actively campaigns against stem cell research, genetic therapies, contraceptives in HIV programmes–"

Cherry flicked her cigarette out of the window. "Can't stand religion myself."

Garrett smiled. "David used to say religions were fairy stories for grown-ups." She registered the pleasure of using David's name out loud. "He hated it all too. He said he could understand the mistakes – we're all human – it was the morality he couldn't accept."

"What did he mean?"

"As a journalist he'd covered stories of the deliberate cover-up of child rape."

"I see."

"They had horrified him."

"Of course."

"He came to think that the very idea of the resurrection and absolution of your sins was immoral, was the exact opposite of what you teach a child: that no-one can or should take away your responsibilities. And he thought a moral act was corrupted if done not for its own sake but out of fear of punishment or for reward in some hereafter."

"Sounds right to me."

"He thought the Old Testament was even worse. He said the God Yahweh was a pro-slavery, sexist, homophobic, ethnic-cleansing racist."

"And what did you say?"

"I said he paid attention to the wrong things."

"After what happened to Spy I hate all that mumbo jumbo."

"David used to say, 'Don't you wish the parables had included simple instructions for making penicillin and quinine? Or a draft declaration of human rights?'"

Cherry smiled. "You wanna hear a joke?"

Garrett nodded.

"Okay, so there's this family in Rome." Cherry crammed a handful of crisps into her mouth. "It's two hundred AD, and Mum and Dad are taking their little boy to the games. In the interval the son begins to cry."

Garrett pulled out to overtake a convoy of camper vans.

"His parents give him Roman ice cream to try to cheer him up. 'You've wanted to come to the Games for ages. Didn't you like the gladiators? And the bears?' The little boy nods his head, sobs and says, 'But didn't you see the lions, at the end?" Cherry gave two loud sniffs. "There was one, all alone in the corner; he was the only one without a Christian.'"

Cherry glanced at Garrett and grinned. A mobile began to ring.

"Christine?" It was a man's voice, hesitant and distant.

"Oh. Rheinnalt."

"George told me you'd been hurt. He said your arm?"

The muscles in Garrett's back tightened. She felt his hands on her waist again. The smell of his aftershave filled the car, sweet and floral, its self-regard feminine.

"It's fine. I've sent you a body."

"George said."

"It would be good to autopsy as soon as possible."

"Of course. Christine, about what happened–"

"Have you had any more results from the Analyzer?"

"Not yet. Listen, I just wanted to say I'm–"

"Is anyone working on it?"

"Yes Shani. Christine I'm sorry."

Garrett watched Cherry light another cigarette.

"It's alright. You've nothing to say sorry for."

Cherry looked over at her. Garrett turned to stare out of her side window. Approaching motorway signs warned of a fork ahead, an exit in two miles.

"Rheinnalt, I'm going to have to call you back."

Garrett put the phone down on the dashboard.

Cherry drove in silence. Garrett looked out of the window. The call back came a minute later, the phone's chirruping ringtone loud in the car. Exit in two hundred yards. No reported delays. Get in lane. Exit in one hundred yards.

The ringing stopped.

The metal and stone of the bridge across the Severn rose up on the road ahead like a strung instrument, graceful in its strength. The estuary shoreline beyond was an unlovely margin of exposed rock pools and mudflats. Over brown water the humps of low Welsh hills gave shape to another country.

The phone began to buzz again.

A lorry tooted its impatience at a delay. Garrett pushed a window button. The fresh summer air that entered the car smelled of grass shavings and diesel exhaust. She picked up the phone.

"Christine–"

"I'm the one who should apologize. I shouldn't have hit you."

"It doesn't matter. Can I see you?"

"Will you make sure Shani looks at that body as soon as it arrives?"

"Of course."

"I'm fairly certain he's the index case."

Garrett listened to the hum of carrier signal.

"How do you know?"

Garrett winced as she searched for change for the toll, trying to work out which was more trouble, her injured arm or being humoured.

"The deceased knew all three of the otherwise unrelated first cases: Lizzie was an ex, Spyder was a friend, and he picked up Fiona Grant at the Brighton festival two weeks ago. My external physical exam showed extreme jaundice and an enlarged liver. That's physical and circumstantial evidence."

"Alright. What do the police say?"

"They're embarrassed by a death in custody." The car sped through the stone arches of the first bridge tower. Suspension cabling strobed past. Garrett picked at Bryce's last question. There was nothing for her anger in it. "I'm at a dead end. All we've got is the body."

"Don't worry about that. We'll autopsy soon as it arrives."

Again the deep current of her anger flowed without resistance. Tiredness seeped up her arm. The wind played a continuous note through the bridge's suspension as they drove under the last tower.

"By the way, one of the chicks has gone missing," Bryce said.

"What?"

"The curlews? I saw them again today. One of the chicks is missing."

"Oh," Garrett said.

"Probably a fox." There was a silence on the line. Garrett studied the river through her window. The last of the water below the road bridge was pocked with black rocks. "Christine? I would like to see you."

"I'm visiting Jason."

"Who?"

"Jason my son."

"Where are you?"

"I've just crossed the River Severn."

They pulled up at a toll gate. Garrett threw a handful of coins into a plastic sieve. They drove under a rising barrier.

"Into Wales?"

"Yes. That's where he lives."

The Welsh hills were close now. Cherry accelerated hard away from the tolls.

"Christine–" In the pause, Garrett heard a man choosing words like stones to step on. When his voice came back it was suddenly loud in her ear. "I'm worried about you."

"You don't need to be. I'm with a friend."

"Okay. I know I don't. Will you call later, just to say you're alright?"

Garrett rang off.

"He sounds keen," Cherry said.

Garrett did not reply. She was glad she had picked up his call. She was still just about part of the team. And if she wanted their results she had to be able to talk to Rheinnalt.

And he had called first. She rubbed at her waist where he had touched her. She remembered her smack – she wasn't sorry about it. She sucked on the memory like a boiled humbug.

Chapter 26

Kirtananda nosed his van through slow traffic on the approach to the Severn Bridge. A lorry had jack-knifed near Llanfihangel, three miles into Wales. In the whine and growl of the engine he heard his dogs, the low animal noises they gave out when they picked up a scent still warm. It took twenty minutes to get through the tolls and reach a clear road. When the four-stroke diesel pushed him back into his seat it made him smile. He was looking forward to the fun he was going to have killing Christine Garrett.

She would probably reach Asari first but he would not be far behind. Which was good. Skyler had made the call to his mother as instructed, but he was still not sure of the boy. Perhaps he would have to kill them both. Arshu had been clear: this doctor had to be stopped, or absorbed. Skyler really believed he could convert her – but if he failed, so what? They were both disposable.

Ahead, a family saloon was hogging the fast lane. Kirtandanda sucked his front teeth. He flashed his beams and honked until it moved out of his way.

Mind you, that night with the scientist and his family, the lad had reacted well enough, shooting when ordered, cool enough afterwards, thinking the woman and her child had escaped. He had not returned the gun – another good sign. The boy was becoming a man. But he was the silent type; they'd not be sure of him for a while.

The cars streamed away from the bridge towards Cardiff, a flow like blood cells into the veins of Wales. As he floated in the busy stream, another premonition tightened his hands on the wheel. It was like the hesitation he'd had queuing in traffic behind the old lady, watching as she struggled to find a gear. What was it this time? Something else – lighter, brighter than compassion.

Fingers tugged absentmindedly at his rainbow dog collar. It was not unusual for him to feel things he didn't understand; that never bothered him; he'd realized long ago that feelings didn't interfere with what you had to do, if you learnt the knack. But as he drove west, he suddenly realised what this exultation was that lit him up like a filament in a bulb, brighter than speed mainlined into an arm above the pulse.

What he was doing *mattered*. He was leaving a mark, part of something that was going to change the world. In this end of times – was that what Arshu called it? – he was more than part of it. He was helping to make it happen.

Ain't that the truth.

He drove easily between the cars and coaches and lorries, full of astonishment. He had never expected to feel this. Nothing he had ever done before had mattered to anyone beyond the reach of his fists and arms or on any stage larger than the fall of his own shadow.

As he looked around – at a businessman talking to himself, his jacket hanging creaseless in the back window, at a coach-load of singing students wearing scarves and spilling beer over each other, at children in the back of an estate sticking out their raspberry tongues – the thousand insults of other lives – he knew what he was looking at.

Endings. Beginnings. A new world coming, healed of its pollutions, its hurts. He knew how fragile the civilized skin was. He'd seen it torn in war, in business, in the gangland neighbourhoods where he had grown up; he'd torn it himself, many times, out of need, under orders, sometimes just for fun. He knew the savagery that lay beneath. This tissue of manners and laws others called civil society, it had given him little; he cared for it less. It was about to be stripped off the bone.

He accelerated hard, past a border sign. *Croeso I Gymru.* Welcome to Wales.

Chapter 27

"Shall we stop for more food?" Cherry asked.

"I'd like to get there as quickly as possible."

"Course. No worries. Might need a short comfort break though."

Steering one-handed, Cherry unzipped her hip pouch. She dug around inside with her fingers with increasing exasperation.

"Here, let's switch."

She pulled over onto the hard shoulder. Garrett climbed into the driver's seat. Cherry stood at the edge of the streaming traffic and searched the contents of her pouch. She began cursing.

"I've lost my stuff!"

A container lorry roared past within inches of her shoulder. Cherry shouted angrily. The slipstream rocked her on her feet.

"Cherry, will you get back in the car? Please."

Garrett drove for some minutes before Cherry spoke.

"It must have been at the festival."

"What do you want to do?"

Cherry swore again. "And I've no money! Not enough!"

"What have you lost?"

"My stash!"

"What was it?"

"My drugs, okay?"

"Will you tell me what they were?"

"Oxies."

They drove in silence for a while.

"OxyContin?"

"Yes."

"How long have you been using it?"

"I was clean for a year. I started again last week."

"What do you want to do?"

Cherry stared out of the window for a long while.

When she spoke it was with sudden enthusiasm. "Don't worry doc. I'm not abandoning you. I might have to make a short stop though, in Aberystwyth." She curled up on the passenger seat. "I don't feel so good. I'm gonna have a nap."

By Swansea five minutes later Cherry was asleep. Glancing over, Garrett saw sweat curling her hair on her forehead. A moment earlier, she had half-expected to be asked to write a prescription. She wondered if Cherry would allow her to introduce her to Dr Chandry, head of the Southwick methadone programme.

She watched over the girl as she drove, seeing the twitches and sweats of starting withdrawal. A few times Cherry shivered in her sleep and called out. Garrett resolved to ask about Dr Chandry as soon as she woke.

The first sign appeared for Aberystwyth. Garrett wondered what Jason was doing. Was he in danger? Was he trying to leave?

She caught a movement in the corner of her eye. She swerved. There was a thump from the nearside front wing. The car lost grip. She steered into the skid. She saw no oncoming traffic and allowed herself to drift into the opposite lane across a bend in the road. The car came to a sliding stop on a grass verge.

Cherry shivered, moaned and turned towards her door. She wrapped arms around her chest, hugging nothing tight to her. Garrett got out of the car. She walked back up the road.

A large badger, over a metre long, lay in a ditch just off the tarmac. It was dead, its head badly smashed on one side. Blood trickled out of its mouth. Garrett stared. She saw Christmas in the cell, and the blood beside his mouth. Garrett realised she was panting. Her hands were shaking.

She glanced up into the sky. Further down the coast, kettles of broad-winged birds wheeled around empty blue. After-images of the smashed, bloody carcass, the red mouth lingered on her sight, as though she had glanced too-directly at the sun. Odd connections formed. Something hard, the stone of an understanding, fell in her mind. Garrett tried to hold herself still and wait.

The first three corpses – two had been drowned, their mouths washed empty; the third – Spyder – his mouth had been full of blood, assumed from biting seizures. Christmas's saliva had been reddened by blood. She remembered the ookineetes, the rogue parasites they had found in Fletcher's blood; cell forms occurring in the mosquito vector, able to move from gut to salivary glands.

Garrett returned to the car. She found her mobile. It showed one intermittent signal bar. The first two call attempts failed.

"Shani Zahra, Parasitology."

"Shani, it's Christine."

"Christine! I tried calling you! Are you alright? Rheinnalt told me about your arm."

"It's fine."

"Are you sure? It sounded horrible!"

"I'm fine, honestly. How are you?"

"I'm good. Much better."

"You sound it."

"Thank you for the tea. Listen, I can't talk now. Are you coming back in?"

"Yes, there is something I must do first."

"The body's arrived by the way. I emailed CDSC. They're tracing the case manager. You've put the cat amongst the pigeons."

"Have you started the autopsy?"

"I'm about to."

"I'd like you to do detailed sections of the salivary glands."

There was a moment's static. "–salivary glands?"

"And check those sections from the first victims."

"Okay. I only wish the timing…" Zahra's voice faded, "…why? Surely–"

"Hello? Hello? Shani?" Garrett looked down at her phone. There was no signal.

Sweat trickled down her back. It was a long shot, but at least it was covered. Zahra would do as she asked.

She got back into the car. Cherry had slept through the accident; the back of her shirt was dark with sweat; occasionally she moaned. Garrett drove on. They reached the coast in under half an hour.

Aberystwyth's crescent of Victorian terraces and retirement bungalows faced out to sea. Surfers, students and pensioners wandered together along the railed promenade. The place rhymed with Brighton. Garrett schooled herself against superstitions. As she drove through, Cherry called out, as if in fear. Garrett remembered her request for a short stop in the coastal town. *No time.*

The coastal road out of town was badly maintained. Garrett steered around potholes to minimise bumps. Pain from her left arm nibbled at her. She almost missed the narrow gravelled turn-off marked by a multicoloured sign.

Asari Valley.

She guided the car into a rutted track. The stony driveway immediately dipped downward. Garrett leaned over the steering column. She could smell dimethyl sulphide: the sea. High hawthorn hedgerows blocked any side view.

Patience. She would know soon enough.

Garrett slowed as she bumped through a small clearing full of rubbish. Footpaths led off between trees. Beyond the clearing the rutted road switched back sharply then dipped down. After fifty yards the trees opened out onto a beach. The road ended in a dry-stone jetty half-submerged in sand.

Garrett pulled up beside a post stuck into the ground. A wooden finger advertised *"Asari Valley"*. A sandy path at the base of the cliffs led off a headland. *Damn it.*

She glanced at Cherry sleeping, the girl's face was beaded with sweat. She was reluctant to wake her; and reluctant for some reason to move. She checked her phone, not surprised to see no signal still. She would have to wait till they were back in Aberystwyth to call the lab.

Back after what?

She stared out of the windscreen, blind to the facing sea, and admitted she was nervous. Why had Jason invited her down here? Cold drenching memories of their last meeting broke over her like, recriminations over money, accusations about drugs, bitter words…

"I don't like your friends, they're aggressive, rude and they exploit you. Can't you see that?"

"You want to keep me in a box labelled 'My child', like a pet mouse, and I won't let you. Dad would've understood."

What had happened to Jason? How had he become so lost?

Should she have done more, taught him something more? She was his mother. She had to take some of the responsibility. She dug out of her fear the buried question she had asked Dr Prenderville: had his upbringing somehow set him up for exploitation? Teaching him to believe in the invisible, in the dream of a man perfected. Had she made him vulnerable to those waiting for him?

Maybe it wasn't too late. Perhaps she could reach him, help him.

She got out of the car and it was cooler at once. The air was fresh, the sun's touch hot but pleasant.

The tension in her eased. The car engine's fan whirred on under the sound of the wind. Garrett watched seagulls surf the breeze inshore, coming over the car, around and back out to sea. The sun was beginning to dip, bringing shoals of light to the surfaces of the water. She saw a small child clutching seaside treasure, laying it beside her on the beach. She remembered his questions still. He had demanded such serious explanations. Why did the starfish have six arms? Why were glass pebbles smooth? How did the seaweed learn to swim? Later, he'd brought his own just-so tales, his reasonings and experiments, to lay at their feet for approval, like a cat mice to its owner. They had spent hours mixing the boy's fantasy with her science and David's quick humour, and in their shared confidences Jason had grown self-assured, quick and easy with achievement, like a champion that always won. Had they prepared him only for success? He had been so lost when David died. Could they have made him more able to cope?

Curling armfuls of water and light carried far up the sloped sands. Garrett closed her eyes and listened to the withdrawing exhalation of the shingle. The touch of the sun was like a facing fire. The suck and sigh of surf surrounded her.

David. David. I miss you. So much. I need you now. We need to talk about Jason.

She turned back to the car. Cherry was still asleep. Garrett looked along the path by the shore. The faint trail slipped in and out of the trees. She decided to explore the headland while she waited for Cherry to wake.

***

Impatience made the start of the Y incision a little deep. Zahra felt a brief wave of nausea. She ignored it and continued cutting.

Why did they call it morning sickness, when it happened in the morning, afternoon and evening? And how could you feel sick and hungry at the same time? She tried to remember if she had any digestive biscuits left in her desk. She was starving.

She completed the first cut and glanced at the clock. This shouldn't take long. If she was fast, she'd be done in twenty minutes.

Her knife slipped on cold tattooed skin.

191

Shit.

Slow down. No point being impatient. Leave that to George.

Right now he was running around like a headless chicken. Short-staffed over the summer break, he had two projects that had gone Alpha – Cuito, Guangdong. And Christine's malaria project was no help.

She pulled down the skin to expose abdominal organs. Tissues were grey.

First sections of lung showed sooty spots. The exposed top of the liver was darkened as if scorched, speckled black. She started to work more carefully.

Abdominal organs were all infected. And lungs and heart. After a little more cutting she was convinced, without blood slides. There was no doubt: Garrett had found another case.

She remembered her last words. With quick slashes of her knife she cut out the submandibular salivary gland. Her nausea and hunger were forgotten.

She carried the lobed gobbet of flesh over to a dissection counter. She cut neat tissue sections. The spongy mass showed the discolouration ran right through.

Imagination gives fear a shape. It is a cursed gift for the neurotic, crude entertainment for the schoolboy. Zahra's imagination was healthy and unrefined but it enabled her to catch with dim enthusiasm at another's. The last words she had heard through the broken signal of Garrett's request from Wales came back to her now, clearer. *Check. First victims.*

Excitement gurgled through her empty gut. She took the sections back to the lab. She started the image analysis programme they had used when Garrett had spotted the first ookineete. She chose Paul Fletcher's case files. His biopsy archive listed the image folders. Had they looked at even half of them? *Right. Analyze irrelevant glands? With all that spare time they'd had.*

Ookineetes. Check. Salivary glands. Okay. The thoughts in her head were for some reason accented the way Garrett spoke, measured, experienced, encouraging. She refined the image analysis, selected the parotid, submandibular and sublingual sections, narrowed the cell forms. Analyze…

An hourglass filled over and over.

Her bladder began to ache above her crossed legs. Garrett's words guttered and flared, throwing indistinct shadows in her again. *Check. Check. Check.* While she waited she logged in to

Sherlock. She searched for the data sets of the previous Brighton cases.

She started the additional exception analyses she'd skipped before. Strings of alphabetic characters streamed across the screen in a digital rain.

Analysing...

The clock on the lab wall ticked. The image analysis window refreshed. It showed a slide from the parotid gland, stained pale pink. Darker purple erythrocyte cells floated in a sunset sea, their interiors speckled with parasites. Zahra leaned forward. She could see half a dozen dark spiky spheres, the unmistakable shape of ookineetes, floating like mines among surrounding blood cells.

Skinner called out as he entered the lab. "Finished already?"

Zahra did not look up. *I'd like you to do detailed sections of the salivary glands.* The half-heard words echoed through the static of memory and intermittent signal, the gain turned up by understanding.

"Shani?"

"Mmm. With you in a sec."

She selected the other three case files. She searched for specific organ sections again. Skinner came to stand behind him. "Shani, I thought I told you to work on–"

"George!" Zahra tried to control her squeaky voice. "Hold on a moment."

Ookineetes... parotid, submandibular and sublingual glands... Analyze. Tiled windows opened one after the other. Ookineetes showed in all of them.

"What's this?"

"Salivary gland sections from all four of the Brighton *falciparum* cases."

Her boss never showed surprise. It was not a pose, just that he had seen everything already. Zahra waited without turning.

"I'll be damned." Skinner's voice was quiet.

The pent-up tiredness and frustration at all the extra hours evaporated. Zahra tasted a primitive, tracked-down joy. It was warm, salty. "It solves the transmission riddle."

"Parasites in human saliva." Skinner stared at the image.

"Yes," Zahra said. "An orally transmissible malaria. And the answer was under our noses all the time! Well, in results we didn't check. Garrett gave us what should have been a sufficient clue days ago, didn't she? I mean *we* are the lab scientists!"

Skinner shook his head. "We didn't check because that isn't natural."

The Sherlock program beeped.

Analysis complete. Species: Falciparum. ***Match:* Chiang-14.** *Exception analyses complete.*

Zahra clicked through to additional information.

Twelve exceptions. Eight outstanding anomalies.

Exception 3 analysis: transgenic material: Species: ***Streptococcus.***

Exception 5 analysis: transgenic material: Species: ***Streptococcus.***

Exception 8 analysis: transgenic material: Species: ***Streptococcus.***

Exception 9 analysis: transgenic material: Species: ***Streptococcus.***

Zahra slumped back in her chair. Dammit! Why hadn't she run those exception analyses the first time? If she hadn't been so distracted...

"Sir, there's something else."

Skinner came to stand behind her.

"Look." She pointed. "You're right. It isn't natural. Sherlock's found transgenic material." She put a hand on her stomach. "*Streptococcus?* An orally-infectious bacterial pathogen. Sir, something's going on. Someone needs to know about this."

Skinner looked slowly around the lab. He seemed to be studying it as if for the first or last time. His gaze returned to Zahra.

"Have you talked to anyone?"

"No."

"Have you been in contact with Christine since she last called?"

"No."

Chapter 28

Kirtananda took the turn off the coastal road one-handed; a front wheel narrowly missed the Asari Valley sign. With his free hand he popped a pill. He considered taking another and decided against it. He needed to pace himself. This past week had become an extended operation. Who knew how long it would be before it was over? One pill, just for the reflexes.

He rolled to a stop. There were no other vehicles in sight. Had he arrived first?

His fingers curled around the butt of his semi-automatic. A thumb released the safety. He pushed open the driver's door then turned back to rummage in the glove box. He found his kartals. After he struck them, he sat still for a full minute.

He took the less-used path up to the headland. From the top there was a clear view of the valley and its approaches. Experience had taught him to take his time, while it was there for the taking. As he climbed the kartals rang on and on in his mind, a pure note that didn't fade.

Arshu had blessed the cymbals. He had explained it all. His was the Warrior's path, his duty to defend Mother Earth, in the Holy War where death was only a door. The note from his kartals would ring past the ending battle, carrying his spirit through into the next life where Arshu would be waiting for him. For five years now that pure note had guided him into every major action, a fixed rail against uncertainty, like a banister up a stair in the dark. It was the purest thing in his life.

From the headland he could see deep into the Valley and far along the beaches. Nothing moved, except sheep and birds.

He switched to field glasses. He noticed the incoming tide. A glitter of light caught his attention down by the south jetty. He adjusted the sights. The sun blinked with him as a gull passed overhead. A fingerpost came into focus and behind it the windscreen of a car. The metal note in his mind shivered and steadied.

***

Kirkpatrick logged on to his terminal in the CDSC building. *Stay calm. Don't panic.* The terminal emitted a loud pop and he flinched.

Unread alerts: 123.

Kirkpatrick began reading. The first messages had come in days ago – that Thursday evening he had left early – from the Brighton hospitals, the Royal and the General. The next cluster was from a Welsh primary care trust, around Aberystwyth, New Quay and Fishguard. Dozens of infections, a few fatalities.

Kirkpatrick fiddled with a plastic golf tee in a trouser pocket. No one knew yet. He scrolled up the screen, forward in time. After the Welsh cluster, more messages from all along the south coast, Portsmouth, Hailsham, Horsham, Crawley…

He bent the golf tee across a knuckle. It was Clarice's fault. She should have been here. She'd have received the alerts. That damned system. Why hadn't they fixed the notify bug?

He continued to page up. So many! He saw first reports from London. They had come in this morning.

What should I do?

He sat motionless, eyes locked on the screen. He took his hand out of his trouser pocket and pulled twice on his nose. It was a twitch he wouldn't be able to rid himself of.

Stay calm.

The desk phone began ringing. The tee snapped between his fingers. Kirkpatrick snatched at the receiver.

That damn damn damn Clarice.

"Hello? Yes. Who?" Kirkpatrick tried to slow himself down. "It's good you called, Captain Skinner." Kirkpatrick stood up, then sat down again. "I need an update. I've a report to make to senior management. We've had some bad news I'm afraid. More infections. Many more. Yes, and deaths. I'm afraid so. What? I'm sorry, what did you say?"

Beside his keyboard, his work mobile began to vibrate and flash. *Unknown number.* Kirkpatrick swung around as though buffeted by contrary winds. "Hold on just a second! I've got a call coming in on another line! Don't go."

Kirkpatrick pressed hold and picked up his mobile. "Hello?"

"May I speak to Simon Kirkpatrick please?"

"Speaking," Kirkpatrick compressed his lips. "I'm on another call at the moment. Who is this?"

"I am Surgeon Commander Charles White, from MI5. I require information on some malaria cases I believe you are dealing with."

Kirkpatrick stared at his keyboard.

"I'm sorry, who did you say you were?"

"Finish your other call then ring me back." An edge sounded in the slow patrician voice on the other end of the line. "My number is eight triple three one thousand. That will take you through to reception, Biological Section, MI5, Whitehall. Ask for me by name. Surgeon Commander Charles White."

"Er–" Kirkpatrick put a hand up to cover his eyes. He pulled on his nose.

"Eight triple three–"

"Eight triple three–"

"One thousand."

"One... thousand."

"Correct. Look it up. I look forward to your call within the next few minutes."

Pop!

Kirkpatrick squinted over his keyboard.

New alert. Sender: Dr Da Costa, The Brighton General Hospital. Subject: new infections.

The desk phone flashed the red warning light for a call on hold. Kirkpatrick's bottom lip began to tremble, unnoticed, for the first time since he was a little boy.

In his ear, the broken connection began beeping.

Chapter 29

A few yards into the trees Garrett put up her good hand. She brushed away a strand of spider's web. Only a thread – but it suggested the path hadn't been used for days. Maybe the commune used this route rarely, preferring the path from the clearing – she'd seen the rubbish dump. Garrett concentrated on the placing of her feet on the increasingly stony ground.

After some minutes she walked out through salt scrub onto a rocky shore. Smooth blues rose to a clear horizon. The sun was hot on her shoulders, a bright warmth banishing the cobwebbed gloom of the trees. She took a steadying breath, grateful for the sunlight's lift.

Maybe she was wrong and her nightmares were just that. Maybe she'd find the commune bustling with life; Jason would be there, healthy, happy, shocked at connections to unusual deaths; and she would be mocked for wanting normal tea. A nervous burst of happiness filled her at the prospect of seeing him.

Above her, a headland jutted out redly towards the sea. Her eyes picked out a fine-grained layer of dark sandstone between lighter bands of Silurian rock, the signature of the Welsh geosyncline. She wondered if Jason had noticed it. On family holidays, they had loved their geology walks. His eyes had become keener than hers.

Large grey turbines stood on the cliff top like a clump of steel flowers, their faces turned towards the wind. Beyond the promontory she could see into a wide sandy bay. The faint sunken trail she was following crossed over dunes and a darkened line of dried seaweed, up through pines again into the cleft of a deep valley.

In the centre of the sandy bay a rocky outcrop rose out of the damp plain of tidal sand. What looked like an arm was raised. Garrett heard a shout.

She approached. A man was seated on top of the rock. His hair was long and bleached by the sun. He wore sandals and a white robe. A short, neatly-trimmed beard accented the hollows in his cheeks.

"Hello Christine."

In the time it took her heart to adjust, Garrett learned how, despite her careful defences, he was part of all her days and always would be, a shadow following her actions, falling on her thoughts.

She vibrated from head to toe at the sound of his voice, plucked with relief. He was safe! She stepped towards the rock her arms ready, then stopped when he made no move. She reminded herself of a resolution.

"Hello Skyler."

"I thought you'd arrive around now." He squinted up at the sun then inclined his head. "I've just completed the Dues of the Seventeenth Hour."

He looked down at her. She didn't know what to say. She glanced up at the exposed geosyncline.

"I–"

"Welcome to Asari Valley."

"Thank you. It's good to see you."

"How was your journey?"

"Not too bad. A little traffic around Cardiff. After that it was fine."

"You've hurt your arm?"

"It's only a cut."

"Does it give you pain?"

"It's fine."

Skyler shrugged a small backpack onto his shoulders. He rose in one smooth motion and stepped down from the rock. "I'm glad you've come. Shall we go up?"

He raised a hand to indicate she walk with him. Garrett looked back the way she had come. "I – I came with a friend. Cherry. She's waiting in the car."

With his left hand Skyler unlooped a short string of brown stones from around his knuckles. His thumb counted beads over his fingers in quick succession; they clicked to a steady rhythm.

"Are you parked at the jetty on the beach?"

Garrett nodded.

He turned and began walking towards the tree line. "You came the long way round. I'll ask Rayan to walk over and drive her up."

Garrett stared at his retreating back. "Are you sure? I can go and get her—"

"Ray won't mind."

***

From the tall sash windows of his office White studied the traffic along Whitehall. His fingers trembled as he lit his fifth cigarette of the afternoon.

He watched a red double-decker overtake a line of parked tourist coaches. The familiar sight was soothing. He had heard somewhere that air traffic controllers often kept fish, and after a shift would unwind by staring into the tank. His fish – the cars moving in slow shrugging lines along the grey tarmac below his window – helped him too.

He thought about his career – until five years ago distinguished and unblemished. One mistake that's all it took; one decision taken under time pressure with limited information. And it had started so quietly, with just a few odd facts, a trickle of infection reports, then increasing evidence of anomaly… Just like now. Was it all happening again? He took a deep drag on his cigarette. *Steady as she goes.*

Simon Kirkpatrick had not sounded in control. Perhaps that was his natural state. Perhaps. White didn't like dealing with unknown quantities. At sea, he had seen many men under stress: everyone reacted differently; some couldn't cope. He returned to his desk.

"Jenny, Charles White here. I need another favour. I'd like some background. On a Simon Kirkpatrick. Works at CDSC Colindale. Project manager. Yes, anything you can dig up. Thank you. Oh and Jenny – Chief's back tomorrow isn't he? Okay great! Can we reach him before if needed? I see. Is it a direct flight? Right."

Major decisions should be taken by the department head. Tomorrow. Not long. White took another drag and partially exhaled a still circle of blue smoke. On screen in front of him was a collated report of all information relating to the current malaria outbreak. It listed all recent alerts received by CDSC. Also included were the Porton Down lab reports. They were full of worrying details: high parasitaemia, unsynchronised broods and rogue cell forms.

The jigsaw was incomplete. White poked at a haphazard collection of papers on his desk, printouts of intelligence and lab reports and the personal notes he had made on the restricted file. He understood all too well that the critical time to control an outbreak was at the start. With each infection the chance of containment reduced.

The smoke ring drifted up slowly, catching his attention again. He sent three smaller rings chasing through its centre, then blew them all away with an impatient sigh. Perhaps this Simon Kirkpatrick would have good news. He pressed the intercom button again.

"Jenny, Charles again. Yes. Yes I know, I just can't help myself. It's your lovely voice. Yes, those too. Okay guilty. I do: two service files, UK army – Major George Skinner, Sergeant Shani Zahra, both working out of the Ring Laboratory at Porton. Also anything you can dig up on a Dr Christine Garrett, an epidemiologist with Sussex CDSC."

Better informed than sorry. He had to be certain to raise the alarm. Otherwise he wouldn't do it. He wouldn't. Not again.

***

The footpath down from the headland was stony and narrow. It cut through spiky gorse and wind-bent pine in sharp switchbacks. Kirtananda knew it the way a child knows fence runs in his back garden. Sweat trickled down his back; adrenaline excited his heart; with the pill, it gave his feet a jumpy energy and let him ski the stones of the path without a stumble.

On some of the lower turns there was a sight of the beach and the car. Kirtananda crossed these open spaces fast. He grinned as he ran. Two misses. He wouldn't miss a third time. Not on home ground.

He thought ahead. The cleanup was almost complete. And the plague was spreading just as Osei had predicted. A new life was about to begin.

When he'd told Arshu that they were nearly done he'd heard the pause. Who knew what calculations had gone on in that vast old soul, in those slow breaths? But then the answer came back, calm and affirming: yes, it was time. He must finish up. Then prepare for the future and his new command, in a healed world.

Kirtananda loved Arshu, loved the man's slow smile and clever words, his wise black eyes and curious way with people.

He sprinted round the last turn down to the beach and stopped at an opening in crouching conifers, where the path ended in a door of sunshine. He breathed in short pants over his tongue, like one of his dogs, a half-opened eye raised against the light. The car was less than fifty yards away. There was someone inside.

***

"Sir, did you get my email on the Kepalua report?" Hanratty stayed at the door.

"No." White scanned his inbox.

"Just sent it you. Thought you should see. I found the story on the newsfeeds."

"What about?"

"An unusual malaria outbreak."

"Where?"

"Kepalua – a group of islands off the south coast of Java. There's a follow-up report yesterday from Jakarta, suggesting a spread to the larger island."

He found the email and read as Hanratty spoke. The information was poor but the similarities – he looked at the date timestamp on the newsfeed. Damn it. Why hadn't the boy been doing his homework? A light began flashing on an extension.

"Why don't I forward you the full reports?" Hanratty eyed the flashing light as he backed out of the door.

White took a deep drag on his cigarette and picked up the phone. "White speaking."

"Er, yes, hello. Is that Surgeon Commander Charles White?"

"Simon Kirkpatrick," White exhaled with his words, "Thank you for calling me back."

"I hadn't realised earlier–"

White sucked on his cigarette. He watched the tip glow orange listening to the man hunt for the end of his sentence. Kirkpatrick's hesitant calculations – of how much pride he could afford – were almost audible.

"The other call was important–"

"That's all right. You may feel you need further proof of my credentials."

"No, I've already checked."

White contemplated the greying end of his cigarette, interested. Offence had turned to caution very quickly. Perhaps the man was a worrier. He tapped ash into a tray. "Good. Now forgive me for being brief but I'm after information, as quickly as possible. I need a status update on this malaria outbreak you have been overseeing. Background detail on the first cases would be good, and on your lab team, and the recent new alerts. I have your reports. I must say they leave a lot to–"

"You won't have the latest information," Kirkpatrick interrupted. "I have just been speaking to one o the researchers. New facts have emerged."

Interrupted, White spat out smoke. "I'm listening."

After a moment he pulled out a pad of paper and began making notes. He covered the sheet and started another. Eventually he stopped writing. He sat still. There was silence on the line.

"Hello?"

White continued to stare at his notes without speaking.

"Hello? Did you understand what I was saying?"

"Please stay on this number. I'll be calling you back."

White hung up. He took a fresh sheet of paper and wrote six points. When he underlined words he pressed too hard and his pen nib caught, splattering ink.

Ongoing outbreak, <u>accelerating.</u>
Brighton. South coast.
<u>On the UK mainland.</u>

<u>Lethal strain.</u>

Possible related Indonesian outbreak.

Possible <u>oral human-to-human transmission.</u>
Possibly due to <u>genetic anomalies</u> indicative of <u>artificial modifications</u>.

White was perfectly still for some minutes.

Not again. Please not again. Not on my watch. He felt physically sick.

But the words he had written on the sheet of paper in front of him would not go away. He had once again underlined a set of linked facts pointing to a terrible threat. Once again, he was responsible for the discovery of a possible outbreak menacing many lives. Only this one was happening faster. And it looked worse, much much worse.

Should he call for a Five committee? Was there time? The infection figures tolled in his head. If his fears about this outbreak were real, every hour, every minute counted now.

It was very quiet in his office. The hands of the mantel clock appeared to be still. He glanced at the picture of the Queen hanging on the wall. Once, on naval duty in the Caribbean during the rainy season, his ship had passed through the eye of a force nine. It was true. It was calm in the dead centre. He had looked up and seen the moon in a clear black sky.

His drifting mind caught at facts, circled the gaps. Missing information always dismayed him. White reached for the phone.

"Jennie, any luck?" His voice shook slightly. He noticed he wanted to clench his teeth. "Okay. Send me through what you've got on the lab team now. Quick as you can, love."

White stared at his screen. He clicked a refresh button a few times. CVs finally arrived in his inbox. They solved nothing.

There were always unknowns. White pinned his notes to the desk with the tip of his pen. He looked at the circled phrases. He added two more.

Possible link to secondary intel on an incident
involving breach of GM protocols

Potential WMD.

He underlined his conclusions again, and again, and again, then caught himself and stood up.

That night in the Caribbean, in the eye of the storm, all directions out were through storm walls. It had been calm and quiet in the centre. But you couldn't stay there forever.

He crossed to the picture of the Queen. With each step he felt closer to some edge, but forced to go on, controlled by events, old and new. A curious feeling overtook him, as though he were looking down on himself.

The reproduction was surprisingly light in its fake gilt frame. He placed it on the floor. Behind where it had hung on the wall was a small metal door with a dial in the centre. He spun the combination, opened the safe and took out a pocket book. Back at his desk he looked up a number and dialled it. He listened to the recording he had heard once before, five years ago. The small of his back felt very cold. He unclenched his teeth. When the recording finished he began to speak.

"Identification: Surgeon Commander Charles White, service MI5, serial number 2340934. Authorization code," White consulted the pocket book again, "849-R43E-2606-XE1234T." White hesitated then continued speaking. "I am raising a COBRA alert. Context: potential weaponized malaria strain active on UK mainland. Risk threat estimate: JTAC Severe Defined. Potential mass destruction capability. Recommendation: convene COBRA immediately."

White hung up. The dread of impending shame hollowed his stomach. But the terrible pressure of hesitation had gone. He had made his decision. He discovered a tiny revival of self-respect. It would not survive a second humiliation but he nurtured it while he could. He would need it in the coming hours.

He took a steadying drag on his cigarette, discovered it had gone out and lit another.

He picked up his pen. Right or wrong, he had work to do. He scratched out a plan. Priority One: start a staff recall; and call Hanratty, he needed him immediately. Two: prep other biosafety labs; liaise with the team at Porton and arrange to share results; maybe go down there. Three: initiate a nation-wide survey of related incidents. Make that Priority Two. He needed that briefing material fast. In his temples, he could feel his pulse against bone.

As he wrote, his thoughts tracked the protocol he had just initiated. His message would have been listened to as he spoke. He didn't know the location but the number he had called was manned round-the-clock by military personnel from JTAC, the Joint Terrorism and Analysis Centre. Calls were being made now. The Chief Medical Officer would be being contacted, along with senior ministers in the Home Office and Health Ministry. Probably the services too, given his threat estimate. He would be called back – or visited in person. White's eyes drifted to the door and the shadow of the bells on the wall. A decision would be taken on the convening of a Cabinet Office Briefing Room meeting.

He had just rung the UK's largest alarm bell. Again. Only this time even more loudly. A Severe Defined Risk was the second highest on a seven-step scale, just below Critical. It had only been reached once before to his knowledge, after the July 2005 London bombings.

Had he panicked again? White blew a large, trembling smoke ring out over his desk. He stared at his notes, at the underlined intelligence. *No.* He had done his duty. And despite what it might mean, the best part of him, the part the sea had helped to train, that had nerved him to make the call, hoped he was wrong a second time.

Chapter 30

They moved through the pines along a footpath of hard earth. The wood offered quiet, the only noise the splash and mutter of water from an unseen stream. Neither spoke. Garrett watched Skyler fold his brown beads over and over his wrist as he walked.

He led her out from under the trees into the open shelter of a wide, bowl-shaped valley. Steep grooved cliffs rose up hundreds of feet on either side, forming an encircling rampart broken only by the narrow gap leading to the sea. It was as though a giant hand had reached down into the earth and scooped out a deep hollow.

A patchwork of small, variously-green meadows covered the valley bottom. At her feet, hundreds of four-petalled blue flowers, *Veronica chamaedry*, fluttered like turquoise butterflies along the edge of the footpath. The stream, noisy in the wood, snaked along the path beside them, silent and fast, covered with a skin of sunlit scales. Distrustful, Garrett had to admit the place was not what she had expected.

"It's beautiful."

Skyler looked pleased and proud.

"Jas – Skyler, I'm worried about leaving my friend Cherry. If she wakes up–"

He pointed to a rise fifty yards ahead. "Come on. I can call to Rayan from up there."

They followed the footpath across sunburned-pale grass. Where they walked, sorrel, thistles and hedge parsley crowded the ground. Garrett noticed darker lawns of moss, how they betrayed nutrient and moisture deposition the way stains discover proteins on a slide. Skyler pointed out livestock, orchards, arable crops. He spoke in boasting rushes, short at first, then more confidently. Garrett was suddenly happy.

They passed five white tepees set on a wide shelf of grass in two straight rows like neatly-stored wizards' hats. There was no-one in sight.

"Skyler, it's very quiet. Are there not many people here right now?"

"Everyone has gone except for Rayan and a couple of others. I'll explain later."

Garrett noticed a muscle jump beside his right eye. When not playing with his prayer beads, his hands were constantly plaiting a nest of fingers. As if yesterday, she saw a boy sat on the edge of his bed lacing fingers together, with a brown smudge on his nose, suggesting Daddy – who likes chocolate a lot, doesn't he – may have emptied the box.

Am I always infantilising you? Why have you asked me here? Is it the infection – are you asking for my help?

When they reached the top of the rise Skyler put two fingers to his mouth. *Coo-weee!* The two-tone call of a tropical bird sounded across the valley. A faint answering cry echoed back from a distant field and Garrett saw the waving of a tiny arm.

"He won't be long," Skyler said. He walked to the edge of a granite ledge that faced into the valley. With slow ceremony he unbuckled a roll mat from under the top flap of his pack and spread it flat on the warm rock. He began to pull out and unfold packages.

"I brought us some lunch, in case you were hungry."

"Thank you!"

Garrett felt the awkwardness of a table turned, a mother fed by her grown child. Skyler folded himself up into a half-lotus on the mat.

Garrett sat down too, her legs straight out, crossed at the ankles. Beneath the rock overhang where they sat an enormous grey Shire with four white stockings grazed between tufts of thistle and willow herb. She saw how the tall magenta and brick-red flowers spread out to the integrated limits of the rock's shade, a living memory of shadow.

"Loosestrife. It's good for our honey. The bees love it." He rummaged in his pack. "Here we are. Try it with the bread. That's fresh, I bake it every morning. And we've got tomatoes – I picked them today, they're very sweet, Trwyn apples, Y Fenni cheese – a cow's cheese–"

Skyler picked up a small loaf of bread, tore it in two and passed half to Garrett with the honey. She could hear the tearing chews of the horse beneath them and discovered she was hungry. Skyler opened a wooden-handled pocket knife, sliced open a large deep-purple tomato and bent to smell.

"So how do you like our Valley?"

"It's very beautiful."

Skyler looked pleased again.

"And the honey?"

"It's delicious. The bread–"

"It tastes of something, doesn't it?"

"Yes."

"That's because wasn't made by a supermarket in some outsourced factory. What you eat comes from the soil here, from the care we take, the faith we keep: it is made out of our lives." He took a leather cord from around his neck and passed it to her. "This Asar was made from local stone."

Garrett looked at the carved image of a many-rayed Eye; the stone was rurbidite, the rust-coloured sandstone she had seen in the cliff. But what held her was a heavy signet ring threaded onto the same cord; it was David's.

"Shall I tell you something about our home?"

"I'd like that."

He held his hand out for the leather cord.

"We sit at the entry point. It is an important stage in every visitor's journey. A sacred place. It is on this spot that most people first hear God."

Garrett blinked. "Did you say God?"

"Yes." Skyler looked amused. He inclined his head, halfway between a shake and a nod. "You think he only exists in the pages of a book? Or paint, reaching to touch a hand across a ceiling? No. He is with us, here, made flesh. And this place is where he likes to teach."

Garrett settled her left arm in her lap.

"You're talking about Arshu?"

Skyler nodded. "Our Teacher. Arshu is the third incarnation of Asari – the resurrected God – Osiris in the Greek."

"Is he here now?" Garrett glanced around. When she heard the gentle mockery in her voice she glanced quickly over at Skyler, alarmed.

Skyler laughed. "No! But he may be, in our next breath. He always arrives alone, unannounced and on foot; and he leaves the same way, without warning, walking with his stick over these fields out to the beach, out of sight and mind, and for all we know, the world."

Skyler tore off a chunk of bread. He began chewing slowly. "Of course many have tried to follow him. None succeed."

"Have you tried?"

"Yes."

"What happened?"

"I tracked him as far as the beach. He rounded the headland and then just vanished. Trust me, I searched for hours. I studied the tracks in the sand. I explored the cliffs, the trees, the shoreline. I couldn't explain it. Some time later, I saw a sail far out to sea. Perhaps it was him." Skyler shrugged then quoted, "*Don't follow in the footsteps of the masters; seek what they sought.*"

"He appears in our Centres all over the world the same way, a sudden brief blessing, then he is gone."

"We are fortunate. He comes here often because this place is sacred to him – it is where he first had his vision of Rebirth. He never stays long, but when he comes he teaches us his Rules of Living. He has shown us how to see and shape the land, to consecrate it so life and belief become one. May I explain?"

Garrett nodded. Skyler straightened up. His words came with the practiced fluency of a teacher on firm ground. Occasionally, to emphasize a point, he tilted his head back and closed his eyes. The gesture discouraged questions.

"Do you know the famous mantra, *Om Mani Padme Hum*?"

Garrett shook her head.

"A rough translation would be, 'Between nadir and zenith lies the jewel in the lotus'. So: in the centre of existence there is male seed and female flower. What does that symbolize? It is a vision of creation in continual divine Coitus. Not a new truth, but one we honour."

Skyler swept his arm over the landscape. "This valley is that ideal made real. It is a Yoni: a sacred womb. Here we are protected and sheltered: the cliffs are high and unscalable, the only entrance through where we sit. Here we are nourished: the earth is fertile. Here we grow: a few hundred of us, individual cells of humanity transforming into a collective the like of which has never been seen."

For a moment Garrett wondered if Jason had a girlfriend. She hoped so. He had never been very good with girls. She would probably be an Asari. Surprised by unexpected jealousy – for a girl that might not even exist – she smiled.

Encouraged, Sky continued. "Within this sacred landscape we have designed our life and homes to reflect our beliefs." He made a curious cupping gesture with his hands. "A*bove, as* *below.* You can see the Tower of Hours," he pointed to a distant white spire standing alone, "And all four Path Houses from here: of Love, Healing, Justice, Force. Yes force, we are not sentimentalists. We take the world as we find it."

Skyler pointed up near the head of the Valley, to where a distant domed roof twinkled in the sun.

"The House of Health and Knowledge will probably interest you most. It's Osei's great work. He has gathered chemists, agriculturalists, bio-engineers... I see you are surprised." He shook his head. "You know Mum, you couldn't ever quite marry up your own faith and science, could you? Not really. Well we have. Don't get me wrong: we are not materialists in any way. We simply use technology where we find it useful; where it has spiritual value."

The Path House of Health.

"Your face! You look so serious! What are you thinking?"

Garrett hesitated. "Skyler, can I talk to you about something?"

"Of course. Anything. But first," Skyler frowned up at the sun. His hand went to the leather cord around his neck. "I'd like to speak to you about my father—"

He stopped. Garrett hitched her left arm higher up where it rested on her thigh; the cut ached. She realized she was frightened.

"Yes?"

"My father—" he stopped again, like a musician making another false start at a memorized piece. Garrett waited. "His death. It was very hard at first – I think I blamed you." He looked up to meet Garrett's eyes. "I don't now. I know it wasn't your fault. It was his kismet – his fate, which we have to accept."

"Thank you. Perhaps I should—"

"No. No. No shoulds." He smiled and shook his head at her. His words lay like a gift between them. They ate in silence together for a while.

"You looked surprised." Skyler smiled at her. "I know it's been a difficult time for you. For me too. For us both. I have taken time to come to terms with things. This place has taught me ways to do that, especially through our meditation practice. I expect you understand that. Christian prayer is a type of meditation." He stopped, waiting for her to say something.

When she didn't reply he continued. "I have found the discipline very helpful."

"In what way?"

"A good question." Skyler sat up straight and his words became practiced again. "Meditation helps cultivate awareness and acceptance. It is useful for seeing clearly then untangling habits of mind. True acceptance is a sort of spell – hard and holy – real magic, not the childish stuff of wizards, but of human transformation."

Garrett considered the proof in his words. *I know it wasn't your fault.*

Skyler dipped his pocket-knife into the honey. She could taste it still on her tongue. He offered her some. She shook her head and thought suddenly about Cherry. Had she woken yet? She'd been so tired, she might sleep for hours. As if he had heard her thought, Skyler nodded towards the distant figure of a man coming towards them on the road.

"Don't worry, Rayan's on his way."

A strange ululating cry echoed out over the valley from the distant white tower. Garrett made out a repeated phrase, *Gurusri-kalki Arshu.* When the call ended a gong sounded five times. Skyler pulled his feet into the full lotus.

"I must perform the Dues of the Hour. Please, join me in meditation if you wish."

He closed his eyes. Garrett waited. He remained still, eyes closed. She felt embarrassed.

"If your old prayers are no longer available to you that's fine. Just focus on your breath."

Garrett had a momentary sense that he was still looking at her, through his closed eyes. She smiled and waited but he remained silent. Beneath them, the horse threw up its head with a snort. The dusty sunshine buzzed with insects.

She studied his face. She noticed wrinkles around his mouth; in the sun-browned skin of his face his eyes were a faded blue; the hair at his temples was lighter than she remembered and streaked with grey. Her beautiful boy was not becoming a man anymore. He was aging. When had that happened? How hadn't she noticed? Had it been sometime in these lost years?

She wanted to reach out and tuck a curl behind his ear, stroke the hair down over his forehead and rub his nose the way that had always made him shake his head. Perhaps she shouldn't think of him that way any more.

"And every time your attention wanders–" Garrett flinched. She felt guilty of prying. "– into the past, to memories, or the future, worrying – escort it back to your breath. Accept and return. That is the required discipline."

The words rose and fell in a rhythm strangely hypnotic, like the swing of a pendulum. She wondered where he had learned that way of speaking. Was it from this man Arshu?

She gazed out over the meadow. As she watched, a single blue butterfly flew up out of the flowers, circled their heads then fluttered down into the grass. In the distance, she could see Rayan making his way towards them. He followed a hedgerow that ran the length of the valley bottom, right past the rock where she sat. The darker foliage was strung through with angelica in long lacy lines.

Garrett felt a certain peace. An hour ago she had been frightened at what she would find, nervous at meeting Jason. Her eyes returned to his face. How confident he was to sit there meditating, comfortable without the need for talking. And to think how the silences of the last few years had been so full of reproach. Was it alright now, just like that? He said he had forgiven her and accepted what had happened. *I know it wasn't your fault.* That's what he had said. That took understanding and courage. She studied his calm face and felt proud. What had happened to change him? Was it this place? She hadn't lied when she had said it was beautiful. It was. She looked at the peaceful valley, at the orchards and distant buildings and the bright stream coiling through the fields. Two years this place had taken him from her.

He had found a home, but what sort of home? She thought of their old family house outside Brighton, and the shut door to David's study. There were square shadows on the walls; the last time Jason had been home he had taken down all the pictures showing his father. What was it he had said then? All attachment is suffering. She studied his motionless, weather-browned face. *What a terrible, cowardly thought by which to live.*

She could see Rayan more clearly now. Black-faced sheep galloped away at his approach.

Chapter 31

Would you believe it? The woman was asleep. Now that was cool.

Kirtananda stepped around the car, his Glock semi-automatic drawn, held at his hip. He stopped by the windscreen and read the sticker above the tax disc. A hospital staff parking permit made out to *Dr C Garrett.* It was her car alright. He peered through the glass. But this woman in the passenger seat was someone else.

The impatience of adrenaline and amphetamines jerked his arm up. Who cares? She had come with her. They must have talked. No loose ends.

A half-eaten apple sat browning on the dashboard shelf next to a packet of B&H gold and two mini pork pies in a cellophane wrapper. An empty crisp packet lay in the woman's lap. Kirtananda glanced up and down the beach. There was no-one in sight. As he screwed a silencer onto the muzzle of his gun, he watched the woman through the side window. Her body was still. Too still. He smashed the window glass. Still the woman did not move. He pushed her forehead with the silencer; her head flopped over to the side at an unnatural angle.

She was already dead. He stared at blood staining a corner of her mouth.

It has begun.

He thought again of the people driving down the motorway, of the old lady having trouble with her car gears outside the hospital. *A healed world coming.* This scene he was looking at would be repeated continually, everywhere.

He leaned in through the shattered glass and pocketed the cigarettes. He hesitated then picked up the pork pies between three fingers, like a waiter forking empty glasses.

He moved quickly back up into the trees. The shore path was still clear but he stayed under cover. Should he return to his cabin for the dogs? Or more firepower? Maybe get the guys. Long experience kept his excitement on a tight leash. When he removed the silencer the metal barrel was cold. Stay on it. She was close now.

He made his way along the shore towards the headland and the Valley. On the way, he tried one of the pork pies. They were bloody brilliant.

Chapter 32

A red double-decker to Peckham Rye roared down Whitehall, covering White in diesel exhaust. The COBRA meeting was due to start in ten minutes. They were walking; access to Downing Street was one of the Metropole's advantages.

"Well let me know as soon as you can." Hanratty broke the connection on his headset. "Damn!"

White waited for the young man to collect himself. A second 138 roared past, closely chased by third, both empty. They passed Horse Guards Parade. Kerbs and grounds were clear of cars. They had been for the last twenty years. White could remember the incident that had resulted in the new parking restrictions – the IRA's mortar attack on Downing Street in '91, carried out from a van parked in the adjacent Avenue – he had felt the blast's shockwave in his office. Could they be dealing with a terrorist incident now?

"Sir, the hospital reports are still being collated. CDSC have reported in but the communication's now carrying a military classification."

"I know," White said. "I sent the order out! James, I need that national survey!"

"I was told it's not being released to us." Hanratty said, his voice defensive and a little breathless as he hurried to keep up with White's long strides. In the distance Big Ben chimed the half-hour, poking up out of the surrounding smog like a wizard's tower, sunlight striking glints off the gilt. "They're sending it up the channels."

He was going into a cabinet-level briefing without up-to-the-minute reports. Great. White felt his stomach muscles tighten.

"Go through the D.G.'s office!" White controlled his voice. It wasn't Hanratty's fault.

They showed their passes at the black steel gates closing off Downing Street. White studied the twelve foot high metal barrier, terrorism on his mind again. It had been erected in 1989 by Margaret Thatcher. Before then, anyone had been able to wander into the street unchallenged. The Cold War, The IRA,

Islamic terrorists: what was that old slogan? Things can only get better. A facile thought. And untrue.

A police officer nodded them through. White led Hanratty down a tall, residential street. To the left the white rusticated buildings of the Foreign Office rose up like a chalk cliff, dominating the facing row of seventeenth century ministerial homes. They passed the black door of Number Ten. Two uniformed policemen stood outside. White glanced at his aide.

"Nervous?"

"A little, sir," Hanratty admitted.

"Don't be. You won't be attending the meeting itself. Your role is communications. I need to know breaking news. You've also got to get those collated reports."

White saw Hanratty consult his phone. He wondered if he had been wise to bring the young man. He was looking overstrung. But he needed Hanratty. There was no-one else until his recalled staff arrived. White didn't know what he would be doing an hour from now but if he was still in a job he might require his own people.

They left the street by a guarded door and entered a small, air-conditioned lobby. White led Hanratty down a spiral staircase, two flights, then along a narrow corridor to another door manned by a plainclothes officer. The building had a confused feel to it, part heritage, part office. White thought of the steel-and-copper-lined basement walls beyond the door.

"Commander Charles White. And James Hanratty."

They waited while the policeman looked up their names on a sheet of paper. White approved. At the highest levels, a person, questions, eye contact: they beat biometrics every time.

"Still hot out there, sir?"

"Beach weather." White replied. "I should be lying beside a pool."

The officer grinned, reading down his sheet. "I'll be in Fuengirola next week."

"Good for you," White said.

The policeman put away his register and held open the door. "Very good sir."

They walked through into an underground hall subdivided into four rooms by glass walls. Three were crammed with computer equipment – terminals, server stacks, router junctions – and small desks where technicians sat, mostly wearing headphones. The facing room, the largest, held a sizeable oval desk and a bank of conference monitors. Two men and a woman sat waiting.

White recognised Roger Thorpe, Metropolitan Deputy Police Commissioner. Thorpe was also liaison to JTAC. White knew the other man too. Colonel Buzz Allcock was Vice-Chief of the Defence Staff, also invited because of the possible terrorist link. Allcock's square shoulders and chiselled face reminded White of the stone memorials along Whitehall.

The woman was his service chief, Dame Frances Burnett, Director General of MI5. When she saw White she rose from the table and came out to meet them.

"Quite a nest you've stirred up for us today, Charlie."

"Frances," White smiled and shook hands. Burnett's lacquered silver hair was matched to her steel-bright eyes, sharp and no-nonsense. Her nod had been required to convene COBRA so fast. He was grateful she was there. Staring at her he remembered a line from his schooldays from a facetious history master. "All power corrupts, but we need the electricity."

"We'll have a full house for you."

White heard the unspoken question: *Again Charles? Again?*

White turned to Hanratty but was beaten to an introduction.

"James Hanratty isn't it?"

White watched Hanratty stammer agreement about his own name. White very much doubted Dame Burnett had known about Hanratty's existence before today. MI5 numbered over three-and-a-half thousand employees at the last count, nearly half recruited in the last three years. But Burnett was always well briefed.

"Do you have the survey data?"

"Not yet."

White could sense Burnett's impatience. He turned to Hanratty, "Chase it again. And check the presentation set up would you?"

Hanratty went to speak to a technician. As they entered the conference room, Burnett added over her shoulder, "By the way, I invited the CDSC manager. They need someone here and he seemed logical."

On cue, a disembodied voice filled the room, "Simon Kirkpatrick," half-human, "...*has entered the conference*," half-machine. One of the monitors came to life with a click and flicker of light. White watched, curious to see how the man matched his mental image. He was dressed in a beige suit and kipper tie patterned with a round motif that could have been golf balls. He smoothed six strands of hair over his otherwise bald head and adjusted his tie.

"Hi, er, hi! Hello! Can you see me?"

The men seated at the table looked up. Allcock said, *sotto voce*, "I'm afraid so."

"Yes, thank you," Burnett called out in a musical voice, hard consonants sounding her vowels like separate bells. "Please wait until we're quorate."

White watched Kirkpatrick's head wobble. The encrypted video link stuttered, turning Kirkpatrick's tie into a brief snow of coloured pixels.

The technician re-entered the room with a remote. "I've loaded your slide deck. These buttons take you forward and back." White nodded. He looked around and wondered what he had started, if he was looking at the very public end of his career.

The technician disappeared in a mouse-like flurry of small steps. Another monitor flickered into life. "Peter Hammond... *has entered the conference.*" White instantly recognised the new face. White-haired, long-nosed and patrician, Sir Peter Hammond was the government's Chief Medical Officer, the most senior health official in the UK government: the Nation's Doctor. He had been sent copies of the lab reports.

"How long's this going to take then?" A tall man, slim with energy, strode into the room carrying a sheaf of files against a creased pink shirt. He gave off an impression of permanent hurry. White recognized Andy Connell, Downing Street's chief spin doctor. With his free hand, the Director of Communications and Strategy for the Prime Minister thumbed a key on an electronic organiser then said, "Oh hello Buzz! They drag you in on this too?"

Connell made his way around the table. White had the image of a bulldog fighting on little sleep. The man's long, jowled face was belligerent and darkened by overwork. Passing Burnett he paused fractionally then moved on, hand extended towards the Colonel. White, an amateur of French chivalric history, recognised the Cut Sublime, Allcock's granite face standing in for mountain scenery inspected to avoid acknowledgement of Burnett's existence.

White was not surprised. The mutual antipathy between Burnett and Connell was public knowledge. On Burnett's appointment – around Christmas two years ago – tabloid headlines had focused on her being female. The coverage had been incessant and increasingly prurient. But only for a week. Burnett was not the sort of woman who took long to master her advantages. Rumour had it that she had made a present of a file to Connell, tied with a ribbon and labelled "Something for the festive season". The stories had dried up as quickly as they had appeared.

Connell dropped heavily into a chair at one end of the table. He took out his organizer and began thumbing in a message. "Right let's make this quick shall we? It's Prime Minister's Questions in the House," Connell inspected his wrist and gave a short bark, "In ten minutes. What are we talking about here?"

Chapter 33

"Rayan, this is Christine."

A young man stood at the edge of the rug where they sat. He wore a purple bandana around his temples and a Tshirt with the Asari logo. He looked from Garrett to Skyler and back then grinned. "Same mouth and nose."

"Her car is parked at the south jetty," Skyler said, his voice brittle with authority. "Her friend's still there... Cherry? Please bring her down here."

Rayan nodded and set off towards the beach. Garrett wondered at the command in Skyler's voice. It reminded her of his father.

"While we're waiting, let me show you some more of our home."

They walked together down into the valley. The footpath they were on joined with another that led down from the cliff top facing the sea. On the forested slopes Garrett could see yellow tracks connecting separate clusters of buildings. Skyler pointed out buildings, crops, the irrigation system. He stopped by a clearing planted with saplings.

"Our newest orchard. I helped the planting two years ago. It's a good spot. These trees are naturally deep rooting and suit this light, sandy soil. We used Arshu's system of Invisible Sympathies."

Garrett remembered Boorman's description of an argument among the vegetables, over delivering food – for a man who had tried to leave. A prisoner, with his family. What was his name? Sikanda? Yes.

Who's Sikanda? Garrett stopped herself from speaking. What had Prenderville said? Wait. Be patient.

"And here's where we process waste." H⸱ ⸱ ⸱ ⸱ ⸱ to a series of stepped water tanks. "The water comes f river Nadis. We use sand filters and reed bed particularly effective. They oxygenate mic gravel: basically they help the system breath

"To support denitrification."

"Exactly. It's a purification process." Skyler began to wave his hands. "Outside this valley, the way our species pollutes its home is a kind of madness. Arshu believes our Earth Mother is sick, that she has been poisoned by primitive tribes competing to satisfy endless cravings. He accepts that we are the disease – we are responsible."

As they walked he continued to move his hands.

"Here we set an example. We understand the land mirrors us, so we begin with ourselves, making the cure within by purifying our minds." He made the strange cupping gesture again. "First we subdue desire. Then by cleansing and transcending ego, we resolve all principles and difference into one truth."

"What truth is that?"

"We are Asari first and last. Can you see the power in that Christine?"

Garrett felt a faint breeze rummage around her ears and ankles. She frowned. "I – I'm not sure I do. I am a woman, daughter, sister, mother, English, European–"

"See? See the Maya? The fog of ego and illusion in your labels?"

He turned away. She wondered if she had offended him. As she caught up with him, she noticed his posture was better than she remembered. He held himself up straight, taller.

"We have dissolved those ancient problems. We have but one identity."

The words of her incomplete thought continued to burst inside her, silent, protesting. *In my time I've been Christian, non-believer, progressive, conservative. At the moment I have good health, the right to vote, opportunities as a medical researcher, responsibilities as a doctor...*

Whitman's line came back to her then, an adamant echo, as she followed Skyler down into the valley. *I contain multitudes.* She remembered how his ending words had comforted her these past years. *Missing me one place search another, I stop somewhere waiting for you.* She was with him at last, close enough to reach out and touch. Why did he seem a world away?

In all your travels, haven't you seen it Jason? We are all different, and not just different as tribes – we are each different differently. If it's cosmic glory you're after it's all around you.

"We have learned that truly to live, one must first die to oneself and be reborn."

He pointed down the track where it climbed towards the end of the Valley. He stared as if looking straight through his hand. "We believe this world is but a shadow cast by the Ideal, this life but a path-house on the eternal Journey of a Soul."

On the other side of the valley Garrett could see a segmented domed roof poking out of the earth like a half-buried egg. Behind it a thickened pole rose up into the air, silvered and topped by a small cowl.

What had he called it? The Path House of Health. Her eyes strayed back to the needling silver chimney. *What was that?* Her patterning mind reached for connection and shied.

They approached the head of the valley. The wide slope of a hill rose above them. Its tilted face of rock and scrub vegetation was dominated by three oval features: two large elliptical pools – small lakes – side-by-side, halfway up the hillside; and set above them, centred high on the grey-browed summit, what looked at first glance like the ruins of a small amphitheatre.

"What is that?" Garrett pointed upward.

"You have arrived at the place of faith. Where all paths start and end. Come. I'll show you."

They crossed a wooden bridge above a weir curved like a smile. As she walked Garrett studied the formations above her. She traced the silver course of the stream down from the wooded summit. It foamed in short falls and trickled through stands of dark pine trees to reach the two mirror-still pools. Fringed with reeds, their calm surfaces reflected the blue of the sky. A memory of Jimmy the Suit staring at the sea came to her, together with old lines he would have recognised. *If I were called in to construct a religion I would make use of water... where any-angled light would congregate endlessly.*

Skyler reached the pools and continued on up along a narrow ridge of broken shales separating the waters. He reached the third and highest oval feature and stopped beside an entrance ramp.

The structure was larger and flatter than Garrett had guessed. It reminded her of an excavated Greek theatre. A wide oval depression formed a shallow basin perhaps a few hundred yards across, paved with white stone unblemished as the corneas of a child. In the centre was a pattern of sunken channels – like a giant labyrinth – dug into the ground, perfectly circular in outline, enclosing a central hole. Like an iris around a pupil, Garrett thought.

"What we teach cannot be learned through a lecture. It must be experienced, sitting alone, listening alone, thinking of nothing, in right meditation, beginning always with the breath. In entering this Valley, you have taken the first step on that journey. And this is the second."

Skyler stretched out his arms.

"Welcome to the Eye of Faith."

He led the way down the ramp. When Garrett reached the bottom her left arm bumped the side wall near her elbow. The pain brightened and faded.

Skyler did not notice her stop. He walked clockwise around the oval perimeter across open ground paved in cut blocks of unpolished marble, sandy underfoot. Set at regular intervals in the outer ashlar walls were stone shelves filled with old, melted wax, and doorways, opening onto bare cells.

"Prayer bays."

Skyler's words echoed off the dressed masonry surfaces, reinforcing their cloistered seclusion. He glanced up at the sun. "I observe the Prime Hours. I will need to pray again soon."

Garrett stopped at a large mosaic design laid into the marble pavement. Hundreds of small gold tiles formed the shape of an eight-spoked wheel. It was large as a man spread-eagled.

"The eightfold noble path," Skyler's raised voice was patient. He waited for her at the next mosaic, a Chi Rho, Roman in style, depicted in red, orange and yellow sandstone.

Dark radial lines ran from each mosaic towards the central circle. A many-rayed eye. Surrounded by faith signs. Garrett blinked. The Asari logo.

"This place is sacred to us."

"It feels like a monastery."

Skyler smiled with approval.

"It is the hub of our community. Some of our greatest achievements occur here. Now you must make a decision: where you wish to walk in from – where your faith starts." When Garrett looked puzzled he pointed down at the Chi Rho and added, "Perhaps here?"

"I haven't been to Mass since your father died."

Skyler looked annoyed, as if she had gone off-script. He considered her for a long while.

"Science. That's your only religion now isn't it?"

"Science can't fairly be described as a religion."

"No?"

"No," Garrett said, almost offended. She wondered how he was able to irritate her so quickly. "It rejects knowledge without evidence."

Skyler walked around the Chi Rho mosaic. He swung his hands in sharp cutting strokes as he spoke. "Your science offers nothing permanent, nothing eternal. No being, no person, no central absolute truth. It is forever explaining God's jokes, and then feeling resentful at being less popular."

Garrett tried to ignore the sneer in his voice. "To require facts–"

"Take reality too seriously," Skyler interrupted, "and you don't see the illusion. To be enlightened is to understand the true nature of this material world: Maya."

Garrett made an effort to summon her patience, as she had endlessly when he had been a child, "Science simply asks, if you wish to claim something is true, to show why."

"Ah Christine, you have all the answers don't you? You think you have lost your faith and found your reason. Don't you understand reason requires an act of faith too? In logic and relevance?" He was sneering again. "You have a long way to go." He shook his head. "Though I will say, it is on a road many still have a distance to travel with you. No matter." He recovered himself. "Just follow me."

He began walking along the radial line away from the Chi Rho. He spoke over his shoulder. "We have outgrown him too but Christ is as good a starting point as any. He was a true teacher of his time. The important thing is to recognise the truth – you know what that is, don't you?"

The bracing motto of the Royal Society, borrowed from Horace's retiring gladiator, ran through Garrett's mind. *Nullius in verba. "Take nobody's word for it."*

"Verified fact," she suggested.

Skyler laughed. "No. There are three sources of truth: scripture, personal witness and true teachings. The last is the strongest, but there are believed to be only three true teachers alive, and only one of those is known to us."

"Arshu."

"Yes. We are blessed. We receive at least one true teaching every year from him."

"How do you know the other two teachers exist?"

"Arshu has told us. One, his own teacher, he will not speak of. The other is the Laughing Master, an adept with a rare gift.

He has been in seclusion on a hidden Pacific Island for the last eighty years, with twenty chosen disciples. No-one else will meet him now before his passing on."

"Why is he called the Laughing Master?"

Skyler smiled. "Have you ever looked between your thoughts, into the place you find yourself and your not-self?" Garrett waited. "There you can also find where a laugh starts."

Garrett stared, puzzled.

"It's the opposite place from where a thought ends. Both are difficult mental journeys. The Laughing Master has made them and chosen to dwell where all laughter starts."

"It sounds a bit premeditated. I thought surprise–"

"Or maybe postmeditated!" Skyler said, delighted. He stopped.

They had reached the edge of the central maze. At opposite points along the circular perimeter, sets of stone steps were cut in the earth. They led down into the dense network of sunken corridors. Garrett could see candles stacked on stone ledges at the foot of the nearest steps. She looked across the narrow passages as they converged in spirals towards the centre. She remembered the prayer labyrinth beneath the picture of the Harrowing in St Andrew's Church. This one was far more complex.

"There are only two entrances that will lead to the centre. We believe the ways to reach Enlightenment are varied – the paths of the Warrior, Farmer, Scientist, Scholar – but the first and most significant fork in the path is the choice between the lives of Action and Contemplation. The two correct entrances represent that choice."

Garrett gazed down into the maze. How had he come to his extraordinary beliefs? The Eye of Faith. Yes of course. It came back to faith.

She remembered first hearing the news of David's death. It had been a sunny day. They had been sitting in the garden having a late tea. Jason had blinked once, a single slow styptic blink. He had not looked straight at her since that moment, until today.

She stared desperately into the Eye, into the central iris. She couldn't hide from her intuition – that faith was a response to fear, of random fate, of loneliness, of unrecoverable loss and death. She felt a surge of sympathy followed by something harder. To be prepared to believe in answers to the most important questions of life – about human nature, right and wrong, the nature of nature – without reasons or facts: it seemed a terrible resignation.

She noticed Skyler studying her with a critical eye, intent as a clockmaker studying the jewelled workings of a timepiece. She found it disconcerting.

"As usual, you present a problem. Your nature seems to me divided. You are a doctor and a research scientist: action and contemplation combined."

"What is this labyrinth for?"

"The Eye of Faith is not a place for the uninitiated." He watched her calm study of the maze with some amusement. "You won't figure it out."

"It does look complex."

"I'll give you a hint if you like."

Garrett looked at Skyler, mildly amused by his air of mystery. He met her gaze.

"Growth."

"Growth?"

"Yes."

"That's it?"

A call echoed out again over the valley from the distant white tower. "I must sit again. Will you join me?"

"Sit?"

"Meditate."

"I – to tell you the truth, I'm still worried about my friend Cherry. She–"

"Ray is getting her!"

"What if she's woken up and can't find me?"

"Look," Skyler let out an angry breath, "It is time for me to perform Dues. If you want to go check on your friend, go!"

"I'm worried she won't know where I am. She's not very well at the moment."

Skyler shrugged. He turned and walked back to the outer perimeter. Garrett followed. He entered one of the prayer bays, took off his sandals and settled into a full lotus facing the centre of the Eye. He placed his sandals side-by-side in front of him.

Garrett stopped at the entrance to the stone cell. She put out a hand then withdrew it. His eyes were already closed. Dust stirred on the marble pavement. Somewhere a bird cawed.

"Skyler, why is there no-one else here?"

He did not reply.

"Skyler?"

The silence remained unbroken.

"Skyler, please–"

Skyler sighed and opened his eyes.

"I told you, most of us have gone. They have joined the Exodus. I will explain when you are ready."

"Why did you ask me to come here?"

Skyler shifted in his place on the ground. He tilted his head back to look at her. "I have been invited to take Sanyas–"

"–what's that?"

"A privilege. It is also a vow, of chastity and separation, a saying goodbye to familiar things, to the world of Maya and illusion, to childhood and family. I'm going away."

"Where?"

"I can't tell you. But I will be gone a long time. In fact, I may not be coming back."

"Is that why you asked me to come? To say goodbye?"

"My teacher Arshu suggested it, to see if you would be interested in joining us." Skyler saw that Garrett was taken aback. "We recruit most of our new devotees through friends and birth families. It is common for us to make this offer, before Sanyas. Afterwards that is not possible."

"What do you mean?"

"Sanyasins have connection to only one family. Asari."

"When did... Arshu... suggest this?"

"Yesterday, just before I called."

Garrett looked around. She frowned. "I need to talk to you about someone who stayed here. Do you know a man called Christmas?"

Skyler laughed. "I know several. Five in fact."

Garrett stared. "Five?"

"Yes. They all took that name last year, when they chose to be part of Rebirth."

"Rebirth? One of them is dead."

Skyler shrugged. "I didn't know any of them. I work in the House of Education." Skyler looked suddenly awkward. "I – I shouldn't have shown impatience with you earlier." He rolled his shoulders. "I must perform my Dues now. I cannot be late. Why don't you look around? I won't be long. Ray should be here soon with your friend."

Garrett stared at Skyler. His eyes were closed again. His breathing was regular and unhurried. She waited but he remained silent. It was as if for him the world had suddenly disappeared.

Behind him the prayer cell was empty. Dust and a few dry leaves had gathered in corners. Garrett noticed a plaque bearing an inscription mounted low on the wall beside the entrance. She bent down to read it.

"Please leave your shoes and mind at the door."

Chapter 34

The Cobra meeting room was radio-secure. Its basement walls were lead and copper-lined. Any outside eavesdropper would hear only silence.

At that moment, there was near-silence inside the room too. General Allcock was staring at the ceiling, his head back. Roger Thorpe had his eyes closed. At the other end of the table Connell tapped at his electronic organizer, visibly bored. Only Sir John Hammond appeared interested, leaning forward on screen, his face creased into a still frown as if facing a wind.

White had decided to give the facts in chronological order. Detailing early case histories he had lost most of his audience. And he was having trouble with his voice. His teeth clenched between each sentence. He clicked on his remote to display a new slide.

"The lab team focused on pathological anomalies but this question of transmission remained unresolved."

"Over the next four days with no further cases it was assumed that, although three people had died, there was no wider implication for public health."

At the other end of the table Connell continued to tap at his organizer. He gave an audible sigh.

"Then yesterday afternoon new information came to light. It appears that administrative errors in neighbouring hospitals and other agencies have resulted in a number of related deaths going unnoticed."

At the words 'administrative errors' Connell put down his organiser.

"How many deaths?" Thorpe asked.

On screen, Kirkpatrick patted his head. White advanced the slide. "By yesterday evening there were a total, not including the first three, of fifteen new cases, including five fatalities, from three hospitals all in the Brighton area." A buzz of talk began around the room. White reflected a moment on the statistics and felt a sudden burst of confidence. Of course he had been right to raise this alarm. Of course he had! This was real, not his own private nightmare. A queer joy, of duty done come what may, shot through him.

"And as of *now*?" Connell demanded loudly.

"In the last twelve hours, there have been a further twenty cases and eight new deaths." White clicked through to a new slide showing a graph. He glanced at Burnett. She gave him a small, distinct nod. The set of her mouth was firm. His voice strengthened "These latest figures, which I received just under an hour ago, suggest the outbreak is continuing to accelerate. We are still waiting for the results from a national data survey," White turned to acknowledge Kirkpatrick who was fiddling with his tie again, "And clarification of many outstanding alerts. There's also a possible related outbreak in Indonesia."

"Confirmed?"

"Not as yet."

"What's the data suggesting—"

"—I know about malaria." Allcock interrupted Hammond. "I was stationed in Singapore eight years." He took the opportunity to be dry. "Last I looked, we don't have swamps or a tropical climate." He looked around the room. "That's the natural environment for malaria."

"True," White agreed. "But recent information indicates that the strain we are dealing with may not be wholly natural."

The room fell silent. At the other end of the table Connell folded his arms.

"The anomalies I mentioned earlier – the high parasitemia and mixed broods – indicated from the start that this strain might be unusual. But it was only this morning, on the discovery of new data by Porton Down, that it became clear that there was a real possibility of an unnatural genesis to this outbreak."

White paused to collect his thoughts. There was no interruption.

"Firstly," White clicked the remote, "Slide images of stained saliva were found containing malaria parasite forms only normally found in the salivary glands of the mosquito vector."

"Again?" Thorpe said irritably.

White stated the implication simply. "This malaria may have the ability for direct human-to-human transmission, infecting orally."

"Like that bird flu?" Allcock demanded.

White nodded, appreciating the quickness of the man. "Not dissimilar. Only the malaria parasite is a thousand times more sophisticated than a virus."

White paused again to show a new slide. "Secondly, genetic tests showed the presence of foreign DNA incompatible with natural mutation."

Thorpe flapped a hand. "Meaning?"

"This malaria could be an artificial – genetically-modified – strain." Burnett explained. Thorpe's eyes widened.

Chapter 35

Kirtananda rounded a turn in a steep sheep-run high up on a ridge on the north side of the Valley. He stopped under the partial shade of a twisted Scots pine, its upper trunk bent nearly horizontal by the coastal wind. Below him the sunlight twinkled off the segmented glass dome of the House of Healing. His body became still, eyes fixed on a point near the summit of the hill at the head of the valley.

Rayan slipped on loose flints as he came around the turn. He squatted down behind Kirtananda; his knees touched his ears. Moment later Dharma appeared on the path, followed by Zakiya and Harith. Dharma reached up and swung himself onto the tree's lowered trunk; his body undulated to unseen music piped through his earbuds. Zakiya and Harith looked at each other, grinned, and dropped down either side of Kirtananda.

Heads turned together. The group became still. They looked with a single gaze at the woman standing beside a stone circle.

Chapter 36

"We have one unconfirmed piece of intelligence that may be related. Two years ago we received information on the theft of an engineered disease agent from a lab that had previously broken GM protocols." White managed to keep his voice even and controlled. "The reported purpose was commercial: the creation of a ground-breaking new vaccine. The pathogen stolen was an unusual strain of malaria."

"I confess the report did not come to mind when I heard about the first deaths. However it did this morning, when I received news of the new infections. I looked up the old case notes."

White clicked the remote.

"The intelligence we have says that a malaria parasite was being genetically re-engineered using transgenic material, specifically sequences from *Streptococcus*, the same cross strain identified in this outbreak. In my opinion, this cannot be a coincidence. A Professor Richardson was responsible. There is some evidence suggesting a live trial might have been conducted, and covered up."

"Covered up?" Connell repeated.

"Development in the UK?" Allcock echoed.

Connell spoke, his voice suggesting limited patience. "Do you have any secondary sources?" White frowned. Connell ducked his head like a parent expecting the right answer, "…any corroborating evidence for the spy story part?"

"No."

"For God's sake." Connell threw his organiser onto the table in disgust. "I haven't got time to sit here listening to Five's rumours." He glanced at Burnett. "Stick to the facts."

White put the remote control down on the table. "There's more. Professor Richardson and his family disappeared soon after the theft of the samples from the lab. They have not been seen since. There was a police investigation. It uncovered evidence that kidnapping might be involved; the case is currently classified as a missing persons. Due to Richardson's clearances and the nature of his protocol violations, intelligence reports were filed but a decision was taken that there was no credible national security threat. That may prove to have been a mistake."

At the end of the table, Connell dropped his head as if he had been shot.

"From where I'm sitting," he raised his head, "There seems to have been rather too many of those."

"We *could* be talking a bioweapon here," Allcock said. "A WMD deployed on the UK mainland!"

"It's a possibility we must consider," White said.

Hammond cleared his throat. "Can I ask–"

"P*ossibility?*" Connell's interruption was scornful. He raised his voice. "Let me make one thing absolutely clear. We've considered the *possibility* of a biological attack three times already this year. Each time it's amounted to nothing and each time we've been accused of negative propaganda, government by fear, all that liberal rubbish. Before we run away with ourselves, before we say or do anything, let's take a step back and look at the facts shall we?"

"We start with the *fact* that this disease has killed a bunch of people..." Connell leaned his chair back on two legs. He sounded bored.

"I wouldn't call it a bunch," White replied.

"...Now some odd test results come up," Connell looked straight at White. He appeared to be developing a dislike for him. As an ex-journalist, he particularly disliked being edited. "We have a two-year-old spook report that might or might not be related," he paused to look around the table then continued. "Now all of a sudden this thing is a WMD attack on the UK mainland. Fact is, we've a bunch of unusual deaths and we'd better find out why."

"I'd agree with that," Hammond said. "We need to repeat the lab research. I'd like to know more about these new cases..."

"Christ!" Connell thumped the table and looked slowly around the room. He was starting to enjoy himself. "Our USP is *competent*, honest government!" He looked around in frustration. "An end to sleaze, whiter-than-white standards in public life, efficient public services. I spend my life getting that message across." He lounged back in his chair. "And then last week we have more cash for honours leaks involving *six* backbench MPs, *eight* peers, seven of them bishops of course–"

"I'm not sure you appreciate the seriousness–" White said.

But Connell brushed aside the interruption, hitting his stride. "Yesterday twenty million identity card records go walkabout in a civil servant's lunch bag. And now–" his eyes bulged, "Now a dozen – or what was it? twenty deaths? – from some bug – turns up yet another intelligence cock-up!"

Connell rose up in his chair. "When news of those deaths gets out this story is going to be big." He closed his eyes and nodded agreement with himself. "Real big. Day after tomorrow, it'll have overtaken the Portland Pigs." He snorted. "Trust me, the one thing the British public love more than their cute animals is to be scared: happens every few months. Look at the fifty Legionnaire's deaths in January: that story ran and ran. And the hysterical reaction to those two hundred Dutch-strain measles cases in Cornwall over Easter! Never mind more are killed every day on our roads..."

His eyes narrowed. "The Street is going to be all over us like a bad rash. If we're going to mount any sort of effective response, any sort of damage-limitation, we need to have all the facts out in one hit."

"We must understand the intelligence errors." Connell switched back to White. He eyed him with suspicion. "W*hat* happened? *How* did it happen? *Who* was responsible?"

White heard the unspoken question. *If the shit hits the fan who can we get it to stick to?*

Hammond cleared his throat again but Connell did not break eye contact with White.

"Well?" From his tone he did not expect a helpful answer.

Chapter 37

Garrett stood above the maze. There was still no sign of Cherry. She decided if she didn't see her in ten minutes she would go back for her herself. She thought of Jason. Did he really meditate every prime-numbered hour round the clock? It made her rule of prayer in the novitiate look almost dissolute.

She studied the twists and turns of the maze's stone corridors laid out beneath her. The path from the closest entrance led, by a circuitous route without paths leading inward, back out to another; she deduced all entrances between those two led to dead ends. By similar eliminations, she quickly identified probable entrances.

The analysis of paths to the centre proved harder. A depth-first tree search following one wall was foiled in the standard way by a secondary maze. And the centre was surrounded by a double spiral path – an old trap. She worked backwards using Themaux's algorithm to narrow the possible combinations. But as the outlines of complete solutions continued to fail, she began to appreciate the sly complicated mind behind the puzzle. It occurred to her that this Arshu might have a sense of humour.

She persisted, much as a player used to winning who meets her match and realises she will probably lose determines to make a game of it anyway. As she paced the perimeter she noticed words carved on one of the low square bollards flanking the nearest steps down into the maze.

"You have only moments to live."

Garrett moved to the next entrance.

"Take your desires for reality."

Looking across the maze walls, touched lightly by vertigo, memories returned from her first WHO assignment to Gujarat, of a trip to the Pakistan border, seeing the Golden Temple in Amritsar and the quotations written on the walls; and the mathematical beauty of a mosque in Lahore, in the arrangement of flowers engraved in tiles and in the emptiness of the prayer rooms. Outside, there had been a line of shoes there too.

"Don't just do something, sit there!"

She stopped reading. She found it depressing.

In a neighbouring meadow, a small herd of brindled cows tore at browned grass. She could see the placid sideways movements of their jaws and the green foam from the chewed cud around their lips.

At least Jason was in good health. He was eating well. He looked fit and tanned and happy. She chewed on this consolation for a while.

On a field high up one side of the valley, she could see a half-harvested patch of wheat shining like a flop of greased hair. Jason had pointed it out as they had walked up, and talked about making flour for bread. From the nearest cluster of buildings a cock crow filled the hazy air.

A whole community was living here, dreaming its dreams, but also growing food, building shelters, rearing children, meditating, withdrawing from the world…

It was a waste maybe, this gazing at a gigantic collective navel – but if it was a happy dream, like a childish wish, perhaps it was harmless. After all, Darwin had played a bassoon to his plants and shouted at worms. And not everyone had to think like a scientist. Even she didn't demand that the dreams of art – a painting or piece of music – be verifiable.

Something Jason had said haunted her. *Some of our greatest achievements occur here.* It chimed in spirit with the carved quotations.

Did he mean in meditating? Achieving some mental state?

It seemed to her there could be no distinction to any thought cultivated by sitting alone on a floor with nothing at stake, no-one in jeopardy. Perhaps concentration could be practiced in some callisthenic mental gym. But just as no thought was a crime, so too with honour – it was in action, in choices surely, that moral virtue had to be achieved.

She had to get it over with and admit it – she couldn't pretend, not even for the time together that might grant. Jason's words were babble to her. Although full of visions and claims to truth, as his voiced thoughts passed through her ears they became papery, insubstantial and fluttering, dry and frail as moth wings, all glory and grails. She tasted dust. As she looked out over the peaceful valley her heart was full of worry.

She remembered her dismay at the trade at Glastonbury, the brisk business done by the homeopathy, dream catcher and faith healing stalls. She could see how, followed step by hopeful step, the logic of those homespun fantasies might lead towards this extraordinary mental construction Jason had described. Pure subjectivity, his words were like transparent bricks in the towers and walls of an invisible castle, built on clouds on top of clouds, floating on air, and all resting on nothing.

What sustained it? Not theory alone. It couldn't, surely?

Jason's most devoutly-uttered words returned like an echo. *Arshu is pure love, pure thought, pure mind.* How he worshipped that man! The perfect father. Did he really think he was a god? Such complete worship must help sustain the illusions.

Suddenly she remembered Christmas dead with a hole in his head, and then a crude drawing of a monkey on a stick, and Prenderville's warnings

What happens when this collective dream collides with reality?

A stray thought rose, of what such total faith and real power might breed together. A tremor ran though her before she steadied herself. A community this small was perhaps powerful to its members, in their minds, in its locality, but no further.

"A rupee for your thoughts?"

"Oh! Jas – Skyler. How was your meditating?" He looked brighter, visibly refreshed.

"Good. I was chanting the million names of Arshu."

"Names," Garrett nodded. "Why?"

His eyes unfocused for a moment. "We are told one of those names is his true name. If I chant through the variations at a thousand names a day, after a thousand days I will have spoken the true name of God."

"Do you believe–"

"I don't believe. I know," Skyler corrected gravely. "Have you solved our maze yet?"

"No."

"No one does unaided. And only one man has solved it with just the help I gave you: Osei, Head of the House of Healing. Don't worry, when you are ready I will tell you the Rule." Skyler faced the centre of the Eye, touched his hands to his forehead and muttered, "Mahatma! Guru-Sri-Kalki Arshu."

Garrett remembered the last time she had heard those words, in Dr Prenderville's study. He had translated for her.

"Skyler, I need to ask you something more about Christmas–"

Skyler made an impatient movement with a hand, as though throwing something away. He looked cross.

"It's likely he was carrying an unusually lethal strain of malaria. It's very important for me to understand how he became infected. Three other people he was recently in contact with died from it."

Skyler stared at Garrett. "Malaria?"

"Yes."

The muscle began to twitch again in Skyler's cheek. "Three people died?"

"Yes."

"None of it has anything to do with us here."

"It's what Christmas died from too."

Skyler's beads began clicking. He glanced past Garrett into the centre of the labyrinth then turned with the look of the scorned. "That's why you're here."

"You invited me, that's why I came. But I hoped I could talk to you about this case. People's lives may be at risk. Please would you help me understand what happened?"

"I told you, I didn't know Christmas, and his death has nothing to do with us here. That's it."

"I am only trying–"

"You think we are responsible." He looked angry.

Garrett became impatient. "Paul Fletcher – Spyder, one of the three first deaths – was also part of this community. Mike Boorman told me you are involved in some important–"

"How do you know about Barindra?" Skyler's voice was harsh.

"I'm in the middle of an investigation. I am trying to understand–"

"How do you know about Barindra?"

"Please, if you know anything –"

"How do you know about Barindra?"

Garrett blinked. "A man called Dr Prenderville put me in contact with him."

"Dr Prenderville. I see." Skyler's mouth twisted. His face was dark with blood.

"He told me a lot of worrying things. I wanted to ask you if they are true."

"You think they are."

"I'm asking because I'm concerned that–"

"–What sort of things?"

"Mike – Barindra – told me he left Asari Valley–"

"Rejection of Arshu is the one sin that cannot be forgiven."

"He said you were once friends. He was worried about you."

"You haven't changed at all have you? For a while, I thought maybe, maybe, you were open to the truth, open to change."

"I won't pretend Jason. I can't believe in your religion–"

"I am not Jason. I'm not your son any more. You will not infantilise me."

"I'm sorry. Skyler. I–"

"What's the matter with you?" Skyler stared into her face. "You make vague paranoid accusations. You undermine me, go behind my back and talk to liars and self-publicists like Prenderville. How do you think that makes me feel?" He shook his head in disgust. "You don't think of other people."

"I don't? What about you calling me twice a year?"

"Dad wouldn't recognise you any more."

"Perhaps neither of us," Garrett said. She couldn't look at him.

"Those jokes you used to tell about the novitiate – how long were you there? Six months? I'm surprised you lasted that long."

Garrett looked up at the surrounding cliffs. White clouds pushed over the high ramparts. Halfway up one side of the Valley, sunlight twinkled on the geodesic dome of the House of Healing.

Skyler sighed. "As usual, you have made me behave less well than I should."

"I made you? How?"

"Okay. You provoke me to say things I regret. Don't you get tired of being clever?"

Garrett flinched from the hatred.

"I can't believe I talked to you about the truth." Skyler said. "What a waste of breath. You can't hear. Even now, you're not telling me what you're really thinking. I can see it in your eyes."

"The truth? About what I really think? Alright I'll tell you what I'm really thinking. I'm frightened. I'm frightened by what I saw on the autopsy tables in Brighton and what we can't explain in the lab. I'm frightened about what has happened to you. I'm frightened by this place and the possibility there is a connection I don't understand. And the one person who could help me will not."

Garrett struggled with herself and lost. She began walking towards the exit ramp.

"There, that's better isn't it? Get the ugly truths out in the open." Garrett was surprised to hear what sounded like amusement.

"I'm going to find my friend, check she's okay. At least I can do that."

"Christine!"

Garrett ignored him. She was angry to discover her cheeks were wet.

"Christine."

Garrett continued to walk away.

"Mother!"

Garrett stopped. She stood with her back to him.

"I thought you weren't meant to call me that."

"I have not yet taken Sanyas."

Garrett watched sunlight play on the segmented glass roof of the House of Healing across the valley. She could see red clots of poppies scattered through the surrounding grass.

"I have learned it's all right to be frightened." The reflective note had returned to Skyler's voice.

Garrett turned around. She forced herself to speak. "I'm sorry."

"Me too."

"You're right. I am sometimes a smart arse."

"That's okay. So am I. Perhaps it runs in the family." Skyler smiled. "Thank you for telling me the truth. I don't understand your fears; but maybe we can talk about them."

Garrett watched the muscle in the side of his face begin to twitch continuously. What was wrong? What was disturbing him so much? Would he ever tell her *his* fears?

"I'd like that." Garrett made a small movement towards the ramp.

"I don't know where they've got to," Skyler said with a shake of his head. "Look, I'll come with you. I know all the paths along the shore."

"I've a better idea."

Garrett looked up, startled. A man stood above them at the top of the ramp. Short, barrel-chested, with cropped red hair, he wore a rainbow dog collar. Four men crowded behind him.

Skyler stepped backward. "Kirt. What are you doing here?"

"Looking for you."

"I'm busy right now."

Kirtananda shook his head. "You should show me more respect."

"Respect? For you?"

"Yes me."

"Why?"

"I will soon be your new acharya."

"You an acharya? Who says?"

"Arshu."

Skyler laughed. When Dharma growled and moved up to his shoulder, Kirtananda raised a restraining arm. Garrett could see the scorn on Skyler's face, mixed with open fear. *What was happening?*

Kirtananda looked down at Skyler and sighed. "You forget your place again. You are not even sanyasin yet."

He tilted his head to one side and studied Skyler. "I can't decide about you. Are you dumb or just ignorant?"

"I think it has to be dumb. You still don't get what's happening do you? You hear the local news recently?"

"I am on retreat. I do not need the stimulus of news," Skyler said.

Garrett watched the two men, Skyler thin, stiff with pride, the other man baiting him, in his look the intense, almost cross-eyed stare of an attack dog. He seemed to have some hold on her son. She feared for him.

"You don't, huh?" Kirtananda looked at Skyler. "It's begun."

"What's begun?" Skyler sounded bored.

"The plague is running."

"Plague?" Garrett said.

"Mother, don't–"

"Mother!" Kirtananda laughed and raised his arms. "Don't you remember what Arshu said: Rebirth through death. Transformation through sorrow. What did you think that meant? Just songs on your guitar?" Kirtananda spat out his disgust.

"You're lying," Skyler said.

"So you haven't seen the local reports of the deaths, in Cardiff and Merthyr Tydvill and Newport? You haven't heard the bulletins today? About the malaria plague?"

When Garrett started forward with a cry Kirtananda drew a gun out from the folds of his robes and pointed it straight at her. She heard the clear snick of the released safety. Behind the snub-nosed barrel the eyes of the gunman held the promise of violence. There was no reasoning with those eyes. She held still.

"Skyler, Arshu is mindful of leadership and succession; right now he is appointing his representatives on each continent. After the cleanup I am to stay here. I will become acharya. You and this woman are no longer needed. She is adding risk."

Garrett recognised the man from the hospital car park. A cold fear ran up her back. *Where's Cherry?*

"Where is –" The look of alarm in Skyler's eyes silenced Garrett before she could finish.

Kirtananda showed his teeth. "It was good of you to deliver her to us."

"You are mad."

"Arshu has spoken."

"This is your madness not his."

"You think too much." Kirtananda sighed. "You always did. Too many answers, to the wrong questions. I am stronger. I have faith. I believe without question." Kirtananda looked at his pistol.

"Wait!"

Kirtananda sighted along the barrel with both eyes open.

"You are making a terrible mistake. I spoke to Arshu this morning! He – he wanted to speak to you, of course. You were not here."

Kirtananda held the gun steady. "You are a fool and he is wise."

"He asked me to give you a message."

Kirtananda shifted his weight. The boy was playing for time.

"You think I'm lying. But I'm not. I swear I'm telling you the truth. Shall I tell you the message?"

Blood pounded in Kirtananda's ears. His men hissed at his back. This boy was irritating as a mosquito. After a moment he jerked his head.

"Arshu said he must speak with my mother when she arrived. He said it had something to do with a promotion. He said you would understand what he meant."

Kirtananda stared at Skyler

"Call him," Skyler said. "Ask him!"

Kirtananda's knuckles whitened. He shook his head from side to side.

Chapter 38

"Can we get back to the current cases?" Hammond said, his voice patient. "I'd like to hear more about the medical context so I can understand the public health implications first. I'm afraid I only received your lab summaries a few minutes before this meeting started. Your later reports didn't get through to me and we have not had time to contact the Surrey and Sussex NHS Trust. You say standard treatments were ineffective in the early cases." The room quietened. "Have we identified alternative protocols yet?"

White nodded. "I have spoken to the chief microbiologist at the Brighton Royal, Dr Da Costa. He reported the first cases and has been treating ten similar cases which have presented in the last twelve hours. He is recommending one of two new Artemesinin-based combinations: Artesunate with either Amodiaquine or Chlorproguanil-Dapsone," Hammond raised his eyebrows then nodded, looking down at some notes as White added, "Together with full blood transfusions every three hours."

At this, Hammond frowned, "For how long?"

"Dr Da Costa claims to have stabilised nine patients this way for more than twelve hours. They remain in a critical condition."

"With full transfusions every three hours?" Hammond echoed. "That's stabilized? Until his blood runs out."

"A point he made to me quite forcibly himself," White said.

"What about the other hospitals?" Allcock asked.

"There are six more in the Brighton area with between one and four cases each. Their reports add nothing new. I would say they are still waking up to the problem."

"What is the overall recovery rate?" Allcock asked impatiently.

White looked at the Colonel. "I don't think I was clear. No patient has recovered so far."

There was a silence.

"Look, what are we looking at, worse case scenario?" Connell said impatiently. No one offered an answer. Connell waved at the graph of infections then looked at the screens. "COME ON! Someone has to stick their neck out and say what we're talking about here. Sir John?"

Hammond shrugged. "At this stage I really couldn't say." Connell raised his voice again and Hammond continued. "If all that we have heard is true," Hammond hesitated, "The first thing we would need to do, as we said, is get some other Level Three labs involved, replicate the results, confirm the oral transmission and genetic modifications, start to understand what we're dealing with–"

"Sir John! Worse case scenario?"

Hammond turned his head as if listening to a voice off screen. "We have case studies for various outbreak types to define NHS emergency response plans," he said. "Many scenarios are considered. You've seen them," he pointed out to Connell.

"I've seen a hundred policy reviews, none of them agree. Some are clearly exaggerated to secure funding streams for unnecessary research," Connell shot back. "Is that your answer? Case studies?" He looked around the room. "Does no one here have the guts to give me a threat assessment?"

"Of course I will." Burnett said. Her voice was calm. "That's what I'm here for."

The room settled.

Connell sat back and smiled. Burnett's gaze came to rest on White's face. He shifted uncomfortably in his seat. "If we are dealing with a GM malaria as lethal and untreatable as currently appears, then estimates depend critically on whether, and then how effectively, this strain can transmit orally." Connell began to grumble again, shifting in his chair. Burnett's voice continued above his, firm and musical. "Now the lab evidence we have is not reliable or specific enough to make a prediction on this count, however we do have epidemiological data for the current outbreak. Unfortunately it's early days and reporting has been unreliable, but... it's all we have to go on."

"Come on Frances, enough already with the ifs, ands, buts, unfortunatelys and howevers. Put your balls," Connell caught himself and grinned, "Put your opinion on the table."

Burnett deployed a sweet smile, her voice unchanged. "I do not deal in certainties. That's a luxury I leave to political speech-writers. However, I presented the facts as we know them to two senior epidemiologists and a bioterrorist expert just before I came to this meeting. They gave me remarkably similar assessments." Burnett began counting her fingers. "Cases present sporadically. We have not seen an extinction event," she paused at a frown from Thorpe and translated, "There has been no incident of localised, catastrophic death. That is good news. It dramatically changes the possible nature of the pathogen. The casualty bounds from both experts ranged from a hundred deaths – this assumes oral transmission proves to be a red herring – to a few thousand plus, assuming appropriate public-health countermeasures – such as the emergency response plans Sir John mentioned – are deployed."

Connell snorted then consulted his watch. "An estimate from one to infinity isn't much use is it? I'm afraid I'm going to have to leave you. The Prime Minister will be on his feet in the House any minute." He swung his chair down to the floor. "But here's what we do: try to refine the," Connell paused, "'estimate' a little. Then consider our response. We'll need a press release. I'll be back in two, maybe three hours, see where we've got to."

He clambered to his feet, turning to the screens. "Given the situation, we'll need that press release ready for when I get back, in time for the evening editions. I'll look over it of course, but try and get the tone right." Connell showed his teeth. "Energetic, exasperated and focused on finding solutions. And I want all the bad news out in one go. We are not going to be seen withholding: we take one hit then we control it. Peter, I'm going to need a paragraph from you. Keep it brief. Non-technical. It should emphasise competent reaction by a world-class, well-resourced health service. We can mention the Emergency Fund, but perhaps not initially. And get more information on this intel cock-up."

He picked up his files.

"I think you haven't grasped what we are facing," White said. "We need more than–"

Connell juggled his files into the crook of an arm. "PMQs have already started. I've got to go. Kick-off the planning, I'll be back tops three hours, see where we've got to," Connell trousered his organiser.

"My recommendation," Burnett's voice cut through the air. Connell's eyes narrowed. "My recommendation," Burnett repeated, "Is that you advise the Prime Minister to cancel PMQs and join us here immediately."

Connell's face showed frank amazement. "Based on your *intelligence*, we might have stopped the country three times already this year. This latest report–"

"A report which will be on your desk within the hour," Burnett interrupted smoothly. "Copies are also being sent to the Attorney General, under Privy Seal, and the heads of JTAC and MI6. Copies of a report – not a dossier – written by my service officers and otherwise *unedited*."

Connell blanched at this last word. Everyone knew what Burnett was talking about. Forced to pause, he looked furious. Like most bullies, the only fists he liked to see were his own. For a moment he was speechless. White watched, fascinated. Burnett continued before Connell managed a reply.

"Some say the word *intelligence* in our service name is an oxymoron." Burnett smiled at Connell, a wide engaging smile, as if meeting him for the first time. "I don't think so. We learn from our mistakes. I understand your need for our intelligence – particularly regarding the very serious threats posed by WMD. You need to be properly advised on courses of action you have already," she looked down at the table then gave her head a little shake, as if freeing it of a small regret, "Have not yet decided upon. Be assured that the report you and others will receive will be the best, untampered-with advice we have. I give you my word on that." Burnett's follow-up punches appeared to thump the remaining wind right out of Connell. Finally he managed a reply. "Frances, you're sticking your neck out a bit on this one aren't you? You'd better be right."

"In the senses you usually mean, I'm not sure being right matters that much."

"Get over it," Connell said savagely.

Burnett smiled again, the sweet, deadly smile of a well-bred Roedean schoolgirl. "If I'm wrong, I can always call for a public inquiry by a well-trained and titled judge asked to focus only on procedural mistakes. The fact that I was right or wrong, that the official reasons for war or public health are actually false or true, might get lost in the smoke don't you think?"

Connell blinked.

"I'd like to go over the medical data again," Hammond said.

"Of course," White said, shuffling paper.

There was a discreet tap at the conference door.

"Excuse me," Hanratty poked his head into the room. He looked agitated. Burnett exchanged a glance with White and nodded to him to continue. She rose and left the room.

Connell stared at the projected slide of rising infections. He appeared unwilling to leave with a fight unfinished. "I can see I'm going to be the one clearing up this spooky mess again."

Chapter 39

Garrett looked out through a barred window. The sky was darkening. Behind her, she knew Skyler was sitting on a bunk bed staring at a metal desk and chair.

"Who is that man?"

"Kirtananda. He's a psychotic killer."

"How long before he proves you were bluffing?"

"Early morning."

"Could it be sooner?"

"Arshu is on a journey at sea. He has a satellite phone which he turns on once a day, six am our time, to maintain contact with the Centres."

"Did Arshu really ask you to invite me here?"

"Kirt told me that's what he said. But he lies."

"Why would Kirtananda want to kill me?"

"I don't know. He likes to kill. That's what he does. He's a killer."

Through the window Garrett could see the tiled dome of the House of Healing. It was perhaps fifty yards away. The rising steel tube she could now see was a chimney – the resemblance to the Porton ventilation was obvious. A biosafety lab, here? She shuddered at the thought of the womb-shaped valley, the geodesic dome buried in its side like an egg waiting to be fertilised. What had been incubating here in seclusion for ten years?

"Who is Sikanda?"

"A scientist. He came here two years ago." Skyler's answer was low and toneless.

"What sort of scientist?"

"A biogeneticist. His field was tropical diseases; malaria vaccine research."

Garrett's eyes traversed the window frame. She had tested the bars; they were unmoving. She had already examined the locked door; it was solid wood with exterior hinges. There were no other exits from the room.

Garrett noticed words, crude graffiti, scratched beside the window in the face of a brick. She bent closer. *Adele. Mummy.* Two words enclosed in a heart made of crosses.

"Who's Adele?"

"What?"

"Who's Adele?"

"She was Sikanda's daughter. How do you—"

"They were kept in this room, weren't they? The family."

"Yes."

"What was Sikanda's real name?"

"Professor Richardson."

"And the men called Christmas?"

"I didn't know them well."

"Do you know what they were supposed to do?"

"They were part of the Rebirth project. One for each continent."

Garrett turned around.

"Christmas," she crossed the room to face Skyler, "The man I found: he was sent out with the infection, wasn't he? Carrying what Sikanda created."

"I don't know."

"What is Rebirth?"

"It's a green ecology project."

"Rebirth – rebirth of what?"

"Mother Earth. That's all I know."

"Where is this man Sikanda now? I need to find him, talk to him."

Skyler shook his head. He carried on shaking it from side to side.

"I killed him." The listlessness had returned to his voice. "Kirtananda ordered me. He tricked me! I was stoned. Jesus! It was a mistake!"

He covered his face with his hands. Garrett stared, horrified. What had happened to him? She looked around the walls, then through them. What was happening outside? When she spoke, her voice was harsh.

"I need to understand what this Sikanda has done."

"Gudrun wouldn't tell me anything about his work." Skyler's hands hooded his eyes now, shielding them from unwanted light. His words came slow, bitter with late acceptance. "She only told me what she thought I wanted to hear."

"Gudrun," Garrett said.

"Now you know everything. There is nothing else I can tell you."

A distant recorded voice called out from across the valley, long repeated syllables. Skyler drew his legs up and crossed them beneath him, placed his hands palms up on his knees, and closed his eyes.

"I must sit and perform my Dues."

Garrett reached out and shook him by the shoulders. His eyes remained closed. His lips began to move soundlessly.

Chapter 40

"I'm putting up on screen a graph from a nation-wide survey conducted at the request of my service two hours ago."

Burnett crossed back to the table. She took the remote from White then nodded through glass walls at a technician.

Connell stood and hitched his trousers. Burnett raised her eyebrows at him. "You need to see this."

He collapsed back into his chair with a sigh. "I'll give you sixty seconds."

The projector light flickered. A graph appeared on screen.

Burnett glanced at Kirkpatrick. "You are looking at data currently 'NATO Eyes Only' so you are all now covered by OSA." She shook her head, "Although I predict this information will be in the public domain by the end of the day."

Allcock leaned forward. "What are those dots?"

"Are they..." Thorpe's voice trailed off into silence.

Burnett clicked the remote again. The image enlarged.

No-one moved.

"God Almighty."

***

It was cool on the cliff top. A breeze was blowing in from the sea. Kirtananda faced into it. The tide was in. Occasionally the dull thud of a heavy wave passed through his feet and he sensed the enormous energy of the water's impact.

The charges were set on the lab. He would set the timers when they left in the morning. No scientific evidence was to be left behind. Arshu-ji had been very clear. Not a problem; he had enough explosives to start a war.

The boys were finishing loading the Bedfords. Then they were done.

A hard unfamiliar object dug into his thigh. He fished a set of keys and a mobile out of a pocket. Garrett's. Yes. Just one last job to do. He smiled.

The boy had played a smart card. Of course the way to make him pay was to make his mother pay first.

He checked the mobile was switched off. He hefted the keys. On an impulse he threw them, far and high out. They fell silently. He waited but could not hear a splash above the sound of the waves below. After a long pause he threw the mobile too.

***

Burnett clicked the remote, showing close-ups. "I'm told initial estimates put the number at around fifty."

"Christ," Allcock said softly

"Are we to understand they all died from this malaria?" Thorpe demanded.

"Yes."

"Colonel," Burnett turned to Allcock, "Given the situation, the military may become involved at some point. That scenario planning–" The officer nodded his head once, as if saluting. This was his language. If you could start to mobilise those resources, it will help Gold Commander's job."

Allcock stood up. "I'm on it."

"The infection rate is being revised upward every half hour."

"Those CDSC reporting errors have cost us dearly," Thorpe observed.

Kirkpatrick fiddled with his tie. There was silence. Allcock left the room.

"Sir John," Burnett said. "We'll need to brief local health trusts immediately."

"Yes," Hammond nodded at the screen where bodies clumped together like dead cells on a Petri dish. "I will also contact our Level Three labs."

"I've done that," White said.

"Good. They will need original biopsy material."

"I can arrange it," Kirkpatrick said. He was ignored.

"We must send early warning briefings to national disease control centres." Hammond said. "The European labs and the CDC in Atlanta, Georgia may be able to help us."

"Good idea," Burnett nodded.

"I will also alert the WHO. We will need to consider the widest quarantine measures."

"What about the Brighton outbreak?" Kirkpatrick asked.

"What about London?" Thorpe added. "We have Operation Sassoon. Should it be activated?"

There was a pause. Burnett turned to Connell. "I think you need to contact the Prime Minister." He stared at her. She threw her voice, shaking him with it like a parent a sleepy child, "We are looking at a state of emergency."

Slowly he began to nod. "Yes. Yes, I agree." He stood up. "This crisis requires a personal response from the PM. Questions will have to be interrupted." Connell addressed the screens on his way out. "Sir John, he may want to visit a hospital in person. Is that possible?"

"Andy, forget it! Right now, the whole country could be a contaminated hot zone."

"Okay, okay!" Connell paused at the door. "The PM will chair the next meeting of this committee. Let's get moving people." He jabbed a finger at White. "Whatever it takes."

***

Garrett stood at the barred window. She could see stars of the summer constellations, Cygnus, Lyra and Aquila. The sky was beginning to lighten at one edge.

She had kept returning to the window, the thinnest point of exit, but it had proved impenetrable. The door was no better, flush and tight-fitting in its frame. She had wasted an hour and broken two fingernails on it.

She glanced at the graffiti beside the window frame. It had been scratched with a sharp point. There was nothing in the cell that could do that. The child must have used her nails.

Garrett went and sat down on the bed.

"Will you speak to me?"

"Skyler? Please? We have so little time."

He continued to chant, as he had all night. The sheer stamina of his effort was undeniable. Garrett couldn't understand how he withstood the boredom, the pointlessness. But of course, he thought there was a point.

"Please talk to me."

The chanting continued. Garrett sat back on the bed, unwilling to move away. She rested against the wall. She noticed an alphabet scratched in higgledy lines in the dirty plaster. Even here, they were teaching their daughter. In such a prison. Such a hopeless place. Lower down, just above the mattress, at head height for a sleeper, she could see a few three-letter words scrawled at an angle. CAT, GAG, TAG, ACT.

Behind her thoughts she could hear Skyler continuing to mutter his syllables, the sounds he believed contained the names of his God. What a ridiculous ritual! What a ridiculous belief – a name, buried in a thousand words. The practice appeared designed to waste a mind, a human life.

Garrett frowned at the scratched words on the wall. Something nagged at her in the old way, at the simple pattern of the lettering. She guessed her mind was playing at distractions, not wishing to think about where she was, about the filthy trapped cell and Jason's droning withdrawal. Anagrams, that was it – they were almost anagrams of each other. Not quite – they were just formed of the same four letters, A, C, G, T.

She thought of the word games she had been drilled in as a child, for exams, patterns of letters in sequence. Miniature codes in similar miniature words.

Beside her, Skyler continued to chant. She wanted to shake him by the shoulder, release him from his voluntary mental prison. She thought of Richardson. Trapped here in this same cell, equally a prisoner. Responsible for an impending plague of a horrific, almost unthinkable scale.

How he must have wished to escape! Or at least get a warning out. But he would have had no unguarded access to computers or telephones. He would not have been allowed to send letters. The only release must have been his work in the lab. Contact only with his family, guards, Bryce perhaps. And of course the organism, the new life form he had created. Garrett stared at the letter triplets on the wall. By manipulating those base pairs hoping for a cure, he had created a monster.

She continued to stare at the scratched words. A, C, G, T. Of course he had chosen those letters to play with. To a geneticist like Richardson, they were distinctive as e, π, x and y to mathematicians, or the constants of physicists. A, C, G, T. Adenine, Cytosine, Guanine and Thymine: the four nucleotide bases on the doubled helical strands of a DNA molecule.

She blinked. Manipulating those base pairs.

Trapped, with no unguarded access to get a message out.

Contact with the organism. Manipulating those base pairs.

To get a message out. Manipulating those base pairs.

To get a message out.

Skyler continued to drone. The letter triplets danced in front of her eyes. Suddenly she knew. Richardson had tried to help. He had sent them a warning. They just hadn't seen it.

Chapter 41

The operations room of JTAC was a basement of Thames House on Millbank. Raised clusters of screens flickered with information dense as a City trading floor. Plain clothes operators sat at workstations chatting through headsets. Server stacks panelled one long wall. Burnett had declined Allcock's offer of Pindar, the hardened MoD command room beneath Whitehall. Better defended, it had arguably less communications facilities – and to have accepted would have passed operational control of her resources to the army.

White watched Hanratty scurry between senior officers, notepad in hand. He looked purposeful and confident. The young man had done some growing up today. White watched the infection summary on the large wall screen. Numbers ticked upwards. Perhaps they all had.

His own brief had narrowed. Burnett had asked him to investigate new foreign intelligence. The data was varied and the geography very dispersed, from Bombay, Cancun and Brisbane, to Cape Town... White glanced at a digital wall clock. 3:53. Burnett had asked for hourly reports.

***

The barred window let in first shadowless light. Was it four? Five? The tower had just sent its call out across the valley. Garrett knelt beside the bed.

"Skyler?"

She laid her head on his crossed ankles.

"Whatever you've done, I still love you."

His lips continued to move, pronouncing sequential variations on nine syllables. Garrett sat down next to him. The thought of what he might have done sickened and angered her. If he would only talk to her, tell what had happened, perhaps she would be able to understand. Perhaps they could start to understand together. But he wouldn't.

Garrett pushed herself back towards the wall with her good hand. She wanted to look at the letter codes again. As she moved a sharp point dug into her thigh through the rough mattress. She frowned and rubbed at the scratch. She explored for the cause. Beneath her hand, under the canvas cover, her fingers felt the outline of a long, thin object.

She picked at a seam until she could rip fabric. Her questing fingers found a fork, snapped in two. One tine was broken.

She went back to the window and scratched a line next to the heart. The broken tine suggested heavier use. With more purpose now, she examined in minute detail around the window edges. She experimented more with the fork. Below the window, the mortar joints broke like sand. Someone had been at work here. Within minutes she discovered five loose bricks, across two of the window bars. Freeing one more brick would release a third bar, just enough of a gap. She hacked at hard, unloosened cement. A few grains chipped off. It was not impossible.

Behind her the chanting had stopped.

"What are you doing?"

Kirtananda cut the connection. Arshu had been quite clear.

The lying bastard.

He checked his Glock. The boys were set. Kirtananda skirted the House of Healing. The charges were set under the lab. The outhouse loomed ahead.

It was the bodies that were the problem. He had considered bagging and taking them, but if anything went wrong, if they were stopped and searched... Then a beautiful idea had occurred to him.

Static from his shortwave hissed. "Boss?"

"Well?"

"I'm done here. Fuck it's muddy. The water's spreading out through the trees and coming round a bit."

"That's fine. Long as it holds for an hour or so."

"Should be fine."

"Okay. Go clean up."

Kirtananda's hand slipped on Tyson's collar. The heavy redbone, ninety pounds of muscle, bone and teeth, jumped against the leash. "Wait up boy."

"We can't get past."

Skyler slipped down behind a tree. They had broken out of the cell without difficulty. The last window bar had come free quickly with their combined efforts. Once out, they had made straight for the woods along the shore, trusting to surprise and speed.

"Zakiya's on the rock. Harith is watching this exit. And Rayan's on the cliff path. I can see them. They've sight of the whole beach. And there'll be someone up top, Dharma or Kirt." Skyler opened his empty hands. "They're all armed."

Garrett nodded. "Is there another way out?"

"Inland. Once out of the valley it's open ground for miles. And Kirt will have it covered."

Skyler shook his head. They stood at the edge of the forest by the beach, panting, heads almost touching. Their voices were at a bare whisper. Leaving the cell they had seen Kirtananda approach. They'd run for the beach; but shortwave was faster.

"So we've got to get out by the shore." Garrett said. "There's some tree cover under the cliff."

"After crossing a hundred yards of open sand?"

"I need to reach the car, check Cherry."

"It's suicide. They're all *armed*."

Garrett rested her weight against the tree. The cut in her left arm was pulsing.

"There's one more thing," Skyler said.

"Yes?"

"I know where there's a gun."

Garrett stared at her son.

Kirtananda stood beside the broken window. This woman was beginning to piss him off. Who did she think she was, special fucking forces? Well she wasn't going to get lucky a third time. Five against two. Unarmed. Home ground.

He returned to the kennels. The dogs hunted best in packs.

The men were set. All exits covered. Shootin' fish in a barrel.

They ran like shadows. A part of Garrett sang with a strange glee. They were together. It had taken this madness, but they were together. She caught up with him on the rise. A shire horse stood asleep beside a hedgerow in the field below.

"I'm holding you up," Garrett said.

"No."

"I am. Don't wait. Go as fast as you can. I'll meet you outside the maze."

Skyler looked straight into her eyes. As he turned to go she grabbed his hand. "Take care."

He reached for her face and held her cheeks. "I'm sorry."

"We're going to get out of here," Garrett said.

Ululating calls echoed off the valley walls. Hunting calls. He kissed her on the forehead.

Then he turned and ran for their lives.

Garrett moved along the path, bent low. The valley had become a giant trap. In front of her, above the facing hill, half the sky had lightened to a deep blue. She thought about routes out. Were they right to go for the gun? Without it they were defenceless, even against the dogs. With it, maybe, just maybe, they could survive. Should she have let Skyler go on ahead? She felt the separation like a physical ache. He was so much faster. And he knew the way.

Ahead, the call note of the dogs rang out, insistent, suddenly excited. Terror clutched at Garrett's heart. A shot rang out, followed by two more. Then silence.

Jason!

Garrett raced down the path. She reached the weir and sprinted over the bridge. On the other side, she lost her footing on loose soil, fell and landed on her injured arm. She rolled to her knees and stopped, teeth clenched.

High on the hillside, just visible in the morning light, grey shapes rose out of the earth, four dogs, followed by a man. They climbed up by the ramp out of the Eye where Skyler should have been waiting! The dogs quartered the ground in circles, noses low. One dog barked and set off down the hill towards the stony ridge between the pools of water.

Garrett crawled backwards towards the bridge until she felt wooden boards beneath her knees. She rolled, landed in the water with a soft splash up to her waist, and waded over to a wooden pier.

When the dogs passed overhead she could hear their snuffling.

"Coming your way. Hold position. She's got to be heading for the beach."

The words ended in a burst of static. Garrett waited thirty heart beats. She couldn't manage longer. She began running, without looking back. Her feet were quick on the ramp down into the oval courtyard of the Eye. Her heart was full of dread of what she might find.

The courtyard was empty. *Jason?*

She crossed to the maze and stopped at the top of a flight of stone steps. Carved lettering was etched in shadow on a low square post.

"Called or uncalled, a god will be present."

The subtle complexity of the spiral corridors mocked her. She had to get through! Jason was in there. Somewhere. She had to reach him.

It was possible. He had done it.

She stood still, a single point of concentration. What had Jason said? The dogs began to call again. She dismissed them from her mind. In the gesture she heard her son's words and the threat of losing that voice was a sharp terror. *And every time your attention wanders, escort it back... That is the required discipline.*

It was possible. *He had done it.* The thought struck her another way: the maze had a solution. And the route had to be one that many could take; it was too much to ask devotees to memorize a long sequence of decisions. There must be a simple rule. What was it Jason had said? *Growth.*

The solution when it hit her was suddenly obvious. It was so simple. The first left, then again the first left, then the second left, then third then fifth then eighth, adding together the last two numbers each time, ignoring all other choices: it was Fibonacci, the simplest rule of population growth. And she had the probable entry points already. After two false starts she chose one with a motif of crossed swords, and threaded the maze in one continuous clockwise spiral without reversal. She entered the central circle.

His body lay face up on the ground. To one side was a hole and a pile of sand.

Garrett studied the bullet holes in his chest and back. She estimated the internal trajectories from entry and exit puncture points and the implied organ damage. The blood loss was already very heavy.

"Mother?"

"Yes, it's me." With a doctor's sense, she stopped her exam. She held him to her. "Shh."

He laughed, a single sob. "You cracked our maze."

"With your help. Shh."

"What are you like? Listen–"

"Shh, you don't need to talk."

"I found the gun! Do you see it?"

"Shh. Shh."

Skyler struggled to sit up. A gout of blood spilled out of one corner of his mouth, black in the dawn light. He spat.

"Don't move," Garrett said.

"Can you see it?"

"Wait. Stay still and I'll look."

Garrett looked around the circle then saw the glinting chunk of metal pressed into the sand beside her legs, beneath where Skyler had been lying.

"Yes. I've got it."

Skyler slumped back against her.

"Good. It cost me enough."

He fought with his breath for a while.

"I hurt."

"I know you do."

They held each other for some time.

"So that's it?" he whispered.

"Shhh."

"Mother? No tourniquet? Bandages? Well – doctor?"

"Shhh."

"Am I going to die?" Skyler lifted his head and looked out over the valley. He coughed. Black spattered Garrett's chest. "I am going to die aren't I? Otherwise you would be fixing me or taking me somewhere." He looked at her, amazed and suddenly desperate. Garrett tried to meet his gaze without fear.

He closed his eyes and began chanting names. A terrible anger rose up and passed through her without resistance. They had no time for it. She held him to her.

A fit of coughing stopped his chant. Skyler's hands gripped her, his eyes clear and shining. "I'm cold. And I'm frightened. I'm frightened."

"I know. It's all right. I'm here. Shhh. It's all right. I'm here. Shhh. It's all right. I'm here. Shhh."

She rocked him in her arms in the old way, until he sighed. With two fingers, she searched for the pulse in his throat. It was faint, but still regular.

A long while later she realised she was staring at the top of his head, so close, she could count hairs. He had been born with an amazing amount of hair. She remembered counting hairs, and toes, and fingers. All starting in blood and mess, the most painful and difficult moment of her life. What an extraordinary achievement it was, a grown man.

His body stiffened in her arms. His eyes opened, but he didn't see her.

"A thousand lifetimes. You promised. Do not forsake me, Arshu! I will wait for you!"

"Shhh. Shhh."

She tried to take his pulse again, now at his wrist. She couldn't find it. She continued rocking.

What a strong child he was! She held his bloody hand and studied the fingers. Like his father's, long and searching. She bent her head and noticed droplets of water splashing on his skin, a tiny patter like the blessing of rain, and realised it was falling out of her eyes.

"You flew my cage."

Garrett froze.

"And you gave my dogs the slip."

She turned. Kirtananda stood on the other side of the sandy circle. One hand held a gun; the other tugged at a leather leash.

"Well, all but Tyson."

The redbone raised his nose and opened his black lips. Through the smile his growl was a bass purr.

"You've caused me a lot of trouble you know that? Now get up. I've a job for you."

Garrett bent her head over Jason's. She rocked him. Kirtananda fired a shot into the sand.

"Get up."

He fired again. A whistle sounded off stonework, short, high-pitched and descending. Garrett leaned further over her son's body, her head almost touching the ground beside him.

"Or do you want me to put more bullets in him?"

Garrett placed Jason's head on the ground. Out of long habit, she put his body in the recovery position then stood up slowly, holding her side as though she had a stitch, a hand inside her shirt just above her belt, where it had become unbuttoned. She turned. Kirtananda's gun was aimed straight at her. A shovel was balanced over his left shoulder. He threw it at her feet.

"Pick it up!"

Garrett's eyes narrowed on the gun.

"Move!"

***

Garrett stumbled down the path through pines. She could feel tears, abstract points on the graph of her cheek, noted like data; in her stomach a tearing pain.

"Faster!"

Despite the care she took – leant slightly over, still clutching her side, light and quick on her feet around obstructions – her left arm was knocked repeatedly. An earthwork loomed ahead, a mud bank crumbling in places from the weight of water pooled above it. She worked around the base. The ground was soft and cold under her feet. Behind her she could hear the growling of the man's dog.

"Now turn around."

Garrett buried the shovel upright into the earth, put a hand under her injured arm and turned round. New blood was staining the bandage.

"Tyson!"

The dog leapt down from the bank with a snarl, his leash trailing behind him. He raced towards Garrett. Her hand slipped inside her shirt where it was unbuttoned above her belt. As Tyson jumped for her throat she fired. Again and again and again. The dog crashed into her. They fell to the ground together, Garrett still firing.

She rolled away and came to her knees. The dog whimpered once and was silent. Garrett stood, her head dizzy with fresh pain. The pistol she had used lay half-submerged in a puddle of muddy water ten feet away.

"You killed my dog." Kirtananda's eyes bulged. "You killed my fucking dog."

"You killed Jason."

"And now I'm gonna kill you."

Kirtananda raised his gun. Garrett stared at the pistol on the ground. It was out of reach. She looked up at Kirtananda. The killer smiled over the barrel, his aim the middle of her forehead. He squeezed the trigger.

Two shots rang out, then the insect whine of a bullet ricocheting off stone. Garrett stared in shock. Somewhere in her mind she registered the fact that she should feel pain. Or nothing. She felt as she had before, detached, a cold grief through all her body. She was still alive.

Another shot rang out. Kirtananda jerked forward as though punched. When he turned around his face wrinkled with disbelief. The next shot lifted him a little. He looked down at his chest in surprise. His feet scrabbled against slipping earth, a last cry shut off when he hit the ground.

"Christine!"

A shout of terrible urgency echoed through the trees. Bryce's head appeared over the top of the bank. When he saw her his eyes closed; his cheeks puffed out with a sigh of relief. He pushed his glasses up his nose with a finger.

"Are you okay?"

Garrett waited for her mind to catch up with what her body had never stopped believing: that she was still alive. She listened to her pulse.

"Wait there! I'm coming down."

Garrett heard stones sliding somewhere and the thud of a landing. Bryce reappeared at the base of the dam beside Kirtananda's body. Garrett could see Kirtananda's back, punctured by bullet holes, and his head folded over at an impossible angle, eyes fixed open. Garrett watched Bryce nudge the body with a foot. It rolled, balanced a moment as though still capable of decision, then tipped over a lip of earth face down into a shallow trench half-filled with seeping water. Garrett closed her eyes.

"Christine."

Garrett felt Bryce's arm around her shoulders. She sensed her body stiffen. His hand touched her hair and held her head against his.

"My son is dead," Garrett's voice was quiet.

They stood together in silence. Garrett's body shook occasionally. After a while Bryce spoke in her ear.

"We must go. Others will be coming."

As he guided her away he stopped to pick up the dropped gun. When Garrett looked back she could see water breaking over the edge of the dam where Kirtananda had fallen, filling the trench, the carcass already half-covered.

***

When they reached the edge of the trees Bryce stopped. He held up a warning hand. Garrett started forward.

"No Christine!" Bryce caught her by the shoulders.

"I need to find his body!"

"There are others with guns." He pulled her back inside the trees.

Garrett pointed to the head of the valley. "I need to go back." She tried to turn round.

Bryce held her. He looked into her eyes then nodded. "Okay."

He studied the paths criss-crossing the open ground.

"This way."

He chose a footpath that climbed high up the side of the valley. He led her stumbling for some minutes along a sheep-run that followed the contour of a ridge. When he stopped to catch his breath Garrett waited beside him. They stood under a twisted Scots pine, its upper trunk bent nearly horizontal by the coastal wind. Below them, the segmented glass dome of the House of Healing was dimly visible under the lightening sky. Garrett's body became still, eyes fixed on a point near the summit at the head of the valley. From her high vantage point she could see down onto the tilted face of the hill straight into the central stone circle of the Eye of Faith. It was empty.

"His body – it's gone!"

"Please. Christine, we must get under cover." Bryce spoke between panted breaths. He looked around then pointed at the dome of the House of Healing below them.

"Quick. This way!"

Garrett continued to stare down into the empty centre of the Eye. "I must find where they have taken his body!"

"Christine!"

He tugged her by the hand.

"Christine! Please! We must get out of sight!"

He pulled her down a steep path stepped with flat stones. Garrett stopped often; when she moved it was with clumsy jerks. They reached the valley floor and crossed to the geodesic dome.

They found an entrance and entered what looked like a gigantic greenhouse.

The air was warm and damp. Soft dawn light filtered in through the domed roof. Paved paths divided ordered beds of plants in stone troughs. In the centre a huge clump of bamboos sprouted up to the glass ceiling.

Bryce turned to her. "We are safe here."

Safe. Garrett swayed on her feet. Bryce reached out and caught her. "It's okay."

A trembling ran through her muscles like the shiver in a horse's flank. Bryce was solid beside her. She swayed a moment in the angle of his arm.

"It's okay now."

Garrett turned her head away.

"Ar gefn ei geffyl gwyn." The Welsh curse was guttural. Bryce held her shoulders. "Can you tell me what happened?"

After a while the trembling stopped. Garrett began to speak.

"I arrived yesterday. Was it yesterday?" She looked up, startled out of her daze. "Cherry – my friend! I came with Cherry. I don't know if she's alright!" Garrett raised her hands, agitated. "Jason sent someone for her! He said they would bring her." She dropped her hands then whispered, "He said... Jason said–"

Her legs give way. Bryce caught her. He lowered her onto the edge of a nearby stone trough planted with tall grasses.

She clung to him, unable to speak. Her stomach heaved. It heaved again. She turned and threw up into the plants, a dry repeated retching.

Panting, she stared down at a tangle of grasses. After some time she became aware of a cloth cleaning her mouth. It was a handkerchief. She took it.

"Thank you."

She cleaned herself up. When she had finished she sat still, staring at nothing. After a while she felt an arm around her shoulders, a chin resting on the top of her head.

"You saved my life," she said. She wiped her mouth again. Her cheek rested against his chest.

"I wouldn't let you be harmed. I've watched over you since we met." From the tower a bell began to toll the hour. Bryce looked out over her head. His mouth began to shape words silently, an ever-varying series of syllables.

Garrett wondered what he meant. She was aware of curious sensations – his warm chest against her cheek, her arms holding her stomach, an acid taste in her mouth – it was like watching someone else's body. She watched herself raise a hand to her forehead and wipe away moisture. She wondered at the sweat.

"I must tell you something," she stared at her glistening hand.

"Tell me everything that happened." Bryce closed his eyes. He continued to mouth silent syllables, in sequences of nine.

"I think these people have engineered the malaria strain we saw in the Brighton cases. That man you shot said a plague is running. They may have released it using human carriers," she shook her head, "Using people like suicide bombers. I think the man I found at the festival, Christmas, was one of them. Garrett clenched her hands. "Someone called Arshu ordered it. They believe he is a God."

She stood up. She looked at the surrounding glass walls. "There was a sniper on the cliff. He might have seen us–"

"Zak's dead. And now Kirt." Bryce smiled. Sunlight mirrored his glasses. "I'm so glad you came here."

Garrett took a step back. "Kirt?"

"I have so much to show you."

Garrett shuddered.

"I do. Truly. And to think Zakiya started in this House." Bryce gave an impatient shake of the head. "I regretted killing him. Not Kirt – he always was a mad dog. But Christine, they're not what I want to talk to you about."

Another spasm rippled from her stomach up and down the length of her body. She stepped back further.

"Rheinnalt, no–"

Steam sighed in faint plumes of artificial rain from hidden piping. She looked up at the sky of hexagon panes. She tried to see through the glass panels.

"I told you, we are safe. Kirt's dogs are leaderless. And anyway they will not dare come in here, not against me. I am Osei, Head of this House. They are nothing. Foot soldiers." He flicked his fingers then looked at her with raindrop eyes.

"How is your arm?"

"Are you Arshu?" she whispered, staring at Bryce in horror.

Bryce laughed. "Am I a living God? No." He saw her consider him and shook his head. "He is a great soul – Mahatma the Indians call it – I am merely his instrument." He gestured with a hand at the greenhouse and the valley beyond. "I cannot show you what he looks like. Images of him are forbidden, only the Asar is allowed. But his presence is all around us. He has enabled all you see."

"Does he order gunmen to murder innocent people?" Garrett whispered.

"I am sorry about the death of your son. It was wrong. I had nothing to do with it. Neither did Arshu."

"I don't believe you." Garrett stepped back from Bryce. Who was he? Her legs began to tremble.

Bryce shook his head. "You don't understand what's really going on. Please Christine, trust me just a little longer?"

When he reached out Garrett flinched. "Don't you dare touch me!"

"Do you remember that day in the lab, when the lab lights went out? When we stood alone together? You were in the dark and frightened, about nothing, by childhood fears. You are in the dark now." He held out his hand. "There is something you must see. Christine – please?"

Garrett thought of Jason's twisted, punctured body in the centre of the Eye of Faith. She thought of the purposes of biology twisted by this man and his associates. Why? Why? *Arshu.* Something in her cried out with anger and a sudden terrible understanding. It was not true what Ivan Karamazov had said, "If God is dead then everything is permitted." Dostoyevsky had been dead wrong. No: it was living belief in gods – in the invented unseen – that could licence anything, beyond morality and decency. Her mind dug into the fear of it like the bright edge of a spade going into mud. What were they trying to do with this malaria?

She felt again the terrible emptiness in her stomach. She shuddered. Not now! She couldn't think of the pain. She couldn't feel it. Not now. She gripped her anger again. Arshu. The malaria. What were they trying to do? The anger stayed. She held onto it, a live animal thing, held onto it for her sanity, against the terrible pain.

"What do you want to show me?"

Bryce gestured. "Everything you see around you is a part of what you must understand. But we have little time: we must go to my lab."

He led the way across the floor of the greenhouse, trailing a hand as if hoping she would take it. They passed a sapling with fleshy, emerald-green leaves and small purple flowers. He paused.

"*Nesiota elliptica* – the Saint Helena Olive. Do you know it? It became extinct in two thousand and three."

Bryce moved on. He stopped by a cluster of tiny open-mouthed orange flowers. "And this is *Aurelius Solebaris*, an orchid indigenous to Borneo. Now it only survives here." Garrett recognised the plant from Bryce's desk in the Porton lab.

"This greenhouse is a small part of Arshu's vision, the start of what I wish to show you. He is a gardener, as much of flowers as of men. Here he has saved many lives – not individuals, whole life forms."

He pointed out larger areas planted out with seed crops.

"In the last hundred years ninety percent of edible fruit and vegetable varieties have been lost to us. Just three plant species – wheat, rice and maize – account for more than half of human energy intake. They are distributed by biotech companies as sterile seed. These beds preserve original wild stock and lost cultivars."

Bryce swept an arm over the plants in front of him.

"There are other seed bank projects – at Svalbard, Kew, the Vavilov Institute – but we are the largest. And this installation – Asari One – is one of five we have around the world. These plants are a commonwealth, a heritage to be saved and shared. Now come, what I must show you is in here. It will explain everything."

Bryce unlocked a door.

***

They passed down a long corridor, the umbilical cord connecting the greenhouse with a brick complex and steel chimney. Bryce led the way into a spacious lab. Glass-fronted cupboards were filled with flasks, bottled reagents and other equipment. A large computer screen dominated one wall. Garrett eyed a pressurised door.

"Do you have a biosafety zone here?"

"Yes." Bryce tapped at a keyboard. "For reasons you'll understand in a moment."

The wall screen blinked and became a pane of electric light. Smaller windows formed and vanished on its surface in quick succession.

Bryce's movements became urgent, his hands agitated. "Christine, I want you to understand me and what it is we are doing."

An hourglass filled over and over on the screen. Bryce stood up.

"I must start at the beginning." A login window appeared and Bryce stooped to enter credentials. "About fifteen years ago our teacher Arshu visited Borneo with the aim of founding a new forest commune. He had already established the large worship communities in Paliputra, Santa Rosa, Oregon, Queensland – and dozens of other centres. But he wanted to build aboriginal faith connections."

"I was also in Borneo. My father – a biologist – had decided my mother and I should go with him on a field trip."

"He didn't understand the danger he was putting us in." The softness left Bryce's face. "The surviving rainforests of this world are a war zone. Three weeks into the trip, we were caught in the crossfire between some tribesmen, settlers and mercenaries of a logging company. My parents were killed. I survived. With Arshu's help."

"Arshu found me under a smoking ruin in the tribal village next to my father's research station. He took care of me. We lived six months in the forest until a plant led us out, the orchid *Aurelius Solebaris*. Arshu had discovered its fruits and, searching for it, we were picked up by a logging company."

Bryce's voice became quiet, conversational. "Tell me, have you heard of the miner's canary?"

Garrett stared.

"Canaries are sensitive to carbon monoxide – which to us is odourless and colourless – so were taken down pits in cages by miners. If a bird died the miners would evacuate." Bryce's eyes did not leave hers. She saw his body settle, joint by joint, from the shoulders down. A hardness – anger? pain? self-control? she couldn't tell – entered his face. "I later found out that *Aurelius Solebaris* was known as a "Climate canary", that is, a species chosen by biologists to signal danger to an ecological system."

Bryce tapped a sequence of keys on the keyboard. Four milky blue-green spheres appeared on the wall screen above tables and charts of data.

"Arshu has explained how its extinction is a parable for us. Watch."

Bryce clicked his mouse. The spheres began to spin.

"You are looking at a simulation. Four, to be precise; global projections of our biosphere, with indicators for climate, ice caps, species populations, forestation etc."

Bryce swung round to face Garrett. His voice became sonorous, lecturing.

Do you know what the projected population of our planet is forty years from now? Eleven billion. *Eleven.* It is now six."

Garrett felt the muscles in her legs begin to tremble again. She wanted to sit down. Bryce saw Garrett's face and raised a hand. "Please. Wait. Just listen."

"Arshu has warned us that the emergent, acute danger is nuclear conflict over inadequate resources." Bryce hit a key and nodded at the screen. The right hand globe flared briefly orange and red before cooling to black. "The world after a thermonuclear war will remain polluted for a hundred half lives of Uranium two-three-two – about twenty million years."

"But Arshu has explained how even if we avoid that event, current demands on resources are creating two further catastrophes: species extinction and mean temperature increases."

Bryce turned back to the keyboard. His long fingers sounded a soft rain. On the wall screen, the middle two globes began to spin.

"Under extreme population pressures, it is the ecocidal destruction of the rainforests that is proving decisive. An area the size of Belgium has been destroyed in the last five months. When canopy edges are compromised, leaf litters dry out. Drought-led fires – which should occur every five hundred years – are occuring every five. Chwarae troi'n chwerw, wrth chwarae gyda thân." His words were soft as he gestured at the screen. The two spinning middle spheres were turning brown, like autumn leaves.

"The trouble is, these rainforests function as our planet's lungs. They suck millions of tonnes of greenhouse gases out of our atmosphere. Within fifty years we will reach a point where the extraction process will fail completely. Our planet will cease to breathe."

He turned his head to her, owlish behind his spectacles. "Have you ever watched your breath for any length of time? Can you imagine what it would be like if it stopped?"

"The consensus on the global warming rate is that it will reach one degree Fahrenheit per decade by twenty thirty and by then will be irreversible."

He tilted his head to one side.

"Do you know that there are more species in ten square meters of rainforest than in all of Europe? Up to ninety percent of all species are in closed tropical forest. You would think we would preserve these places like treasure houses."

He pushed his glasses up his nose with the fork of two fingers.

"Instead we destroy them. More than fifty thousand species become extinct annually. That's over a hundred *a day*."

Bryce's glasses glinted at Garrett. Behind them, his eyes were intense in their still regard.

"And it's not just on land. Every exploited marine species will be commercially extinct by 2048."

"Rheinnalt?" Garrett said. Her appeal was direct, to his over-bright eyes. She leaned against a lab bench. She was having trouble standing.

"Let me quote you this statement signed in 1992 by the majority of Nobel prize winners then alive. *Human beings and the natural world are on a collision course... if not checked... our current practices... may so alter the living world that it will be unable to sustain life in the manner that we know... no more than one or a few decades remain before the chance to avert the threats we now confront will be lost.* "

Bryce shook his head. "Dawnsio ar y dibyn. We dance on the edge of a cliff. While the politicians argue and businessmen fiddle their carbon tax reports, our planet burns."

Bryce hit runs of keys. Numbers appeared below the globes.

"Look at my four scenarios. Do you see them?"

"The world middle-left is the result of global warming by twelve degrees. Life is fugitive, it has ceased to exist as we know it. The last time the planet warmed by seven degrees so quickly, almost everything on Earth died."

"The next world has warmed by eight degrees. Humanity has survived but most life forms haven't. It took ten million years for Nature to recover from the last mass extinction event. This man-made one will be far worse."

"Of course my models only confirmed Arshu's first prophesy." Bryce walked towards the wall screen. "But fifteen years ago he had a vision of an alternative."

Bryce gestured at the last spinning globe, still serene, still milky blue-green.

"The world on the left has a viable biosphere. More than that, it is thriving. Mankind is in balance with the earth. We comprise a few million prudent gardeners, not a pestilence of billions."

"Pestilence?" Garrett whispered. She couldn't control the shaking in her legs. She felt the sweat again on her forehead.

"Christine, as biologists we understand genetics. That allows us to see truly; our sight is unveiled. Have you considered honestly, rationally, how we are more likely to survive?" He waited only long enough for her silence. "We are scientists. It is our duty to follow the evidence is it not, wherever it leads? And we are granted power beyond that of ordinary men and women; we have tools that can change the world. That carries a terrible responsibility. Responsibility that requires action."

Garrett stared into Bryce's eyes. They were black and shining and alive in their twitching purpose. She saw the madness of complete certainty. A feverish chill swept through her body.

"What have you done?"

"We have started a cull."

Garrett stared at Bryce in horror. She saw his hands mimic sadness, in his eyes and the gestures of his hands.

"Do you not concede the logic?"

"Rheinnalt?" Garrett whispered. She remembered her nightmare of school children playing with dynamite. Understanding swept through her trembling body. She raised her right hand to visor her eyes. From somewhere unexpected she noticed tears for the man who had lost and been lost. And all the anger was in the understanding.

"What have you done?" Garrett whispered again.

"You were right about the malaria strain. The disease that killed your three cases in Brighton is an engineered orally-transmissible hybrid of falciparum-streptococcus, very infectious and lethal. Its name is Krissa. It was carried by the man you know as Christmas."

Garrett let out a sigh with her whole body.

"It was created by accident, by an old colleague at Kronos, my first laboratory."

"Sikanda."

"Yes – or Professor Richardson as he was then known. Like many great scientific discoveries it was a mistake. Richardson had ignored protocols and introduced foreign sequences into the

Plasmodium genome. He was chasing the first malaria vaccine, and had a good candidate. The unexpected side-effect of oral transmission was to be his crowning stroke of genius: a free, fast distribution mechanism, able to reach the most remote of areas. But the vaccine strain turned out to be viable and pathological, lethally so. I had transferred to Porton searching for a disease agent, but when Richardson told me about his failed project I realised we had found what we needed."

Bryce bent to tap a few keys. A new window opened on the screen. "Shall I tell you what happens next? Arshu has seen it all."

Garrett gripped the lab bench with both hands. She looked around the closed lab. On the screen a newscaster was speaking. There was no sound.

"The first outbreak is established here in the UK. Last night we saw the beginnings of the media frenzy and official reaction. I expect a state of emergency will have been declared by now."

Bryce turned from his keyboard and began to pace back and forth in the narrow corridor between the lab benches. "The international reaction will begin soon."

"As the death toll rises, so will the panic. The first foreign case will provoke counter-measures of incredible brutality." His words came faster now, with scripted urgency. "The UK will be sealed off from continental Europe. The French will close surrounding airspace. Any attempted international flights will be shot down. The Channel tunnel will be shut; a complete naval blockade will prevent ferries and merchant shipping out of British ports." Bryce's eyes contacted then swept past Garrett's, his voice a pre-recorded chant.

"But the measures will be too late. This pathogen will not respect borders or the delayed measures of bureaucrats."

"Stop it."

"I can't."

"Please try."

"There are four other vectors, on separate continents. According to my models, new outbreaks are already incubating in a dozen countries. Within a week from now, genuine Krissa cases – among a flood of false positives – will be identified on every major landmass, despite the best efforts of governments and the WHO. We know it will be successful because of our trial. We sent the first vector out early to a remote island chain."

"Where?" Garrett whispered. She leaned against the lab bench and cradled her injured left arm in her right. She tried to stop the shivers in her body but found she couldn't.

"Kepalua. It's off the south coast of Java in Indonesia. There were thirty deaths in two weeks," Bryce shrugged, "hardly an international incident. But when we had confirmed the contagion the others started their journeys. The UK's vector went first – he didn't wait as long as instructed, not that it matters. By the end of the month, Krissa will be a worldwide pandemic." Bryce looked past Garrett. He spoke out of an often-rehearsed future. On-screen a map of the UK appeared behind the newscaster's head.

"The first reaction of governments will be to reach for the gun. Martial law will be declared. Cold war protocols will be activated." Bryce shrugged. "They will discover barriers designed for radiation are not effective against Krissa. All that the Plasmodium needs to destroy a human group, whatever the size, is a single infected carrier cell. And remember, the modern world has never faced a serious global biological attack. It is simply not equipped to deal with it."

"I see you are wondering how I am so certain. Arshu dreams with his eyes open. He has seen it. It will come to pass."

On the screen the map of the UK was speckled with clusters of red dots, like a body with chickenpox.

"The breakdown of modern society will be unexpectedly rapid. Our technologies are dependent on people, the weakest links in all the chains. They will not turn up to work; they will desert public spaces; they will stay at home. Transport systems will falter and stop; the airwaves, landlines, the Internet will fall silent; our skies and highways and railways and shipping lanes will empty; power stations will stop generating. Across all our great cities the lights will go out."

Garrett listened to the soft, reasonable voice. She stared in frozen horror at the man in front of her, at his smile of prophecy. Behind his head the newscaster had been replaced by the prime minister looking grave, mouthing silent words.

"Soon, the loggers' chain saws will stop, for the first time in fifty years. All around the globe, factory trawler fleets will put in to port, and stay there. The world's five-hundred-million-strong car fleet will slow down, park, and start rusting along with fertilizer spreaders and combine harvesters. Mines will shut and power station chimneys stop belching smoke."

"Arshu predicts fifty-year carbon emission targets will be met within nine months. The atmosphere will stabilize, and then begin to repair itself – incredibly quickly in most of the models I have run. The ice caps will grow back over the poles. Glaciers will reappear in the high Himalayas. Water tables will replenish themselves and rivers run clean and full. The Colorado, Yangtze and Ganges will reach the sea again for the first time in decades."

"Arshu says we will be pleasantly surprised at the speed of recovery of the land, once the business of industrialized agriculture is ended. The tropical rain forests will begin to recover. Whales will repopulate their depleted oceanic nurseries. Fish stocks will see explosive expansion. The great coral reefs – Pulley Ridge, Belize, the Barrier, those rainforests of the oceans – will bloom again."

"Of course some damage – plastics, nitrogen – is irreversible." Bryce's eyes twinkled, "But I think we will be surprised at how resilient Mother Nature is, given a fighting chance."

"And then there's us," Bryce focussed on Garrett, his gaze confiding.

"Us?" Her voice sounded all right to her. She felt sick inside. She closed her eyes but the voice continued, relentless.

"–*Homo sapiens*, that unwise race of primates. Krissa is a powerful pathogen, unlike any I have seen," Bryce glanced at the screen. The newscaster was back. "We have run models."

"Absolute quarantine is really the only effective barrier. Countries with biological warfare reaction plans will activate pre-prepared research facilities. Some protocols will prove effective. A few command and control structures will survive, although blind, deaf, dumb and impotent."

"The Cold War paranoids, who have dug their own bunkers and filled them with tinned goods, and those few within effective reach of resources and the intelligence to use them without delay, they will have a chance."

On her closed eyelids, Garrett saw again Jason's punctured body. She remembered his questions, asking why she was doing nothing. Tears ran down her cheeks. She wanted to slip to the floor, to curl up and cover her ears. Above all, she wanted the voice to stop.

"And of course no disease is perfect. Certain blood groups confer limited resistance. Some lucky few will discover they have inherited some rare unpredictable immunity: a ten thousandth is the lower predictions of my models. Why do you flinch? The current human population is six point six billion. That means there will still be about sixty million survivors."

Garrett shivered and opened her eyes. She felt cold and hot at the same time. She looked around at the walls, at the television screen spewing its Technicolor infection news, at the blank windows tuned to a dead channel. Bryce continued to speak.

"Of course some knowledge will be lost. With the rioting and looting will come the destruction of many libraries, museum collections and electronic data stores. But just as Mother Nature is resilient, so are we. Haven't we proved we are her equal?"

Bryce stared up into the fluorescent lights. He spoke from a faraway private place. "Isolated individuals will find each other. Scattered bands will form communities. Talents will be shared. Farmers and gardeners will husband seed and animal stocks. Technologists will reassemble our networks. Librarians will work to rescue our intellectual heritage. And everywhere, on all continents, we Asari will be there to guide the process."

Bryce raised a hand in front of his face as though to scold, or trace a warning sign in the air. "The human animal only breeds in pairs, and we rear our young over decades. So we will have the space of many centuries to reflect and understand."

Bryce gestured at the screen. "Our earthly ark, sinking beneath the sheer weight of human numbers, is being suddenly lightened and set on a wiser course. We have given our race a second chance. Yes, we will survive. But we will be changed." Bryce bowed his head. "As Arshu says, we will have learnt a necessary lesson."

**

Garrett looked around at the walls. She met Bryce's eyes. There was nowhere else to turn.

"And you? Will you be one of the survivors?" she whispered.

"Will I?" Bryce smiled. "Will we?"

He stepped towards her.

"Why do you think I came back here? It was for you. I am going on the Exodus. It will be a long trip. I don't know when I will be back here." He held out his hand. "I want you to come with me."

"Rheinnalt—"

"Osei please. You know me truly now." His outstretched hand opened. His voice trembled with excitement. "I want you to meet Arshu. If you come with me you will have that chance."

"Where is the Exodus?"

"It is hidden. I am one of the few who know the way. He's there. Waiting for Rebirth."

Bryce looked at her, his eyes were shining.

"You have no idea what it is like – the silence, the peace – when you meet Arshu for the first time." Bryce dropped his hands. "He's not a charlatan, not some tourist baba, or spiritual huckster like those televangelists. He is a true visionary, a great soul gifted with second sight, a man who radiates love through his whole being. Imagine meeting someone who can be relied upon, who can tell us answers, solve our problems." He opened his arms, like a preacher extending an invitation. "It is liberating."

"You have grown up with the endless chatter of voices, knowing only a world of competing opinions," he put his hands up over his ears and his voice was mocking, "Of opposed theories, where all the prizes go to those with the loudest voices, or worse, to the naysayers and sceptics for whom nothing is sacred. I don't believe you are one of those. But how many of us have been properly trained to recognise a great soul when he walks amongst us? How many know how to still the chatter of our modern minds, and accept the peace he brings, the love he offers? I want you to have that chance. As I had. When you see him, you will understand. Will you come with me?"

"Rheinnalt, you must give me all Richardson's research notes and samples." Her appeal was direct, simple, like a mother to a child.

Bryce frowned. "What for?"

"So that we can try to follow the work and find some defence. Find a cure."

"That would be a waste of time."

"Why?"

"Because we have a cure already."

Garrett stared at Bryce. The shine to his eyes made them appear separately alive.

"It was always a part of Arshu's plan. And I can't claim any credit for the work – that belongs to Sikanda." He waved a hand like a confident conjurer over a top hat. "It was the first instruction I gave him when he joined us." Bryce began to pace the room again in slow steps. "I pointed out it was the only chance of limiting the damage that his new strain might cause if it got out into the general population. He was in no position to argue. He came up with a new protocol. It was brilliantly simple."

"The strain has a deliberate weakness to an engineered protein. Sikanda described it as a chemical Achilles heel." Bryce smiled. "He called the prophylaxis protein Paris."

"There is a cure," Garrett said. A cold still point formed in her stomach. She calculated the geometry of the lab room.

"But it is not for others."

There is a cure. Garrett's thoughts narrowed, swept out beyond the walls of the room. *Where?* She took the smallest of steps. She held the tremors in her body in check. She judged distances again.

"How effective is it?"

"Completely. Remember, Paris isn't a drug designed to cure a disease. It's a drug for a disease *designed to be cured.*"

Garrett took another step forward.

"We have a limited stock of the drug. But Christine, if you come with us–" His gaze was intimate as an unwelcome kiss. When he saw her reaction he looked confused for a moment, like a lover caught out offering a bribe. "Please, come with me. Meet Arshu. Then you will understand."

He strode over to the wall screen and pointed at the spinning worlds. "Look at the evidence!"

In three large bounds Garrett crossed the fifteen feet, her eyes fixed on Bryce's gun beside the keyboard. As she reached out, her hand shook badly and knocked the gun away. She trapped it with splayed fingers. The metal was cold and heavy in her hand. She raised the muzzle to point at Bryce's back and thumbed off the safety.

He cocked his head to one side, like a listening bird, then turned round. Garrett stepped backwards and glanced to either side.

"What are you going to do? Fight your way out?" Garrett kept the gun trained on Bryce's chest. Her hand trembled. "You wouldn't make it five yards. Those gunmen out there are not amateurs. And they will already have the whole valley covered. They are searching for their leader's murderer."

"I must tell what I know."

"Without me, you are standing in a death trap."

"Then help me."

The gun sights wavered but stayed pointed at Bryce's chest. Bryce studied her, head still on one side. He ignored the gun.

"Rheinnalt, please? Stop this madness."

"You haven't been listening, have you? Madness is trying to stop true prophesy. Look," Bryce gestured at the screen. The speckled map was visible in a corner. "It is already real."

"We can stop–"

"Madness is allowing the destruction of ninety-nine percent of life on earth when you have a chance to prevent it. Madness is knowingly repeating the mistakes of the past. Put down that gun."

Garrett stepped back again. His calmness alarmed her and she was having trouble with her hand. The gun shook badly.

Bryce shook his head. "You wouldn't use it against me anyway."

"Not willingly." Garrett kept the gun aimed at Bryce's chest. "But I must try to stop the disease. And I will shoot in self-defence."

"No you won't."

"Help me publish the cure." She allowed herself a personal appeal. "Rheinnalt? We could do it together. Stop the deaths."

He was still a moment. She had touched him.

"I came because of you. You know that don't you?" His voice was soft. "I hoped you would understand."

"Would your father have understood?"

Bryce blinked.

"You told me he taught you a lot. Was it to kill indiscriminately? To commit mass murder?" Garrett looked at the gun sights, corrected her aim. She wondered what it would be like to pull the trigger, to fire a metal bullet. She wondered if she could do it. She had treated gunshot wounds.

"He was a good man but in many ways he was naïve." He cocked his head, like a bird listening to a distant call. Garrett recognised the attitude of attention from Jason, listening to the invisible. "I understand that now. Seeing your parents for what they are is part of growing up."

"Would your father have agreed with what you are doing?"

"I don't need his approval," Garrett saw a brief flash of anger, "but good has come of his death, and my mother's."

"Good? Help me Rheinnalt. Please?"

He shook his head sadly. "You haven't been listening."

"What you are doing is an atrocity."

"It is sanity. It is salvation."

"So the dead will just be unlucky," Garrett said bitterly.

"Everybody dies of something."

"Even your own people. Like Christmas."

"He welcomed his fate."

"Like my son?"

Bryce was silent a moment. "I regret Skyler's death. I told you it was not on my order. I even warned him. He ignored me." He paused then continued. "He chose his own fate. He became involved with Sikanda and his family, treading where he had no business. He was visiting their cell."

Garrett sagged against the edge of the desk. The pain of the loss rose and fell inside her, uncontrollable and unending, sucking her down in a black hopeless whirl. She saw the cell again, and Jason sitting on the bunk praying. Garrett stared at Bryce. The cell. She blinked with both eyes. *The cell.*

Suddenly she knew. She knew where to find the cure.

The slim hope bobbed up in her mind, small but certain. She clung to it, let it carry her briefly out of the helplessness, the unfathomed waiting grief. For a moment her mind cleared, free of the black pain. She tested the hope. Yes – it was possible. The anger she had felt in the greenhouse returned, strengthened with the sudden hope. She sensed she would pay a price but she clutched at it. The brutal energy steadied her. She stepped away, glancing once behind her towards the door leading to the greenhouse. When she looked back she noticed Bryce's right hand down by his hip. She remembered the gun he had picked up.

"Don't Rheinnalt. If you won't help, don't try to stop me. I will shoot."

He shook his head. "You wouldn't shoot me."

He reached behind his back. Garrett hesitated, checked her aim. He pulled out the other gun. He looked down at it as though counting change in his palm.

"There. That was easy, wasn't it?" He looked up at her, smiled, then raised his gun. "What you don't understand Christine, is the strength that faith gives–"

She pulled the trigger. There was a click. Nothing more. She looked at the gun. No bullets.

"I had to test you." His head twitched sideways. "I didn't think you would do it."

Despair rose in her again. She watched obsession curdle into mistrust. She knew what it would become.

"You realise I must kill you now." He looked angry, as though it were her fault. He pointed at the screen. "Krissa is spreading and during this time we must remain hidden. All over the world our communes are empty. We will not return for years, not until Arshu says the time has come for us to lead."

"The only thing that can stop us is if we are discovered. Arshu said you were a threat. I told him no. But I was wrong. He was right, as always."

"He told me you must be tested, your faith, in me, in us. And like any experiment," his voice was quiet, sad, "The outcome is always uncertain. You failed, Christine."

He raised his gun.

***

"I'm sorry Christine."

Garrett found in Bryce's eyes only calculation. A click sounded between them as he thumbed off the safety.

"Rheinnalt–"

Bryce's eyes narrowed in their aim. His fingers tightened around the gun butt.

"Before you kill me would you like me to tell you how Professor Richardson's message will be found by the authorities?"

Bryce's eyes adjusted focus. The pistol did not move. Garrett felt a moment of vertigo, looking down through another eye on two strangers faced off like arguing lovers. A memory of familiarity returned. She suppressed it with a shiver; it would cripple her for the effort to come. She studied the question lurking in Bryce's eyes. The understanding of him was intimate and offensive, but it calmed her. He wouldn't kill her. Not before he had heard what she had to say. He needed to know. She would confide in him. After that, he wouldn't be able to do without her.

He would start by asking what message.

"What message?"

"The message he threatened you with." Bryce gave no reaction. "Before he was killed."

Bryce was silent. Garrett used her anger to ignore the trembling in her legs.

"You were right to take him seriously. The threat was real." The silenced muzzle of the pistol nosed at her, within spitting distance but out of reach.

"What are you talking about?"

"The message was real." Garrett watched the gun track to the left then right then back centre.

"I don't have time for fantasy," Bryce said. "It's too late."

"Yes. How could he send a message? He must have been lying."

Bryce shook his head. Garrett watched his hand shift its grip on the pistol. His fingers tightened again. She spoke quickly. "Just think: a brilliant geneticist, a leader in his field, kidnapped, trapped in a lab without access to the outside world, unable to call for help. How could such a man have got a message out beyond the walls of his prison?"

"What had he got access to? His wife and daughter?" Garrett shook her head. "Also prisoners. What about the tools of his trade? Test tubes, microscopes, organic reagents? No – all going nowhere, certainly not out of the lab."

Bryce smiled. Garrett watched the gun. "But there was one thing that was leaving. Something the professor had intimate day-to-day access to. Something designed to leave, to make its own way, its own living you might say, in the outer world."

Bryce became still.

"Yes. The organism itself." Garrett said. "His creation, the very thing he was forced to work on."

Garrett found the trembling calmed a little more with each purpose-filled word. She watched Bryce consider. She saw the dismissive shake of the gun.

"It's true it couldn't speak for itself. It couldn't be told to post a letter or make a telephone call. But remember our professor is brilliant."

Her voice became hard and cold as steel wheels set on a fixed rail. "You are not sentimental so it's important you understand what I am suggesting. Real possibilities. My life depends on it. And perhaps the lives of many others."

Garrett looked past the gun, past the man to the terrible, useful fact that she knew him. If she showed fear he would assume desperate imagination, not fact. But he would yield to a real threat to his obscene plan. A threat he understood. She forced herself to imagine a young medical intern requiring a lecture, and started casually.

"You know, computer scientists who work in computational genomics often observe that the mechanisms of biogenetics read like a communications protocol. Base pairs versus ASCII encoding sets, protein transcription versus data transmission, error handling through redundancy: genetics is an apparatus of chemical communication. Creationists have described it as the divine script, the genome as God's book of creation."

"So, you're a trapped geneticist," Garrett shook her head, "your only working medium an organism of your own creation. You need to get a message out. *Why not use God's own script?*"

Bryce stepped back. Implications fractured in his eyes. Garrett plunged on, committed to his education.

"Yes. You begin to see. As I did last night. So how? How could you communicate genetically? Is it really possible? Remember how a human message is stored in a document on a computer: it is a string of binary digits. Those ones and zeros represent letters – A is **1000001**, B is 1000010, C is 1000011 – put them together and you make words, so 10000111**0000001**1000010 is CAB. Use enough binary digits and you can store many words, many sentences – a message of any length. All you need to write that binary document are the translation codes."

Bryce blinked. Garrett controlled a shiver with her anger. She saw her thought unfolding between them. She began to speak more quickly.

"Now consider a genome. It's also a document of sorts, made up not of ones and zeros but strings of acids. The twisted strands of DNA are like long sentences written in a chemical language – their natural function is to define protein expression and so forms of life. But if you can write natural language into binary files, why not into this chemical book? All you need is to define translation codes between the genetic letters and a human alphabet."

Bryce was motionless. Garrett continued, twisting her crystalline idea on its axis, turning it for him to see entire.

"Of course unlike the binary system – where each symbol has only two possible values, one or zero – in this biochemical language each letter can be one of four possible acids, adenine, cytosine, guanine and thymine: A, C, G and T for short. That means instead of seven binary digits, sequences of just three acids would provide enough patterns to represent all of the twenty-six Roman letters. Let's say **AAA** is A, AAG is B, AAT is C. Then the word CAB would be represented by AAT**AAA**AAG. To write the word CAB chemically, you would just have to create this sequence of acids on a strand of the DNA, starting adenine (A), adenine (A), thymine (T), and ending in guanine (G). We already have adequate genetic modification techniques to do this work."

"Now, think about stringing these triplets together. What do you have? What have you written into the very genome of the creature you have created? Words. Sentences. More: a *message.*"

Bryce's eyes were unfocussed. Garrett continued, relentless. His doubt could kill her.

"I am not fantasizing. Last night, I saw a strange group of three-letter words scribbled on the wall of the cell where I was held: CAT, GAG, TAG, ACT. At first I thought they were a parent's attempt to teach his child simple words." Garrett shook her head. She studied the muzzle of Bryce's gun. "It was the use of those letters, A, G, T and C that gave it away. I realised I was looking at parts of a translation table."

Bryce shook his head.

"But where can such a message be written, is that what you're thinking? Surely a creature's DNA cannot be hijacked in such a way without catastrophic functional changes? Well every freshman geneticist knows the curious fact that over ninety percent of any genome is non-functioning: junk DNA, evolution's graveyard."

Bryce was unreadable. Did he not believe her? She continued to explain.

"What about space? Well, the entire human genome occupies a total of just over three billion DNA base pairs in twenty-three pairs of chromosomes, and has a data size of approximately seven hundred and fifty megabytes, which is slightly larger than the capacity of a standard Compact Disc, the rough equivalent of a pickup truck full of books. Admittedly the malaria parasite Plasmodium falciparum is smaller. It has fourteen chromosomes, twenty-three million base pairs of DNA. Around a megabyte of data. But that's still the equivalent of five hundred pages or a short novel. The junk, ninety percent? That's four hundred and fifty pages. Plenty of scribble room there."

"You're too smart to make the mistake of hoping that such a message will not be discovered, if it is there." Garrett gestured at the television screen. "This outbreak will trigger massive resources directed at understanding the disease agent. The strain will be sequenced. The sequence will be analysed. If the professor encoded a message, it will be flagged very clearly, very simply. I would guess a long sequence of the same acid at the start of the message would do the trick. Twenty adenine bases all in a row would catch the attention: that would never occur naturally. And the encoding pattern, he will have kept it simple – after all, this message is meant to be read, isn't it? Yes. If it's there it will be found."

Garrett's blunt words sped through the air between them. Blood stained Bryce's face. Suddenly his gun looked very small and crude.

"The question is, if there is a message... *What did he write?*"

"If it's only precise, adequate instructions to recreate this cure then when other researchers discover the professor's recipe in his message you may still be safe. But there is another possibility."

***

"What if the professor has told the whole story? Described your organisation. Named it. Identified this place. Do you believe a worldwide manhunt would not trace one of your groups? Interrogate then find all the others? Find this Exodus location? *Find Arshu?*"

Silence.

"What will they do with him?"

Garrett's question hung in the space between them.

"Of course, there may be no message. You may be safe. And even if there is a message, it may not lead back here. Arshu may be safe."

Garrett and Bryce stared at each other across the gun. Had she miscalculated? She continued to fire reasoned points, the only bullets she had, straight at Bryce.

"But I think you need to know, don't you?"

"New labs will already be studying Krissa. But we had a week's head start. We've already sequenced the genome. And we know where the dataset is: sitting on that Analyzer in Porton."

The gun did not waver in its aim. Garrett did not stop speaking.

"You don't believe me? Dial in now. Let's see."

Bryce stirred, as if from sleep. "We can't."

Garrett glanced at the screens. She felt a spike of panic. "Neither of us can afford to waste time. You need to know what that genome is saying. So do I. Every hour, every minute counts!"

Bryce stared at a point in space between them. He spoke slowly, word by word as the thoughts formed. "The Analyzer stores its data on a local drive."

He gave a slight shake of his head. "And it's on a Level Four subnet – Porton protocols won't allow those devices to be accessed remotely."

"Then there's only one way to reach that data." Garrett raised her voice, forced eye contact. "You weren't trained on that equipment were you? I was. You're going to need someone who can analyze the sequence for you fast." Garrett targeted her words at the muzzle of the gun.

"You need me."

Chapter 42

Four hundred feet below ground Zahra sat alone in the level four Parasitology lab in the midst of a firefly swarm of machine LEDs. She rubbed with the heel of her hand at the small of her back through her safety suit. She was beginning to feel the weight.

Sherlock's discs hummed at her elbow. It had been a long and furious day. There had been briefings all afternoon and evening, endless online conferences and meetings with other labs. Somewhere in the upper offices Skinner was waiting to be interviewed by some official. They were in shock.

It was hard to believe. The government had identified the Brighton malaria strain as a *weapon*. They said it must have been deliberately released. No-one credible had yet claimed responsibility.

Health trust reports were still coming in from across England – Portsmouth, Salisbury, Exeter – and each new infection centre had provoked fresh anxiety. They had escalated to level four protocols.

Inside the lab, the overhead fluorescent lights had been burning for eighteen hours. Zahra felt a strange sense of inversion. The pathogen was *out there*. It was meant to be the other way round.

She moved her hand around to her stomach. She had felt another kick that morning. It was such a strange feeling, her baby growing inside her, quickening unseen, part of her yet more than her. When they had discovered the transmission danger, afterwards, it had been a surprise to realise her first thought had been for the baby. *The baby!* Her baby. Her baby. She repeated the phrase to herself as if to ward off danger. She'd have to start thinking about names! She stroked her stomach. He? – She? – was safer inside.

Rheinnalt had called to say he was on his way in. He had sounded strained. He said Christine might be with him. Sounded like there was something between the two of them. Hard to believe.

The guys on annual leave would arrive over the next few days – MacLeish tomorrow, back from a family holiday in the Scottish Borders. He'd called from his car.

Zahra glanced at the wall clock. *Enough.* She logged off. Skinner had ordered her to get at least a couple of hours sleep; there were cots set up upstairs. She stood stiffly. She had to be careful. The baby probably needed her to sleep too. If she could.

At the hatch Zahra glanced back. She rolled her shoulders. It would be good if Christine was in; she'd be a help. She stepped out and spun the door handle.

In the empty lab, one of the overhead ceiling lights flickered. The fluorescent tube ticked away quietly as an element burned down in its partial vacuum. The sound was loud in the empty space, above the purring of air conditioning and spinning hard drives.

After a few minutes the lights went out.

***

Bryce refused to let Garrett search for Jason's body or check on Cherry. At the top of the path out of the valley Garrett looked back. She could just make out the oval depression of the Eye. She didn't want to leave him. Words from the St. Matthew's Passion rose through her. 'Ich will hier bei dir stehen.'

I would stand here beside thee. But you are gone.

Bryce nudged her in the waist with the gun. "Go!"

Garrett turned away. She stumbled along the track up to the headland.

They took Bryce's car. He directed her to drive inland, up linked river valleys eastward. On their right the moon swung back and forth like a roving searchlight. To the north the peaks of Snowdonia rose purple against the shaded base of the sky. Bryce turned on the radio.

...particularly affected are towns along the English south coast, including Brighton, Hove and Seaford.

There was a sudden, muffled groan. The sound rose in pitch and grew, becoming something between a scream and a roar, as if the sky were being torn in two from top to bottom. Garrett caught sight of a pointed fleck like a dart sliding with alien speed and straightness down the horizon. Bryce gave no reaction. He sat motionless beside her, the gun held in his lap.

She kept driving, fast, along curving roads, with an empty stomach. Jason's last dry kiss remained on her forehead. The ache of separation hollowed her. Tears formed and she refused them. She buried the image of the broken body out of reach.

They passed through tall black mining villages with brick sprawls and stone centres and names without vowels. The shapes of the surrounding countryside blurred together in the sweep of headlights, like a picture rubbed out by a child's hand. A trembling at the edge of her vision warned her of exhaustion.

Through the intermittent interference from the hills, a clearer, ministerial voice pierced the static.

"Make no mistake: we are under attack. This artificial disease has been designed to infect and to kill. It's been released within our borders and has already taken many lives. The safest place is indoors, at home, with your family. Your NHS trusts will give up-to-the-minute bulletins."

Bryce turned up the volume, as though interested in a match report.

"We may be physically apart but we must be together in spirit, and in our shared determination to survive this terrible attack. We should keep hope. We have the finest public health service in the world. Our scientists are at work. And we are not alone. Others have been attacked – in Indonesia, and maybe America. We have friends across the globe pledging their support and help. Together we will defeat this plague, this cowardly attack. Stay with your families. Remain calm. Be of good faith."

"They do not understand what they are facing."

Garrett did not reply. They had stopped at a set of lights in a railhead town of fifteen thousand souls. The place was still ending its bank holiday. Two young women in matching pink skirts stumbled down the pavement arm in arm, smoking and laughing. They ran a few yards. One of them held a can of lager at arm's length. She toasted something invisible, fell, and was hauled up by her friend. Behind them, a red neon sign in a lace-curtained window advertised "A sage". The two girls studied the occupants of the car at the lights.

Garrett drove on. The same thoughts kept recurring. How fast was the outbreak spreading? Had it reached here?

She steadied herself, reaching down beneath the surging fear, the bone tiredness, the pain in her left arm, to the cold clear currents of her old confidence; a confidence founded on understanding.

"What happened after you lost your parents? When you left the forest?"

"Why do you want to know?"

"Don't you want to tell me?"

Garrett slowed through a tight corner and accelerated out. The car's automatic gearbox changed up with a sliding jerk of momentum. When she glanced back at Bryce, he was staring down the approaching straight.

"Arshu came back to the valley with me – to my old family home – and we founded Asari together. He encouraged me to continue my studies and then to take a research position. Arshu has always been fascinated by the potential of science. The Asari greenhouse and seed bank, and the lab – he understood and supported our wishes before we had them." Bryce waved a hand in front of him. "It is hard to explain unless you have experienced it. When you share a vision, you think with one mind, act with one body. With Arshu, he knows our thoughts."

"You really believe that?"

Bryce looked sideways at Garrett. "You told me you brought your son up a Catholic. You must once have believed in a man who was all love? You knelt to him; you ate his body and drank his blood. That vision is clouded, unequal to our times. But the great Christian innovation, the finding and promotion of the perfect man over all, has not been lost. I've found it alive, made flesh in front of my eyes, Christ once again. I hear and see him."

"If he is a man, he is a primate, a mammal."

Bryce shook his head. "What happened? How did you lose your faith so completely?"

The road twisted in the headlights, fifty feet above a snaking river course. Garrett thought of Jason, then of Cherry's adamant smile.

"I grew up." Her voice was bitter.

"I think you blame your faith for what has happened to you. You are angry–"

There was a rumble as the car tyres clipped a line of cat's eyes. Garrett corrected position.

"Yes I'm angry. And yes, I blame the 'faithful' for harming, for taking from me, those I love."

"Faith is a hard gift–"

"Faith is childish. And deep down you know it."

A blind corner approached too fast. When she stabbed at the brakes the back wheels began to skid. Bryce put out a hand and held the dashboard.

"You condemn what gave birth to your own science."

Garrett steered into the turn, threshold braking until the tyres gripped. She accelerated hard out of the corner into the straight. The morning star was visible overhead, a sharp silver point nailed into grey.

Did he really want an argument? *Now?* After what had happened? She let the anger dry on her cheeks. At least it stopped her thinking about what she had buried. She continued to drive fast above the winding river, steering into the turns.

"Religion gave us our first chemistry, our first psychology, our first medicine. But in this century its claims are usually wrong–" as she drove through the sharp bends, Bryce's head began to jerk back and forth as though punched by an invisible fist, "–often immoral and always man-made. And those who hold to superstitions simply for comfort or by convention give cover to terrible misunderstandings; they prepare the ground out of which can grow truly pathological thinking."

"You mean us."

"Yes."

"You detest me for my faith."

"No I don't. I judge and hate what you do because of it."

"Did you not follow my thought experiment? Isn't it reasonable?"

"It is inhuman."

"Perhaps – compared to current human behaviour, which is psychotic. But it is right to take the necessary steps to avoid disaster. We are engaged in a holy war."

"Holy?" Garrett couldn't keep the contempt out of her voice.

"A war against the unbelief of planetary suicide."

"Salvation through mass murder?"

"A war fought with a new vision, combining the Eastern and Western Enlightenments. What we do is both spiritual and scientific."

"You're not a scientist. You are a lab assistant. You provided Professor Richardson with facilities and resources to manufacture your cure and pathogen, but you didn't create them. You use wind power but you couldn't invent the technology. You have a climate-controlled greenhouse – I doubt you built the components yourself. You've only enough knowledge to exploit and misuse. That is all."

"Not true."

"You need me to decode a genome for you."

Leaving the city Garrett drove north as she was told along unlit country roads. She understood Bryce's caution. East of Cardiff the barrier of the Severn River forms the English-Welsh border and the two motorway bridges are monitored with cameras. Darkened villages swept past as road signs: Tideham, Stroat, Lydney. Bryce gave directions at each junction.

There are different silences between two people, between the dull, the embarrassed, the married or old friends. And there is the preoccupied silence of the dressing room before fights and matches with no waste of words or pretence of society.

The River Severn rejoined them for the run into Gloucester. They used the small road bridges on the outskirts of the city and turned to push south through the sleeping Cotswolds, through a road maze bordered by neat high hedges and haunted by religious memorials at every fork and crossroad.

***

The grasslands beyond the Porton Down chain link fence were standing grey waves, the sky above a blank white. At one point Garrett heard the faraway pant of a chopper coming in from the east. The aircraft flew unseen above the thick tree canopy shielding their parking spot. Bryce gave no reaction.

The guardhouse was barely a hundred yards away. Garrett could see a soldier on duty. It would take just seconds to sprint over and raise the alarm. But she sat still. Bryce had been clear.

"Understand I cannot allow any threat to our plans. If you try to escape, or draw attention to yourself in any way, I will shoot you. If necessary, I will shoot myself too –and early knowledge of a possible cure will die with us."

"Do not be mistaken. I do not fear death. This life is but a link in a chain. And Arshu will be waiting for me in the next."

Garrett was certain he would act as he promised. She was trapped in the knowledge that if a message existed, buried in junk DNA, it could be some time before someone stumbled upon it; and the smallest delay would cost countless lives. The speckled map from the news broadcast remained vivid in her mind.

She sat silent in her seat, hands folded like sleeping birds in her lap. Deep in her stomach she could feel waiting the loss and the trembling. The terrible pain was not gone: she knew it would return. But right now, for what she needed to do, she refused it, refused to think back to the valley, to the stone circle and what she had left there.

She held fast to her anger, let it make of her one piece, a single purpose, forged around the revelation of a possible cure. During the drive she had thought back, step by step over the last few years, since Skyler had first spoken of Asari. Each memory, re-evaluated, drew her purpose afresh over her anger, sharper each time. That was enough. She could not afford to feel more.

She had applied herself to the problem of finding a possible message, composing a series of regular expressions: powerful pattern-matching programs useable by Sherlock, each a single complex mathematical sentence.

The red and white road barrier beside the guard house rose and fell like a salute as a car passed through the fence. Garrett wondered if Micky was on duty. She shuffled her limited options but could see no way out of the cul-de-sac she had escaped down.

She was under no illusion: she had bought some hours, maybe enough to locate the cure; past that point she became expendable. He would make a quick clean end to it. He had the gun. She felt herself studied.

"When I met you I thought you were one of the walking wounded." The amusement was back in Bryce's voice. "I underestimate you. Again and again. And even when I decide not to, still I do. I cannot get your measure, Christine. "You look all claw and beak." She stared straight ahead. I know you are planning algorithms, analyzing chances, options–"

She did hate him then; hated most his understanding of her.

"Alright. Let's go." His command when it came, was abrupt.

She drove down to the gate. They were waved through without delay. Garrett drove across the grey meadows. The sky lightened a notch. Faint colour washed into the land.

She circled past the regimental HQ and drove out towards the lab compound. Five or six cars were parked out front. A busy morning. Garrett felt a lift of hope and glanced at Bryce. He was smiling. Her hopes sank back. He knew this complex. He understood its layout, its systems. He would not miscalculate.

He raised the barrier with his security card then directed her to a loading bay at the back of the main building.

"Move."

He took the car keys. The gun pushed her in the back towards a short flight of steps. They led up to a metal security shutter. Bryce swiped his security card then tapped a code into a keypad. Garrett heard the surprised glissando of an electric motor starting. The shutter rattled up, revealing a collection of crane-yellow flatbed trolleys and yard ramps, and at the back, a service lift. It rose out of the shaft when called, cables pulling smoothly upward as though hand over hand. Prodded into work, Garrett heaved at the heavy lattice gate. When it opened, in a concertinaed crash of metal, the unyielding finger poked her back again.

Garrett stumbled onto the lift floor. Looking down as she crossed the gap she glimpsed the plunging dark and felt a warm draught. She smelled hydraulic oil and something else, trapped and alive.

***

The lift squeaked as it descended, small metallic cries. Something else settled in her stomach with her weight at the bottom of the shaft. The lift opened onto a curving access corridor. Cold conditioned air poured into the spaces of her clothing. Fluorescent overhead light held no heat striking her face.

Bryce dug the gun into her kidneys. As they stepped forward their partnering footsteps scratched at the metal floor of the lift. Garrett sensed again the encircling concrete, the corridors and contained rooms, like the deep burrow of an oversized rodent. The underground pressed on her. A question shivered in her mind: *Am I just helping him?*

They stopped together, an arrested tango. The gun reminded her of the lead.

Wait! Think! What should I do?

Her thoughts took sudden flight, passing through the tons of surrounding earth, up and out, to consider from above the base, the inland and coastal towns, the speckled map of a country under attack...

The gun dug harder into her back. She wondered what a bullet would feel like. Hot? Like a needle? When she didn't move the gun pushed harder, bruising her spine. Her thoughts continued past her anger to the thought of other outbreak specialists at work, other doctors and researchers. There was another chance; she had to take it.

"Out!"

Garrett blinked, back in the lift, her back bruised. She took a breath and stepped out of the lift.

***

The outer access corridor was empty. They passed the door to the Bacteriology lab. Their shoes squeaked on the thick gloss floor-paint. They reached Parasitology. Bryce used his card. The door shut behind them.

So here we are again.

Pieces of equipment remembered themselves to her: a double-headed microscope, the microtome beside it, the submarine door into level III. Bryce pushed Garrett over to his desk.

The laptop vibrated in its docking station as it woke from cold standby. Garrett noticed a spare laptop battery beside the keyboard. The screens around the lab were blank, showing only power standby, except for one, Zahra's, where tropical fish swam back and forth.

Bryce reached out to flick a video switch. "Let's use the overhead projector shall we? It would be a shame to miss any of the show." He pulled out a stool for himself a few feet to the left and slightly behind her.

Garrett bent over the keyboard. "I'm going to connect to the dataset for the sequenced Krissa genome. Then I'll start a pattern recognition script."

She navigated folders, found the data file, started the pattern recognizer and keyed in the five regular expressions she had composed in her head on the journey. A window popped up with a message above an empty bar. *"Fourteen chromosomes in dataset. Processing one of fourteen..."* The bar began filling up from left to right, making level progress, like the predetermined flight of a bullet.

Garrett glared down at the keyboard. She estimated distances.

On screen the status window refreshed. The pattern recogniser had found nothing in the first chromosome. Bryce told off his lips, loudly. He held the gun two-handed, angled across his knees.

"Processing two of fourteen..."

The progress bar emptied and began refilling. Garrett let go of the mouse. The laptop battery, a narrow bar of black metal, lay six inches from her left hand. When she shifted her feet the on-screen cursor moved. In her peripheral vision, gold winked at her from Bryce's spectacles.

"How did Christmas survive for so long?" Garrett said.

The screen flickered. *"Processing three of fourteen..."*

"Christmas was O negative. That blood type confers a limited resistance to Krissa. The parasite cells don't clog the blood, cerebral hernias do not occur. Salivary glands are still colonised, so the carrier is still infectious, but he stays alive longer. That makes an O negative carrier a lethal vector."

"Processing four of fourteen..."

"A human mosquito, if you like."

Bryce watched, hypnotized by the progress bar. Garrett moved her feet again. She shifted her left hand. They watched the screen fill and refresh, fill and refresh, again and again without result. *Five of fourteen, six...*

Perhaps she had been wrong about the message. Or her regular expressions contained errors, or weren't checking for the right pattern. She had made an assumption: that Richardson wanted his message to be found. Her expressions looked for unnatural runs of base pairs to signal the quote-unquote of a message start and end. Then they trialled various candidate ciphers. Each was tested simply, against the two strongest patterns in English she could think of: the most frequently occurring letter – "E" – and words – "The", "Of", "And" – delimited by spaces. Primitive, but the best she could manage in the time.

"Processing seven of fourteen..."

"You were very lucky to survive Kirtananda at the hospital."

"Processing eight of fourteen..."

"His team don't usually make mistakes." Bryce's voice trailed off.

"Significant unnatural sequence identified. Processing... Processing..."

"Well, well," Bryce said softly, moving off his stool. His feet touched the ground. The gun still pointed at Garrett's back.

Okay. Careful! Don't rush. He will wait. He must wait. The battery lay under her fingertips.

"Unnatural sequence end detected. EBCDIC pattern match confirmed. Translating..."

Bryce leaned forward. Garrett let weight collect in her knees and onto the balls of her feet.

A lower text pane began to fill. As they read, the progress bar continued to fill and empty. *"Translating... Translating..."*

```
                    Cipher match analysis

        Trial scheme 3 indicated by letter and word frequency
                            analysis

              Encoding        EBCDIC
              Cipher          Baconian translation
              Probability     very high
              Start sequence  GGGGGGGGGGGGGGGGG
              Start location  Chromosome 8
                              Base Pair 1,102,223
              End sequence    GGGGGGGGGGGGGGGGG
              End location    Chromosome 8
                              Base Pair 1,124,007

                        Text translation

                             TITLE
        Termination protocol for malaria parasite Achilles, genome
                     carrier of this message.

                            AUTHOR
                   Professor Stephen Richardson

                           ABSTRACT
     The following compounds, collectively named Paris, will show
        significant immediate growth-inhibition rising to lethal
       effects for the parasitic infection by protozoa of strain
             Achilles. In addition, active ingredients in this
     pharmaceutical composition have a high selective toxicity.
     They contain no poisonous atoms such as antimony and arsenic
     and will not harm mammalian cells. Confirmed by in vivo assay
                             test.

                     METHODS AND MATERIALS
        Synthesis of 3-dibutylamino-7-diethylamino phenoxazinium perchlorate (Compound A-
     8). A mixture of 3-dibutylaminophenol (1.0 mL, 4.43 mmol) and N,N-diethyl-4-
     nitrosoaniline (790 mg, 4.43 mmol) was suspended in ethanol (55 mL) at room
     temperature.
        60% aqueous solution of perchloric acid (0.5 mL) was added by dropping to the
     suspension. The resulting mixture was refluxed with heating for 3 hours and cooled to
     a room temperature. It was then concentrated under reduced pressure to half an initial
     volume of its solvent, and cooled to 0° C. The resulting precipitate was removed by
     filtration and filtrate was concentrated. The concentrated crude material was purified
     by means of silica chromatography (eluate: chloroform:ethyl acetate=9:1) to give a
     crude compound. The resulting crude compound was dissolved into methano and cooled to
     0° C.
```

```
        Then a few drops of diethylether were added for crystallization. The resulting
dark blue crystal was filtered to give -dibutylamino-7-diethylamino phenoxazinium
perchlorate (33.3 mg, isolation yield of 2%).

        1H-NMR(400 MHz, CD3OD) δ: 7.77 (d, 2H, J=9.8 Hz), 7.38 (dd, 1H, J=9.8, 2.6 Hz),
7.35 (dd, 1H, J=9.8, 2.6 Hz), 3.77 (q, 4H, J=7.1 Hz), 3.70(q, 4H, J=7.8 Hz), 1.74 (m,
4H), 1.46 (m, 4H), 1.35 (t,6H, J=7.1 Hz), 1.02 (t, 6H, J=7.5 Hz). FAB-MS 380.

                                CLINICAL USE
        Pharmaceutically effective amount and administration route or means of the
compounds according to the present invention may be optionally selected depending on
therapeutic strategy, and the age, weight, sex, general health conditions and racial
(genetic) background of a patient. Generally, the compounds may be administered in an
amount of 1 mg~10,000 mg/day/70 kg of a body weight, more generally 50 mg~2,000
mg/day/70 kg of a body weight.
```

Scan completed.

Chromosome 8, Base Pair 1,102,223. Start sequence Gs. Encoding EBCDIC. EBCDIC, the old IBM mainframe encoding chosen by an old-school scientist. Garrett breathed out. She felt a lumpy mixture of pity and respect. *Well done professor.* She repeated the information in her mind, over and over.

She looked at Bryce. There was only a description of a formula. Their gaze held. What was between them was completed.

"Paris." He smiled. "Nothing more. Good old Sikanda. Always the scientist." He turned away. His voice was gentle, tender with her. "Christine–"

He raised the gun.

She threw her left hand like a punch, fingers opening. The battery extended her reach by a short flight. It hit the side of Bryce's head. He grunted and dropped to his knees.

The gun fell. It bounced hard, a pin ball rattling over the floor, off a lab bench, a wall, across the floor again, and stopped under the trap of Garrett's foot.

Bryce brought a hand down from the side of his head. The fingers were bloody. He looked up at the screen, dazed.

Garrett picked up the gun. It was heavy in her hand. She checked the safety was off.

"You were going to kill me," Her voice was as steady as her hand.

Bryce smeared the blood over his fingertips. "Life is a deadly business."

The outer lab door gave a decompressing hiss. Zahra ducked her head through the hatch.

"Sounds like I'm not the only one who can't sleep!"

Bryce hit Garrett low down, around her hips. Her left arm slammed into a bench as she went down. Pain lit up the nerves and for a moment she saw nothing. She heard Bryce roll past, chasing a released rattle. The rattling stopped.

"Hello?"

She was moving then, in between the lab benches, left, left, right, through the maze, quiet as quiet can be, except for her arm shrieking.

"Shani!" Bryce's shout echoed around the lab.

"Rheinnalt! What on earth…?"

"Help! I'm hurt."

"Hurt? How?"

"It's Christine!"

Garrett crouched low. Bryce was approaching Zahra, two lab benches away. *Making sure it's two against one. Then two against none. Then one against none, with no one left to tell.*

Stay on the move, stay low, out of sight. He has the gun. *Shani is bait for me, I'm bait for her.*

Must get the message out.

"Christine? What's going on here?"

"Be careful! Look, she hit me. I was lucky, I got her gun but she's still dangerous. Can you see her?"

"Why did Christine hit you?"

Garrett kept her head down. *He's backtracking, down the left side, looking along the rows. Use the cross benches.*

"Why is she dangerous? Rheinnalt!"

"Can you see her, Shani?"

Garrett placed her feet with care, her knees bent. *Track his voice. Stay low. Keep moving. Go for the exit. Predictable, but I must get the message out. Ah!*

Garrett stopped, crouched beneath the double-headed microscope. Pain throbbed blackly in her left arm. Zahra stood in front of the exit hatch, looking straight at her. Garrett held her breath. She could kill her with a word. Less. With a pointed finger.

"Shani, listen to me! We don't have much time. I think Christine was using us." Bryce's voice approached. Zahra and Garrett continued to stare at each other.

"We must find her! We don't know what she is capable of!"

Bryce's voice moved behind Garrett's back. She scuttled down another narrow corridor between lab benches.

"Rheinnalt? What are you–"

The silenced bullets sounded two soft thuds. The shots spun Zahra around. Bryce lowered the gun. He breathed in the smell drifting off the muzzle of the silencer. It reminded him of melted hair. *One down.*

Now finish it. It has to be done. Make it quick.

A dozen lab benches: she's in there, a mouse in the maze. Don't underestimate her this time. What is she after? *Getting the message out.* So where? Watch the workstations. There's the exit door, centre of the wall. Covered. Good. Now it's simple. Sweep the room. It has to be done.

Garrett crouched, panting, beside Zahra's body. The young girl lay curled on the floor hugging her belly. Blood stained the front and back of her shirt and trousers. Her eyes were open, wide with shock.

"Where were you hit?" Garrett whispered. She leant down to place her ear beside Zahra's lips to catch the reply.

"Left arm and leg."

Garrett looked around. She saw a computer under a nearby desk. Working quickly, she unplugged two USB cables. She tied one high on Zahra's left arm, using her teeth to pull it tight.

As she worked she listened. She could hear nothing except the hum of air conditioning and computers. *Where was he?*

She explored the exit wound in Zahra's left thigh with her fingertips. Anger tightened her chest, her throat. She tied another tourniquet then arranged clothing to hide the cables. Zahra looked frightened. Garrett leaned down to whisper, maintaining the precise calm and steady eye contact of a prescribing doctor.

"I can't move you. Close your eyes and stay still." Garrett listened. She could hear nothing except the pounding blood in her ears. "If I stay with you he will kill us both. Do you understand? Don't move."

Zahra nodded. She closed her eyes. Blood lay in a bright red pool around her body. Garrett tested the tourniquets. A squeak of floor paint sounded to her right.

She moved fast, by reflex, behind a bench. Thoughts repeated in her mind on a tight loop: draw him away. Get the message out. Must get the message out!

The exit was a few feet away. It was the only way out. Bryce knew it, and knew what she was thinking.

A sudden memory of a chessboard superimposed on the lab. Jason, a smart twelve-year-old in an endgame, just kings and pawns left, both clocks running down, her red flag up, his move simplifying, removing options, leaving her in Zugzwang: all choices losing.

An old response surfaced, bloody-minded, refusing, complicating... She turned round. Right, left, right, keep using the cross benches, keep moving, back, away from the exit. *Quick.* Pain seeping through my arm. Ignore it. Shattered glass from a monitor. Pick up that long shard. Keep moving. Faster!

She stared at the security keypad beside the Level III hatch.

***

She remembered Zahra's words. *No actually. We took a much more cultural, historical approach. Two numbers we could all remember, rotated every six months.* Dates. She had guessed at the time. And heard her key a four digit number to confirm.

Her fingers punched numbers.

2020. Enter. Invalid code.

Don't look round. Keep trying.

2019. Enter. Invalid code.

2018. Enter. Invalid code.

Garrett stopped. *Think.* Scientists choosing dates? She began punching numbers again.

Einstein. Special Relativity. 1905. Enter. Invalid code.

Okay. The General Theory. 1916. Enter. Invalid code.

Damn it! Garrett glanced behind her. Bryce was criss-crossing between benches, sweeping thoroughly as he advanced.

Newton. Principia. 1687. Enter. Invalid code.

Copernicus. 1543. Enter. Invalid code.

"Christine!" Bryce's voice held a brutal note. "Christine?"

Don't look! *Think!* A committee of biologists. *Biologists!*

1859. Enter. Invalid code.

"I'm sorry Christine."

Damn it! The other one!

1953. Enter.

The door hissed.

Garrett pulled hard on the hatch wheel. Metal squealed, loud in her ears. She pushed hard, darted through the gap. The sound of the ricocheting bullet fell from a high-pitch, a plucked snapping string. She followed through, using her momentum to swing the hatch door closed, one-handed, with a clang. Spin the wheel to reset the lock.

Down the changing rooms in a rush. Biosafety suits. Grab one. A helmet. Glance back – he knows the code. Must gamble some time. Slash. Slash. Slash. Slash. Slash. Slash. Slash. Slash. Slash. Slash. Slash.

Go! Another keypad. The other date. 1859. Enter.

The door hissed.

Yes! Close the door. Quick!

Bryce entered the changing rooms with care. He moved past rows of lockers, inspected the changing cubicles, peered beneath each door before opening. All empty.

The box of gloves and helmets too small to conceal a person. Where was she? *Where was she?*

There!

Garrett's face looked back at him through the toughened plexiglass of the Level IV lab observation window. Clever. Clever. As always, she surprised him.

Never mind. She was finally trapped. At the centre of the maze. Time to finish it.

Bryce turned to the biosafety suits. He swore. Long jagged cuts. In all of them. He looked back at the window. Garrett held up a handful of glistening glass: culture dishes, stoppered sample tubes, a solution flask. She threw them onto the floor. She returned to the containment freezers and came back with another handful of glass. She threw again. Bryce stared.

Free agents, God knows how many. Broken glass. He glanced at the suits then back at Garrett.

She was out of reach. And she knew everything.

For a brief moment he didn't know what to do. It was an unusual feeling, vertiginous, like falling off a cliff in the dark. But brief.

He nodded at her once then walked over to the alarms in the wall. He smashed the plate glass, reached in and pulled down on the red handle. A voice began speaking through a tannoy in perfect Queen's English.

"Warning: this is a biosafety containment alarm. It cannot be aborted. Please do not proceed unless there has been a level four or higher containment incident."

Bryce twisted the handle two full turns. Yellow lights began flashing behind him.

"Warning: this is a biosafety containment alarm. It cannot be aborted. Please do not proceed unless there has been a level four or higher..."

Bryce pulled the handle down fully. The precise voice echoed now more loudly, all around the walls.

"May I have your attention please. A level four containment incident has been raised in sector two. This sector is being sealed. All level four labs will be sealed in... one minute, level three in... two minutes. The facility will be sealed in... ten minutes. Personnel in all sectors, please exit immediately. I repeat: personnel in all sectors, please exit immediately. This is not a drill."

Bryce sat on a changing bench and cleaned his head and hands of blood. He heard the Level 4 door locks activate, the thud of the deadbolts quick-fire silenced rounds.

"May I have your attention please. A level four containment incident has been raised in sector two. This sector is being sealed. All level four labs will be sealed in... one minute, level three in... two minutes. The facility will be sealed in... ten minutes. Personnel in all sectors, please exit immediately. I repeat: personnel in all sectors, please exit immediately. This is not a drill."

The English voice was certain as a judge pronouncing sentence. He reviewed the containment protocols: power and fresh air would be cut to all sectors very soon; after ten minutes, no overrides would be allowed, all exits sealed, lift shafts filled with quick-set concrete foam: at that point, there would be no possibility of appeal.

He had underestimated her. *Again.* But for the last time. In the Level II lab Bryce stopped at his desk. The screen was still showing Richardson's message. He hit *Cancel*. A message box appeared. *Warning: analysis macro and output has not been saved. Do you wish to save?* He clicked *No*. The program returned to its start menu.

On the way out he saw Zahra's body lying on its side in a pool of blood.

Half-a-dozen lab technicians waited by the lifts, calling out questions. The panic was controlled. Outside, a slight breeze brought fresh air, like a reviving breath. He headed back to the service lift and his car. Shadows were shortening over the ground. He could see the sun's orange disc already rising behind a stand of birch trees.

It had been close. Very close. *That message.* Buried in junk DNA. Yes, it might be found. Some accident might reveal it, or some talented researcher spot it. Eventually. After weeks, months maybe. After it was too late. The Rebirth was still safe.

He looked at the elegant silver birches and thought of Christine. The regret was sharp. He had offered her everything: life, a future, salvation; she had chosen the dark. He remembered her fear of the black underground space. The labs would be dark. He thought of Arshu, the love he felt for him, the absolute loyalty he owed. He had had no choice.

One tree stood over the others. Its falls of golden leaves hung over the fence, almost but not quite touching the ground.

Chapter 43

"May I have your attention please. A level four containment incident has been raised in sector two. Sector two has been sealed. The facility will be sealed in... three minutes. Personnel in all sectors, please exit immediately. I repeat: personnel in all sectors, please exit immediately. This is not a drill."

He had not looked back at her as he had left. And he understood what would happen to her. *Don't think of him.*

She looked around. A dozen feet away, a yellow alarm light flashed above the exit door.

Must get the message out. Three minutes! The door! The airlock.

On the other side of the lab the freezer cabinet doors stood open. She looked down. The rubbersoled boots of her safety suit were wet. The surrounding floor, darkened with spilt liquid, was frosted with grains of thawing tissue and splinters of broken glass. Spilled liquids were evaporating into the air. She remembered Zahra's recitation of the freezers' contents, with the cross-sector comparison project underway: Cholera, Ebola, Tularaemia, Typhoid, Hantaviruses, Botulinum Toxin spores, Encephalitis, Anthrax... and she had thrown everything she could.

Would the rubber boots puncture? Well, stand here forever or else take the risk, Christine. She took two sliding steps. Glass scratched like fingernails. Sweat trickled down her arms.

She reached the airlock with a minute and a half to spare.

The door was controlled by large buttons marked with Open and Close chevrons, like the passenger doors on trains. She pressed Open.

Come on!

She pressed again. The door did not move. Open. Close. Open. Close. Open. Open. Open. Come on!

"...The facility will be sealed in... thirty seconds..."

She thought again about the released disease agents: Nipah, the haemorrhagic viruses, Poxes, MDRTB, Yellow fever...

The airlock door wouldn't open. Of course it wouldn't. It shouldn't. She stood in the most lethal place in human history.

The lights shut off.

"May I have your attention please. This facility has now been sealed."

Garrett stared into the darkness. There were no equipment lights. And she could no longer hear the hiss of air conditioning.

***

Operating mode: ISOLATION. Power remaining: 52 minutes.

Letters and numbers blinked lime green at the bottom of her vision. The digits shifted humourlessly.

Operating mode: ISOLATION. Power remaining: 51 minutes.

It was quiet, the only sound the low buzz of the helmet filters. She thought of the lab air lines. Pointless without power. She thought again of the spilled contents of the bio-containment freezers in the surrounding air. She refocused on the countdown. Fifty-one minutes of helmet power. Fifty-one minutes of clean, filtered air.

She stared past the constant subtitle. Behind it was black on black, matching the black pain seeping out of the cut below her left elbow. She cradled the forearm against her stomach. She found the pain slippery and hard to control, increasing with the silence.

Cold began to seep into her suit. It was tempting to stop for a while, sit down perhaps. She forced herself to move. She tried not to think of the glass.

A hand outstretched, she sidled around the edges of the lab, along benches, the observation window, walls. In her shuffle, she felt suddenly old, uncertain.

It was Bryce who had reduced her to this. She trembled. He was responsible. The thought spiked repeatedly through her.

Step-by-step she explored the limits of her cage. She returned repeatedly to the airlock, always trying the door buttons as if for a reward. She moved into the middle of the room. By touch alone, she made an inventory of the lab equipment. It was slow fruitless work.

One thought kept repeating: only she and Bryce knew of the message hidden on chromosome eight.

Must escape. Must tell.

When she blundered into a freezer she cried out. Pain darkened her arm, then flooded through her body. She almost blacked out. Fresh blood trickled along the fingers of her useless hand. The thought of blood loss dismayed her out of all proportion.

"No!"

Her feet were cold and wet – was that blood too? She shook herself. *Stop it.* She peered into the blackness behind the countdown. Must continue.

She blundered on. Blood thudded in her head. She always tried the power switches, on centrifuges, microscopes, the freezers. After a while she realised she'd exchanged hope of escape for a new craving – for light, any spark or glow or flame, to push back the blackness.

It was the animal instinct to be still, and exhaustion – physical and of logic – that drove her to ground in the end. She remembered the containment protocols. She felt her pulse miss and catch. The lift shafts would be sealed by now. She kicked down deeper, for purchase, and found nothing. She stopped in a corner and sat on the floor. After a few minutes, she made a pillow of her right arm on her knees.

Thirty-five minutes.

She closed her eyes against the subtitles. Tiredness swept through her with the cold. A loosening, like the release of sleep, slowed her circling thoughts. She opened her eyes briefly. *Thirty-four minutes.*

***

What do you reach for in your extremity? Your fears? Your lover? Your God?

Garrett saw Jason's punctured body in her arms, the image in her mind's eye vivid as light stained through the memory of film, his mouthing 'mother' silently, once, eyes closing, lips beginning to mutter his holy syllables; she understood then, and accepted his giving up of her in that moment for the peace he had learned to find. Acceptance. To see the facts as they are, not as wished, an objective subject. A hard and holy spell he had called it. He had been right about that much.

Under her closed eyelids beneath the blanketing dark she sought memories of his childhood. His first steps, holding a single finger; his tantrums at night, a three-foot-long body rigid from head to toes with the injustice of bedtimes. After some minutes she stopped. The memories were not bearable.

She sat absolutely still. Further movement was a waste of energy. Jason's spell returned like an offered gift. Perhaps clearing her mind was not. She raised her head and settled her back against the wall.

Operating mode: ISOLATION. Power remaining: 12 minutes.

Time. She dealt with that first. A breath every three seconds. Twelve minutes. Two hundred and forty breaths left to her. So be it. Take one.

Next: Rheinnalt Bryce. The only other person who knew of the existence of the Paris formula. The man who had trapped her here. He was out of reach. Let him go.

Now the plague: how many were already infected? In Brighton, Glastonbury, Aberystwyth, London… as a doctor she knew only too well the horrors they would face and the possible numbers of dead.

Something flickered behind her eyes. She didn't want to die. For a moment an ancient impulse bowed her head. She waited in silence, like a lover for a single word. She realised she was straining to hear a voice, to see some light. She turned her head. The dark was an uninterrupted wall around her.

Two hundred and thirty-one breaths. Two hundred and thirty breaths. Two… hundred and… twenty-nine... Panic filled her mind, together with the image of the Harrowing in St Andrew's Church. *The one sin that cannot be forgiven.* She didn't want to die. *Just one prayer.* She felt her balance go. Without thought, her weight settled on a knee. *It is never too late for Confession.* She considered the offer.

No.

Her thoughts steadied. She opened her eyes. Fear of the closed underground space rushed through her and she accepted it, again and again, as it burned away. She waited. The silence held.

The focus of her attention swept round and round the lab, her mind a still centre as she stared into the black. Keep thinking. Keep searching.

She returned again to what she knew of the complex and its systems. It was based on a ring design. *Yes.* What else?

Concentric circles of increasing biosafety, sectored by labs of different specialisms. That's right. *What else?*

Level II led on to level III led on to level IV and so on. *What else?* The lift shafts had filled already. What else? At the centre there was a level V storage facility.

Operating mode: ISOLATION. Power remaining: 11 minutes.

She rose to her full height in the dark. Breathe. Steady – use every breath. Plenty of time to be cold and still. Her feet moved inside her rubber galoshes. Now think again.

She was in the Sector II Level IV lab. Near the centre.

Yes.

An idea loomed through her fears, suddenly visible, clear and entire. Level V was accessed through the Level IV labs.

There was another door.

She moved by touch and shuffle to the spot marked in her memory, opposite the airlock. It felt good to be up and moving again, even if she was heading away from the exit. The exercise warmed her blood. Her free hand reached out to wipe the walls, head-high down to her feet, a gesture like a wizard's incantation; except she guided her hand along a curve differentiated to maximize probabilities with a minimum of movement.

Operating mode: ISOLATION. Power remaining: 10 minutes.

There! A wheel. Set low, hip-high, recessed into the metal, with a keypad, just as she remembered. It would be red. The door fit into its frame fingernail tight.

How had she missed it earlier? She had been tired, frightened, reaching out only head and chest high. Use the keypad!

1953. Enter.

The door hissed. Garrett smiled at her thin victory. The predictability of scientists! Her smile widened. With her good hand she gripped the wheel and turned.

Operating mode: ISOLATION. Power remaining: 9 minutes.

The room beyond was small. She explored by touch. There were fridges, and a series of doors set in the circular wall allowing entry from other sectors, each secured via a keypad.

Operating mode: ISOLATION. Power remaining: 8 minutes.

Her dates didn't work. Nor obvious number patterns. She used precious breaths trying every combination she could think of, at every door.

7 minutes.

All these doors and she was still trapped! She turned round and round. The new room had felt like a brief escape. To know it was only an extension of her prison was too bitter to accept. There must be another way!

Operating mode: ISOLATION. Power remaining: 6 minutes.

Garrett stared at the merciless countdown in her face plate. It would not stop.

Six minutes! She squinted. Or five? For a moment she was uncertain. Six. She turned slightly. Five? She shook her head. Six. Five. Six. Five. She moved towards the centre of the room.

An LED chip of light of the same lime green as her face plate countdown glowed unmoving, separated now from that number. Garrett felt carefully. Her gloved fingers explored the outline of a thin tablet resting on top of one of the fridges. A cord extended out of one side. Power. Off. But the LED was still on. Battery power.

***

*Operating mode: ISOLATION. Power remaining: **4 minutes**. Warning: please exit the lab or reattach helmet to a power source.*

Garrett found the laptop catch. She opened the lid. Dead keys rattled beneath her fingers.

The power switch had a positive click. The machine vibrated with the shiver of a waking animal. Garrett stared spellbound at the dazzle of white lettering spinning for a memory chip check. The electronic fire lit the storage room, making of the grey walls a cave where her shadow moved. She looked around her, wondering.

*Operating mode: ISOLATION. Power remaining: **2 minutes**. Warning: please exit the lab or reattach helmet to a power source.*

Garrett tapped in login credentials. The machine gurgled. Garrett waited. *Come on! Faster!* The machine gurgled more. *Come on!* Like a baby, it would not be hurried.

*Operating mode: ISOLATION. Power remaining: **1 minutes**. Warning: please exit the lab or reattach helmet to a power source.*

The machine showed a desktop. Garrett requested a network link. The machine thought a moment, muttered something inaudible then agreed to initiate a connection.

Garrett watched the electric paint dry and tried not to watch the countdown. *Okay, where's the silver lining here?* She tried to grin. She considered one piece of luck, a fact of modern infrastructures, that power and communications are delivered by separate distribution networks: occasionally useful, during miners' strikes, or trapped in sealed military biosafety labs... She smiled, then winced at fresh pain in her left arm.

A beep announced a connection.

Operating mode: ISOLATION. Power remaining: **30 seconds.** *Warning: please exit the lab or reattach helmet to a power source.*

She accessed her webmail, her mind a white pin of concentration. Time for one sentence. To all staff. *Send.* She checked the Sent Messages listing.

Christine Garrett	
To:	**ALL_STAFF;**
Subject:	**UK malaria outbreak**
Sent:	23 July 2020 10:54
Importance:	High

The agent causing the UK malaria outbreak carries a message in its genome at Chromosome 8, Base Pair 1,102,223, start sequence Gs, encoding EBCDIC, with manufacturing instructions for an antidote.

Dr Christine Garrett

<<<<<<<<<<<<<<<<<<<<<<<<<<<<<<<<<<<<<<<<<<<<<<<<<<<<<<<<<<<<<<<<<<<<<<<<<<<<<<
This email is intended for the named recipient only. If you have received it in error you have no authority to use, disclose, store or copy any of its contents and you should destroy it and inform the sender. Whilst this email and associated attachments will have been checked for known viruses whilst within WHO systems we can accept no responsibility once it has left our systems. Communications on WHO's computer systems may be monitored and/or recorded to secure the effective operation of the system and for other lawful purposes.
<<<<<<<<<<<<<<<<<<<<<<<<<<<<<<<<<<<<<<<<<<<<<<<<<<<<<<<<<<<<<<<<<<<<<<<<<<<<<<

Garrett re-read the message. Done! She sat back.

After a moment something like a shrug leaned her towards the laptop again. She clicked "Forward" then typed an address.

To: george.skinner@dstl.porton.mil. Send.

Operating mode: ISOLATION. **No power remaining.** *Exit the lab or reattach helmet to a power source.*

Garrett closed her eyes. Adrenaline drained away. She had done what was necessary. She felt the dizzying spin of blood pressure loss. In that moment she lost her bearings, lost track of her breaths and the countdown. Time slowed.

Her mind reached beyond the lab, beyond the great buried wheel of sealed rooms around her, up above Salisbury Plain, the Cotswolds, England, out among specks of rock and gas circling in an endless day, out farther to where clusters and whorls of stars retreated before greater wheels, mathematical and chemical. Successive moments distanced, became fixed panes of sensation in a spinning apparatus filled with light. She glimpsed her life not starting and ending, not as causes and events, simply a succession of moments, whole as it would always have been, in the eternal cinema of the present.

Eternal recurrence: the thought visited her fleetingly and she remembered the Eye of Faith and its ring of paved stones with their carved inscriptions of heaven and rebirth. Accepting her fear, she saw the childishness behind the wishes.

Illuminated by the pain flooding her body, events replayed in her mind. *Not the end. It seems like it at first. But it's not... Every day I see him all around me. And I am him in so many small ways. How I cook a meal, read a newspaper, write a letter...* Her words to Cherry came back to her. Then, without possibility of action, she reached back further and chose at last the consolation of memory.

Jason was running beside her in a grey dawn, holding her hand, forever quicker on his feet, a faint smile on his lips when he glanced at her. The image faded as her sight dimmed, but her life lay still and present, out of time, like linked scenes in a film lying dark on the reel.

She bent her head until the visor of her helmet rested on her arms. In the gloves of her suit her fingers clenched reflexively around the memory of Jason's hand as they ran through the valley.

Chapter 44

"Shani's still in there!"

White faced an angry department head outside the entrance to the lab complex. He had arrived at the base barely an hour ago, after reassignment to profile the Porton team. His interview with Major Skinner – the research manager facing him – had been interrupted by the alarm.

"Sir!" A military policeman approached in a hurry. "Sir, we've just been told–"

"Wait up," White extended his hand for Major Skinner to continue.

"One of my team, Shani Zahra's missing," Skinner gestured at the guard standing a little way off, "Gary saw her in the lobby maybe twenty minutes ago. She took the lift down to the labs. No one's seen her since."

Skinner's phone beeped at his belt. He ignored it. White turned to the MP who spoke in rapid bursts, like a semi-automatic.

"Sir, we've completed a physical perimeter inspection. All exits secured."

"Signals?"

"They're running full diagnostics remotely. All offsite admin servers and routers are still up. They've just reported the containment alarm was raised in Sector II, Level III."

"That's my lab."

White's eyes flicked back to Skinner. "It's possible your man raised the alarm." He turned back to the MP. "What else?"

"The main lift access shaft has been sealed. System monitors are showing all sectors, all levels locked down. The service shaft is registering an error. It is being checked."

"The DeCon team?"

"On its way."

"Thank you sergeant. Keep me informed."

"Yes sir. Oh, sir, Gold command is being set up in Whitehall."

"Who is it?"

"General Allcock."

The MP retreated to a black Land Rover whiskered with aerials. White turned back to Skinner. Something in the other man's face caught his attention.

"What is it?"

"I think you need to read this." Skinner passed over his phone.

```
"The   agent   causing   the   UK   malaria   outbreak
carries  a  message  in  its  genome  at  Chromosome  8,
Base  Pair  1,102,223,  start  sequence  Gs,  encoding
EBCDIC,  with  manufacture  instructions  for  an
antidote.  Dr  Christine  Garrett."
```

White's eyes focused past the other man, over his shoulder. Three vehicles had appeared on the road between the lab complex and the Porton base. White looked back at the message. It had a ghostly quality, as if sent from the grave.

"If it's true–" Skinner did not complete his sentence.

"Forward it to me." White tapped at his own phone. "CDSC can look into it."

Garrett's e-mail was sent on to Colindale and the other investigating labs. White left a voicemail with his service head then dialled a number. The vehicles on the road could be seen more clearly now, green four-tonners moving at speed. "Yes. I need an e-mail trace. *Now.*"

The lorries approached the compound. The racing throb of their diesels could be heard from a distance. The vehicles entered the compound and circled to a stop in a roar of dust. A small group in white biohazard suits jumped out of the back of the first. A uniformed officer coordinated unloading with barked orders.

The trace report was short and simple. White nodded at the lab. "The e-mail came through routers in this complex." He did not sound surprised.

"Christine's in there too," Skinner whispered.

"Colonel Scales, Bronze scene commander." The uniformed officer stood in front of White. "Who are you?"

White made introductions then briefed him. "Colonel, we've got two, possibly more, people inside."

"Alive?"

"We don't know. But as of five minutes ago, it appears Dr Christine Garrett was alive enough to send this." White showed the officer the email they had received and explained the trace.

"Sir," the MP approached again, "The service lift shaft did not seal. There was a fail on the sealant trigger."

"Can it be repaired?" Colonel Scales asked. "Can we seal the shaft?"

"Wait!" Skinner interrupted. "It's possible to override the door locks remotely, isn't it? I saw it done in training."

"My orders–" Colonel Scales began.

"Commander," Skinner spoke low and fast to White, "The information in this e-mail, if true–"

"My duty–" Colonel Scales began again.

Skinner raised his phone. "–could save hundreds of thousands of lives, maybe avert a catastrophe. Christine Garrett may know more, if we're not too late." He pointed into the ground. "That lift shaft is a chance. If we don't use it, if we seal it, we may be bottling in that lab our best hope of stopping this disease."

"Major, are you suggesting we break containment protocols?" Colonel Scales said, openly astonished.

"Containment! The epidemic is already running! Early cases are dying. Hundreds are infected. Transmission is happening across the country!" Skinner swept his arm across the surrounding fields. "The disease is *out*."

There was an awkward silence.

"Colonel, *is* it possible to override the door locks?" White asked.

"I should remind you, this lab contains Level V weaponized agents," the Bronze commander said stiffly.

"Colonel, is it possible to override the door locks?"

Colonel Scales did not look prepared to reply.

"Sergeant?" White asked the MP standing beside the colonel.

The man looked from one officer to the other. White's waiting silence forced him to speak. "Theoretically, yes."

"How?"

"Signals are already accessing the admin servers. They have root authority."

"I will not authorize any action that will compromise the integrity of this facility without direct orders from Gold command," Colonel Scales said. He turned on his heel. Discussion was over.

White called Whitehall. Dame Frances Burnett had received his voicemail. She had called Sir Peter Hammond directly. They set up a conference call with a WHO lab which had been forwarded Garrett's email.

They waited four minutes, the time it took their top biogeneticist to check twenty-four amino acids – the message start sequence – in a dataset he had received the previous evening. While they waited, White explained the situation to Burnett. When they had confirmation, she put him through to General Allcock personally.

Decisions took ten more minutes, time Skinner was aware they didn't have.

Chapter 45

Zahra squinted at the wall. Long hand on the five, short on the four. She closed her eyes then opened them again. Long hand on the nine. How had that happened? Only an hour now till visiting.

Who'd be first through the door? The usual suspects. Her Mum. George Skinner. Fly hopefully. A strange man – he had an earring – but she liked him. He brought her jokes instead of flowers. Her eyes closed. When she opened them again the clock hands had straightened out. She looked over at the other bed. Christine lay still, her left arm bound in white at her side. Her face was closed, the skin pale. When she had first woken, her open eyes had looked like two holes in snow.

Zahra had been told about the final lab operation at Porton. The DeCon team, led by Skinner, had worked fast. They had reached Garrett where she had sealed herself in Level V. Her helmet had still been running on reserve power, as cautious in its warnings as a fuel-empty light. She had been quarantined. Screened. Stained slides had shown the presence of the Krissa infection. Nothing else.

Her own survival was thanks to the tourniquets; they had stopped critical blood loss. The paramedics had found her unconscious through body shock and reduced blood pressure. She put a hand on her stomach. The foetus was stable.

They owed Jim – Mr Da Costa the nurses called him – the room. Soon after they had transferred he had arranged it. He said he'd noticed the messages back and forth. Said he thought the nurses had better things to do than run between the two of them all day. Said conversation was good for recovery but they shouldn't stay up too late. He had been formal, like he was writing a prescription. *Three chats a day, after meals.*

Zahra glanced over at a rustle of starched sheets. Ah! And was that a smile? Well, something. Not much of a smiler, is Christine. Too tough for her own good.

"Hi."

That's better. Her eyes look okay. Still a little dull. That'll be the morphine.

"Nearly showtime."

"Oh, is it? What time?"

"Six." Zahra glanced up at a knock at the door. She pushed a pillow up behind her back, adjusted her hair. Garrett watched then did likewise. They looked at each other and nodded. "Come in!"

Zahra smiled. "Hello Fly!"

"How you doing, girls?" Fly stepped into the room. "I brought someone to say hello."

"George!" Zahra smiled.

"Ladies."

The men crossed to the beds.

"We've been told we can't stay long," Fly said. "She been behaving herself?" he asked Garrett.

Garrett met his careful, measuring stare. "No."

"I'm not the one caught trying to get out of bed," Zahra protested.

"Jim says you're not out of the woods," Skinner cautioned.

"Jim's just a worrier." Zahra frowned at Skinner.

"He is," Fly agreed, looking from Zahra to Skinner. Something passed between the three of them, easy to miss, like the flight of a bird.

"Why can't you stay long?" Zahra asked. She rubbed at the side of her stomach with the heel of her hand.

Fly shrugged. "Apparently Christine's got to talk to some big cheese."

Fly went over and hugged Garrett.

"My turn," Skinner said over Fly's shoulder.

The visitors found chairs. They spoke of Cherry. Fly had attended her funeral. He had given a short speech.

Garrett said little during the conversation. She listened, and nodded. Skinner sat beside her. He spoke often to her, small exchanges, about pain relief, her arm, bits of news. His sentences were paced slow, to match her stamina. She replied mostly with single words. She had learned that he had spent a lot of time with her while she was unconscious, watching the monitors, the drips, as she recovered from critical blood loss. It had left them comfortable with each other without speaking. It was an odd bond – inherited half-conscious, like a parent's – and she wasn't sure how she felt about it yet. She wasn't a child.

It was easiest when they chatted medicine. Something done before. Skinner had new statistics on the epidemic. Mostly good news. Paris was effective, and easy to manufacture and distribute; because it was water soluble it could be added to public water supplies. With a cure, public co-operation was high. Regional Epidemic Centres were controlling re-infection. The conversation became technical.

Fly interrupted, leaning over to kiss Garrett on the cheek. "You did good," he said. When she started to speak he held her with his old, weighing eyes a moment. The memory of Cherry was between them. Then he shook his head slightly. "You did better than good."

He went out for teas. Garrett lay back and closed her eyes.

"I'm a very busy man."

"I don't care how busy you are. You'll wait your turn. This is a hospital not a government ministry. It's bad enough having police officers on my ward day and night." The head nurse pointed at the clock. "Come back in twenty minutes. I suggest you wait in reception."

Andy Connell took out his organiser. The head nurse stared. "And I'd appreciate your turning that off while you're in the hospital."

She picked up a sheaf of papers and bustled away down a corridor. Connell stared after her.

"Yes matron," he said, sotto voce.

White watched the other man holster his phone like a defeated gunfighter. "I don't think they call them that any more."

"Nice legs," Connell said, still staring after the nurse. "Come on, let's go outside. I need a fag."

They found a windy corner away from the expectant dads and doctors on breaks.

"We've found another commune. South Peru. Near the Aguada Blancas."

"Sounds lovely." Connell offered a cigarette. White shook his head. "And?"

"Same setting as the others: a deep coastal river valley. That makes thirteen now."

"Don't tell me: there was no-one there." Connell lit his cigarette.

"Some squatters moved in six months ago. They know nothing except useless gossip." White spread his empty hands.

"It's the same pattern: nobody left behind with hard information."

"Anyone saw them on the move?"

One of the expecting Dads came over for a light and company. Connell scowled at him. He went away.

"We traced a large group of travellers to a small port called Arica across the border in Chile. We think it was them from the MO. They embarked the day they arrived, all of them, on a vessel leased in advance for cash, their crews let go. The destination filed was San Juan de Lurigancho. They never arrived. That was a year ago."

Connell sucked on his cigarette and contemplated the glowing tip. "Where the fuck do you think they all went Charles?"

White shrugged. "Pick an ocean. The five ships we know about are all under three hundred tons, so aren't required to have AIS transponders. My guess is they rendezvoused with a bigger vessel and were scuttled."

"What about the people we've picked up here in Wales?"

"We were lucky. They were expecting to leave any day. One of them handled the drug money, knew the other communes, the banks... otherwise we wouldn't have got this far. The group appears to be obsessed with secrecy."

"And no-one's spilled on where the others went?"

"No. They don't know."

"What about the other four suicide vectors?"

White shook his head. "Same. I'm certain none of them were told. It's impressive when you think about it. I wish our compartments were that tight."

"Christine Garrett–"

"We intercepted this note this morning, addressed to her." White took a saffron-orange slip of paper from his wallet and passed it to Connell.

"The story is not yet ended, it has not yet become history,
And the secret life it holds
can break out tomorrow in you or in me."
Gershom Scholem

I will never forget you.
Osei

"Osei?"

"We think it's the researcher from Porton," White said. "Bryce."

"Do you think he'll come after her?" Connell watched the traffic passing along the road in front of the hospital. "He'd be mad to right now."

White shrugged and shook his head. "Unfortunately it doesn't look like we'll catch him any time soon. This group, if they stay gone, well we aren't going to find their tracks in the sea."

Connell flicked ash. His mouth twisted. "So stay on the money. The pressure we're putting on the Swiss–"

"I've an update for you there. We got the information an hour back."

Connell gave a bully's smile of pleasure. His hand said gimme.

"Three years ago the group liquidated their assets. Converted to cash deposits, then over a three-month period withdrew the lot, physically; paper bonds stacked like bricks in sacks. And there was a lot. An astonishing amount. In over a dozen separate Zurich investment houses. Bottom line: the money's gone too."

"Jesus." Connell stared at the other man. "You've got nothing."

When the two men returned to the Emergency Unit the head nurse was back at her station. Her voice rang out across the ward.

"You can go in now. Excuse me!"

Connell's face darkened as he turned.

"One at a time thank you."

"George definitely likes you," Zahra said.

Garrett raised a warning eyebrow.

"And he's very polite." Zahra considered this then added, "Maybe too polite. I don't know about you but I like–"

She stopped as the door opened to let in a new visitor. He had inquisitive eyes. They took in and dismissed Zahra in one glance. "Christine. Andy Connell. <u>Andy</u>."

Garrett blinked. First name terms. The man was barely in the room. She watched him wait for her reply. His eyes, ears looked open to all signals. She was reminded of a hare. Why was he here?

His hands were clasped over his crotch. "I'm here on behalf of the Prime Minister." They managed some small talk. The man dropped a few more names. He returned to his boss. "He wishes to convey to you the debt of thanks that this country owes you. And to acknowledge your bravery."

He was waiting again. He wanted something from her. What? She understood that he had pushed hard for this interview.

"Well it's very good of you to pop down and say hello," Zahra said firmly. "And you can thank Him too. But Christine needs to rest now."

"I don't think you quite–" Connell started. Garrett saw the hare show its teeth, then think better of it and wait, ears flat and open. Garrett said nothing. "Of course. Well I won't disturb you any longer. Perhaps when you're feeling better you'd like to join the PM at Number Ten? He'd be delighted to see you. Consider it a standing invitation."

"*Perhaps you'd like to join the PM at Number Ten?*" Zahra mimicked when he had left. She rolled her eyes.

They had one more visitor. Surgeon-Commander White was an old soldier, with old-world courtesy. He sat with them talking about field hospitals he had known.

When he spoke about Garrett's courage it was a soldier's statement of what was expected but still needed to be recognized, out of a long history of example.

"Andy Connell saw you earlier."

"Yes."

"Look here. I don't usually give advice. I find the free sort not usually worth a damn." White hesitated a moment. "But I'll break my rule in this case."

"You haven't yet left this hospital room." White glanced at the window. "Out there a savage animal is waiting for you. It's called the media and it likes to eat the living and the famous. The more alive, the more infamous, the better."

"You're a celebrity. Maybe not next month, next year. But as of today, your picture is front page. In a biosafety suit, helmet off. Holding your arm on a stretcher halfway into an ambulance. Arriving here, halfway out of an ambulance." White shook his head. "Everyone has a camera in their pocket nowadays. The pictures can't be stopped."

"Andy is one of the few people who can control that animal. And even he can only do it briefly, but maybe long enough for the agenda to move on. It always does. He will want to honour you. Let him. Cut a deal. Use him. He's already using you."

After the visitors had left they slept. Zahra woke first. She listened to the familiar noises of the hospital through the walls. She thought of the way Fly spoke about Cherry; he dealt with his loss by speaking about it. Garrett didn't. But Garrett was different.

Zahra watched the evening sun throw the bright square of the window across Garrett's bed. It moved across the covers like a negative shadow. It was late by the time it reached her face, lending the skin warmth and eventually drawing some gold from her hair.

Garrett accepted her luck at face value. Daytime, she chatted with Zahra and read magazines; television was too intrusive. She never mentioned Jason. More visitors came. She found if she concentrated hard she could arrange all the facts she had heard in order long enough to understand them. Her mind cleared as the Dilaudid dosage went down.

She took each day as it came. The worst time was when she was awake and Zahra asleep. She began to notice a routine: the changing of the drips, check-ups, meals arriving and leaving, the long echoing nights. Time restarted. Her strength returned. The nursing staff began to insist she finish her meals. The need to endure was hard to endure.

At night she watched the hands of the clock turn through the long hours. Daytime, she watched the sun's shadow move across her bed. Mostly she slept.

***

Jim Da Costa kept them both a full month. By then the Reaction programme had the epidemic under full control. The early death toll had peaked at two thousand. With the wide availability of Paris, fatalities were rare, due mainly to delayed reporting.

The disease had become just another story, one picture in the rolling wallpaper of news. Reinnalt Bryce provided the only sustaining interest, as public enemy number one, a monster enlarged by his disappearance. Her own exposure had been brief. She had taken White's advice. Andy Connell had got his boss her public handshake at her hospital bedside; the tabloids were muzzled.

In the end, impatient with Da Costa's caution, she checked herself out of the hospital. She went back to her large echoing house overlooking a suburb of Brighton. A water pipe had burst and flooded the basement. September was mild, occasionally drizzly, colder than expected.

The chilly home was silent. After a month sharing a room with Zahra it was hard to adjust. The girl's chatter had been a sort of sunshine. Without that protective weather Garrett discovered it was best to have voices in the house. She left the television on in the background, something she had always hated.

She took a sabbatical but tried to keep busy. The house needed sorting out. She went through David's study. No point shying away any more. She kept only what she had to – his notebooks, a decent jumper, an old pair of reading glasses which worked for her too. Sorted lives; boxes for keeping, black bags for throwing.

She kept meaning to start Jason's room.

Zahra stayed in touch, mainly by text. About random happenings across the day or night – gossip about the baby, bad jokes, conveyed messages. "Fly says…" "George asks…" "When you coming over?" A little of that sunshine still filtered through. George Skinner e-mailed. News. Some gossip. Her replies were brief, to discourage.

She rose early. The grey autumn mornings brought no warmth and she disliked the cold bed. One night late in September she first had the dream. It started with a phone call.

"Hello mother."

The rhythm of her heart adjusted.

"Mum you there?"

"Jason?"

"It's my duty call."

Another adjustment of the heart.

"Good to hear your voice," she said. She listened at the phone as though at a door.

"Everyone is saying you saved the world. I guess you think you were right after all. Just as you always were."

"It's not like that."

"True or false. Your world is so simple. You're the great scientist and that simplifies life for you, doesn't it?"

"No." She felt a sharp pain in her mouth.

"People must be such a disappointment. Unsolveable. Chaotic. Uncontrollable."

"I don't want to control anyone."

"You tried to control me. You couldn't listen."

Garrett was silent a moment. "I was wrong."

She clenched her teeth against more words even though it tasted like blackmail. She listened, but he was gone.

She sat up in bed and shook her head to free it of the dream. She found blood in her mouth.

It was still the middle of the night. She went down to the kitchen for a drink. She rinsed around her teeth and felt with her fingertips where she had bitten her cheek. She ran water into the sink over her wrists then stood at the back window watching for first light, holding her elbows for an hour; she waited unrewarded, like darkness at a mirror. Down the hall, she could see the boxes and bags stacked by the study door.

She spent the morning sorting through old photos and data disks. By lunchtime she'd had enough. She sat at the kitchen table and watched the television. The afternoon stretched out before her.

The silence in the rest of the house was unbearable. She put on her boots and walked down to the beach. Wandering aimlessly she found a row of deckchairs and sat down. A few seats along, a tramp was singing tunelessly to himself.

"Hello Jimmy."

He looked alarmed and began to polish his eyebrows.

"It's Christine, remember?"

"Oh yes! Hi Christine. Nice to see you again. You been busy?"

Garrett smiled. "How have you been, Jimmy?"

They talked about the beach. Then about children. Jimmy pointed to a girl running between windbreaks with a bowed kite.

"My son used to love kites," Garrett said.

Jimmy reached down beneath his deckchair. He produced an opened bottle and took a swig. His head nodded up and down as he followed the kite. The child was learning to pull on the strings.

"He used to make them with his father."

Garrett talked about Jason. Jimmy nodded, smiling at her from time to time, and at the sea and the sky. He watched the child pulling the kite up the wind, hand over hand, as though it were the weight of a bucket of water.

"Children bring out the best in us. And the worst." Jimmy took a drink.

Garrett found herself describing her dream.

"He accused me of not listening. I – I didn't." She was silent a moment. "Not in the way he needed." Garrett tried to sit up but slipped back in the sling of the deckchair. "There was always this gap – just like after David died." Garrett shook her head. "If I'd just listened–" She shook her head again. "I see that now."

The kite was up, tugged up, a coloured wing held back by the thinnest thread. Garrett stared at Jimmy without seeing him. "Instead I told him why he was wrong."

"Why did you do that?"

"Because he was! Christ Jimmy, don't you read the news?" Garrett tasted bitter anger on her tongue.

"No." Jimmy smiled. "I read this beach. It tells me what I need to know." He raised an arm. The little girl with the kite was running again. Jimmy's hand followed a failed flight in small loops before dropping back into his lap.

"He was misguided." Garrett stared at the sea. An outgoing wave drew back over the pebbles in a soft roar.

Jimmy watched the child with the kite. She was crying. The string had broken. A man stood over the little girl, explaining as he wound a loose end around a plastic handle.

Jimmy emptied his bottle and stood up. "Come on."

Garrett didn't move.

"I want to show you something."

He marched out across the pebbles. Garrett closed her eyes.

"Come on slow coach!"

The faint cry reached her through the sound of the surf. Garrett squinted against the low sun. She could see Jimmy waving his straw hat.

She wondered if he had ever undergone an evaluation, whether he could be helped. She watched him wandering up and down at the edge of the water. He was looking down, intent, as if searching for something lost. She stood up and walked down to him.

"Look."

He held out a handful of glass pebbles.

"Aren't they beautiful? When they're dry it's like they're covered in frost; they're hard to spot. But when you dip them in

the sea you can see their clear colours. Doesn't it remind you of–
" The roar of a wave downed his words. Garrett looked out
across the beach, each stone a hope, and thought of the faith
healer's remedies and of medical trials. "Come on, I'll show you
where to look."

They wandered along the hissing shingle, feet bare. Garrett
strung her boots around her neck.

"If you see a blue one show me! They're very rare! I once
found one this big!"

"Do you have it?"

"Oh no, I throw what I collect away at the end of the day. I
can always find more." He swept his arm out to take in the beach
and the sea beyond. "They'll never run out."

When they tired of searching for pebbles they found a bench
to sit on at the end of the pier. The sun had gone down, leaving a
sky sprinkled with stars. Garrett listened to the withdrawing
sighs of the sea and the breath of the night wind.

Jimmy pointed. "Such a beautiful star."

Garrett identified the planet Venus near the horizon on the
ecliptic. She held herself still.

"Jimmy I miss my son."

They sat still together a while. Jimmy turned to her.

"Christine! I remember you! You're the one who likes
Larkin."

Garrett gave Jimmy a faint smile.

"Remember the almost truth?" He nodded at the sea.

Garrett watched then said softly, "The waves come in
undated, between the rocks."

Jimmy tilted his head.

"What will survive of us is love," Garrett whispered. She
bent over her empty stomach and held her knees. She began to
cry, deep repeated sobs she couldn't stop. Salt water fell into the
sea below. Jimmy sat beside her humming a tune on one note,
over and over, as the waves crashed ceaselessly into the legs of
the pier.

When Garrett opened her eyes the sky overhead was dark.
She felt emptied out, exhausted as though she had run all night.
She took a deep clean breath. Beside her, Jimmy's eyes were
two glints.

"I'm hungry. Think I'll go up the beach. You?"

Garrett shook her head.

She sat until she grew cold then began walking. The movement entered her thoughts, calming them step by step. She walked up onto the South Downs, pushed by an urge to climb higher. The chalk footpath was slippery with evening dew.

Feathery seeds of thistledown floated past. Hundreds, thousands of the delicate parachutes drifted through the air. Garrett watched the complex patterns they made around her, intricately changing, careless beyond comprehension, a snowfall of genes. *Asteraceae Cirsium.* She reached out and caught one. She studied the seed as though it could unlock a secret.

It started to rain. Garrett stopped beneath a sheltering Holm oak. Further along the coast she could see the emerging constellation of Brighton. The lights of thousands of ordinary lives stood out against the dark. It was suppertime. Meals were being prepared, newspapers read, arguments had; ordinary people speaking their minds and listening, making and sharing a common sense. She studied the notch in the sky made by a church steeple, the highest point in the land, then her eyes lifted as she thought of higher, more rational hopes, her attention caught by what looked like a fast-moving star. Envisat II? Hubble?

From her vantage point she could see a beaded thread of lights leading out into the dark. Brighton Pier. She scratched at her left arm just below the elbow and remembered the five men sent out with death in their veins: human mosquitoes, part of a divine plan. They had been lucky.

Was Arshu still alive? Had he ever existed? She thought of the black cave in the painting of the Harrowing in St Andrew's, and the dark empty centre of the Eye of Faith in Asari Valley. *Superstition.* The needed fight.

A trickle of water found its way inside her collar. She shivered. The lights along the coast were no longer visible. It didn't look like she should wait.

She started down the footpath, careful of her footing on the wet chalk. Leaves somersaulted on the wind and wrapped her feet. Sycamore keys whirled past. She walked on in the falling silence of the rain.

THE END

Nicholas Lim

Report on malaria epidemics in continental plover flocks
to the WHO SEAN, Jakata Indonesia

Molecular epidemiology findings
Executive Summary, August 2028

This report sets out the findings of the SEAN Emergency Epidemiology Group after preliminary investigations into recent malaria epidemics in continental plover flocks. Following molecular assays, it is beyond doubt that the unusual infection is a mutation of the Krissa strain, highly lethal and orally-transmissible. The infamous "Krissa message" was found at its original location on Chromosome 8 at Base Pair 1,102,223. There are minor differences due to transcription errors but the encoded name "Professor Stephen Richardson" is still carried in the malaria's genome unaltered.

The most plausible explanation for the new disease is that a transfer event took place through digestion of inappropriately-disposed-of corpses. Crab plovers are scavenging birds. Possible sites have been identified off Sumatra and Kalimantan. Rapid dispersal of the bird malaria appears to have occurred along migration routes out of the Indonesian Archipelago. The new strain is now so widespread it is effectively ineradicable. Fortunately the antidote appears to be still fully effective. WHO SEAN has commissioned an immediate follow-on study into the threat of future transfer events, reservoirs of infection and mutation.

"Even if the open windows of science at first make us shiver
after the cozy indoor warmth of traditional humanizing myths,
in the end the fresh air brings vigour,
and the great spaces have a splendour of their own."
Bertrand Russell, *What I Believe*

ABOUT THE AUTHOR

Nicholas Lim lives in London with his wife and two sons. An Oxford and Faber Academy graduate, he has been writing and editing for over twenty years, publishing poems and short stories in a number of award-winning anthologies. *The Pattern Maker* is his first novel and won the Pen Factor prize in 2012. If you would like to get updates on other stories by Nicholas Lim, please subscribe to the author's newsletter by visiting www.nicholasrobertlim.co.uk.

We hope you enjoyed reading *The Pattern Maker*.
Please share your thoughts here http://smarturl.it/PMReview
and receive a free short story by Nicholas Lim
as a thank you for your support.

Richmond Press

Printed in Great Britain
by Amazon

74913178R00203